For my daughter, Eliza
May you always 'Be more Iona'

Also by Clare Pooley

The Authenticity Project

'Brilliant contemporary story, full of food for thought. Clare Pooley is amazing'

'The perfect read. A great follow up [to] *The Authenticity Project*'

'The fantastic cast of eclectic characters will steal your heart and have you rooting for their happy endings'

'A delightful story . . . heart-warming and funny, I am completely charmed by the author'

'Such a joyful book'

'I loved Clare's last book and this was just as good'

'A great novel with some truly wonderful characters'

'The mood-lifting feel-good book of the year'

THE
People on
PLATFORM 5

CLARE POOLEY

PENGUIN BOOKS

TRANSWORLD PUBLISHERS
Penguin Random House, One Embassy Gardens,
8 Viaduct Gardens, London SW11 7BW
www.penguin.co.uk

Transworld is part of the Penguin Random House group of companies
whose addresses can be found at global.penguinrandomhouse.com

Penguin
Random House
UK

First published in Great Britain in 2022 by Bantam Press
an imprint of Transworld Publishers
Penguin paperback edition published 2023

A CIP catalogue record for this book
is available from the British Library.

ISBN
9781804990971

Typeset in Sabon LT Std by Jouve (UK), Milton Keynes.
Printed and bound in Great Britain by Clays Ltd, Elcograf S.p.A.

The authorized representative in the EEA is Penguin Random House Ireland,
Morrison Chambers, 32 Nassau Street, Dublin D02 YH68.

Penguin Random House is committed to a sustainable
future for our business, our readers and our planet. This book
is made from Forest Stewardship Council® certified paper.

MIX
Paper from
responsible sources
FSC® C018179
FSC
www.fsc.org

'Trains are wonderful.
To travel by train is to see nature
and human beings, towns and churches
and rivers, in fact, to see life.'

AGATHA CHRISTIE

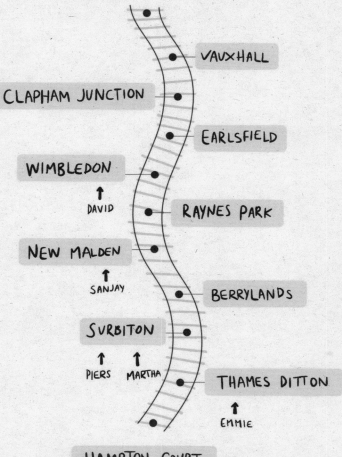

Iona

08:05 Hampton Court to Waterloo

Until the point when a man started dying right in front of her on the 08:05, Iona's day had been just like any other.

She always left the house at half past seven. It took her an average of twenty minutes to walk to the station in heels, which meant she'd usually arrive fifteen minutes before her train left for Waterloo. Two minutes later if she was wearing the Louboutins.

Arriving in good time was crucial if she wanted to secure her usual seat in her usual carriage, which she did. While novelty was a wonderful thing when it came to fashion, or film, or even patisserie, it was not welcome on her daily commute.

Some time ago, Iona's editor had suggested that she start *working from home*. It was, he'd told her, all the rage, and her job could be done just as well remotely. He'd tried to cajole her out of her office space with sweet talk of an extra hour in bed and more flexibility, and, when that didn't work, had attempted to drive her out by making her do something awful called *hot desking*, which – she learned – was corporate speak for *sharing*. Even as a child, Iona had never liked sharing. That little incident with the Barbie doll was still seared in her memory and, no doubt, her classmates' as well. No, boundaries were necessary. Luckily, Iona's colleagues quickly became familiar with which was her preferred desk, and it morphed from hot to decidedly frigid.

Iona loved going into the office. She enjoyed rubbing shoulders with all the youth, who taught her the latest lingo, played her their favourite new tracks and told her what to watch on Netflix. It was important to keep at least one finger plugged into the zeitgeist, especially in her profession. Bea, bless her, wasn't much help on that front.

She wasn't, however, looking forward to today very much. Her latest editor had scheduled a three-hundred-and-sixty-degree appraisal, which sounded altogether too intimate. At her age (fifty-seven), one didn't like to be appraised too closely, and certainly not from every angle. Some things were best left to the imagination. Or not thought about at all, to be honest.

Anyhow, what did he know? Much like policemen and doctors, her editors seemed to get younger and younger with each passing year. This one, believe it or not, was conceived after the World Wide Web. He'd never known a world where phones were tethered to the wall and you had to look up facts in the *Encyclopaedia Britannica*.

Iona thought back, somewhat wistfully, to her annual

appraisals when she'd first started at the magazine, nearly thirty years ago. They didn't call them 'appraisals' then, of course. They were called 'lunch', and they happened at the Savoy Grill. The only downside was having to politely remove her editor's fat, sweaty hand from her thigh on a regular basis, but she was quite adept at that, and it was almost worth it for the sole meunière, deftly detached from the bone by a subservient waiter with a French accent, and washed down with a chilled bottle of Chablis. She tried to remember the last time someone – other than Bea – had attempted to grope her under a table, and couldn't. Not since the early nineties, in any case.

Iona checked her reflection in the hall mirror. She'd gone for her favourite red suit today – the one that shouted *I mean business* and *Don't even think about it, mister.*

'Lulu!' she called, only to discover the French bulldog already sitting right by her feet, ready to go. Another creature of habit. She leaned down to attach the lead to Lulu's hot-pink collar, studded with diamanté spelling out her name. Bea didn't approve of Lulu's accessories. *Darling, she's a dog, not a child*, she'd said on numerous occasions. Iona was quite aware of that. Children these days were rather selfish, lazy and entitled, she thought. Not like darling Lulu at all.

Iona opened the front door and called up the stairs, as she always did, 'Bye bye, Bea! I'm off to the office. I'll miss you!'

The advantage of boarding the train at Hampton Court was that it was the end of the line, or the beginning, depending, of course, on which way you were travelling. There was a life lesson there, thought Iona. In her experience, most endings turned out to be beginnings in disguise. She should make a note of that one for the column. So, the trains were always – as long as you arrived early enough – relatively empty. This meant that Iona could usually occupy her favourite seat (seventh aisle seat on the right, facing forward, at a table) in her favourite carriage: number three. Iona had always preferred odd numbers to evens. She didn't like things to be too round or convenient.

Iona sat down, putting Lulu on the seat beside her, and began arranging her things in front of her. Her Thermos filled with green tea, just chock-a-block with age-defying antioxidants; a bone china cup and matching saucer, because drinking tea out of plastic was beyond the pale in any circumstance; her latest mail and her iPad. It was just ten stops to Waterloo, and the thirty-six-minute journey was the perfect opportunity to prepare for the day ahead.

As the train became busier and busier with each stop, Iona worked happily in her little bubble, wonderfully anonymous and blending into the background. Just one of thousands of identikit commuters, none of whom paid her the blindest bit of attention. Certainly, no one would talk to her, or to anyone else. Everyone knew the Second Rule of Commuting: you may nod to someone if you've seen them on a significant number of occasions, even – *in extremis* – exchange a wry smile or an eye-roll at one of the guard's announcements over the tannoy, but you never, ever talk. Unless you were a nutter. Which she wasn't, despite what they said.

An unfamiliar noise made Iona look up. She recognized the man sitting in front of her. He wasn't usually on this train, but she often saw him on her return journey, on the 18:17 from Waterloo. She'd noticed him because of his exquisite tailoring, which ordinarily she would have admired, but it was rather ruined by an extraordinary sense of entitlement which only really comes with being white, male, heterosexual and excessively solvent. This was evidenced by his penchant for manspreading, and talking extremely loudly on his mobile phone about *the markets* and *positions*. She'd once heard him refer to his wife as *the ball and chain*. He'd always get off at Surbiton, which struck her as a little incongruous. She gave all the passengers she recognized pet names, and he was Smart-But-Sexist Surbiton.

Right now, he did not look quite so pleased with himself. If anything, he seemed in distress. He was leaning forward, clutching at his throat, and emitting a volley of sounds somewhere between a cough and a vomit. The girl sitting next to him – a pretty young thing, with red hair in a plait, and dewy skin that she no doubt took for granted but would, one day, remember fondly – said, rather nervously, 'Are you okay?' He was, quite obviously, not okay. He looked up, trying to communicate something to them, but his words seemed jammed in his throat. He gestured towards a half-eaten fruit salad on the table in front of him.

'I think he's choking on one of his strawberries. Or maybe a grape,' said the girl. This was obviously an emergency. It hardly mattered precisely which piece of fruit was involved. The girl put down the book she was reading and patted him on the back, between his shoulder blades. It was the sort of gentle pat that was often accompanied by the words *good dog*, and not at all what the situation required.

'Here, do it harder,' said Iona, leaning forward across the table and giving him a hefty thump with a closed fist, which she found rather more enjoyable than she should have done, given the circumstances. For a moment, there was silence, and she thought he was better, but then the choking sounds started again. His face had turned a mottled purple, and his lips had started to lose their colour.

Was he going to die, right here on the 8.05? Before they even got to Waterloo?

Piers

08:13 Surbiton to Waterloo

Piers's day was not going at all to plan. For a start, this was not his usual train. He liked to be in the City before the markets opened, but today's routine had been thrown completely off course due to Candida firing the au pair the day before.

Magda had been their third au pair this year, and Piers had held out high hopes for her lasting at least until the end of the school term. Then they'd returned early from a disastrous weekend away *en famille* to discover Magda in bed with the landscape gardener, and cocaine residue and a rolled up banknote on a hardback copy of *The Gruffalo*. Piers might have been able to persuade Candida to let Magda off with a warning, since she'd been off duty at the time, but the besmirching of the children's favourite bedtime story had been the final straw. *How can I read that story again without imagining Tomaso exploring Magda's deep, dark wood?* Candida had yelled.

Things had gone further downhill when Piers had finally boarded a train at Surbiton, to discover that the only free seat, at a table for four, was opposite the weird lady and her flat-faced, wheezy dog. Piers didn't usually see her in the morning, but she was an irritatingly familiar sight on his return journey. He obviously wasn't the only commuter who tried hard to avoid her, since she was often flanked by the only unoccupied seats.

Crazy Dog Woman was looking even more ridiculous than usual, wearing a crimson suit upholstered in a tweed fabric that would have been much more at home covering the furniture in a primary school.

Piers did a quick mental calculation on the pros and cons of standing until he got to Waterloo versus sitting opposite the sofa in heels. Then he noticed that the girl sitting next to the empty seat was rather gorgeous. He was pretty sure he'd seen her on the train before. Piers recognized the little gap between her two front teeth – a tiny imperfection that tipped the balance of her face from blandly pretty to captivating. He may even have winked at her – one of those silent moments of communion shared by those attractive and successful commuters who found themselves stranded in a sea of mediocre humanity, like high-performance racing cars in a Lidl car park.

She was in her late twenties, probably, wearing a tight pink skirt, which he was sure displayed a perfect pair of legs, sadly hidden under the table, with a white T-shirt and a black blazer. She must have some trendy media job that allowed dressing down all week, not just on Fridays. Having some eye candy for the journey swung the balance in favour of sitting down.

Piers pulled out his phone to check on his key positions. He'd lost so much money last week that he needed this week to be spectacular. He sent out a silent prayer to the gods of the markets, while taking a grape from the small fruit salad he'd picked up at the convenience store by the station. He'd spent so long trying to get the kids to eat their breakfast while fending off cries of *Where's Magda? We want Magda!* that he'd neglected to eat his own. He'd hovered over the pain au chocolat in the bakery section, but Candida had banned him from eating pastries as she said he was getting fat. *Fat?!?* He was actually in remarkably good shape for his age. Still, he held his stomach in, just in case, conscious of the girl sitting next to him.

Piers goggled at the numbers on his screen. Surely that couldn't be right? Dartington Digital had been a dead cert. He took a sharp, involuntary intake of breath, then felt something lodge deep in the back of his throat. He tried to breathe, but it just settled in further. He attempted a cough, but it had no impact on the obstruction whatsoever. *Stay calm*, he told himself. *Think. It's only a grape.* But he could feel himself being overwhelmed by a wave of fear and helplessness.

Piers banged his hands on the table and widened his eyes at the women around him in a silent plea. He felt someone pat his back in a motion that was more massage than the extreme surgery required. Then, thank goodness, a sharp, hard thump that surely must do the job? With a huge sense of relief, he felt the grape shift slightly. Before it settled back into position.

I cannot die right here, right now, he thought. *Not on*

this ghastly commuter train surrounded by nobodies and weirdos. Then, an even worse thought: *If I die today, Candida will find out. She'll realize what I've been doing, and the kids will grow up knowing what a loser their father really is.*

From his position, hunched over the table, Piers could see the red suit standing up, like a volcano erupting, and a loud voice bellowed, 'IS THERE A DOCTOR ON THE TRAIN?!?' *Please, please*, he thought, *let there be a doctor on the train.* He'd give up everything he had just to be able to breathe again. *Are you listening, Universe? You can have it all.*

Piers closed his eyes, but he could still see red – either the ghost of the crimson tweed, or the blistering of blood vessels behind his eyeballs.

'I'm a nurse!' he heard from somewhere behind him. Then, within a few seconds that felt like an eternity, two arms clenched round him from behind, and he was pulled up from his crouching position, the arms thrusting deep into his stomach – once, twice, three times.

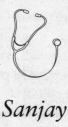

Sanjay

08:19 New Malden to Waterloo

Today was going to be *the* day, thought Sanjay as he made his way to New Malden station to catch his usual train. The day he finally plucked up the courage to speak to The Girl On The Train. He'd even worked out what he was going to say. She always carried a book with her. A proper one, not a Kindle or an audio book. It was one of the (many) reasons he knew they'd be perfect together. Last week, he'd noted that she was reading a novel called *Rebecca*, so he'd bought himself a copy from his local bookshop, and read the first few chapters over the weekend. Which meant that today, presuming she was still reading it, he could ask her what she thought of Mrs Danvers. The perfect conversation starter. Original, friendly and intelligent.

Sanjay looked out for his two housemates. They worked at the same hospital as him, but were currently on nights, so they often passed each other in the morning – Sanjay heading north, all fresh-faced and relatively energetic, James and Ethan going south, pale, exhausted and smelling of disinfectant. A window into his near future.

Sanjay stood at the point on the platform, near the snack counter, where Carriage 3 usually stopped, since he'd learned, after weeks of trial and error, that this was the section of the train she was most likely to be on. *Great book*, he practised in his head. *What do you think of Mrs Danvers? I'm Sanjay, by the way. Do you take this train often?* No, no, scrap that last bit. Definitely too creepy.

As soon as Sanjay boarded the train, he could see that today was, indeed, turning out to be his lucky day. There she was, sitting at a table for four with Rainbow Lady, her dog and a slightly plump middle-aged man in an expensive suit. Sanjay had spotted him several times before. He was just the type of arrogant high-flyer that Sanjay used to see being wheeled into A&E with a perforated stress-induced stomach ulcer, or a suspected heart attack brought on by a recreational cocaine habit, yelling *I have private medical insurance!* He obviously thought himself better than most mere mortals and had scant respect for the personal space of others.

Sanjay was, however, very fond of Rainbow Lady, who he'd seen many times on his journey to work, but never spoken to. Obviously. In a world where almost everyone wore black, navy or shades of grey, she chose emerald greens, turquoise blues and livid purples. Today she did not disappoint. She was dressed in a suit made from a bright red tweed that made her look like one of the strawberry creams that were always left in the bottom of a family-sized tin of Quality Street.

Could he ask her to move her dog so he could join her table? After all, the dog presumably didn't have a season ticket and having an animal on the seat must contravene every health and safety rule. The problem was, Sanjay both admired and was terrified of Rainbow Lady in equal measure. He wasn't the only one. However crowded the train, few people dared ask her to move her pet. And if they did, they didn't make the same mistake again. Not even the guard.

He stood, holding a metal pole for balance, trying to work out how to get close enough to the girl to start up a conversation. He'd never done this before. All his previous dates were with women he'd met at college, work or on a dating app where they'd exchange banter for days, tentatively swapping nuggets of personal information, before actually meeting IRL. This was old-school, and it was terrifying. There was a reason why no one did this any more.

Considering that there were around eighty people packed into a relatively small metal casing, the carriage was, as always, remarkably quiet. Just the sound of the wheels on the track, the tinny noise from someone's headphones and the occasional cough. Then, cutting through the silence like a juggernaut, a voice:

'IS THERE A DOCTOR ON THE TRAIN?!?'

His prayers had been answered in the most unexpected and extraordinary way. He cleared his throat and said, with as much authority as he could muster, 'I'm a nurse!'

The crowds parted deferentially, people contorting their bodies out of his path, ushering him forwards through a multitude of odours – coffee, perfume, sweat – towards Rainbow Lady, his girl and the man who was quite obviously choking.

This scenario had been covered in the first term at nursing college. Emergency First Aid, Module One: The Heimlich Manoeuvre.

Sanjay's training took over as he clicked into autopilot. With more strength than he'd known he possessed, he hauled the man up from his seat from behind, clutched his arms around his belly and pulled as hard as he could, right into the diaphragm. Three times. It felt as if the whole train held its breath in sympathy; then, with a huge cough, the offending grape was expelled from the man's mouth with remarkable velocity, landing with a satisfying plop in the cup of tea sitting in front of Rainbow Lady.

The cup rattled on its saucer, then settled back into position, as the entire carriage erupted in applause. Sanjay could feel himself blushing.

'Ahh, it was a grape,' said Rainbow Lady, staring into her tea, as if this had all been part of a children's party game called Guess The Hidden Object.

'Thank you so much. I think you just saved my life,' said the man, his words coming out with effort, and one at a time, as if they were still navigating their way around the memory of the grape. 'What's your name?'

'Sanjay,' said Sanjay. 'You're welcome. All part of the job.'

'I'm Piers. I really can't thank you enough,' he said, as the colour gradually returned to his face.

THE NEXT STATION IS WATERLOO, announced the voice on the tannoy. Sanjay started to panic. He was being patted on the back and congratulated by one stranger after another, which was really gratifying, but there was only one person he wanted to speak to, and he was missing his chance. Everyone stood and started moving towards the doors, propelling him forwards, like an unwilling lemming being pushed towards the cliff. He looked back at her in desperation.

'What do you think of Mrs Danvers?' he blurted out. She looked totally confused. She wasn't even reading that book this morning. She was clutching a copy of Michelle Obama's autobiography. Now he looked like a deranged stalker. Perhaps he *was* a deranged stalker.

He'd blown it. There was no coming back from that.

Emmie

Emmie was feeling far too shaky to go straight to the office, so she ducked into her favourite independent family-owned coffee shop instead, pulling her reusable cup out of her bag.

'Hey, Emmie!' said the barista. 'How's it going?'

'Not great, actually,' said Emmie, before she could stop herself and replace the words with her usual, socially acceptable, *Good, thanks!* As a point of principle, she hated the idea of being one of those people who griped about their insignificant first-world problems, when every day there were people sleeping on the street, or struggling to feed their children.

The barista paused and frowned, waiting for her to continue.

'Someone nearly died on my train this morning. He choked on a grape,' said Emmie.

'But he's still alive, no?' said the barista. Emmie nodded. 'No permanent disabilities?' She shook her head. 'So, this is a cause for celebration! A cinnamon swirl, perhaps?'

Emmie couldn't even begin to explain why she wasn't feeling in the slightest celebratory. She'd started her day, as usual, doing her stretches and counting her many blessings, and then – *BAM!* – before she'd even got to Waterloo she was confronted with her own sense of mortality. The realization that one day, totally out of the blue, you could go from being a happy, healthy person to . . . not being at all.

And what use had she been when the man sitting next to her was dying? Emmie, who'd always thought of herself as resourceful and good in a crisis, had sat there impotently while two strangers had saved his life. When the chips were down, her gut reaction had been flight rather than fight. All she'd been able to do was think, *What if that happened to me? What if I were hit by a bus today, blown up by a terrorist or electrocuted by a dodgy computer cable? What would I leave behind? What have I achieved?*

Emmie thought about the project she'd been working on for the past month – the fully integrated digital ad campaign for a 'challenger' brand of loo roll. She imagined her eulogy: *Thanks to Emmie's strategic and creative genius, a few more people were able to discover the luxury of a slightly quilted, lightly perfumed toilet paper.*

As a teenager, she'd spent a month sleeping in a tree to protect a local forest from destruction and much of her school holidays volunteering at a soup kitchen. Her nickname had been Hermione, because her friends claimed that if they'd had House Elves at their school, Emmie would most definitely have campaigned for their liberation. Yet here she was, at twenty-nine, doing nothing that would even remotely change her corner of Thames Ditton, let alone the world, and sitting idly by while people choked to death.

Emmie remembered the nurse from the train that morning. He was so calm. So competent. So – and she forgave herself for a moment of shallowness – *good-looking*. He really *was* making a difference. Saving lives before he'd even got to work.

Perhaps she should retrain as a nurse. Was it too late? Maybe not, but the fact that she was renowned for fainting at the sight of a nosebleed or an ingrowing toenail was a probable indication that medicine wasn't the ideal career for her.

What was it Gorgeous Hero Nurse had called after her as she'd left the train? It had sounded very much like *What do you think of Mrs Danvers?* But it couldn't have been, because that wouldn't make any sense at all. All that drama was muddling her brain.

Emmie sat down at her desk and plugged in her laptop, buzzed by the combination of caffeine, adrenaline and determination. She was going to start using all her experience and talent for something *good*. Perhaps she could pitch for a charity client, persuade Joey to let her take them on pro bono? He'd bite at that if they could win some awards with the creative work.

She pulled up her email. She'd check for anything important, write her priority list for the day, then spend some time on her new project.

Emmie scanned down the list of unread messages. One, right at the top, stood out, partly because the name made her smile. A.friend@gmail.com. The subject was *You*. Was it from a headhunter? She opened it and scanned the brief text.

THAT PINK SKIRT MAKES YOU LOOK LIKE A TART. HOW DO YOU EXPECT ANYONE TO TAKE YOU SERIOUSLY? A FRIEND.

Emmie swivelled her chair around, as if the author might be standing right behind her, waiting to see her reaction. But, of course, they weren't.

Emmie read the email again, her buzz from earlier drowned out by a tidal wave of anger, shame and embarrassment. She looked down at the skirt she'd picked out that morning. A hot-pink pencil skirt that had made her feel feisty, successful and sexy. Now she just wanted to rip it off and throw it in the office bin.

The open-plan space was already filled with people. Her colleagues. Her friends. People she respected, and had thought respected her. She scanned their faces and body language, looking for clues as to who could have sent her that email just – she checked the time stamp – ten minutes ago. But everyone looked just the same as they did every other day.

Emmie, however, didn't think she'd ever feel the same in this office again.

Iona

18:17 Waterloo to Hampton Court

Iona was floored by a wave of that particular form of dread that accompanies finding an HR person in your meeting with your boss. Brenda – head of 'Human Resources', which she still thought of as 'Personnel' but had been renamed at some point in the nineties – was sitting next to her editor at the meeting room table, looking officious. This, in itself, meant nothing, since officious was Brenda's natural resting face, but it just added to Iona's general sense of impending doom.

'Hello, everyone,' Iona said, cursing herself for the slight tremble in her voice. 'Do two people count as everyone? Maybe I should have said *Hello, both* or *Hi, you two*.' She was blabbering. She trained her eyes on her editor, in the vain hope that refusing to make eye contact with Brenda might cause her to disappear. Her editor's name was Ed. Had he changed his name to match his job? She wouldn't put it past him.

'Uh, would you mind leaving the dog outside, Iona?' said Ed, aiming his finger at darling Lulu like a member of a firing squad. Which perhaps he was.

Iona reversed out of the open door, lest one of them tried to shoot her in the back.

'Could you possibly babysit for a few minutes?' she asked Ed's 'Executive Assistant', the modern equivalent of a secretary, but without the shorthand. She looked gratifyingly thrilled. No doubt it would make a nice change from being Ed's underpaid and undervalued henchwoman. 'She loves it if you scratch her in the soft bits, just behind her ears.' Then, because she always overdid it when she was nervous, she added, 'Don't we all?' along with a forced, high-pitched laugh. Ed's assistant shrank back in her chair, looking startled.

'*Once more unto the breach, dear friends*,' muttered Iona under her breath as she walked into the room again, spine aligned, head held high, just like she used to walk on to the stage, back in the day.

'Sit, sit,' said Ed, gesturing at a row of brightly coloured, empty chairs around the meeting room table. Iona chose the one to the right, hoping that the combination of tangerine-orange chair and crimson suit might do permanent damage to Brenda's retinas. She took a notebook and newly sharpened pencil out of her handbag. She wasn't intending to make any notes, but she could always use the pencil to stab Ed through the hand if necessary. The thought cheered her up a little.

'So, before going into a detailed appraisal, I wanted to talk to you about the *big picture*,' said Ed, steepling his fingers in front of him and looking serious, like a schoolboy pretending to be a bank manager. He reeled off details of falling circulations, lower revenues, higher overheads, all the numbers floating past Iona like radioactive pollen on the breeze while she tried to look interested and intelligent.

'You see,' he said finally, 'we need to concentrate more on our digital offering and pull in a younger audience, and that means making sure all our content is modern and relevant. And, to put it bluntly, we're concerned that *Ask Iona* feels just a little ...' He paused, searching for the most appropriate adjective before settling on '. . . old-fashioned.' Ed was apparently unable to demonstrate creative flair even with his insults.

Iona felt sick. *Stop it*, she told herself firmly. *Stand up and fight. Think Boudicca, Queen of the Celts.* So, she gathered her ragtag army, and climbed aboard her chariot.

'Are you saying that I'm *too old*, Ed?' she said, pausing to enjoy the sight of the HR lady blanching, which only made the line where her foundation ended and her chins began more apparent. 'Because, as a magazine therapist, life experience is crucial. And I have experienced it all. Sexism, ageism, homophobia.' She dropped the words like landmines, which of course they were. If she could acquire a disability, which at her age was a distinct possibility, she'd have practically a full house of potential discrimination cases. *Navigate your way around those, Brenda-from-HR.*

'Of course I'm not saying that,' said Ed. 'I'm just giving you a challenge.' Iona understood immediately that in this context 'challenge' was code for 'ultimatum'. 'Anyhow, maybe downscaling could be a positive move for you. You'd be able to spend more time with the grandchildren.' She gave him an extremely hard stare and cracked her knuckles, which always made Ed wince.

Brenda cleared her throat and fiddled with her lanyard. 'Oh. No grandchildren. Of course not,' stammered Ed. Did he mean 'of course not' because she was obviously too young for grandchildren, or because she was too lesbian?

'Let's not rush into anything. We'll give it another month and see if you can revolutionize your pages. Bring them up to date. Make them sizzle. Think *millennial*. That's where the future is.' He forced his face into a smile, and it almost cracked at the effort.

'Sure,' said Iona, writing SIZZLE on her notepad, followed by WANKER. 'But let me just remind you, Ed, how critical the problem pages are for the magazine. People depend on them. And I don't think I'm being too dramatic when I say that *lives* depend on them. And our readers enjoy them. After all, many of them say they only buy the magazine for my pages.' *Take that, pathetic Roman centurion.*

'I'm sure they used to, Iona,' said Ed, picking up his sword and plunging it into her heart. 'But when did anyone last say that? Mmm?'

Iona didn't go straight back to her desk. Instead, she walked directly to the toilets, eyes trained on the ugly, yet practical, carpet, still slightly tacky underfoot from all the spilled fruit punch at the last office party. She locked herself into one of the cubicles and sat on the closed seat, with Lulu on her lap, breathing in the melange of pine-fresh chemicals, various bodily excretions and dog. She started to cry. Not pretty crying, but the explosive sort that came accompanied by rivers of snot and running mascara. This job was her life. It was the reason she got up in the morning. It gave her purpose. It was *who she was*. What would she be without it? And who else would employ a magazine therapist who was rapidly approaching sixty and had been in the same job for almost thirty years? How had it gone from accolades, acolytes and awards ceremonies to this?

Iona tried to summon up some anger but was just too weary. The old days, when she'd been ferociously busy juggling a social column and advice page with occasional restaurant reviews and travel pieces, had been tiring, but not being busy *enough* was exhausting. She was tired of exuding a confidence she'd not felt for real in years. She was tired of constantly having to look occupied, when she'd had all her responsibilities – bar her advice pages – gradually stripped away.

She'd learned to spin out every task over hours, and to angle her computer screen so no one could tell that rather than working, she was actually planning fantasy holidays with Bea on perfect coral atolls or stalking old school friends on Facebook.

Life, of course, was not a competition. But, had it been one, Iona had imagined herself well in the lead. Over the years she'd secretly mocked the life choices of her contemporaries, as – one by one – they'd pulled over on to the hard shoulder of the career expressway, in favour of popping out one child after another and pandering to the needs of ungrateful, selfish husbands who'd once looked passably handsome but had grown beer bellies, nose hair and fungal toenails.

But now, she looked at their pictures of children's graduation ceremonies, multi-generational feasts around scrubbed pine kitchen tables and, even, tiny newborn grandchildren blinking with unfocused eyes at the camera, and she wondered if, just maybe, they were winning after all. At least they weren't weeping into the neck of a lapdog on a lavatory.

Iona heard the door to the toilets open, and the sound of two sets of heels clacking against the tiled floor. She lifted her feet on to the seat, pulling her knees into her chest and burying her face further into Lulu's fur to muffle the sound of her sobbing.

'God, I hate Mondays,' she heard one of the women say.

She realized, to her relief, that it was Marina, one of the features editors. She and Marina were good friends, despite Marina being nearly thirty years younger than her. They always exchanged a bit of 'banter' at the water cooler and had even been out for lunch together a few times. Marina would fill Iona in on all the office gossip and, in exchange, Iona gave her free advice on her tangled love life. She and Marina also respected each other as fellow professionals, women at the peak of their powers. Perhaps she should come out of her lavatorial hidey-hole and confide in her friend. A problem shared, and all that. Maybe she could suggest another lunch. A restoratively boozy one.

'Me too,' said Brenda-from-HR. 'Although I hate Wednesdays even more. You know, neither here nor there.'

'Hey, was that the old dinosaur I saw you and Ed talking to?' said Marina. 'Are you finally getting around to making her extinct? What are you planning? An ice age or a meteor strike?'

So much for female solidarity.

*

Iona was more relieved than usual to find her train home waiting for her at Platform 5, Waterloo. At least this part of the day was reassuringly predictable. She boarded at her favourite carriage, then swore to herself and accidentally squeezed Lulu, making her yelp. There was Grape Man – what was his name? Piers. That was it. He was sitting just across the aisle from the only spare seat. He was bound to want to start up a conversation, and much as she'd usually revel in someone's profuse gratitude, right now she just wanted to sit quietly and imagine herself in a world where she still mattered.

Iona sighed, and sat down. She opened her handbag and took out her glass and flask of ready-mixed gin and tonic, along with a ziplock plastic bag containing a couple of slices of lemon. She waited for the inevitable interruption. But it didn't happen. She looked over at Piers, who was leaning back in his seat as if he could bend it to his will, and had his thighs splayed so far apart that the old woman sitting next to him was pinned up against the window like a Roman blind. He caught Iona's eye and she thought, for a second, he was about to speak, but then his gaze slid away and lighted on his mobile, which he grabbed and started punching with a dictatorial index finger.

Iona felt awkward. Then annoyed at herself for allowing this . . . *oaf* to unsettle her. Surely the done thing – the *only* thing to do – when confronted by someone who, just a few hours previously, had *helped save your life* was to say thank you? Or, at least, hello? A casual nod, even? Perhaps he didn't recognize her? Not possible, surely? The only thing Iona had never been accused of was being forgettable.

'Darling,' he said into his phone, in a tone and volume that showed no consideration at all for the serenity of his fellow passengers. 'Could you nip down to the cellar and bring up a bottle of the Pouilly-Fumé and put it in the fridge to chill? No, not that one. The *grand cru*. One of the ones we brought back from that ghastly villa holiday in the Loire with the Pinkertons.'

Lulu, sitting on Iona's lap, began to growl. Iona felt the barrel of her body expand, like a set of bagpipes filling up with air, then she swivelled towards Piers and issued a cacophony of high-pitched barks.

Piers jabbed at his phone, terminating his conversation without saying goodbye, and glared at Iona.

'What on earth is wrong with that ridiculous dog?' he shouted.

Iona was used to people being rude to her, and she could – perhaps – ignore Piers's ingratitude and boorishness, but she was not going to let him insult Lulu.

'Lulu,' she said, 'is not ridiculous. She is, in fact, highly intelligent. She is also a feminist and, as such, she calls out toxic masculinity wherever she finds it.'

Piers's mouth dropped open, and he picked up his copy of the *Evening Standard*, opening it in front of his face like a veil. Iona was quite, quite sure that they were never going to look at each other, let alone speak, ever again. And thank the Lord for that.

Sanjay

Sanjay had transferred from Accident and Emergency to Oncology two months previously. It was, in many ways, an improvement. A&E had been hectic, chaotic and endlessly stressful, punctuated by the sounds of alarms, crying, and urgent instructions issued in staccato. It had also left him feeling a bit lost. Sending a small child home with a broken arm now safely stowed in a cast, clutching a sticker for bravery, was lovely and heart-warming, but so often he would transfer people to the wards and never get to hear the end of their story. You couldn't build relationships with patients in A&E, you usually just came in at the most dramatic part of the plot and were pulled out before the resolution.

Oncology played more to Sanjay's strengths, which was why he'd requested the transfer. He'd be able to see the same patients, week in, week out, over a period of months. Years, even, in some cases. He already knew the regulars – the names of their children and grandchildren, the contents of their dreams and their nightmares, and how to make their treatment pathway as manageable as possible. This was why he'd gone to nursing college – to heal hearts and minds as well as bodies. When he'd written that in his application form, he hadn't just been trotting out the clichés, he'd genuinely meant it.

The problem, Sanjay was finding, was that the more entangled he became with the lives of his patients, the less he was able to cope with the unhappy endings. For every handful of people he sent home with a benign cyst or a five-year all-clear, there would be one with an incurable recurrence that had spread to the liver, the bones and the brain. There were mothers of young children he'd watch growing weaker and weaker with every round of chemotherapy, losing first their hair, their eyelashes and eyebrows, then their sense of humour and, eventually, their hope.

The consultants Sanjay worked with seemed inured to all this. They were able to 'compartmentalize'. They could deal with tragedy, injustice and lives shattered, then take off their white coats at the end of the day and head out for a beer or two without, it seemed, a care in the world. How did they do that? Sanjay's compartments all appeared to be linked together. He couldn't stop one thing leaking into the next. He would wake up in the middle of the night thinking about the tumour markers in Mr Robinson's latest blood work, or remember the liberal scattering of dark shadows in Mrs Green's PET scan while he was trying to eat his dinner.

'Thank you, nurse,' said Mrs Harrison ('Please-call-me-Julie') as he applied a dressing to the site of her biopsy, right by her left armpit. 'Do you think it'll be okay?' She looked at him with eyes that conveyed hope and fear, in a tussle for supremacy.

'Do try not to worry, Julie,' he said, as he sidelined the question and rifled through his mental filing cabinet for the accepted form of wording. 'Nine out of ten breast lumps are benign. But you did absolutely the right thing, seeing your GP straight away, just to be on the safe side.'

This was, of course, true, but Sanjay had seen the expression on the face of the sonographer as he noted down the measurements of the – worryingly large and uneven – dark mass on the screen. Nothing that Julie would have been able to pick up on, but Sanjay had learned to recognize the slight narrowing of the eyes and the tensing of the fingers on the computer mouse.

'I know, I know, but I worry about my kids. They're only little. Six and four. You want to see some pictures?' said Julie, pulling out her phone. Sanjay did not want to see the photos – it would just make things harder. If only he could just concentrate on case numbers, prognoses and treatment plans, not bereaved children and bucket lists that would never be completed.

'I'd love to,' he said, with a warm smile.

After cooing at the pictures of two happy, secure, gap-toothed kids with no idea their whole world might soon fall apart, he sent Julie off with the impossible instruction to keep busy and to try not to think about it until she came back for the biopsy results in five days' time.

Sanjay ducked into the empty family room, also known as the room-for-really-bad-news. You didn't ask a couple to 'take a seat in the family room' when you were anticipating a happy conversation. He helped himself to a cup of water from the cooler in the corner and sat down on one of the armchairs surrounded by the ghosts of words like *terminal*, *riddled*, *do-not-resuscitate order* and *end-of-life pathway*. Did all that shock and grief seep into the soft furnishings? He imagined it oozing out of the cushions and curtains, a toxic, viscous sludge gradually filling the room and drowning him.

Sanjay's hand shook, spilling water on the floor. He put the cup down and tried hard to take long, deep breaths. His heart felt as if it were trying to beat its way out of his ribcage. He pressed a palm, hard enough to bruise, against his breastbone, as if he could force it back into place.

What would Julie say, or all those people on the train on Monday, who thought him some sort of hero, if they knew about his regular and debilitating panic attacks? What if they could see him hiding in the family room, the toilets or the store cupboard, bent double, head in his hands as he waited until he could breathe normally again?

What use was a cancer nurse with a fear of death?

It was probably just as well he'd blown it with The Girl On The Train. Even if she agreed to a date, she'd soon find out what a fake he was, and that would be the end of that.

Martha

08:13 Surbiton to Waterloo

Martha tiptoed past the closed bedroom door, trying to ignore the muffled groans and rhythmic banging of the headboard against the wall, coming from inside. It was unpleasant enough, imagining old people *doing it*; even worse when one of them was your mother. And worse than that, when the other one wasn't your father.

This boyfriend, Richard ('Please-don't-call-me-Dick-ha-ha'), appeared to be sticking around. She counted the months back on her fingers. It had been nearly a year, and Martha kept finding more and more man stuff in their house. Shaving foam in the bathroom, boxer shorts in the laundry cupboard, and even a little toolbox in the hallway, which he'd never actually used but she suspected he'd left there in order to appear manly and useful.

Martha wondered if Richard knew how old her mother was, or if Kate had spun her usual line about having had

Martha at a 'ridiculously young age. Barely in my twenties.' It was her birthday coming up, so perhaps Martha should bake her a cake and ice HAPPY FORTY-FIFTH BIRTH-DAY on the top in multi-colours. That would really set the cat among the pigeons, not least because her mother hadn't touched refined sugar since last century.

Maybe scaring this one off wasn't a good idea, though. His replacement could be worse. And there would be a replacement, since her mother, like nature, abhorred a vacuum. She abhorred the vacuum cleaner too, come to think of it. Their house was a mess.

Martha walked to the station on autopilot, thinking about her text exchange last night with Freddie. She really liked him. He wasn't popular, obviously. He was slightly awkward and a bit of an outsider, but she was hardly one to hold *that* against him. He was actually super clever and surprisingly funny.

Freddie didn't make her swoon like the heroines did in Jane Austen novels. There was no heart pounding, bosom heaving or loosening of corsets. Not that she wore a corset, and her bosoms weren't large enough to heave. But having a boy to talk about, she'd discovered, was important. When all the cool girls huddled in the corner whispering and giggling, she'd have someone to whisper and giggle about too. She would be one of the gang. She hugged the thought to her like a hot water bottle.

Martha spent a lot of her time feeling like David Attenborough narrating a nature documentary. She was an observer, studying a foreign species, trying to work out their habits and rituals, so she could move among them without being rejected or picked on. Did other teenagers do this naturally? Or were they all struggling to work out the rules? The rules that always seemed to change just as soon as you had them all worked out. What brands to wear, music to listen to, words to use, people to follow on social media, actors to idolize. It was a jungle.

The train was almost full when it pulled into Surbiton station. There was only one free seat in the carriage, and Martha walked towards it. She was about to sit down, when one of those typical alpha-male banker types, approaching from the other direction, flung himself forward, knocking her out of the way. He spread out in the seat, pulled a laptop out from his briefcase and opened it on the table in front of him, like a dog cocking his leg against a lamp post to mark his territory.

'Oh, great,' said Martha, not realizing she'd spoken out loud until he turned and looked up at her.

'Sorry, love,' he said with a grin he no doubt thought was endearing. 'There are winners and losers in life, and in this instance – you're the loser.'

Martha felt herself flush. She didn't know what to say. She wanted to get away, but the aisles were too crowded. Something buzzed in her pocket. Once, then twice, then a determined volley of alerts. She pulled her phone out and stared at it, grateful for the distraction. The Year 10 group chat was going crazy with some inane gossip or other.

Martha scrolled back through the messages, the words blurring and her stomach clenching. Surely not? No. No.

No. It couldn't be her. She was being paranoid. Then she reached the original source of all the electronic chatter – the laughs, the jeers, the disgust, the outrage – and she felt her stomach contract further, as a wave of bile forced itself up her throat.

'For fuck's sake!' yelled Seat Stealer, as she vomited all over his keyboard. 'Do you have any idea how much this laptop costs?'

Martha heard a whine on the other side of her, and looked down into the eyes of a familiar French bulldog who, in that second, seemed to see right into her soul.

'How dare you!' shouted the woman holding the dog. Martha flinched, assuming she was also yelling at her, before realizing the woman was staring straight at Seat Stealer. Martha had seen her on the train many times before. She was the Magic Handbag Lady. 'Can't you see the poor girl's not well? God, I should have done the world a favour and left you to choke the other day.'

'I'm the injured party here, actually!' said the man, gesturing at his laptop in disgust.

'Well, there are winners and losers in life, and in this instance, you're the loser,' said Magic Handbag Lady, which on any ordinary day might have made Martha smile.

As the two grown-ups were trading insults, Martha had a flashback to the scene in *Jurassic World* where the T. rex and the Indominus rex turn on each other, allowing the defenceless humans to escape unnoticed, and, as the doors opened at the next station, she pushed her way out of the carriage and ran.

Martha wove her way through the crowds of commuters, her throat still burning with the remnants of stomach acid, feeling the endless stream of notifications puncturing her phone like shrapnel, and knew that there were some situations it was impossible to outpace.

Iona

08:05 Hampton Court to Waterloo

Iona had never suffered from writer's block before. Quite the reverse. Usually, she had to corral the words back in, bring them to heel. But since *that meeting* a week ago, the words which usually flowed so naturally sputtered out in twos and threes, only to be deleted shortly after they hit the screen. Every time she'd manage to piece together a whole paragraph, she'd look at it thinking: *Does it SIZZLE? Is it MILLENNIAL enough?* Just when she needed her talent and her confidence more than ever, they'd deserted her.

She'd thought about enlisting the help of some of the 'millennials' in the office, but perhaps all of them – like Marina – thought her a dinosaur and were secretly hoping she'd just shuffle off to a retirement village in a pair of beige slacks with an elasticated waist and sensible shoes, freeing up an additional 'hot' desk. And besides, asking for help at work would mean showing weakness, and she really couldn't afford to do that right now.

Iona sipped her tea as she watched the passengers boarding the train at New Malden. There was Sanjay, the heroic nurse who'd saved the life of that ungrateful misogynistic asshole last week. He sat down at the spare seat opposite her. They nodded at each other and smiled awkwardly.

Iona found herself at a loss as to the required etiquette. Her recent exchanges with Piers had only served as salutary reminders that engaging with strangers on the train was not a good idea *at all*. That's why there was an unwritten law against it. But she and Sanjay had shared *a moment*. They were joined together, like it or not, by a brush with death. So, what were the rules now? God, it was difficult being British sometimes.

Iona stared out of the window, into the back gardens of terraced houses, the children's swing sets, tiny fishponds, washing lines and greenhouses. Each a little clue about the family who lived inside. Anything to avoid an eye contact which would make her dilemma more acute.

The train slowed down, then shuddered to a halt.

As the minutes ticked past with no sign of movement, Iona and her fellow passengers grew increasingly restless. The silence was punctuated by sighs and groans, the tapping on phone screens and the shuffling of feet. Finally, a tinny and – given the circumstances – irritatingly chirpy voice came through on the tannoy.

'Apologies for this delay to your service this morning, which is caused by a signal failure at Vauxhall. Hopefully we'll be on our way shortly.'

'Oh dear, they'll be terribly worried about us at the office,' whispered Iona to Lulu, wishing this were true. If they were stuck here all morning, would anyone even notice? Lulu gazed up at her, eyes like two chocolate buttons melting in the sun, and licked her on the nose.

She turned towards Sanjay, who was drumming his fingers rhythmically on the table in front of them. His jaw was clenched so tight that she could see a muscle twitching near his earlobe, and his breathing had become shallow and rapid. It was no good. She was going to have to say something.

'Are you okay, Sanjay?' she said, in the same voice she used to calm down Lulu whenever another – less polite – dog barked at her in the park. He looked up, startled, as if he'd forgotten where he was.

'Uh, yes. Thanks. It's just I'm going to be really late for my shift,' he said.

'We'll be on our way soon, I'm sure,' said Iona. 'And it's hardly life and death, is it?' Then she stopped, realizing her error. 'Oh dear, perhaps in your case it is?'

Sanjay laughed, a little awkwardly. 'Oh, I'm not that indispensable!' he said. 'I'm in oncology, so my patients tend to die a bit more slowly than that. More than half don't die at all, thank goodness.'

'Well then,' said Iona. 'There's no need to worry, is there? You know, I could have done with your nursing prowess on the train yesterday. I was sitting right here, and a schoolgirl threw up all over the laptop of Smart-But-Sexist Surbiton!'

'Who?' said Sanjay.

'You know, Grape Guy. Piers. The one whose life you

saved. Where have you been, anyhow? I've not seen you at all since then. I was beginning to think you'd been some kind of heavenly apparition. Although, if you had been, I'm not sure why you'd have bothered saving *him*. It may have looked like regular vomit, but it was actually liquid karma.'

'Uh, I've been sitting down the other end of the train. Deliberately, to be honest,' said Sanjay.

'You've been avoiding me?' asked Iona, realizing once the words were already out of her mouth that her encounter with Ed and HR was making her uncharacteristically paranoid and needy. *Stop it, Iona. The poor boy can sit where he likes. You're going to scare him off.*

'No. Not you, no, not at all,' he said, tripping over his multiple denials. Bless. '*Her.* The Girl On The Train.'

'What girl on the train?' asked Iona, mystified. 'Isn't that a film? And didn't she murder someone? Or perhaps she didn't. I can't actually remember. So *twisty.*'

'The one you were sitting opposite when that man – Piers – was choking,' he said.

Iona frowned, playing back the scene frame by frame in her head.

'Oh!' she said, locating the requisite image with a sense of triumph. 'You mean Impossibly-Pretty Thames Ditton!'

'Is that what you call her?' he said, smiling at last. 'It suits her. Do you give everyone nicknames? Do you have a name for me, too?'

'Of course!' she said, before remembering that she'd called him Too-Good-To-Be-True New Malden on account of the way he seemed almost suspiciously nice. He always gave up his seat for old ladies and pregnant women, said sorry when other people trod on his foot, and had one of those gloriously warm and empathetic smiles. If you were casting for a psychological thriller with a killer twist, where the least likely character turned out to be the serial murderer, you'd cast Sanjay.

'I called you Probably-In-The-Caring-Professions New Malden, because you're always so thoughtful towards everyone,' she said, rapidly employing skills honed by decades of editing, rearranging and substituting words. *Nice swerve, baby. She's still got it.*

'Wow, how perceptive of you,' said Sanjay.

'Well, it is a particular skill of mine,' she replied. 'I'm rarely wrong. So, why have you been avoiding the fair flame-haired maiden of Thames Ditton?'

'Oh, it really doesn't matter,' said Sanjay, blushing in a way that was completely endearing, and only aroused Iona's curiosity.

'Go on, you can tell me,' she said in a stage whisper, reaching across the table and patting his hand. 'I'm the soul of discretion.' This wasn't entirely true, obviously, but he wasn't to know that discretion, in Iona's world, was more of a stretch target than an *actualité*.

Iona knew that the best way to persuade someone to talk is to stay quiet. People, when confronted with silence, feel the overwhelming urge to fill it with something. So she sipped her tea and waited. She watched Sanjay struggle with the decision, then gradually assume the resigned air of someone who was about to spill the beans, and Iona knew she'd won.

'Well, you see, I was about to ask her out on a date, the

day Piers choked, but now she just thinks I'm a complete idiot. I've only ever talked to her that once, and I totally crashed and burned,' he said.

'Just because she's impossibly pretty doesn't mean she's also nice, you know. You'd probably find she's not the right girl for you at all if you actually did get to know her,' said Iona. 'Perhaps she's mean to puppies and follows Katie Hopkins on Twitter.'

'It's not just that she's gorgeous. I'm not that shallow,' said Sanjay. 'She reads actual books, you know. Every morning. Really interesting ones. And she can do the whole of the *Times* quick crossword before we get to Waterloo. And when she listens to music on her headphones, she closes her eyes and moves her fingers in the air like she's playing an imaginary keyboard. And she smiles at complete strangers like she really means it. And she has this little scattering of freckles like a constellation across the bridge of her nose. And—'

Iona held up her hand. 'Okay, stop! Stop, for the love of God, before I vomit too. Believe me, you don't want that. The carriage reeked of stomach acid all the way to Waterloo. It quite put me off my tea. You've convinced me. Although I still suspect that her "playing an imaginary keyboard with her eyes closed" wouldn't win you over if she were ugly. So, you want to get to know her better, right?'

'Yes! I don't even know her name!' said Sanjay. 'And I can't exactly call her Impossibly-Pretty Thames Ditton, can I?'

'Well, Sanjay. It's your lucky day, because One: I like you. Two: I owe you one, since thanks to you, I don't have the death of a fellow commuter on my conscience. And Three: I am a professional!' said Iona, illustrating each point with an additional finger in the air.

'You're a matchmaker?' said Sanjay.

'No! I'm a magazine therapist!' she replied.

'Oh, you mean an agony aunt?' said Sanjay.

She sighed, liking him a teeny tiny bit less. Just as well he was starting from a high base.

'All you need to do, Sanjay, is to sit with me in Carriage Three whenever you can, and I will engineer it all for you, just you wait.'

Iona sat back in her seat, stroking Lulu and smiling to herself. She could feel a rather poetic quid pro quo coming on. This was going to be *fun*. And Sanjay and Impossibly-Pretty Thames Ditton were both millennials, weren't they? Getting to know them both better – to watch a little love affair blossom, even – would be perfect research for her column. At the very least, it would give her something else to think about. She couldn't wait to tell Bea. Bea was a sucker for a good romance.

The train jerked and started moving forward, accompanied by a collective sigh of relief from the passengers.

Piers

18:17 Waterloo to Surbiton

The harder Piers tried to rectify the situation, the worse it got. He thought back a few years, to the days when he'd been nicknamed Midas, and every stock he'd touched turned to gold. He'd felt invulnerable. A Master of the Universe. Now, whatever he so much as looked at turned to sludge. He knew that the problem was he *cared* too much. You had to approach the markets with a certain insouciance, sidle up to them stealthily, like trying to chat up a pretty barmaid. The more it mattered, the more desperate they thought you were, the more likely the numbers were to throw a drink in your face and ban you from the pub. And right now, it mattered *a lot*. More than it ever had.

He stared down at his polished Gucci loafers as he walked towards Platform 5 on autopilot. His shoes, like his Rolex watch and his Hermès ties, always gave him a certain amount of reassurance. Nothing really bad could happen to a man in Gucci loafers, could it?

By the time he boarded the train, it was about to leave, so was already crowded. He could see only one available place and it was, as always, opposite Crazy Dog Woman. The train equivalent of the restricted-view theatre seat. The least popular seat in the house. Just as he'd thought his day couldn't get any worse.

As if Piers's life wasn't screwed up enough right now, this lady was seriously messing with his regular commute. For a start, she made him feel irritatingly *beholden*. He and she were connected for ever by his near-death experience. Piers hated feeling beholden. He liked the satisfying simplicity of knowing that everything he was, everything he owned, was down to him, and him alone.

The other reason he dreaded sitting near this woman was that she obviously hated him. Being hated was another thing Piers didn't like. One of his great skills was making people warm to him. He was a chameleon – he could play the charmer, the intellectual, the confidante, the joker – whatever the particular situation required. And yet, this woman had yelled at him. In public, *twice*. She'd accused him of 'toxic masculinity'. Ordinarily, he'd have taken that as a backhanded compliment, but she obviously hadn't meant it as one. And now, she was glaring at him again.

Much as Piers hated to be the first to capitulate in a fight, in this case it would be in his interests to do so. He wanted his commute to return to the comfortable place it had been. The gentle segue on rails from his work life to his home life.

At least this woman was *interesting*. In his rarefied world of high finance, members' clubs and fancy catered dinner parties, he never came across people like her. And she'd be a challenge. If he could make her like him, it would prove he'd still 'got it'. One thing he'd always liked – until recently, at least – was a challenge.

Piers sat down, cautiously, on the seat opposite Crazy Dog Woman. He summoned up the most appropriate sentiments and prepared to switch on the full beam of his charm. But although he'd marshalled the required words into order, they just wouldn't come out of his mouth, like belligerent striking workers refusing to cross a picket line. He waited, until the silence between them became unbearable, then he cleared his throat and tried again.

'I think we got off on the wrong foot,' he said, the words, once released, coming out in a torrent. 'And I suppose I really should thank you, for helping me out the other day.'

She raised one eyebrow at him – a facial feat that he'd always wanted to be able to achieve, but had never managed, despite hours of practising in front of a mirror. He added a grudging envy to the list of negative emotions he felt about his travelling companion.

'You *suppose you should*, or are you actually grateful?' she said, making him squirm, which nobody had done since his boss had asked him to justify a particularly large expense claim, involving scandalously priced champagne at a strip club.

'Uh, no, I really am grateful, honestly,' he said, discovering as he spoke the words that they were surprisingly true. 'I thought I was going to die.' She gave him another hard stare and said nothing.

'I'm Piers Sanders,' he said, with his most winning smile, holding his hand out across the table like an olive branch. She said nothing and crossed her arms across her capacious, slightly crêpey bosom, leaving his hand hanging awkwardly.

'Oh, don't be like that,' he said. 'I am trying here! At least tell me your name. Can't we start over?'

'Iona Iverson,' she said, finally, proffering her hand reluctantly. He shook it. It was all rings and nails, digging into his palm. Was she deliberately squeezing too hard, to make him wince? Surely not.

'Tell me, Iona,' he said. 'Why did you, and your cute little dog, describe me as *toxic*? I'm wounded. Seriously!' He clutched his chest with both hands, and gave her his soulful Labrador puppy look, the one he used to employ when he wanted the latest female intern to fetch his dry cleaning or a box of doughnuts, back when that sort of entirely reasonable request didn't get you hauled into HR.

'I just know your type,' she said, showing no sign of thawing.

'Oh? And what is my "type"?' He put slightly aggressive air quotes around the word 'type' before he could stop himself.

'The *type* that uses those irritating air quotes. That talks too loudly. That manspreads and mansplains. That believes they're better than other people. The type that judges everything by its cost and thinks the accumulation of money is the most important thing in life. The type that assumes an obviously faked charm can get them out of any situation—'

'Stop!' he said. He hadn't been expecting a list quite that

long, and there were people listening – although not, he hoped, agreeing. 'Look, you don't know me, and I think you're guilty of some heinous stereotyping. I'm not at all what you'd expect.'

'Go on, then,' she said. 'Surprise me.'

Oh God. He'd walked right into that one. There were more surprising facts about Piers's life than he cared to admit, but he'd spent decades not sharing those, and he wasn't about to start now.

Iona pulled a large silver hip flask and a glass out of her extraordinarily commodious handbag. That thing was like a Tardis, holding – it seemed – beverages for every occasion, and God knows what else. He wouldn't be at all surprised if she produced a lightsaber next. Or a wand.

As Piers rifled through the possible responses to Iona's challenge, searching for the elusive sweet spot between the too obvious and the too personal, he wondered whether his travelling companion was actually a Jedi Knight or a Grand High Witch, because he felt an overwhelming urge to *confess*. Perhaps he really could tell this complete stranger what he'd been doing. Maybe that would be a release of sorts, stop the toxic stew of secrets from churning around in his stomach, poisoning everything. Or maybe it would tip over the first of a whole damn row of dominoes, causing a knock-on effect that could end who knows where. Finally, he settled on a truth. Not, by a long shot, the whole truth, but the original one. The one that had started it all.

'I hate my job,' he said. 'Not just a little bit. I really, really hate it.'

He watched her face soften just slightly into a semblance of a smile.

'Well, well. You win,' she said. 'I actually wasn't expecting that at all. What is your job?'

'I'm in the City. A futures trader. Do you know what that means?'

'Yes. It means patronizing, arrogant tosser. No! Silly me. It means rich, patronizing, arrogant tosser,' said Iona. Piers decided to let that one slide. Besides, it was hardly something he'd not heard before.

'Well, I used to love it, but not . . . any more,' he said.

Piers had become so accustomed recently to cover-ups and evasions that the honesty of this statement felt strange on his lips. He'd given away way too much. He quickly deflected the subject back to her, and away from himself.

'Do you love what you do, Iona?'

'Oh, yes. I do, actually. More than anything. Except Bea, of course,' she said, clutching her hands to her chest and spinning the most vulgar of her rings, the one that had left a dent in his palm, so that the large ruby caught the light, turned it red, and splintered it on to the window next to her, making it look unnervingly like the aftermath of a crime scene.

'Bea?' he asked.

'My wife,' she replied. 'We've been together thirty-five years, and got married as soon as it was legal. The love of my life. Are you married?'

'Yes. She's called Candida,' he said.

'Yikes. Like the yeast infection?' said Iona.

'Well, your wife's named after an *insect*. Candida is an ancient saint's name, actually,' he explained, as he'd heard Candida do many times. 'From the Latin for "pure white".'

'So, a racist yeast infection. Why is it that white is synonymous with pure, innocent, virginal, whereas black signifies malevolence and depression?' She glared at him as if he'd invented the language.

Piers didn't think he'd ever been as glad to see the sign reading SURBITON slide into view.

As Piers walked towards his Porsche Carrera in the station car park, he pressed his key fob, causing all the lights to flash in a way that signalled *successful man approaching* to any onlookers.

He thought about his accidentally divulged truth. When had he started hating his job? He wasn't entirely sure. The knowledge had crept up on him gradually. The problem was, it was more than a job – it was a whole lifestyle, a personality, a belief system. It was wound around his organs like a giant parasite that couldn't be removed without killing its host. If he were no longer a trader, then who would he be?

Plus, there were the practicalities. Without the ridiculously high salary and bonuses he'd become accustomed to, he'd never be able to cover the monthly payments on the Porsche. Certainly not the mortgage interest on the house. They'd moved from Wimbledon to the less salubrious, but cheaper, Surbiton two years ago, because Candida wanted a swimming pool and a tennis court, and a separate apartment for the au pair.

That was something else he'd not be able to afford if he

changed careers: his wife. Candida, much like his car, his suit and his watch, was a status symbol. A trophy wife. She'd been the proof that he'd made it, the icing on the cake of his new, impressive life.

And now that icing had solidified into cement, keeping his feet trapped in the life he was no longer sure he wanted while the waters slowly rose around him.

Iona

Iona breathed hard on the album, then brushed it off with her sleeve and placed it on the turntable.

'Do you remember this one, sweetheart?' she called back over her shoulder to Bea.

'Dolly Parton. It always reminds me of that night, when you first got your job at the magazine. What show was I in then?' said Bea.

'*Les Misérables*,' said Iona, taking Bea's hand in hers and twirling her round to the music. 'Third prostitute and random guest at the wedding. I crashed the backstage during the interval, and we celebrated my new job offer in the wardrobe room. Do you remember?'

'Of course I do! Making out behind a rail of French military costumes. I missed my cue for the wedding scene, which completely messed up the choreography!' said Bea, and she tipped her head back and laughed, looking – just for a moment – exactly like the woman she'd been back then, nearly thirty years ago.

They'd been so broke, after buying the house, and Iona couldn't believe her luck when someone offered to *pay her* to go to parties and then gossip about them, which was how she spent all her time anyway.

'Remember how we went out for dinner with some of the cast, and I climbed on to the bar and pranced down it in six-inch heels while the chorus of Les Mis sang "Nine To Five"?' she said, as Bea spun her expertly. They never could agree on who took the lead when they were dancing.

Dolly had, of course, been talking about 9 a.m. to 5 p.m., whereas Iona generally worked from 9 p.m. to 5 a.m. What energy they'd had in those days! Although they'd always slept in until mid-afternoon.

'You'll never guess what I found when I was clearing out my desk drawers the other day,' said Iona, breaking away as Dolly's voice gave way to the final instrumental. She walked over to her handbag and pulled out a silver rectangular box. 'Look!'

'It's the Dictator!' said Bea. The magazine had given Iona the use of one of their drivers, who would ferry her and Bea between parties, then drive them back to East Molesey at the end of the night. A Dictaphone sat in the back seat of the car, and as they left each party, they'd relay descriptions of the guests, the ambiance and the gossip in increasingly slurred tones on to its minuscule cassettes. Iona called it 'the Dictator' since it always insisted on knowing all the details, however much they just wanted to get home and sleep. 'Do you still have any of the tapes?'

'I think most of them were archived, but I found this one, from 1993. You want to listen?' said Iona. Bea nodded, sat in the armchair and kicked off her shoes. Iona squinted at the tiny buttons, before selecting the one labelled PLAY.

So, we've just left the Quaglino's reopening party, she heard herself say in a voice that seemed to come from a different world, which she supposed it did. *They say Terence Conran spent a fortune on the refurb. How much did he spend, darling?*

I don't know. But millions. Squillions, even, came the reply.

'That's me!' squealed Bea.

'Of course it is, darling,' said Iona. 'Shush. Let's listen.'

Who was there? asked a male voice.

'That's your driver! What was his name?' said Bea.

'Darren,' Iona replied.

EVERYONE was there, obviously, said young Iona, *but the real gossip was about who WASN'T there. We were all expecting Princess Di to show up, but she never did. Rumour has it she's too furious about those photos of her exercising at the gym that were printed in the* Daily Mirror.

You can't entirely blame her! said young Bea. *She was using the weight machines. The one that trims your inner thighs. You could see her crotch! Not exactly princessy!*

Even princesses have crotches, honey. Anyhow, she was wearing a leotard and Lycra shorts; it was hardly Sharon Stone in Basic Instinct. *Can't see why it would stop her showing up at the biggest event in town*, said young Iona, showing a remarkable lack of empathy in old Iona's opinion.

What did you eat? asked Darren, who was always responsibly and irritatingly sober, and Iona suspected had been briefed by the magazine to make sure they never forgot to log all the relevant details on the Dictator.

Huge platters of fruits de mer! replied young Iona. *Prawns, lobster, crab, oysters – all nestled in crushed ice. I loved it. Bea didn't, did you, darling?*

Too many legs, apart from the oysters, which didn't have enough, said young Bea, making old Bea snort with laughter. Iona clicked STOP on the Dictaphone and pulled Bea to her feet as Dolly started singing 'Jolene'. She hugged Bea tightly to her, resting her chin on Bea's shoulder.

'I think they're going to fire me, darling,' she said, dropping the words into the empty air behind Bea's back.

'Why on earth would they do that?' said Bea, and Iona could feel the muscles of her back stiffen with outrage. 'You're their star!'

'I used to be, honey, but not any more,' said Iona.

'Well, you'll always be my star,' said Bea. 'Always. The brightest star in the sky. What's the brightest star called?'

'It's called Sirius,' said Iona.

'Well, you're my Sirius,' said Bea.

'Siriusly?' said Iona, pulling Bea even more tightly towards her and forcing a small laugh to muffle the sound of her crying.

Sanjay

08:19 New Malden to Waterloo

As Sanjay boarded the train, he heard a piercing whistle. Not from the guard, but from inside the carriage. The sort of whistle that involves putting two fingers inside your mouth, like a farmer calling his sheepdog. He looked, along with everyone else in the carriage, towards the source of the sound. It was Iona, waving at him wildly.

Sanjay's stomach lurched as he saw that, just like on the day of the grape, about two weeks ago, she was sitting next to The Girl On The Train. This was it. His opportunity. This time, he was not going to mess it up.

Sanjay walked towards them, trying so hard to look casual that he was conscious of the movements of every single muscle in his body.

The Girl On The Train had a book in front of her, as always, her place held by a leather bookmark. She was obviously not

56

the kind of person who turned the corners of the pages or, even worse, broke the spine.

'Good morning, Iona!' he said, channelling a nonchalant James Bond greeting Miss Moneypenny.

'Sanjay, darling!' she replied, as she picked up Lulu from the seat opposite her, and put her on her lap.

'Here. Lulu doesn't mind giving up her seat for a bona fide nursing hero, do you, sweet pea? It'll do her good to learn how to share. It's called *hot desking*, you know. It's all the rage,' she said to the dog, who didn't look entirely thrilled about the change of location.

Sanjay sat in the newly vacated seat while he tried to corral his thoughts, which were racing around like frightened sheep, into some semblance of order.

'Sanjay, this is Emmie. With an IE, not a Y,' said Iona, gesturing at The Girl On The Train, who now had an actual name. 'Almost a palindrome, but not quite.'

What on earth was a palindrome? It sounded like a medical ailment, but not one he'd ever come across.

'I remember you!' said Emmie, with a smile that created a dimple, just on one side. Her hair today was tied into a sort of knot, from which a few tendrils had escaped. 'You're the incredible nurse who came to the rescue when that man was dying right next to me!'

Sanjay could feel himself blushing. He tried to convey action hero vibes, but suspected he looked more like a flustered Moneypenny than a suave Bond.

'Wasn't he just amazing?' said Iona, like a proud mother after watching a Nativity play performance. 'Sanjay, Emmie is in digital advertising. She does all sorts of clever things with websites and social media for big brands who want to be in with the youth.' Iona gave him a pointed stare which clearly translated as *now it's your turn to say something interesting*.

'Wow,' he said.

'Well,' said Emmie, 'it's not half as impressive as what you do. I mean, you actually save lives. I've seen you do it! So calm and in control. I just get people to buy more washing powder or loo roll. It must be really rewarding, helping people like that.'

'I guess,' replied Sanjay. He searched for the perfect anecdote about his job – one that portrayed him as caring but strong. Heroic, yet humble. Just as he was about to launch himself into it, Iona's eyes widened, and she started jerking her head to the side. Was she having a seizure? No, she was trying to communicate something to him. Sanjay stared back at her helplessly, trying to work out the code. He was sure she was trying to help him, but she was just making him more agitated.

Sanjay felt a sharp kick on his ankle and yelped, then glared at Iona who just widened her eyes further and jerked her head again, towards the window. Sanjay turned to his right. He'd not really been aware of the man sitting next to him at all. Partly because he'd been so busy looking at Emmie, but also because the man was so bland.

Sanjay had noticed that the suit brigade on the train – the lawyers, bankers, accountants and suchlike – tended to wear a type of uniform. They all chose suits in grey or navy, with plain or striped shirts in inoffensive colours, and brogue-style shoes. Some of them tried to break out, to show a spark of originality and individuality, to say *I'm more interesting than you might think*, by wearing an amusingly patterned tie, or brightly striped socks, or witty cufflinks. Not this guy. He was definitely not the comedy-tie type. Everything he wore looked designed to blend into the background. Most men, as they aged, developed distinguishing features – bulbous noses, jowls or hairy ears. He had none of that. Nothing memorable or significant.

Now Sanjay saw that the man was sitting in front of an open lunch box containing a sandwich, a banana and a Kit-Kat. Did people still do lunch boxes? Surely that was what Pret A Manger was for? In his hand, shaking slightly, was a slip of paper which he was staring at, open-mouthed.

Iona kicked him again and mouthed, less silently than she intended, 'What does it SAY?' jerking her head towards the piece of paper.

'Can I help you?' the man said to Iona, much to Sanjay's mortification. Iona, however, was completely unembarrassed and undeterred.

'Actually, I was wondering if I could help *you*,' she said. 'That piece of paper seems to be bothering you.'

Iona reached over and, to Sanjay's surprise, the man passed the paper to her.

'I CAN'T DO THIS ANY MORE,' read Iona. 'Good God, it's a cry for help from your *sandwich*. No wonder you look a bit stunned.'

'I think it's more likely to be from my wife, actually,' said the man.

'She must really hate making your lunch,' said Emmie,

leaning forward, her arm on the table, so close to Sanjay's that he could feel the heat emanating from her skin.

'I suspect it runs a little deeper than that, dear,' said Iona. 'I'm Iona Iverson, and this is Emmie and Sanjay. What's your name?'

'David Harman,' replied the man.

'You must be new to this train!' said Iona. 'I've not seen you before.'

'No, I've been taking it every weekday for decades, actually,' said David. 'I've seen you many times.'

'Oh. Gosh. Silly me,' said Iona. It was the first time Sanjay had seen her look discombobulated, but she rallied in no time.

'Did you know your wife wasn't happy, David Harman?' she said.

It turned out that having broken every norm of commuting already, there was no stopping Iona, who now thought it okay to get involved in everybody's business. Where would it end? Sanjay also had the sense that everyone else around them was only pretending to read their papers or listen to their music. They were actually following every word. Had they had become the in-house entertainment?

'No! I know we've been a bit . . . stuck in a rut,' replied David. 'But we've been married nearly forty years! It's hardly going to be all fire and romance at our age, is it?' Then he paused and looked reflective. 'I suppose I should have guessed something was up, because of the granola,' he said.

'The granola?' echoed Iona.

'Yes. We've been eating the same breakfast every morning

for about a decade. I have wholemeal toast with that spread that's supposed to lower your cholesterol, and a lightly poached egg, and Olivia has Weetabix. If it's the weekend, I add a thin slice of smoked salmon and she adds a chopped banana and some honey.' *Where was this going?* wondered Sanjay. Were they going to get a real-time outline of David's entire weekly routine?

'Anyhow,' he continued in a monotone. He was not a natural raconteur. 'A couple of weeks ago she switched to *granola*. For no apparent reason. It looks like there's only a small step from granola to impending divorce, doesn't it? I bet they don't put that in the small print on the packet.' He exhaled hard and leaned back in his seat, as if he'd just been punched in the stomach. Which, in a way, he had.

'Well, before you start suing the granola manufacturers or assuming the worst, try talking to her. I bet you haven't listened to her properly for years, have you?' Iona glared at David, which was the last thing the poor man needed right now. 'We "women of a certain age" just want to be seen, heard, made to feel like we matter. We need to know that we're not irrelevant or surplus to requirements,' said Iona, who seemed to be taking this all rather personally.

'Are you a marriage guidance counsellor?' asked David.

'She's a magazine therapist,' said Sanjay. Then, before David could say anything else, he added, 'Not an agony aunt.'

'Well, quite,' said Iona. She looked as if she were about to add something, but was interrupted by the guard's voice announcing their imminent arrival at Waterloo.

Everyone began to jostle into position to exit the train.

Somehow, Emmie was already at the carriage doors. She turned, as if she could feel Sanjay staring after her, and waved at him. 'Have a great day,' she mouthed, or something along those lines.

'Sanjay,' said Iona, in a tone that implied *I'm not angry, just disappointed.* 'You're going to have to try a little harder, you know. I can't do this all on my own.'

All day, whenever he had a few free minutes between dealing with patients and catching up on his admin, Sanjay replayed the events of that morning in his head, cringing as he remembered his lines: 'Wow,' and 'I guess.' Iona was quite right. Surely he could have done better than that? Perhaps he would have done, had he not been completely blindsided by that man, whose name he'd forgotten, and his talking sandwich.

He spotted Julie Harrison in the waiting room: someone with much bigger problems than his.

'How are you feeling, Julie?' he asked.

'Oh, you remembered me,' she said, smiling at him. 'I'm scared, Sanjay.'

Julie was sitting in the waiting room next to her husband, who looked even more frightened than she did. He was clutching an open newspaper, but Sanjay suspected he wasn't actually reading it, since he seemed to be staring blankly at a point on the featureless wall in front of him.

'I know you are,' he said, taking her hand in both of his. 'The waiting is the worst bit. Once you know what you're dealing with, we can make a plan, and it'll all seem more manageable.'

'And it might turn out to be a false alarm, right? A cyst or something, like my friend Sally had,' said Julie, looking at him beseechingly, as if he had the power to make it so. He wished he did.

'Yes, of course, it could be,' he said. Although it wasn't. He'd had a quick look at Julie's file, waiting in the consultant's in-tray. It was a sizable grade three, triple-negative invasive ductal carcinoma. In nursing school, they'd been taught that cancers came in a whole variety of types. Like viral infections that can range from a common cold to Ebola, cancers cover a spectrum from the relatively easily curable to the sort that will most probably kill you within weeks. Julie's cancer, he knew, was closer to the Ebola end of the field.

'I'll come and find you after you've seen the consultant,' he said.

The family room was already occupied by a clutch of weeping relatives, so Sanjay slipped into the storage cupboard. He leaned his back against the wall, then slid down to the floor where he sat among the dust balls, head on his knees, next to an abandoned pair of crutches, feeling the sweat beading on his forehead and taking deep gulps of air.

As he often did, because he found the words hypnotically soothing and distracting, he recited the elements of the periodic table in his head, in order of atomic number: *Hydrogen, helium, lithium, beryllium, boron, carbon, nitrogen* ... By the time he reached number thirty-seven on the third round – the often overlooked, but actually quite interesting, rubidium – his thoughts had stilled, his breathing calmed, and his heart stopped pounding.

Emmie

'Take a seat, Emmie,' said Joey, her boss. Emmie pulled out a chair between Jen, her favourite copywriter and good friend, and Tim, the latest floppy-haired and somewhat vacuous office intern. She watched as Tim wrote EMMY on his company-branded notepad, underneath JOEY and JEN. She resisted the urge to reach across him and correct his spelling with a red pen.

They had to tiptoe around Tim's well-intentioned ineptitude, since his father was their chief toilet roll client. He'd signed off on an ad last week with the headline BECAUSE YOUR AMAZING, and Joey had just smiled tightly and told him to chalk it up to experience. Anyone else making an error like that would have been assigned to the office coffee and bagel run for at least a week.

'Hartford Pharmaceuticals are coming in next week to discuss their latest new brand launch, and they sent a briefing pack over in advance, so we can quickly reach light speed, hitting the ground running with some category-redefining, expectation-busting early creative concepts,' said Joey. Emmie wondered whether he spoke the same way at home: *Really launch yourselves into those bowls of Rice Krispies, kids. Let's smash through those nutritional guidelines and redefine the breakfast paradigm.*

Joey leaned down and picked up a plastic bag which he emptied into the middle of the table. He looked around at the team, as if disappointed that no one had given him a standing ovation.

'Diet pills,' he said. 'As yet unnamed – that's part of our brief. The easy way to melt away the pounds and achieve the body you've always wanted.' Tim wrote DIET PILLS on his pad and underlined it.

'Hallelujah! It's the Holy Grail,' said Jen, picking up one of the blister packs of tablets, popping two into her hand and knocking them back with a glug of her sugar-laden Frappuccino. 'Perhaps they can do something about my arse.'

'You have a fabulous arse,' said Emmie, for the hundred and twelfth time. 'You only hate it because of the patriarchy.'

'Bollocks. I hate it because of the cellulite,' said Jen.

Tim wrote PATRIARCHY and SELLULIGHT on his pad.

'Anyhow,' said Emmie, 'I bet you they don't actually work. Look, it says here *causes weight loss as part of a calorie-controlled diet*. Doesn't *anything* cause weight loss as part of a calorie-controlled diet?'

'Settle down, kids,' said Joey, who was only five years older than Emmie. Nobody in their office was older than forty. Where did all the middle-aged advertising people go? 'So, what we need is a state-of-the-art web presence, digital advertising on all the usual social media, targeting young, body-conscious girls. And we'll have a kick-ass influencer campaign, obviously. The story needs to be something along the lines of *I felt so fat and hated myself, but then I found the answer to my prayers in this little box. Now I have the body, and the man, I truly deserve.* Simples.'

'You've got to be kidding, Joey,' said Emmie. 'You want us to create a campaign based on making women who already feel terrible about themselves for no reason feel even worse?'

'I'm sorry if it offends you,' said Joey, looking offended, 'but isn't that what we do? We highlight an issue and provide a solution. That's what we're paid for – to sell the dream.'

'This isn't selling a dream, though, is it? It's selling shame and discontent. I'm honestly not comfortable working on this one, Joey,' said Emmie.

Joey sighed. 'Emmie, why on earth did you decide to go into advertising if you have such an inflexible conscience? But fine. The last thing I want is you being all holier-than-thou in front of our highest-billing client. You can swap with Sophie and take the toothpaste brief. Hopefully she'll be less of a . . .'

Emmie braced herself for the arrival of her least favourite word.

'. . . snowflake,' finished Joey, as predicted.

Tim picked up his pencil and drew a heavy line through EMMY.

Emmie got up and left the room, knowing that she'd just used up the majority of the brownie points it'd taken months of hard work to accumulate. She knew she was one of Joey's top performers but, even so, she could only push it so far.

She was going to have to do something spectacular with the toothpaste or she'd find herself on the list for the next 'office downsizing'. Or 're-sizing', as Joey had rebranded it.

She remembered her train journey that morning, and Sanjay – the nurse who'd stopped that man choking a couple of weeks ago. What on earth would he think of her if he knew that she spent her days finding ways of making people feel dissatisfied, then selling them solutions that they neither wanted nor needed? Not that he'd waste time thinking of her – he'd have far more important life-or-death-type things on his mind.

Emmie had chosen this career because she'd thought it would be creative, young, fun and vibrant. It was all those things, and most of the time she loved it. She just hadn't expected it to make her feel so *grubby*. Still, she had a plan now. She was going to pitch for clients who were doing something *good*, who'd help her regain her self-respect. Environmentalists, food banks, animal shelters. Surely there must be loads of charities looking for help from a hotshot agency like this one?

She'd just been blown temporarily off course by that stupid email which had completely knocked her confidence. At least it appeared to have been a one-off. She'd been opening her emails warily for days in case another toxic message was lurking there, but so far nothing.

Emmie's phone pinged and she looked down, expecting to see a supportive message from Jen, sent surreptitiously from the meeting Emmie had just vacated, but it was a text from an unknown number. She knew, before she even opened it, who it would be from.

YOU THINK YOU'RE SO CLEVER, BUT WE ALL KNOW YOU'RE A FAKE.

Emmie's fingers fumbled and dropped her phone. She bent down to pick it up, scanning the open-plan office again for clues. Who was doing this? Who hated her that much? Who on earth could be so underhand and cowardly?

Who is this? she typed with slippery thumbs, ignoring her own advice to clients on dealing with trolls: NEVER ENGAGE. It turned out that was easier said than done. She watched as three dots appeared on her screen. They were replying. Then, just two words appeared:

A FRIEND.

This was no friend of hers. But nor was it some random stranger. It was someone who knew her email address and her phone number, and could see the clothes she was wearing.

And the worst thing was, although she knew she should just delete them and discount them, those words were already burrowing into her subconscious and festering.

Emmie had always been surprised by her success, had secretly suspected it was just a fluke, and had worried that one day her extraordinary run of luck might peter out.

Now it looked as if maybe it had.

Iona

08:05 Hampton Court to Waterloo

Iona was so busy reading through the latest letters sent to *Ask Iona* that she didn't even notice Emmie until she'd sat down on the seat opposite.

'Oh, wow. Actual letters,' she said. 'I didn't think people wrote those any more.'

'They don't generally,' said Iona. 'More's the pity. But, strangely, when they're writing to a magazine therapist they often do. I guess it feels more private, more personal than an email. I can tell a lot just from the handwriting, you know. It conveys not just character, but emotion and mental state, too.'

'What does that one say?' asked Emmie, nodding at the paper in Iona's hand. 'Can you tell me?' Iona had discovered that everyone was fascinated by other people's problems. It was why drivers slow down on the motorway as they pass the site of a car crash, and it was why she was so successful. *Had been* so successful, she corrected.

'Sure. They're all anonymous, in any case. This one is from a mum who's worried about her teenaged son. She caught him watching porn on his iPad. That's an easy one.' She smiled at Emmie in a way that said *caring, professional and wise*. She often reminded her readers that 90 per cent of communication is non-verbal. The train, which had been stationary for a few minutes, lurched forward as they pulled out of New Malden station, causing some of Iona's tea to slop over the edge of the cup. Thank heavens for saucers. No sign of Sanjay. Drat. He'd missed his opportunity. Again. Foolish boy.

'So, what are you going to tell her?' asked Emmie, looking genuinely interested. Such a charming girl; she could see why Sanjay was so smitten.

'Well, I'm going to advise her to check all the parental controls on her internet service, and I have a very helpful pamphlet on online security that I'll send to her,' said Iona, who was rather proud of her technical know-how. How many *dinosaurs* knew their way around internet security issues, huh?

'Parental controls?' said Emmie, looking at her as if she were a little dim. 'Every boy learns to navigate their way around those by the time they're about ten. And they *all* watch porn. Surely he's just doing what every other perfectly normal teenaged boy is doing?' Iona prickled. Maybe Emmie wasn't right for Sanjay after all. She was a little bit *know-it-all*. Nobody liked a clever-clogs.

'So, what would you suggest then, dear?' she said, trying to sound fascinated rather than narky.

'Well,' said Emmie, 'She could see it as an *opportunity*.' She looked at Iona a little nervously.

'Go on,' said Iona, 'I'm interested.' She realized that she actually was. Maybe Emmie could throw a 'sizzling millennial' perspective on the whole thing.

'She could talk to him about how pornography isn't real. I mean, actual girls don't look like those girls, do they? And actual sex certainly shouldn't be like that sex. She'd be doing all his future girlfriends a service, wouldn't she?' said Emmie.

To be fair, the girl had a point. Iona wasn't sure whether to be pleased or annoyed, so she settled for both.

'Rather an awkward conversation, don't you think?' said Iona.

'Well, that's no bad thing, is it?' said Emmie. 'He'll be so mortified about having to discuss sex with his mum that maybe it'll put him off the porn for a while!'

'Well, quite,' she said. 'You're quite good at this, you know. That is precisely what I was going on to say, in fact. So many young boys these days, for example, have no idea that pubic hair is *a thing*, because porn stars don't have any, so if they do ever come across it in real life, they're disgusted. Why should women feel forced to make themselves look like a prepubescent child? I myself have always favoured a 1970s "natural woman" style. A lush Lady Garden, with the occasional prune to stop things getting completely out of control. Wild and proud, that's what I say!'

Emmie was looking a bit stunned, slightly queasy, even. Oh dear. Had she gone a little over the top? Young people today were so sensitive.

'Iona,' she whispered, leaning over the table between them. 'You do know everyone is listening, don't you?'

'Oh, don't be silly, dear. They're all far too busy with their newspapers and iPhones and stuff to listen in to our little conversation,' she said.

'So, do you live near Hampton Court Palace?' asked Emmie, which was such a non sequitur that it took Iona a while to effect the mental U-turn required.

'Yes,' she replied. 'Bea and I bought a house by the river in East Molesey nearly thirty years ago. We'd just moved back to the UK from Paris, and were horrified at the prices in central London. East Molesey seemed like the perfect compromise. Only a short train journey to town, and right by the Thames, the Palace and Bushy Park.' She was going to refer back to their earlier conversation with a witty pun on '*Bushy* Park', but Emmie cut in before she had a chance.

'I've always meant to go to the Palace,' said Emmie. 'I was fascinated by the Tudors at school. Do you think the headless ghost of Anne Boleyn stills haunts the place?'

'Oh, my goodness. You must go!' said Iona. 'There's the most fabulous maze in the grounds. I've spent years learning how to navigate my way seamlessly around it. It's great fun.' Then she had an idea. A brilliant one.

'Tell you what!' she said. 'I could show you around! Why don't we go this Sunday, ten a.m.? Are you free?' She held her breath, waiting for the answer.

'Sunday. Um, I'm not sure . . .' stuttered Emmie. Iona could tell she was searching around for an excuse, but couldn't let this opportunity slip.

'Please,' she said, allowing herself, just this once, to sound a little needy. Sometimes the ends justified the means.

'Oh, okay. Why not? Thank you. I'll see you then, if not

before,' said Emmie. Iona gave herself a mental high-five. 'Oh, by the way, I meant to show you this.' Emmie reached into her pocket and pulled a photo up on her mobile. It was a young girl with ridiculous hair, face obscured by a lurid green face-pack, lying in a bath full of bubbles, reading a copy of *Modern Woman*. 'Isn't that your magazine that Fizz is reading?'

'Yes, it is,' said Iona. 'Who on earth is Fizz? What sort of a name is that? I mean, it's fine for a canned drink, or a bath bomb, but for an actual human being?!?'

'She's a TikTok sensation,' said Emmie. 'I met her through work, but she's become a good friend of mine. You should get her to do a column for your magazine. I bet she'd love that. I'll ask her, if you like.'

'That's really kind of you, Emmie,' said Iona. 'I'll see what my editor says.' She had no intention of talking to Ed, obviously. She was teetering on a knife-edge already, without bothering him with C-list celebrities on a children's video-sharing app. But it was sweet of Emmie, in any case.

The train drew into Waterloo station, and Emmie shrugged on her coat and put her phone back in the pocket.

'See you on Sunday!' she said as she dashed off.

Iona smiled to herself. She collected her things together, picked up Lulu and made her way, along with the crowd, to the train doors. She felt a hand on her arm, and turned to look at a man, around her age, staring earnestly at her.

'I love a full muff, too,' he said. 'So hard to find these days.' And he gave her an exaggerated wink.

Oh, for goodness' sake. You'd expect that the one benefit of ageing would be not having to deal with that sort of thing. Iona turned to him with the smile of a shark scenting blood in the water.

'You're fond of the ladies, are you?' she said.

'Certainly am,' he replied. 'You interested?'

'Absolutely not,' said Iona. 'You see, I'm rather fond of the ladies too, which I expect – actually, *I very much hope –* is the only thing we have in common.'

Martha

Martha had taken to getting to school twenty minutes earlier than usual. That way she could navigate the corridors before they got too busy. Ever since her very personal picture had been shared to the Year 10 group chat, she'd been constantly tuned to fight-or-flight mode.

Nowhere felt safe. Even the previously hallowed peace of the library had been besmirched. Yesterday, Martha had left her file on one of the library tables while she was searching for a book, and when she'd opened it later, an enlarged print of *that photo* had fallen out. Someone had drawn an arrow in red Sharpie, pointing at the most embarrassing bit, and had written A HANDY PLACE TO STASH MORE BOOKS?

She had thought about skipping school altogether – blotting her perfect attendance record for ever – but what would she do with all those acres of empty time other than berate herself over and over again for having been so utterly stupid?

Martha didn't blame Freddie, despite the whole thing having been his idea.

He'd begged her to send him a photo of herself naked, legs apart. He'd told her he'd seen *loads* of vaginas already, and it really wasn't a big deal. That's what everyone did when they liked someone, he'd said. And Martha was trying very hard to be just like everyone else.

It turned out, however, that Freddie was just as inept and naive about all this stuff as she was, since he'd been so excited to receive Martha's pic that he'd sent it on, triumphantly, to his best friend. Freddie's friend was so amused that quiet, studious Freddie, who was usually more aroused by a neat line of computer code than girls, had scored a nude, that he shared it with one other boy. That boy uploaded it to WhatsApp. It had only been there for ten minutes before he'd regretted it and taken it down, but by then it had been screenshotted numerous times and shared everywhere. All that lay between anonymity and notoriety, it transpired, was nine hours and four reckless decisions.

Freddie was distraught, but it was too late for him to take it back now. He also, funnily enough, no longer wanted to be her boyfriend and had disappeared back into the safety of the computer department.

Martha hadn't told her parents. They'd be so disappointed in her and, worse, they'd each blame the other. It had taken years after the divorce for them to stop the constant bickering over her head, and the last thing she wanted to do was to reignite that fire.

Her small group of friends had been horrified on her behalf, and had said all the right, sympathetic, things. But then they'd gradually distanced themselves from her, as if her stupidity were catching. They'd 'forget' to save her a place at lunch or to tell her when they were meeting up after school. They'd also apparently gone collectively deaf, since they no longer heard her when she called after them in the corridor.

Martha had, of course, considered telling the school authorities, but that was only going to get hapless Freddie into terrible trouble – expelled, even – and it wouldn't put the genie back in the bottle. They'd probably do some kind of ghastly school assembly on data privacy and internet security, using her as the cautionary tale, the poster girl for idiocy, which would just keep the incident current for even longer. They'd ban the picture, obviously – tell everyone to delete it immediately. But everyone knew that nothing could be permanently erased these days, and the only thing more alluring than a nude pic was a banned nude pic.

Martha reached the Year 10 lockers and stopped dead in her tracks. Draped across them was a home-made banner, fashioned, it seemed, from somebody's bedsheet and reading STOP SLUT-SHAMING!

Martha felt her cheeks burning. She knew who'd done it. She'd become a cause célèbre among the group of older girls who were always railing against everyday sexism and misogyny. They were only trying to be supportive, but didn't they see that even their well-meaning banner was branding her a slut? Ironic, since she was possibly the only virgin in Year 10, along with Freddie. Anyhow, they didn't want to be her friends, just her protectors, and their suffocating concern only made her feel weaker and more pathetic. More of a target.

Martha could see some of the popular kids approaching. David Attenborough piped up in her head again. *See the group – no, the 'cackle' – of hyenas. They've picked up the scent of the wounded wildebeest calf, separated from the migrating herd, and they close in for the kill.*

She reached up and pulled down the banner, crumpling it into a large ball which she shoved into her locker, where it lurked like a malignant tumour to be excised at a later date, and ducked into the relative safety of the empty geography room. She'd only taken that stupid picture because she desperately wanted to fit in, and now she was more isolated than ever.

She walked over to the globe on the teacher's desk and spun it around with her finger. This world was just a small speck in the universe. She planted her finger on Britain, blotting out all but Cornwall, North Norfolk and the Outer Hebrides. Such a tiny island. And she was just one of millions of minuscule people populating it. So why did she feel like everyone was focusing on *her*? She wished she could go back to the comfortable anonymity she'd never appreciated until now. She didn't care any more about being popular, or even accepted. It was too late for that. She'd settle for being invisible.

Martha sat down at one of the desks, enjoying the last few minutes of solitude before the bell rang for class.

She jumped as there was a tap on the window, right next to her. Then another tap, and a third. Three phones were being pushed against the glass from the playground outside. Three screens dancing along the windowsill, displaying three identical pictures. Six legs thrust akimbo. Multiple reminders of Martha's humiliation.

When was it all going to stop?

Piers

18:17 Waterloo to Surbiton

Piers strode quickly down Platform 5, eyes fixed straight ahead as he passed the third carriage. That woman had made a small hole in a huge can of worms last time he sat with her, and he knew that if she prised it open any further, a whole nest of the things would come swarming out, and he'd never get the lid back on again.

He walked right to the end carriage, which was relatively empty, and took a seat at a table for four. Piers reached into his inside breast pocket and pulled out a battered leather notebook. One of his key rituals was writing his numbers each day into the book with a pencil. Old-school. The rituals were important, as they were signals to the gods of the markets that he meant business and should not be messed with. He, for example, always cracked his knuckles then flexed his fingers before making a significant trade, an action that used to elicit whoops and hollers, and even chants of *Midas! Midas! Midas!* from the trading floor. Not any longer, obviously.

Piers's heart sank as he compared the number at the bottom of today's page with the one on the page before. He was down another 15 per cent. How could that be possible? His heart took a further plunge into the abyss when he saw a flash of violent colour out of the corner of his eye. Was she following him?

'Piers!' she said, dispelling any hope that she might have wandered into his carriage for an altogether different reason. 'I thought I spotted you walking past! Look, since we're now on speaking terms, there's something I've been dying to ask you.' Oh God. He said nothing, since he had no intention of encouraging her. She sat down opposite him, placing her dog on the seat next to her, regardless.

'I need to hear all about the Grape of Wrath,' she said. 'What was it like, the dying thing? Did you have an out-of-body experience and look down on yourself from the ceiling? Did you see your life flash before your eyes?'

Piers squirmed in his seat. This felt like a military interrogation, and he had the uncomfortable sensation that all the passengers around them were listening in.

'Uh, no, I didn't, actually,' he said. 'Isn't that just when you're drowning? I mainly thought about my kids growing up without a father.' This was, in fact, another lie. This was what he realized he *should* have been thinking about, but he was hardly going to confess the truth to a full carriage of eavesdroppers.

'Did it make you decide to do something good? Give all your money to charity?' said Iona. Piers shook his head but felt himself flush as he remembered his hastily offered vow to the Universe. That didn't count, surely? It was extracted under torture conditions and therefore exempted by the Geneva Convention.

How could this woman see inside his head? Still, at least she seemed to have forgotten their conversation from last week.

'Was it staring death in the face that made you realize how much you hated your job? You know, a *What's it all for? Why have I wasted my life?* moment?' Oh, she hadn't forgotten, then. He sighed and checked his watch, calculating how long he had to put up with this before he reached his stop. Eighteen minutes.

'Not really, no,' he said. 'The truth sort of crept up on me over a number of years.'

'But you said you used to love it. What *did* you love about it, at the beginning?' she said, her eyes boring into him so intently that he found himself rifling through the locked filing cabinet of his past, looking for answers.

'Numbers,' he said finally. 'That's what I loved about it. I've always enjoyed playing with numbers.' He stopped, wondering if he could just leave it at that, and waited for Iona to move the conversation on, but she didn't. She just looked at him, silently, until he found himself talking again.

'You see, my childhood was rather . . . chaotic,' he said.

'Chaotic how?' said Iona, leaning forward.

'Uh, the usual things, I guess. An unemployed, often absent, father who spent his dole money at the bookies. Alcoholic mother. I'm sure you know the score. Then I discovered maths, and it was so . . . orderly, inevitable, controlled and neat. Quite the opposite of the rest of my life. And it turned out I was really good at it.'

'And it was maths that helped you escape your child-hood?' asked Iona.

'Yes. Well, it was Mr Lunnon, my maths teacher, to be fair. He spotted me and put me forward for the school's talented-and-gifted programme, and that opened all sorts of doors for me. Extra lessons, and competitions all over the country. Then, when I was applying to universities, he helped me with my UCAS form and coached me for my interviews. I was the first in my family to go to university, and the first from my school to read mathematics at Oxford. I owe everything to him.'

God, he felt rather tearful. And guilty. When had he last contacted Mr Lunnon? Was he still alive, even? Had he ever actually said thank you? Surely he had?

Perhaps it was the unexpected wave of emotion that made him proffer another confession, something he'd not told a soul, the thought that he'd take out in the sleepless early hours of the morning and turn around in his hands like a crystal ball.

'That's what I'd really like to be, in an ideal world,' he said. 'A teacher. I'd like to change someone else's life, the way he changed mine. You know, give something back, rather than just moving money around. It'd be like life coming full circle.'

Iona leaned back in her seat and smiled at him, genuinely. As if she might actually like him just a little bit. Or dislike him a little less. The thought cheered him up, which was strange since he really shouldn't give a toss what she thought of him.

'Well, that's the second time you've surprised me,' she said. 'And it's your lucky day, because I might be able to help.'

'Why would you want to help me, Iona?' he asked. Not in an aggressive way, but because he was genuinely interested in the answer. He tried to remember when he'd last wanted to help anyone who wasn't actually related to him, or who didn't have a direct impact on his own career or wellbeing.

'Well, what would be the point of saving your life if I didn't try to make sure you made the most of it?' she replied. 'Anyhow, helping people is my raison d'être. Or in your case, thanks to that errant grape, you could say it was a *raisin* d'être! See what I did there?!?'

Iona laughed so hard at her own joke that it completely negated the need for anyone else to join in, thank goodness.

'Well, that's very kind of you, but there's no point. You see, it's not an ideal world, is it? Apart from anything else, my wife would loathe the idea of me being a teacher,' he said, standing up as the train, finally, drew into Surbiton station.

'Well, talk to her at least,' Iona called to his retreating back, as he headed towards the door. 'I'm sure all she wants is for you to be happy.'

'Are you asleep, Minty?' whispered Piers. In the dim glow of the night-light he saw Minty's duvet shifting, and a small, plump arm reached towards him, her clenched hand opening out like a startled starfish.

'Daddy! You're home!' she squealed.

'How was school today, gorgeous?' he said, leaning over to kiss her warm cheek and inhale the scent of Johnson's Baby Shampoo and strawberry-flavoured toothpaste.

'Cool. Ava's daddy came into assembly to talk about his job,' said Minty.

'What does Ava's daddy do?' asked Piers.

'He's a vet. That's a doctor for sick animals. He works at London Zoo. He brought a meerkat. A real one! It was soooo cute,' said Minty.

A *meerkat*?!? That was just cheating! How was any other parent supposed to compete with that?

'Can you do an assembly, Daddy?' said Minty.

'Sure I can, Pickle,' said Piers, tucking the duvet back around his daughter. 'I can tell your friends all about investment banking and how we make lots of money by guessing which stocks and shares are going to go up and which are going to go down.'

Minty frowned, looking entirely unconvinced. And who could blame her?

'So, I've found a fabulous new nanny,' said Candida in between mouthfuls of Marks & Spencer's risotto primavera. Candida, who'd been to finishing school, never spoke with her mouth full or rested her elbows on the table, and always used a pressed linen napkin.

'Oh?' said Piers.

'Uh huh. I've had it with au pairs, barely out of school, with all their adolescent angst and *issues*. Remember the Danish one who used to eat everything in the fridge in the middle of the night? And the girl who had loud nightmares in Romanian that would wake up the kids? Not to mention Magda and her apparent drug problem and loose morals.' She shuddered. But at least she hadn't brought up the Dutch au pair. Perhaps that little episode had finally been swept under the carpet.

'This time we're getting a properly trained, experienced nanny,' Candida continued. 'With a raft of glowing references. She's called Fiona, looks reassuringly like Mrs Doubtfire, and used to work for a second cousin of Sophie Wessex.' He must have looked blank because she added, 'Prince Edward's wife. The nice but mousey one. I always say *if in doubt, throw money at the problem*. You taught me that.' She beamed at him.

Did he really used to say that? He probably had. How arrogant and stupid of him. And how much money had she 'thrown at the problem' exactly?

'Darling,' he said, treading cautiously. 'Have you thought about maybe bringing up the children yourself? They're not babies any more. Minty is at school already, and Theo will be going next year.'

Candida looked horrified. 'But Piers, what about my *work*?' she said. 'I'm not some sort of 1950s housewife who's happy wearing a pinny while baking pies and getting your slippers and gin and tonic ready for your return from the City, you know.'

Piers, who viewed himself as forward-thinking, would totally buy into this argument if Candida were actually earning anything. However, her 'job' was costing him a fortune. She'd opened a designer boutique on the high street, where the rents were astronomical, and she only occasionally flogged a dress to one of her friends at mates' rates. A substantial amount of stock, still labelled for sale, seemed to magically appear in her own wardrobe, and she insisted on hiring a sales assistant, since she couldn't possibly be tied to the till all day. Still, this was obviously a battle he was not going to win today.

Piers had been watching Candida's glass of wine. He'd learned, from years of experience, that the optimal time to broach a difficult subject was after the first two glasses – when she was feeling relaxed – but before the third, which often made her belligerent and argumentative.

'Candida?' he said, resting one toe on the extremely thin ice. 'What would you say if I told you I was thinking of retraining as a maths teacher?'

Candida laughed. That fabulous unconstrained laugh that had made him turn to look across the dance floor at her, the night they'd met, at the Hurlingham Club, ten years ago.

'I'd tell you that if I'd wanted to be a teacher's wife, I'd have married a teacher! Imagine that! Me! *Tatler*'s most eligible!' she said. Then she paused, searching his face.

'Oh God. You're being serious, aren't you?' she said. 'You're only thirty-eight. Isn't that a bit young for a mid-life crisis? Why don't you buy yourself a flashy sports car or something? No, wait, you've done that already!' She grinned at him, flashing the neat little veneers that had cost him as much as a small car. He knew that under all that fake porcelain, her actual teeth had been filed into tiny sharp daggers. There was a metaphor there somewhere.

'How about a Harley-Davidson, then? I might even be

able to overlook a brief affair with the receptionist, so long as she's not much younger than me, and you promise not to fall in love with her.' He didn't reply.

'I'm only joking,' she said. 'Obviously.'

'I'm not, though,' he said. 'I'm miserable in the City. I have been for years. And I'm no good at it any more. As soon as it stopped being a game, as soon as it *mattered*, I lost my nerve.'

'Don't be silly, darling,' she said. 'You're a *genius*! That's why they call you Midas, isn't it?'

'But don't you want me to be happy?' he asked, remembering Iona's parting shot from earlier.

'Of course I do! You know how caring I am. That's why I'm such a good mother! But I'd like you to be happy *and* rich. Look, think of the *children*. A teacher's salary wouldn't pay their prep school fees, let alone Eton and Benenden. And it wouldn't pay for all this.' She waved expansively at their house, filled with all the *stuff* chosen by Candida's expensive interior designer. All the lamps, vases, rugs and throw cushions that had to be replaced whenever they went out of fashion.

'And do you really want to be the one to tell Minty she'll have to give back her pony?' Candida continued. 'She was upset enough about Magda going, imagine how she'd feel about losing the pony.'

'Do we honestly need all that, though?' he said. 'Would it really be so dreadful if the kids went to state school, for example, and Minty had a hamster? Or a goldfish? I'd have killed for a hamster at her age.'

'Oh God, here we go again! *I was so hard done by that I*

had to keep a woodlouse in a matchbox as a pet,' said Candida, mimicking his voice.

'It was an earwig,' said Piers. 'Eric.'

Candida smiled at him in the same way she smiled at Theo when he said he wanted one more bedtime story. A smile that said *I love you, but no. You do not have enough points on the reward chart to be allowed special privileges.*

'I tell you what,' she said. 'Why don't you just keep going until the kids have finished school, and then you can do whatever you want. You could teach then, if it really is the limit of your ambition. Or we could sell up, buy a boat and sail around the world, naked apart from artfully tied bandanas. Or go and rediscover ourselves in a Buddhist retreat in Thailand. Why not focus on "rich" for now, and then you can do "happy" later on? How about that?'

After the kids left school? In *fifteen years*. Some murderers served less time than that.

'Sure,' he said, as Candida finished her third glass of wine. And she smiled at him, trying to hide the look that was a combination of relief and victory.

What was he going to do now? How could he tell her that the decision was already – to a rather large extent – out of his hands?

Sanjay

08:35 New Malden to Waterloo

By the time Sanjay got to the station, his usual train had been and gone. He was running really slow today. Everything felt sluggish, even after the takeaway two-shot espresso he'd knocked back on the way.

He'd had a terrible night's sleep. He'd stayed up late since, in a rare coalescence of shifts, he, James and Ethan were all home at the same time. They'd spent hours gaming, ending the evening with a *Star Wars*-type challenge that involved flying spaceships through a meteor shower, shooting obstacles and aliens out of their paths. This had morphed into a vivid, technicolour nightmare, in which several of Sanjay's patients, friends and family had sprouted rapidly growing and proliferating tumours from various parts of their bodies, which he'd had to shoot away with a laser gun resembling a giant syringe, while his mum, who was a lawyer, kept popping up and shouting *Stop that, or I'll see you in court!*

'What took you so long, gorgeous?' said a voice behind him, making him jump. He turned around and there, sitting on a bench, hiding behind a copy of *The Times* and looking like a spy in a Cold War movie, waiting to exchange brief-cases, was Iona.

This was incredibly disconcerting, since last time Sanjay had seen her, a large growth had been appearing from her left ear, expanding like a balloon being filled with helium. He'd fired at it, and had accidentally blown off her head. He was relieved to see her still in one piece.

'What are *you* doing here, Iona?' he said. 'This isn't your station.'

'Let's not get possessive about stations, dear heart. This isn't my station, but nor is it *your* station. It's a station for the people. Or anyone with a ticket, in any case,' she said.

'Stop being so obtuse, Iona! You know what I mean. This isn't the station you usually use,' he said.

'I'm actually here looking for you,' said Iona. 'You weren't on my train this morning, or yesterday, for that matter. And I needed to see you before the weekend.'

'Why?' he asked, feeling increasingly uneasy. He should have known never to get involved with a total stranger on a train. Unless it was Emmie, obviously. And that wasn't going too well either, was it?

'Look, the train's here. Let's get on and I shall explain all!' she said.

Sanjay and Iona boarded at Carriage 3, obviously. Iona stared up the train, frowning. She pushed her way past the people standing in the aisle, ignoring the mutterings and expletives, Sanjay following red-faced in her wake saying *sorry, excuse me, sorry* on behalf of them both, until she reached her usual table for four.

'Good morning,' she said to the businessman sitting in the aisle seat facing forward. 'I believe you're sitting in my seat.' Lulu emitted a low growl, as if to emphasize the point. Now who was getting possessive? Sanjay was going to enjoy seeing this one play out. No one *ever* gave up their seat on this train without a fight. He would always leap up for an obviously pregnant lady, of course, or someone who looked infirm, but he was unusual.

'Oh, sorry,' said the man, standing up and vacating the seat.

How did she do that?

'So kind,' said Iona, sitting down, Lulu on her lap, and arranging her things on the table in front of her.

Sanjay was, naturally, left standing. Iona leaned towards him and whispered: 'Just as well that chap doesn't know the Fourth Rule of Commuting.'

'What's that?' said Sanjay, wondering if there was a pamphlet he should have read.

'Never surrender a seat once occupied!' said Iona. 'So, the reason I had to find you so urgently is I need you to come somewhere with me on Sunday, ten a.m. You are free, aren't you?'

'Yes,' he said, then cursed himself for not finding out what Iona had in mind before offering up his availability on a plate.

'Thank goodness for that!' said Iona. 'We're going to the Hampton Court Maze!'

'Uh, great. But why?' said Sanjay.

'Because I haven't been there for ages, and it's my favourite place,' said Iona.

'Why don't you take Bea?' said Sanjay.

'She doesn't like the maze,' said Iona. 'She keeps getting lost.'

'Isn't that the whole point of a maze?' said Sanjay.

'And I thought you'd enjoy it,' said Iona, ignoring him. 'I thought you might like to spend the morning with me. But of course you wouldn't. You have far more interesting things to do with your time than spending it with a boring middle-aged lady, I'm sure.' Iona sniffed and looked scarily as if she might be about to cry.

Sanjay felt awful. Iona obviously didn't have many friends, and it was very flattering that she'd chosen him to invite, and now he'd just made her feel bad. His mum would be so disappointed in him. She'd told him it was incredibly bad manners to turn down a girl who'd plucked up the courage to ask you to dance or go on a date. Sanjay didn't think Iona was who she'd had in mind when she said that, but even so.

'No, no!' he said. 'I'd love to come. I can't think of anything more fun!'

'Great. That's settled, then,' said Iona, rallying remarkably quickly.

The train pulled into Wimbledon station and the woman sitting opposite Iona stood up to leave. Sanjay sank gratefully into the empty seat.

'Sanjay!' Iona hissed in his ear. 'Stand up! Quick!'

'Why?' he asked. 'I've only just sat down! What about the Fourth Rule of Commuting?'

'This is one of the well-known exceptions,' said Iona.

'What exceptions?' said Sanjay.

'Never give up a seat once occupied *unless Iona tells you to*,' said Iona. 'Look! It's the man with the talking sandwich. You remember! I need to catch up with him. Yoo hoo!' yelled Iona, gesturing at the seat Sanjay's bottom was unwilling to let go. 'There's a free seat over here!'

The man, whose name Sanjay couldn't recall, looked a little terrified. He sat down, somewhat cautiously, in the seat Sanjay had just vacated, no doubt still warm from the imprint of Sanjay's buttocks.

'Hi, Iona. Hi, Sanjay,' he said.

'Hi, Daniel!' said Sanjay with relief, as it finally came back to him.

'David,' said David, sounding resigned, as if people often got his name wrong.

'Now, how did it go the other night?' asked Iona. 'Did you talk to your wife about the note? More importantly, did you *listen* to her?'

'Yes, of course I did. But I think I may have left it too late,' said David, looking bleak. 'It was a bit like putting a sticking plaster over a gushing arterial wound.'

'You need a tourniquet for that,' said Sanjay, who was feeling a little left out.

'Well, quite,' said Iona. Then, turning to David, added, 'He's a nurse.' Sanjay couldn't see her rolling her eyes, but could tell she was by the tone of her voice. 'So, what did she say?'

'We can't talk about this here,' said David. 'It's hardly private.' He had a point, thought Sanjay, but not one that Iona was interested in, clearly.

'Don't be daft. That's the great thing about the anonymity of the train. No one pays anyone else the blindest bit of attention. Now, tell me what happened. What did you say your wife's name was?' said Iona.

'Olivia. She wants to sell the house and buy somewhere of her own. Possibly abroad. She says she wants change. Adventure. Passion,' said David.

'Well, don't we all!' said Iona. Then, realizing that David was looking rather mystified, she added, 'Or maybe not. When did you last surprise your wife? Take her somewhere new and exciting?'

'Uh, I'm not sure,' said David. 'To be honest, since our daughter, Bella, left home, we've fallen into a bit of a rut. We don't even talk much any more. All our conversations used to be about her, you see. I think Bella was the beating heart of our family, and when she went, she left us rattling around in a useless shell.'

'Oh yes, the empty nest. You're not alone in feeling like that, you know,' said Iona. She patted David on the knee, making him look alarmed rather than comforted. 'It's quite, quite common. I even have a leaflet about it. When did she leave home?'

'Ten years ago,' said David. 'Then, a few years later, she moved to Australia.'

'Ten years is rather a long time to leave a marriage without a functioning heart, David,' said Iona. 'You can hardly blame Olivia for wanting something more.'

'You need a defibrillator,' said Sanjay. They both ignored him.

'Well, I realize that now, obviously,' David said to Iona,

94

looking more than a little exasperated. 'But it's too late. That's what she said.'

'Not necessarily,' said Iona. 'You just need to convince her that she can have change and adventure and passion *with you.*' Sanjay suspected *that* was going to be an uphill struggle. David looked like a man better acquainted with a cardigan and comfortable slippers than with passion or adventure.

'It's so easy to let a marriage become tired and mundane,' continued Iona. 'One minute you're telling her she has eyes that hold a whole galaxy of stars, and the next it's *are those knickers dirty, because I'm putting a dark wash on.*' David looked as if he wasn't sure what was the most shocking: the idea of his wife's metaphorically dirty knickers or the thought of him putting a wash on – dark or otherwise.

'You need to remind her why she fell in love with you in the first place!' said Iona. 'Damn, we're at Waterloo. Let's chat more next time! I have to dash – team *brainstorming.*' It was obvious from the way she said 'brainstorming' exactly what she thought of that idea.

Iona picked up her huge handbag, tucked Lulu under her arm and bustled off, leaving David looking a little stunned. 'See you on Sunday, Sanjay!' she called back to him. 'Don't be late!'

'You should count yourself lucky, mate,' said a voice from the other side of the aisle to David. 'I've been trying to get rid of my missus for years.'

So much for 'the anonymity of the train'.

Sanjay felt his phone buzz in his pocket. There was a text alert on his screen.

Mum: MY FRIEND ANITA IS COMING FOR LUNCH ON SUNDAY.

Meera always texted in caps. Sanjay sighed. He knew where this was going.

That's nice, he replied.

Mum: SHALL I ASK HER TO BRING HER DAUGHTER? SHE'S YOUR AGE.

As he wondered how to reply, Sanjay's finger hovered over his screen. He knew from experience that the best strategy was to change the subject.

What are you working on at the moment? he asked. Meera's work was the only thing that could compete with the minutiae of her children's lives for her attention.

Mum: A FORCED MARRIAGE CASE. FASCIN-ATING, BUT TRAGIC.

Do you see the irony? typed Sanjay, before he could stop himself.

Mum: I'M NOT SUGGESTING YOU MARRY ANYONE! 😠 I JUST DON'T WANT YOU TO BE LONELY 😢.

Thanks, but I'm not lonely, typed Sanjay, then wondered if this were true. He was hardly ever alone, but that wasn't exactly the same as not being lonely, was it?

Are these clients paying you? he asked, as he always did.

I'M CHARGING AS MUCH AS THEY CAN AFFORD, said Meera, which, of course, meant they were paying nothing. Luckily Meera's legal practice was constantly bailed out by Sanjay's dad's taxi business. They even shared a property: legal advice (often free) upstairs, and mini-cabs downstairs. Meera had a habit of persuading the drivers to give her clients free rides to and from court appearances, much to his dad's annoyance.

ANITA'S DAUGHTER IS A DENTAL HYGIENIST, said Meera, who was also adept at changing the subject.

SO MAKE SURE YOU BRUSH YOUR TEETH REALLY WELL BEFORE YOU COME FOR LUNCH!

Thanks Mum, but I'm already busy on Sunday, typed Sanjay.

It looked like Iona had done him a favour after all. There was nothing more awkward and humiliating than a middle-aged woman setting you up on a date.

Iona

The 'brainstorming' session was being held in the Clark Kent room. On Ed's arrival, one of his more revolutionary ideas had been to rename all the meeting rooms in the office after famous journalists. They must have run out of real ones. Iona had been campaigning for months to have Clark Kent renamed as Nora Ephron, to no avail. It was a sad indictment of Ed's hiring policy that more of their employees had heard of Clark Kent than the incomparable Nora.

Iona had been excused from the weekly brainstorming meetings in the past, due to – she imagined – her seniority, but one of the results of her 'three-hundred-and-sixty-degree appraisal' was her attendance being deemed mandatory. Active and enthusiastic participation in team sessions was, according to Ed, one of her KPIs. She hadn't wanted to confess that she had no idea what a KPI was, and had Googled it as soon as she'd got back to her desk. It was, apparently, a 'Key Performance Indicator'. She was still none the wiser. It sounded like a diagnostic tool a locksmith might use.

'Welcome, everyone, welcome!' said Ed, who was standing by a flip chart wielding a set of primary-coloured pens. 'And remember, there is no such thing as a bad idea!'

This was patently untrue. What about the Sinclair C5? Or prawn-cocktail-flavoured crisps? Or that candle for sale on Goop called *This Smells Like My Vagina*? But perhaps Ed genuinely believed it, as he'd executed many very bad ideas since he'd been in charge. This meeting room, for one. In the good old days there'd been a large, oval table in the centre, surrounded by practical chairs. Now the room was filled with garishly coloured beanbags which, Ed insisted, helped the creativity flow.

The beanbags didn't help Iona's creativity at all. For a start, she was always worried that someone would be able to see her pants. And secondly, these things were like quicksand. Once she was *in* one of them, she found it almost impossible to get *out* again. Her only options were to ask someone to give her a hand, which was totally humiliating, or to flip over on to her hands and knees first, then get into a standing position from there. Everyone else seemed to be able to manage it. Perhaps because they were younger and more flexible, or maybe they'd just had more practice, having grown up in the beanbag era. Iona resolved to buy herself a beanbag so she could do some training sessions at home. In the meantime, she had to find excuses to stay in Clark Kent until after everyone else had left, so no one would see her floundering around on the floor like a fish out of water. Which, she supposed, she was.

Iona gritted her teeth and lowered herself on to a bright yellow bag. She'd left Lulu with Ed's assistant, as Lulu would not like this set-up *at all*. She was a traditionalist.

'Iona!' said the man in the emerald-green beanbag on her left. She turned to see Olly, Head of Socials, which, she'd discovered after a rather humiliating misunderstanding, now meant things like Twitter and Instagram, not parties.

'Yes?' she said, hoping he wasn't going to ask her to 'friend' him on Facebook.

'You set the magazine's Twitter feed on fire this week. Bravo!'

'Did I?' she asked. How on earth had she done that? She wasn't even on Twitter, which had always seemed too *angry* for her tastes. Lots of people alternately firing insults at each other, then posting pictures of kittens. *Racism! Misogyny! Homophobia! Look at my lovely fluffy cat!*

'Yes! That little riff you did on pornography and pubic hair was shared *thousands* of times. I was quite taken aback, TBH, as I'd expected you to come up with some standard guff about parental controls,' said Olly.

'Good God, no,' said Iona. 'Every boy worth his salt knows his way around parental controls by the time he's about ten, you know.' She spotted Ed looking over at them quizzically and raised her voice a few notches. 'Anyhow, I'm most glad I could help you with some *sizzling millennial* content.' Take that, Ed, and stick it up your KPIs.

'Right, team!' said Ed. 'Settle down! I want to kick this morning off by asking Olly to share some super-exciting news with you all. Olly, the floor is yours.'

Olly leaped out of his beanbag without even using his hands, in an unnecessarily show-offy manner, plugged his iPad into a cable at the front of the room and a bar chart beamed on to the large screen on the wall. Modern technology was miraculous, but Iona felt a wave of nostalgia for the days of overhead projectors and acetates, and being able to say *next slide please*, in a polite yet imperious tone, to the minion operating the carousel.

'As you're all aware,' he said, 'our readership has been getting older and older. The median age of our readers is nearly fifty.' He said *fifty* as if it were an incomprehensibly large number of years. He would learn one day that fifty years could in fact disappear in the bat of an eyelid. 'So, it is *vital* that we pull in younger readers before our current ones literally die off.'

Ed was nodding away so vigorously that she could picture his head flying loose from his shoulders and rolling among the beanbags, like a macabre game of bagatelle. It was a less distressing image than one might expect.

'So, what we need is *influencers* who can lead the way, and pull in their legions of followers. Influencers like this . . .' and he motioned towards the new picture on the screen. A picture Iona was sure she had seen before. She frowned, trying to think where. Then she remembered she shouldn't frown, since it only encouraged the beauty editor to slip her another business card of a Botox specialist.

On the train! That's where she'd seen it! Emmie had shown her that exact same picture.

'We didn't set this up, or pay for it, but Fizz – the *actual blue-tick-verified* Fizz – posted this pic a few days ago captioned "every girl needs me-time", and, as you can see, the magazine she's chosen to take into the bath is *our magazine*. This is exactly the sort of coverage we need. Fizz is the archetypal *Modern Woman*. I've reached out to her via her socials and her agent, but I've not heard anything back – she probably never checks her DMs.' When, Iona wondered, had people started *reaching out*, instead of merely calling? Apart from the Americans, obviously, who'd no doubt been doing it for years, along with *circling back* and *thinking outside the box*. 'So, I'm hoping that one of you lot might have an in somehow? Anyone?' He looked around the room, his eyes resting on each person, one by one, except for her.

'Hold on a second,' said Ed, raising his palm to Olly like a traffic policeman. 'We should circle back a moment in case anyone doesn't know who Fizz is.' He looked so pointedly straight at Iona that everyone else's eyes turned to face her as well. 'Iona probably thinks she's a canned drink!' he said with a guffaw.

'You are funny, Ed,' she said in her steeliest voice. 'She's actually a TikTok sensation and, it so happens, a very close friend of a very close friend of mine. If you like, I'll see if I can arrange for us to take her out for lunch to discuss a possible partnership. I believe she likes the Savoy Grill.' Iona, of course, knew nothing of the sort, but how could anyone *not* like the Savoy Grill?

Everyone stared at Iona with such incredulity and, if she wasn't mistaken, a soupçon of admiration, that she realized she was actually enjoying herself. She wished she could flounce out of the room in triumph, leaving them to their silly 'idea generation sessions', but sadly flouncing anywhere wasn't an option; she was stuck in this damn beanbag until lunchtime.

Piers

18:17 Waterloo to Surbiton

It was a testament to how badly Piers's day was going that his conversation on the train home with Iona was turning out to be its highlight. He'd actually loitered around on Platform 5 deliberately, to ensure they were on the same train.

Piers's opinion of Iona had completely changed since last night, when he'd spent an hour or more scrolling through articles about her on the internet. It turned out that she and Bea had been 'It Girls', back in the eighties and nineties. They'd been constantly pictured at parties and premieres and on private planes and flashy holidays. Iona was tall, willowy, blonde and aloof. Bea was an even taller, statu-esque Black girl who wore her hair in braids cascading down to her waist, or piled on top of her head in increas-ingly elaborate twists, and had eyes that seemed to leap from the page across the intervening decades to challenge him.

'I Googled you,' he admitted. 'You were fabulous. I loved your nickname: Iona Yacht.' Piers tried to sound insouciant since, in a rare moment of self-awareness, he knew how shallow his new interest in Iona made him appear.

'Those were the days,' she said. 'I never did own a yacht, actually. I just spent a fair amount of time on other people's. I used to write social columns before I moved to problem pages. Bea and I were invited to *everything*. Paid to turn up, even. In those days, believe it or not, it was quite outré to be overtly gay. "Lipstick lesbians", the press called us. The paparazzi followed us everywhere.'

'I bet they did,' said Piers, taking in – for the first time – Iona's dramatic bone structure and startling cobalt-blue eyes. Why had he not noticed before? Was he really so shallow that he couldn't see past the slightly sagging skin and the creases? He suspected he was.

'You do realize, you've been talking about me in the past tense, don't you?' said Iona. 'From "It Girl" to "Past-It Girl" in three short decades.' She looked incredibly sad. Oh God, he did hope she wasn't going to cry. Not on the train, surely? There were probably laws against that sort of behaviour on public transport. If there weren't, there should be.

Out of the corner of his eye, Piers could see several of their fellow passengers surreptitiously typing *Iona Yacht* into Google. He'd noticed that whereas people used to avoid sitting near Iona, now the seats in her vicinity were rarely vacant. She seemed to have become the in-carriage soap opera. Did that make him a supporting actor in Season One?

'I'm sorry,' he said.

'Don't worry,' she replied, flapping her hand in front of her face as if she could wave back the advancing tears – or the advancing years. Or both. 'Everyone does it. The tragedy is that I am just the same woman I was back then. I still feel twenty-seven.'

'Ah, but I bet you're so much wiser now,' said Piers.

'I am,' said Iona. 'But that's not the way today's youth-obsessed society views me, is it? Anyone over the age of fifty is deemed irrelevant, it seems. Dinosaurs.'

'I'm sure that's not true,' said Piers, ignoring the fact that he'd believed exactly that until last night. 'Anyhow, I love dinosaurs. You have no idea how much time I spent in the Natural History Museum as a child.' He didn't add that much of the museum's appeal was that it was free to enter, warm and safe, and that for a few hours he could lose himself in the throng of happy families, believing himself a part of them.

'Back then, I couldn't walk out dressed in a bin bag without bringing traffic to a standstill,' said Iona with a sniff. 'Now, I could walk down the street naked and no one would pay the slightest bit of attention.' Piers thought this highly unlikely. Actually, he didn't really want to think of Iona naked at all. That sort of image could seriously ruin one's day.

'You know, in Japan, elders are venerated, looked up to. Perhaps Bea and I should move there. Pity I don't like raw fish. Or karaoke. Still,' she continued, 'better than being an Inuit. They leave their elderly on ice floes to die.'

'I don't think they do that any more, Iona. Not for centuries, in fact,' said Piers.

'Anyhow, let's talk about more interesting things. You. How's it going with the career change?' said Iona, peering at him through narrowed eyes, giving him the impression of being scanned by a supermarket checkout machine before being declared an unexpected item in the bagging area.

'I haven't got very far, to be honest,' said Piers. 'I have no idea how to go about retraining. Perhaps I'm too old.' He didn't want to confess the real reason he'd abandoned the idea of teaching so quickly: Candida's total lack of support. It felt disloyal somehow.

'Nonsense. You're just a baby. Not even forty, I bet. What you need to do is to talk it all through with an actual teacher. They can give you an inside track. Do you know any?'

Piers pictured all the friends that had come to Candida's last drinks party – City lawyers, bankers, hedge-fund managers, venture capitalists, CEOs, and a sprinkling of media people for colour. Not one single teacher. They'd have been eaten alive. Served up by the hired-in uniformed waiting staff alongside the smoked salmon blinis and prawn tempura, and washed down with chilled vintage Pol Roger.

'No, I don't think I do,' he said. He discounted Minty's Year 1 schoolteacher. He couldn't confide in her without the risk of it getting back to Candida, and besides, if he were to teach, he'd want to inspire troubled teenagers, not over-privileged five-year-olds.

'Mmmm. Well, I'm sure something will turn up,' said Iona. 'In my experience, something usually does.'

'Sure,' said Piers, wondering what strange, simplistic

universe Iona lived in. They pulled into Surbiton station, and he got off the train to return in his banker's car to his banker's house and his banker's wife.

This was just a waste of Iona's time, and his own. He had far more pressing issues to worry about.

Sanjay

Walking through the Hampton Court Palace gardens, with their perfectly cut lawns, majestic fountains and formal parterres, Sanjay could feel the knots in his neck and shoulders begin to loosen slightly. It was so easy when you spent the majority of your waking hours in the harsh, artificial light and brutally sanitized interiors of a London hospital to forget how healing the outdoors could be. All this beauty lay just a few miles from Sanjay's home, and yet it was the first time he'd been here.

It was one of those perfect mornings, when winter shows the first signs of ceding to spring. There was a cloudless blue sky, but a slight chill in the air and a low mist hanging over the lakes. The first exploratory flowers – snowdrops and crocuses – were pushing their way through the cold ground.

Sanjay felt like one of the magical creatures of Narnia, seeing the evidence of the White Witch's powers diminishing. A beaver, maybe. Or a faun. He'd rather be a faun.

The Hampton Court Palace Maze is the oldest surviving

hedge maze, commissioned around 1700, recited Sanjay in his head. He'd spent hours last night reading up on the history of the palace and the maze so that he and Iona wouldn't find themselves stuck for conversation. He'd never, funnily enough, been on an outing with a virtual stranger thirty years older than him, and was more than a little apprehensive about it. Goodness knows why she'd suggested he come, or why he'd agreed. Things just seemed to happen when he was around Iona, without him having any control over them whatsoever.

'Sanjay!' called Iona, so loudly that the heron, who'd been waiting so patiently while his photo was taken by a crowd of Japanese tourists that Sanjay had assumed he was made from plastic, took flight. 'Over here!'

Iona was waiting by the entrance to the maze. She was wearing a long, emerald-green velvet frock coat, with a showy fake fur collar, large gold buttons and braiding, which looked very much in keeping with her regal surroundings. And clumpy, black Doc Martens boots, which very much didn't.

'Look,' she said, pointing into the distance. 'Isn't that Emmie over there?'

Sanjay's heart seemed to stop beating as he followed the direction of Iona's index finger. Surely not? And yet there she was. Unmistakably, incredibly Emmie.

While it was impossible to discern any features from this far away, she wove between the groups of tourists and gaggles of Canadian geese in the exact same way she'd sweep through Carriage 3 in the mornings. All energy and optimism, as if she couldn't wait to get to wherever she was going, as if the day were a ripe peach just waiting to be plucked. Oh God. Why had he chosen that imagery?

What on earth was she doing here? The answer, of course, was staring him in the face. Actually, he realized as he turned to glare at Iona, she was determinedly *not* looking at his face.

'Emmie! Yoo hoo! We're here!' she called.

'Iona!' said Emmie, slightly breathless, her cheeks pink from the chill. 'How fabulous is this place? Hi, Sanjay! I didn't know you were coming too!'

'No, I didn't know you were coming either,' said Sanjay. They both turned to look at Iona, but she was bent over, tying the lace on one of her Doc Martens.

'Have you been here before?' said Emmie, smiling at him.

'Uh, no,' he stuttered.

It was ironic that Sanjay, who was known at the hospital for being able to talk to *anyone*, for turning strangers into friends in less than the time it took fetch a cup of tea from the vending machine, was so struck dumb whenever he was with Emmie. She'd look at him, expectantly, and it felt as if his tongue were expanding to fill his mouth, turning into an inebriated slug, totally unable to move in any useful way. Simultaneously, his mind would drain of all coherent thought. She must think him a total imbecile. He cursed Iona for her ham-fisted matchmaking. She could at least have given him some warning.

'I love your boots, Iona,' said Emmie, who'd obviously given up on him. 'Are they the vegan ones?'

'Hardly!' said Iona, frowning. 'They're footwear, darling.

They're neither vegan nor carnivores, on account of being inanimate objects and not needing to eat.'

Emmie obviously didn't know quite how to respond to that, because she changed the subject.

'This maze is *huge*. I wonder if Henry the Eighth used to come here to escape his current wife and flirt with the one he was lining up to take her place,' she said.

'I doubt it,' replied Sanjay, leaping gratefully on one of the facts he'd absorbed last night. 'He'd been dead more than a hundred years before it was planted. It was William the Third's idea.' Oh God, now he just sounded like an arrogant swot. 'I think,' he added, trying to soften the edges.

Emmie spotted a peacock strutting past the fountain, looking disdainfully at the tourists as if wondering why they were trespassing in his gardens. She walked away to take his picture, giving Sanjay a chance to accost Iona.

'Iona,' said Sanjay, 'I'm sure you thought this would be a good idea, but—'

'Darling, it really *is* a good idea,' she butted in. 'A marvellous one, actually. Just you wait and see. I shall remind you of your ingratitude at the wedding.'

He sighed.

'Well, since you've landed us in this embarrassing situation, could you at least do me a favour, and get lost?'

'Get lost?' said Iona, looking rather hurt. 'You want me to leave?'

'No! I mean get lost in the maze. You know, so Emmie and I can have some time on our own,' he clarified.

'Well, that's hardly realistic, is it, sweetheart? I am a veritable *grandmaster* of this maze. Why don't you two get lost, which shouldn't be too difficult, and I'll wait for you in the centre?' said Iona, as Emmie walked back towards them.

'Shall we queue up for tickets?' she said.

'I've bought them already,' said Iona, pulling three tickets out of her handbag. 'No, no, I insist. My treat. I see it as my way of paying back the NHS. Now, you two go in together, and I'll go separately. I don't want to ruin the whole maze experience for you by showing you which way to go! That'd be no fun at all! I'll wait for you in the middle.'

'The average time taken to reach the centre is twenty minutes,' said Sanjay, regurgitating more of the Hampton Court website.

'Well, there's a challenge,' said Iona. 'See if you can beat it!'

How hard could it be to find the middle? There were only so many different paths to take, so they had to stumble across it eventually. Sanjay and Emmie could hear the shouts of triumph as people discovered it, and they all seemed so close by, and yet so hard to find.

'It's just around this next bend!' said Sanjay. 'I'm sure of it!' He rounded the corner only to find a dead end. One that looked rather familiar. But that was part of the problem: one hedge looked very much like any other hedge. Iona must be getting terribly bored waiting for them to show up.

'We're just going around in circles,' he said. 'We need a ball of string, like Theseus in the Labyrinth!' He was quite pleased with that one. Emmie seemed like the kind of girl who'd appreciate a knowledge of the Greek myths.

'That's so true!' said Emmie. 'Did you bring any provisions?

We may be here a while. Perhaps they'll find us in a few weeks' time – just two desiccated husks.'

'I think we need a system,' said Sanjay, attempting to sound decisive and manly. The kind of person you could trust your heart with. 'Why don't we try only taking the right-hand branches?'

That didn't work. Nor did alternating left and right.

'I think we're overthinking this,' said Emmie. 'Have you noticed all these kids seem to be able to find their way in and out? Let's do what they do and just go with the flow, run randomly, and see where it takes us?'

Emmie took his hand in hers, and they ran, laughing around corners, swerving around slow-moving groups of tourists, until they fell triumphantly into the centre. A large open space with a bench in the middle. An empty bench.

'Where's Iona?' said Sanjay, sitting down next to Emmie. He clung on to the edge of the bench to stop himself giving in to the urge to put his arm around her shoulders.

'No idea,' said Emmie, still out of breath. 'Do you think she got bored and left? Or perhaps she's been eaten by the Minotaur.'

'I'm not sure even the Minotaur would have the nerve to take on Iona,' said Sanjay. 'Before he'd know what was happening, she'd be giving him *that look* and saying, *What is it that's making you so angry? Tell me about your relationship with your mother. I'm a magazine therapist, you know.*'

Emmie laughed, making Sanjay feel like he'd won the lottery.

'Iona!' shouted Emmie. 'Iona! Are you there?'

'Nearly there, darlings!' he heard her shout back. 'Thought

I'd give you a head start.' She sounded close by, and he could see a flash of emerald through one of the hedges.

'That was such fun, wasn't it?' said Emmie. Sanjay grinned and nodded. As soon as they'd stopped worrying about where they were going, he'd also stopped thinking about where he and Emmie were heading. For the first time, he was feeling totally relaxed in her company, as if she were just another one of his patients – a gorgeous one, without cancer.

'Iona!' she shouted.

'Be with you in a second!' came a voice which sounded further away than it had last time.

Sanjay was just wondering whether he should tell Emmie how much he liked her when Iona crashed through the gap in the hedge, looking more flustered than he'd ever seen her. Her elaborate hairdo had fallen over to one side, and there was a small branch sticking out of it, like a sprig of holly in a Christmas pudding.

'Well done!' she said, panting slightly, and leaning against the back of the bench for support, her hand gripping it so tightly that her knuckles had drained of colour, accentuating the crimson red of her fingernails. 'You made it! You were pretty fast, actually. You obviously make a perfect team. Fabulous, isn't it?'

'Totally!' said Emmie. 'I must bring Toby here. He'd love it.'

There was a silence, then Sanjay found himself asking the question he really, really did not want to know the answer to.

'Who's Toby?'

'My boyfriend,' said Emmie. 'He loves puzzles. He's brilliant at them. I guess that's why he's so good at coding. He has his own tech company.'

Oh, good for him, thought Sanjay, wondering how it was possible to dislike someone you'd never met so intensely.

Iona

How could triumph turn to disaster quite so quickly?

Iona had *finally* found the centre of the maze – they must have moved things around since she was last here – and seen her two young lovebirds sitting cosily on the bench together, only to hear Emmie announce that she had a boyfriend already.

Sanjay had an unconvincing smile fixed on his face like a carnival mask. It was clear that the only theatre he was destined for was the operating theatre. Still, all was not yet lost. Perhaps this 'boyfriend' was a fairly new and casual relationship, easily dislodged.

'Have you and Toby been together long?' she asked, sitting next to Emmie on the bench, forcing her to move even closer to Sanjay.

'Nearly two years,' said Emmie.

Two years to Iona was a mere blink of the eye, but she imagined that to Sanjay and Emmie it seemed like an eternity. Maybe it was a long-distance relationship, going rather stale and running out of steam. At least she wasn't wearing a wedding ring. Iona had made sure to check on the train before she'd suggested this outing. It was always important to do your research.

'But you're not married?' said Iona.

'Not yet, no,' replied Emmie. 'But we've been living together for ages, so I guess we might as well be.'

Bugger.

'You should have brought Bea, Iona. I'd have loved to meet her,' said Emmie.

'I should have done,' she said. 'I've told her all about you two. She's dying to meet you both. Now, why don't we go and find ourselves some coffee? I need to pick your brains about your lovely friend, Fizz. I'm hoping she'll come out for lunch with me and my editor. Then you two should explore the Palace! I have to get back for darling Lulu. She hates me being away too long.'

'Can you show us the quick way out?' asked Emmie.

'No, no,' she said. 'That would be cheating. You guys go in front, and I'll just follow on behind you.'

Since she was having a coffee with two millennials who, quite frankly, owed her one, even if things hadn't gone entirely to plan, Iona took the opportunity to pull her notebook out of her bag and surreptitiously check her most recent list of readers' problems.

'Darlings,' she said. 'Hypothetically speaking, if a girl around your age fancied her best friend's ex-boyfriend, should she go for it or not?' Emmie and Sanjay looked at her rather strangely, so she added, 'Just wondering,' which didn't help much.

'Well, she needs to consider the Girlfriend Code, obviously,' said Emmie. *Code? What code?* Iona's fingers itched to pull her notebook out, but she held them in her lap and said, 'Of course. Out of interest, how would you describe the Girlfriend Code, Emmie?'

'The Code says you never mess around with a girlfriend's ex without getting the go-ahead from her first. Also, she should bear in mind that there's probably a good reason why they split up. She should make sure she has all the relevant info before plunging in,' said Emmie.

The phone sitting on the café table in front of them started buzzing, and skittering across the polished surface. The name on the screen said TOBY, and it was accompanied by a picture of a man with eyes the pale blue of a frozen lake, and one of those irritating hipster beards that all the youngsters in Iona's office had taken to growing.

'Do you mind if I get this?' asked Emmie, picking up her phone and her coffee without waiting for a response, and walking away from the table.

'Don't look so glum, Sanjay,' said Iona as she pulled her notebook out and scribbled furiously.

'Did you see that picture?' said Sanjay. 'He looked like a . . .'

'Hunk,' said Iona, at the same time as Sanjay said, 'Twat.'

'Was that a ski lift he was sitting on?' said Sanjay.

'Yes.'

'I've never been skiing.'

'It's overrated,' said Iona. 'Lots of braying Sloanes with dodgy fashion sense and expensive planks strapped to their feet.' Sanjay sighed.

'It's hopeless, Iona,' he said.

'It's never, ever hopeless,' she replied. 'I do not want to hear that word in my vicinity. You know, Bea was practically standing at the altar, about to marry a very influential, but crashingly dull, man ten years older than her, when she ran off to London with me.'

Iona paused, thrown by an image of Bea and herself shrieking as they tried to navigate the Place de la Concorde in a buttercup-yellow convertible VW Beetle.

They'd filled the car with as many of their favourite possessions as they could squeeze into it, leaving all the other remnants of their past lives behind. They'd put the roof down to give them more space and did their best to keep everything in, but lost Nigel the yucca plant and Iona's grandmother's teapot somewhere on the road to Calais.

The car had had no working seatbelts, so Bea – who was the only one plucky enough to drive on the right-hand side of the road – would fling her arm out sideways to protect Iona whenever she had to brake suddenly. *Darling, I'm so glad you care!* Iona had shouted above the noise of the traffic.

The car image was replaced, in a sharp jump cut, by one of Bea's wedding veil, fluttering in the wind, a giant lace-trimmed albatross, as she launched it off the back of the cross-channel ferry.

'Two hundred and fifty wedding presents had to be boxed up and returned,' she said.

'How brave,' said Sanjay.

'I thought it rather wasteful, actually. Some of those gifts were amazing,' said Iona.

'No, I meant how brave she was, following her heart like that,' said Sanjay.

'She had no choice, sweet pea,' said Iona. 'Neither of us did. Sometimes fate just shows you the way to go and you have no option but to follow. And if this is your fate, it will happen. Just you wait. It's absolutely not over until the fat lady sings.'

Emmie

Weekend expeditions with people she barely knew were not something Emmie usually did. She'd only agreed to this one because of her long-running obsession with Iona.

Emmie had been secretly stalking Iona for nearly a year – as long as she'd been taking the Thames Ditton to Waterloo train. She'd spotted Iona straight away – how could you not? She was exactly the sort of woman Emmie wanted to be when she was old. She was totally individual – iconic, even – and obviously didn't care at all what anyone thought of her.

Iona reminded Emmie of a poem she'd learned at school. *When I am an old woman, I shall wear purple . . .*

Whenever Emmie had the opportunity, she'd sit near Iona and glance at her surreptitiously from behind her book, trying to work out what her backstory was. Perhaps she'd been a prima ballerina. It would explain that posture. A child prodigy who'd had the world at her feet until an overenthusiastic lift by her Russian ballet partner had damaged her spine, causing her to retire at the age of twenty-three. Or maybe she was a famous cello player, who'd not played professionally since an Italian conductor had broken her heart by running off with the second clarinettist.

Thanks to Piers and his wayward grape, Emmie had discovered Iona's actual name and profession, and had described the whole incident to Fizz after one of their meetings.

'Iona Yacht!' Fizz had yelled. 'You met the actual Iona Yacht! She was an influencer before they'd even been invented. My mum was *obsessed* by her. She used to read me her columns every weekend when I was a kid. So, she's an agony aunt for a magazine? How gorgeously retro! I haven't read an actual magazine for years. I'm going to buy hers *right now*. Which one is it?'

'*Modern Woman*,' said Emmie.

'Ugh. What a truly ghastly title,' said Fizz. 'I had no idea she was still around, let alone *commuting*. How unlikely. I assumed she'd been killed in some tragic but terribly glamorous accident, like Isadora Duncan.'

Emmie had looked up Isadora Duncan. She was a dancer who'd died at the age of fifty when her headscarf had been tangled in the wheels and axle of the convertible she was riding in, on the French Riviera. Fizz was quite right. If Iona were to die, that was exactly the sort of way she'd go. On the other hand, it was quite possible that Iona was immortal. Maybe she'd just regenerate like Doctor Who, and come back in the body of Scarlett Johansson.

Fizz had begged Emmie for an introduction, and it sounded, from what Iona had said, as if effecting that was going to be easier than she'd imagined. She felt an irrational twinge of jealousy at the idea of Fizz and Iona becoming BFFs.

'Guess what, gorgeous?' said Toby on the other end of a crackly line. 'I've made your favourite. Roast beef and all the trimmings. Yorkshire puddings, even.'

'But Toby,' she said, trying not to let her irritation leak into her voice, 'I told you to eat without me. I'm at Hampton Court, remember?'

'Oh God, how stupid of me!' said Toby, and she could tell from his tone that he was bashing his forehead with the heel of his hand, as he always did when he'd forgotten something important.

'I've only been here an hour. We've done the maze, but I was hoping to go around the palace kitchens with Sanjay. Do you mind?' said Emmie, realizing as she did just how much she was enjoying making a new friend.

Most of Emmie's old friends had drifted away since she'd moved in with Toby. It was what happened when you were in a serious relationship, she supposed, and she lived miles away from them all now, in Thames Ditton. Toby had wanted to move out of town so they could buy a house big enough for an eventual family, but she often felt isolated.

It was ironic that she had so much more space than she'd had in her tiny shared flat in Dalston, yet sometimes she found suburbia suffocating. Claustrophobic. She missed her old flatmates, and having a circle of friends just walking distance from the same pub.

'Sanjay?' said Toby. 'I thought you were meeting a sixty-year-old woman?'

'I am,' she said. 'Iona. But she invited Sanjay along too, another guy from the train. He's a nurse.'

'Oh, cool,' said Toby, although Emmie suspected he was just a bit jealous. Men had such fragile egos. She supposed she should take it as a compliment – the fact that he was convinced everyone wanted to sleep with her.

She looked over towards Sanjay and Iona, heads together, talking urgently. It was just as well this wasn't a video call. If Toby knew how good-looking Sanjay was, he'd definitely be jealous. If you were a casting director for *Casualty* and were looking for a man to play a nurse who was both clever and kind, and who all the patients would have secret crushes on, you'd cast Sanjay. He had a gorgeous mop of black hair, which was slightly too long so he had to keep blowing it out of his eyes. And those eyes were a deep brown, made up of more individual shades than brown ought to have, and ringed by the sort of lashes she spent a fortune on mascara to achieve.

It was obvious Sanjay was great at his job, too. He was so calm in a crisis and really empathetic. The kind of person you'd happily discuss your embarrassing symptoms with. Unless you fancied him. Which she didn't.

'Honestly, Emmie,' said Toby. 'Don't worry about me. You have fun with your friends. It was my stupid mistake, after all. I'll chuck your half of the lunch in the bin. I'm afraid it won't really keep, or freeze, even.'

Emmie sighed, readjusting the vision of the way her day would play out in her head.

'Don't do that, hon,' she said. 'If I leave now, I can be home by one p.m. Will that work?'

'Perfect!' said Toby, sounding like his old self. 'Can't wait. I love you so much! Have I told you that?'

'About a million times,' said Emmie, smiling. 'I love you too, and not just because you make a mean roast potato.'

Iona and her ever-increasing circle were not the first people Emmie had met on public transport. Almost exactly two years ago, she'd been taking the tube to work from Dalston. She'd reached into her handbag for her wallet as she approached the barrier, but it had gone. She was completely stuck, with no way of getting through the turnstile, no money, no bank cards, and – much worse than any of that – she'd lost her favourite photo of her mother, holding her as a baby, kissing the top of her soft, bald head.

'You look like you need help,' a voice had said from behind her. And there he was. A foot taller than her at least. Her knight, not in shining armour, but wrapped in a soft, navy cashmere coat and smelling of citrus and sandalwood. He'd persuaded the guard to let her through the turnstile, and had lent her twenty pounds, on the proviso that she go out for dinner with him that evening.

Emmie had always prided herself on her strength and independence, but it meant that often in relationships, she was the one who made all the decisions, who set the pace and direction. Toby didn't let her do that. He adored her, he told her regularly, and wanted to look after her, and – much as she hated to admit it – relinquishing some of that control was actually a huge relief.

Emmie hadn't told Toby about the horrible anonymous messages she'd been getting at work. She knew he'd be furious on her behalf, but there wasn't anything he could do, and she didn't want that unpleasantness leaching into their home life, her safe space. Anyhow, just being with Toby stopped her worrying about all that. She was sure that if she didn't engage, whoever it was would get bored with tormenting her.

Emmie let herself into the immaculate tiled entrance hall. She could smell the beef roasting in the oven, and hear Toby singing enthusiastically to the radio, but missing some of the notes and muddling the lyrics as always.

She took off her shoes and put them neatly in the 'shoe area'. Toby had a place for everything. He hated mess and clutter, so their house was like a show home. Even Marie Kondō would be impressed. When they'd moved in, they'd spent an evening drinking champagne and going through all of Emmie's knick-knacks. He'd held them up, one by one, saying, 'Does this spark joy, Emmie?' as they'd decided what to keep, what to throw away and what to give to charity.

Emmie, in a warm hazy fug of champagne, had leaned over and kissed him. 'Does this spark joy, Toby?' she'd said. Then they'd sparked their personal brand of joy for hours, surrounded by overflowing charity shop bags.

'Emmie, you're back!' said Toby, pouring her a glass of red wine. 'Come here, chef's perks.' And he pulled her towards him and kissed her as if he'd not seen her for weeks.

How perfect was this? It had been a lovely morning, but she was so glad she'd come back home.

Sanjay

08:19 New Malden to Waterloo

Sanjay didn't notice the girl sitting opposite him straight away; he was too busy thinking about Julie's first chemo session that morning. He'd promised he'd be there to hold her hand. The train pulled in at Raynes Park and a group of noisy schoolgirls got on. That's when he noticed her. She was wearing the same uniform as them, although hers was a much neater version, and she stiffened, like a deer in the crosshairs of a rifle, the tension crackling in the air between them.

'Oh God, let's move carriages,' said one of the new passengers, in a voice so loud and forced that it was obviously designed to catch their attention.

'Why?' asked one of her friends.

'Look who's sitting in this one. It's Martha.' She drawled out the name to three times its usual length, like a taunt.

The group swivelled as one to look in their direction, and

the girl opposite Sanjay shrank down into her seat, as if it could suck her up like a black hole, transporting her through a vortex into a more benign universe.

Sanjay remembered that feeling. He'd spent his school years alternately trying to stand out – to be picked for the football team or noticed by a girl he liked – and trying to disappear – to not have his dinner money stolen or be singled out for ritual humiliation in the playground by the cool kids. He desperately wanted to tell this girl that it would all be okay. That it was temporary. That bullies are usually miserable themselves, which is why they lash out at others.

But that's not the way it works on trains. Not in this city, anyway. You turn a blind eye, like everyone else in their vicinity was doing. Not their business. Not their problem. Sanjay had once seen a woman get on a train with her skirt tucked into the back of her tights. Nobody had said a word, they'd just let her get off at Waterloo and disappear into the crowd. Sanjay had felt guilty for the rest of the day.

Then Sanjay thought about Iona, and what she would have done if she'd been on that train that morning. She'd never have let someone suffer that humiliation, and there was no way she'd let this one lie either.

Be more Iona, he said to himself.

He turned to his fellow passenger. She had features made of acute angles that looked a bit too large for her face. It was, he knew, the sort of face she would grow into, that would morph from awkward to stunning as she grew older. The more conventionally pretty teenagers would become bland and forgettable over time, while she'd blossom. He was, however, certain that she neither knew this, nor would she believe it if he told her.

'Hey,' he said, in the tone he used for children coming round from a general anaesthetic. 'I'm Sanjay. I'm guessing you're Martha, right?'

Martha didn't reply, just shrank even further back into her seat.

'Don't worry, they've buggered off,' he told her. 'I remember kids like that really well. They used to call me the p-word and tell me to go back to where I came from. I tried to explain that I was born in Wembley, and my heritage is Indian, not Pakistani, but they weren't interested, obviously. Anyhow, you know where they are now?'

'No,' she replied, still looking nervously towards the carriage doors.

'Well, one of them works at the sewage plant at Berrylands – and not behind a desk, if you get my drift. One is long-term unemployed and, I suspect, has a gambling addiction, and the other went to prison for grievous bodily harm in his early twenties.' This was actually a lie. Sanjay had no idea what had become of his childhood tormentors, but he liked to invent various miserable outcomes for them. Despite what people imagined, being a nurse didn't make him a saint.

'Don't get me wrong, I'm not celebrating over what happened to them – I'm just telling you because people who bully usually have more problems themselves than you are ever aware of,' he said.

'And what did you do?' she asked, looking him in the eye for the first time.

'I became a nurse,' he replied.

'Cool,' said Martha, and she actually smiled, just a little. One of the best things about his career was the way his job title made people smile.

'So, why are they picking on you?' asked Sanjay. 'Is it because you're super clever and they're just jealous?'

'I wish,' she replied. 'No, I did something really, really stupid. This is all my own fault. My friends are all avoiding me, like it's catching or something. I've been completely ghosted.'

Sanjay didn't want to risk scaring Martha away by asking exactly what she'd done. He could remember being at school well enough to guess the sort of thing. He had absolutely no idea how to help. But he did know who would.

'Hey, Martha,' he said. 'Have you met Iona on this train? She's the woman with the big hair, great clothes and French bulldog who often has a seat to herself.'

Martha nodded vigorously.

'Of course I have! I didn't know her name. I call her Magic Handbag Lady, since I reckon that bag is a portal to another universe. More things come out of it than could ever have gone into it,' she said. 'She stood up for me when I was sick on the way to school the other day, actually.'

'That sounds just like Iona!' Sanjay grinned, putting two and two together, but choosing not to tell Martha that Iona had mentioned the vomiting incident. The poor girl was being gossiped about enough already.

'Oh, and that's not her dog, by the way, it's her daemon,' said Martha.

'Her demon?' said Sanjay.

'Daemon,' corrected Martha. 'Haven't you read *His Dark Materials*? A daemon is like your soul outside your body, in animal form. You can never be separated. I mean, have you ever seen her without the dog?'

'Er, no,' said Sanjay.

'See,' said Martha. He wasn't sure that he did see.

'Well, next time you see Iona and her demon on the train – she's always in this carriage, number three – tell her what you've told me. I bet you she'll know what to do. She's amazing.' He paused, then added, 'Just don't call her an agony aunt. Or let her organize a date for you.'

Iona

Iona had forgotten how much she missed The Savoy. While the world around it had changed enormously in the twenty years since she'd been a regular visitor, it was a reassuring constant, an oasis of timelessness, nestled between The Strand and the River Thames.

You could tell it had been built by a theatrical impresario, as it always gave her the sense of walking on to a stage, and the art deco style lent it a sprinkling of old Hollywood glamour. Iona had dressed accordingly and was wearing a vibrant orange 1920s-inspired dress in silk and velvet. Lulu was sporting an orange feather attached to her diamanté collar.

'Iona,' said Ed, in his best *I am your boss, and don't you forget it* voice, the one he seemed especially fond of. 'There is no way they are going to let you take that dog into the restaurant. Not in a fancy place like this. It would break every health and safety regulation. It might be a good idea if you just took her home, rather than humiliate me. I can do this meeting just as well on my own. Better, probably.'

'Isn't this just beautiful, honey? I told you you'd love it,' said Iona to Lulu, who was tucked under her arm, ignoring the increasingly agitated editor alongside her, who sighed theatrically.

They walked up to an imperious-looking maître d' standing guard at the doors to the Grill, the sound of Iona's stiletto heels on the marble floor echoing around the foyer.

'Ed Lancaster,' said Ed. 'Editor-in-Chief of *Modern Woman*.' Iona had discovered that the more intimidated he felt, the more obnoxious he became. *In Chief*. What did that even mean?!? 'I have a reservation for three. I'm meeting Fizz – the influencer. You'll probably have heard of her. I'd like your best table, please, and a media discount, obviously.'

He made, Iona noticed, no mention of her at all. One of the many things Ed had to learn is that you must never shit on people on your way up the greasy pole, as they will only shit on you on your way back down. Iona, luckily, had spent her glory days *paying it forward*, and sometimes, often when she least expected it, those little debts were repaid magnificently – as, she anticipated, was about to happen right now. She crossed her fingers behind her back and waited.

The maître d' peered silently at Ed over the top of his spectacles, then turned to Iona and smiled broadly, taking her by both shoulders and kissing her showily on each cheek.

'Iona, darling,' he said. 'Why have you stayed away from us for so long? We've missed you! You've not changed an iota! Now, dogs are strictly not allowed in the restaurant . . .' Ed shot her a triumphant look. 'But obviously the rules don't apply to you! I had put you in the corner over there, since no one told me you were coming.' He glared at Ed, assuming, correctly, that this was his oversight, and gestured towards the restaurant equivalent of Siberia. 'But I shall move you to your old table, with the river view. The Chancellor of the Exchequer can sit elsewhere. Follow me.'

'Thank you, darling François,' said Iona, resisting the urge to check the expression on Ed's face. 'And how is the lovely Nicole?'

'Older, but still just as beautiful. In fact, she is like one of our delicious cheeses; she gets better with age,' he said, with a wink. 'Although please don't tell her I compared her to a Stilton.'

Iona laughed, and mimed zipping her lips together. She remembered François as a junior waiter, when he spoke with an East End accent and was called Frank. He was constantly being clipped around the ear by the maître d' for minor infringements, like placing a knife on the table with the blade facing right instead of left, or missing a fingerprint smudge on a silver wine coaster. Iona had signed a napkin for Nicole, a chambermaid he'd been dating, and would slip them both complimentary tickets she and Bea had been sent for the latest West End shows.

They sat down at the best table in the room, which was groaning under the weight of bone china and crystal glasses. Iona tried very hard not to look victorious but was not sure she'd succeeded.

'Are you sure Fizz wanted to come here?' said Ed, trying to sidle his way back on to the ground he'd lost. 'I wouldn't have thought this was her style *at all*. Far too old-fashioned. She'd prefer some hipster place in Shoreditch, surely?'

'No, no, this is her favourite,' said Iona, who – to be honest – was feeling a little apprehensive. After all, she'd never met Fizz, and hadn't even heard of her until two weeks ago, somewhere between Hampton Court and Waterloo. Since then, she'd watched a few of her strange little videos, and wasn't at all sure they'd like each other.

What was it with young people and the obsession they had with sharing *every single little detail* of their lives? Where was the mystique? The enigma? When she and Bea had been constantly in the press, the public had known which parties they'd attended, what they wore and who they hung out with, but didn't know where they lived, let alone what they ate for breakfast. Which, by the way, never involved an avocado, smashed or otherwise. Their home had always been off limits – their haven.

Nothing, it appeared, was off limits with Fizz. After just a few minutes of scrolling, Iona knew which side of the bed she slept on, all about her Nutella addiction, and what she had tattooed on her left buttock. Don't ask.

Ed looked over her shoulder and she watched his whole manner change, like a snake shedding its skin, morphing from bored and irritated to gushing and obsequious.

'Fizz!' he said. 'It's so good to meet you IRL! I am such a huge fan!' He didn't pay Iona any attention at all, let alone introduce her to their guest. She might as well have been another overly large table decoration they just had to talk around.

'Oh, you're so sweet,' said Fizz. 'What an extraordinary

place. I'd never have thought of coming somewhere like this. It's not my kind of scene *at all*.' She was, Iona decided, every bit as irritating as she'd suspected. She buttered a piece of freshly baked bread roll and fed it surreptitiously to Lulu. At least they'd both get a good lunch out of this ghastly charade. Iona made a mental note to order the most expensive dishes on the menu.

'I thought you might say that,' Ed said, glaring at Iona in a manner that reeked of *I told you so*.

'No, this is just *fabulous*. Totally unique. I'm so *over* all those cookie-cutter, try-too-hard Shoreditch places. I bet this was your idea, Iona,' she said, turning to Iona and beaming at her with her wild hair colourings, random piercings and perfect teeth. Iona could feel herself thawing.

'Hey, I passed this bloke on the way in who I'm sure I know from somewhere,' said Fizz, gesturing towards the Chancellor of the Exchequer.

'Fizz,' said Ed, in a voice so oleaginous that you could slip on it and dislocate a hip. 'I am *so* glad that you are a fan of my little magazine.' *His* little magazine?

'I'm not, actually,' said Fizz, tickling Lulu under the chin and blowing her kisses. 'But I am a *huge* fan of Iona.'

Iona melted a little more. At this rate, the only thing left of her by the end of lunch would be a little puddle on the floor. It was, she thought, quite possible that she and Fizz were going to become the very best of friends.

'Just imagine – Iona Yacht!' Fizz continued.

'Do you?' said Ed, perking up enormously. 'How amazing. Where is it moored?'

'Ha ha, you are funny, Ted,' said Fizz. 'No, that's what

they used to call Iona. You must know that! You are so, so lucky to have her!'

'Aren't I,' said Ed, through teeth more gritted than an Alpine road in midwinter.

Iona smiled, and felt a weight that had been resting on her shoulders for several years start to shift slightly. She was beginning to feel, just a little bit, like the woman Fizz thought she was. The woman she'd used to be.

Maybe it was all going to be okay after all.

Iona

18:17 Waterloo to Hampton Court

Iona was on such a high after her fabulous lunch that she walked into Carriage 3 as if she were walking on to the yacht she'd never actually owned. Fizz had agreed to write a weekly column for the magazine on *What's Hot and What's Not*, and Ed was convinced it would pull in young readers in their thousands.

Iona frowned. Bizarrely, her carriage was often packed these days, even when the rest of the train was fairly empty. She should probably switch to another one, but Lulu hated change and besides, this carriage held so many memories.

Iona paused, and let herself be enveloped, just for a few precious moments, in one of them. The one she and Bea called 'The Day of the Suit', from about ten years ago.

She replayed the scene in her head, watching herself sitting down at her usual seat and pulling her things out of her bag. She'd been so immersed in mixing her drink – it had been negronis back then – that it had taken her a while to notice the woman sitting opposite her. She was dressed in a pinstriped three-piece suit, with a flamboyant silk tie, and a spotted handkerchief poking cheerily out of her jacket pocket. Her face was hidden behind a copy of the *Evening Standard*, but Iona had recognized the notes of Jo Malone's lime, basil and mandarin perfume, and the hands holding the newspaper. Beautiful, black hands, with perfectly buffed fingernails and elegant, long fingers that could – in another life – have belonged to a concert pianist. Bea's hands.

'Do you take this train often?' Iona had said to her partner, in her lowest, most husky voice.

Bea lowered her newspaper and looked at her quizzically, as if seeing her for the first time.

'I could be persuaded to,' she said, folding her paper and holding out a hand for Iona to shake as the train pulled in at Vauxhall. 'My name's Beatrice. Delighted to make your acquaintance.'

'Has anyone ever told you how incredibly attractive you are?' said Iona, by the time they'd left Wimbledon.

By Raynes Park, Bea had her hand on Iona's knee, and by Berrylands they were kissing passionately across the table.

At Thames Ditton, they'd been thrown off the train.

'I'll have none of that lewd behaviour on my watch,' the guard had shouted at them. 'It's disgusting.'

Judging by the looks on the faces of several of their fellow passengers, he hadn't been the only one to disapprove, but there was one girl, in her early twenties probably, who stood up in her seat and applauded as the train pulled out of Thames Ditton station, leaving them standing on the platform.

'Where on earth did you find that suit?' said Iona.

'The Major next door was having a clear-out,' said Bea. 'The wardrobe lady at the theatre altered it for me, and I couldn't resist giving it a bit of an outing. It felt like that sort of suit that would pick up a beautiful stranger on a train.'

'Well, that's lovely, but now we'll have to walk home,' sighed Iona. 'I can't face getting on another train this evening. Don't you think we should be a little more *discreet*, maybe? Stop drawing so much attention to ourselves?'

Bea had stepped back and looked at her in horror.

'Darling, what is the point of being *alive* if you go through life unnoticed, without standing out and making waves? And for every pig-headed bigot, like that train guard, there'll be a girl like the one who applauded, who – just maybe – had been struggling with her own sexuality and whose life may now be very different because of people like us, who refuse to be discreet and stop drawing so much attention to ourselves.'

'You're right, Bea. Of course you are, my darling,' said Iona, taking Bea's hand in hers as they started the walk back to Hampton Court. Because Bea was always right.

Now, a decade later, Iona looked over towards that very same seat. It had a briefcase on it. Piers's briefcase. He'd saved it for her. How lovely. And his coat was reserving the seat next to it for Lulu.

It was rare, recently, that Iona didn't find one of her new friends sitting at her table on her journey. Why had it taken her so long to see her train carriage as a fascinating portal into other people's stories, rather than just a way of getting from A to B? At a time when her life had felt like it was totally unravelling, her train gang had stopped her brooding. It was never a good idea to brood. Unless, of course, you were a chicken.

'Piers!' she said. 'How kind of you to save Lulu and me a seat!'

'It wasn't exactly easy,' said Piers. 'I had to ignore endless pointed looks and tutting and act totally pig-headed and thick-skinned.'

'That must have been difficult for you,' said Iona. 'Well, what a lovely way to end a fabulous day. This calls for gin and tonics. Luckily, I have two glasses. And nuts. And napkins.'

'Have you got a whole delicatessen in there, Iona?' said Piers.

'It's the Fifth Rule of Commuting,' said Iona. 'Always come prepared for any eventuality. I can also sort you out if you ladder your tights, get bitten by a mosquito or start your period unexpectedly.'

'That would certainly be unexpected,' said Piers.

'Same,' said Iona. 'That tampon's been in my bag since 2014.'

Piers looked a little uncomfortable. He was obviously not entirely at ease with female biology.

'Too much information?' said Iona. 'Why don't you tell me how your day's been?'

'Not so good,' Piers said, with an expression that looked very much worse than *not so good*. She felt like Winnie-the-Pooh bumping into Eeyore in the Hundred Acre Wood. She was just a little annoyed at Piers for bringing down the mood.

'Want to talk about it?' she asked, squashing her irritation. She had, she told herself firmly, enough *joie de vivre* of her own right now to be able to spread a little around.

'Have you ever had the feeling that your whole life is like a Jenga tower, and if one more piece is removed the whole thing is just going to come crashing down?' he asked her.

'Actually, yes, I have,' said Iona, batting away the unwelcome image of Brenda-from-HR. And just as she was about to ask him to explain what, or who, was removing bricks from the Jenga tower of his life, they were interrupted.

'Excuse me,' said a young, somewhat timid, voice. 'Is your name Iona?'

'Yes, it is,' said Iona. 'Why do you ask?'

'I'm Martha. Sanjay told me to find you,' said the girl, who was all elbows and knees, with a couple of enviable cheekbones thrown in, and couldn't be much older than fifteen. Although, to be fair, anyone under the age of forty looked about fifteen to Iona.

'Sit, sit,' said Iona, shooing Lulu off her seat and brushing the dog hairs she'd left behind on to the floor. Martha looked nervously at Piers, as if he might lean over and bite her at any moment, reminding Iona that she'd seen Martha on the train before.

'Don't worry about Piers, sweetheart,' she said. 'He's perfectly tame now, and very sorry about yelling at you when you were ill. Aren't you, Piers?' Iona gave him a stern look.

'Oh, it's you,' said Piers. 'The vomiter. Still, no harm done that couldn't be fixed by giving vast sums of cash to my local computer repair store. I'm sorry for shouting.' Martha didn't look entirely reassured.

'Now,' said Iona. 'Any friend of Sanjay's is a friend of mine. Tell me how I can help? You don't mind, do you, Piers?' Piers did look a little put out, actually, but Iona ignored him. These train journeys were short, and she needed to spread her time out fairly.

Quietly, and haltingly, using gestures and grimaces to get her story across without resorting to language that was too florid or embarrassing, Martha told Iona about the photo and the bullying. 'So, you see, I don't want to tell the teachers, I can't talk to my parents because they don't live together and it's all . . . complicated. They'll both blame me and each other, and it'll cause even more arguments. And, right now, I don't have any friends.'

'Sounds like another wobbly tower of bricks,' said Piers.

Martha stopped and stared at Piers, unsure how to respond.

'Ignore him, sweetheart. He's having a career crisis, which we're going to deal with another time,' said Iona, giving Piers her handy 'back in your box' look.

'Even before all of this, I never really fitted in, and now I never will. I don't know what to do.' She began to cry, wiping her eyes on the cuffs of her school blazer, and Lulu, who had an extremely highly developed sense of empathy for a dog, and was probably a renowned therapist in a previous life, started whining.

'Good God. Since when have you wanted to *fit in*?' said Iona. 'I can't think of anything worse. My wife, Bea, says the whole point of life is to stand out, not to fit in.' She rolled up her metaphorical sleeves and got to work. 'So, if you're not prepared to talk to the authorities' – she paused as Martha shook her head vigorously – 'then this is not the sort of problem we can deal with head on. Talking about the photo is only going to draw more attention to it – add fuel to the fire, so to speak. So, we have to approach the issue *sideways*. Sort of sneak up on it, like a game of Grandmother's Footsteps.' Martha looked blank. Iona sighed. 'One of the games we used to play before the World Wide Web,' she explained.

'I still don't get what you mean?' said Martha.

'The point is, if you want to stop them thinking of you as . . .'

'Naked girl,' finished Martha.

'Well, quite,' said Iona. 'If you want to stop them thinking of you as *that*, you have to get them thinking of you as *something else*. It's a distraction technique. Replace one image with another.'

'So I need to do something *worse*?' said Martha.

'Well, that's one potential strategy,' said Iona, 'but I don't recommend it. No, you need to do something way, way *better*! Think Kim Kardashian!'

Martha looked sceptical.

'Does everyone call Kimmy "the sex tape girl"?' Iona said. 'No, of course they don't! Because Kim has given them so many other things to talk about that they barely remember the tape.'

'What tape?' said Martha.

'My point precisely,' said Iona. 'So, what's your *thing*?'

'My thing?' repeated Martha, looking confused.

'Yes. Everyone needs a thing. Music? Art? Sport?' Martha still looked blank. This was going to be hard work. 'Piers's thing' – she gestured at Piers, who'd thought he'd been totally forgotten – 'is numbers. I know, it's a funny thing to have a thing about, but each to their own.'

'What's your thing?' Martha asked.

'Well, dear heart, why do you think Sanjay told you to find me?' She paused and raised her eyebrows at a nonplussed Martha. 'Because *this* is my thing!' She smiled her 'mysterious benefactor' smile. 'Helping people. I'm a professional.'

'You're a psychotherapist?' asked Martha.

'Sort of,' she replied. 'A magazine therapist.'

'Oh. Like a journo-stroke-psychotherapist mash-up? Cool,' said Martha, who, it appeared, was a bright child.

'Exactly,' said Iona.

'I'm not sure I have a thing,' said Martha. 'I quite like acting. At least, I used to. I haven't done any for ages.'

'Bingo!' said Iona, slamming her hands down on the table, almost knocking over her gin and tonic. 'I myself used to be on the stage, as did Bea. It's where we met. The magic of acting is it takes you out of yourself. It allows you to try on other people's clothes and inhabit different worlds. It's the perfect therapy when real life is too hard. Instead of people thinking of you as Naked Girl, they'll start describing you as Martha-the-fabulous-actress. Martha-who-lights-up-the-stage-and-has-the-audience-on-their-feet. See? Now, how do we start? Is there a school play?'

'Yes. *Romeo and Juliet*, which is my English set text. They're auditioning soon, I think,' said Martha, looking equal parts terrified and excited. 'But my mum will never let me do it.'

'Why on earth not?' asked Iona.

'Because she says this is a *crucial year*.' Martha looked stern and put air speech marks around the final two words in an impersonation, Iona guessed, of her mother. See, a natural actor. 'I have my GCSEs next year, and my maths teacher says at this rate I'm on course for a total car crash. Mum will argue that rehearsals would take up too much homework time. Bet you she does.'

'Mmmm,' said Iona, thinking how the Universe really did work in mysterious ways. 'What you really need is a private maths tutor. Someone who'd give you some lessons for free. Like an aspiring teacher who needs some real-life practice . . .' She let the words hang in the air, waiting. There was no response.

'I mean, it wouldn't be asking too much, would it? It's not like *saving someone's life* or anything, is it?'

Still nothing.

'You know, there's a fabulous Buddhist saying that goes: *When the pupil is ready, the teacher appears* . . .' said Iona, with a loaded emphasis on *teacher*.

Piers cleared his throat. 'I'll help if you like,' he said. 'Since we often take the same train, we could spend the time usefully. So long as you promise not to vomit on me again.'

Et voilà!

Emmie

Emmie felt like she'd accidentally stumbled on to the set of a Hollywood movie.

She was sitting in her favourite Italian restaurant, lit by the flattering glow of flickering candles, halfway through a bowl of spaghetti vongole, and Toby was kneeling on the floor in front of her, holding an open box containing a glittering diamond solitaire ring. Any minute now, the director would shout *Cut!* and all the waiters would wander off-stage to drink tea out of polystyrene cups and vape.

'Do you realize that when our children ask how you proposed they're not going to believe this story? It's far too perfect,' she said. 'I can hardly believe it myself.'

'Look, I don't want to rush you, but I'm kind of on tenterhooks here, and I'm getting cramp in my calf. Does that mention of our hypothetical children mean yes?' he asked.

'Of course, yes! I'd love to be your wife!' she replied. Toby grinned and turned around to face the silent and expectant room.

'She said yes!' he shouted, and the whole restaurant cheered and whooped in response, probably out of relief that they didn't have to witness a public and traumatic rejection, which might put a downer on their own evenings.

Toby hugged her tightly, as if he were worried that she might change her mind and run away, and the waiters pulled out a bottle of champagne they must have had chilling under the table in anticipation. Although she noted they'd left the cork in the bottle, just in case.

He'd choreographed it as beautifully as he'd designed their house – every detail thought through, every eventuality anticipated. Even the ring fitted perfectly, she thought as she twisted it round, running her thumb over the sharp edges of the diamond, wondering if she'd ever get used to the weight of it on her finger.

'How did you get the size just right?' she asked him.

'Uh, I measured your finger while you were sleeping. It was really hard, actually! I was terrified you'd wake up and think I had some weird kind of finger fetish. You do like it, don't you? I did check that the stone was ethically sourced, because I knew you'd want to be sure.'

'I love it!' said Emmie, perhaps a little too enthusiastically. If she were being really picky, which she wasn't, she'd confess that she'd always dreamed of an emerald engagement ring, but she couldn't exactly expect Toby to know that, and if he'd asked her what sort of ring she'd wanted, he wouldn't have been able to surprise her like this, would he?

People had often said to Emmie that *when you know, you know*, and she'd thought it a particularly smug and unhelpful cliché. But now she knew exactly what they meant. She couldn't imagine her life without Toby in it. Since she'd met him, their relationship had expanded to fill almost her entire world. Nobody had ever loved her with the intensity that he did, and this moment proved it.

She looked around her, trying to soak up every single detail – the smell of garlic and freshly baked bread, the feel of the starched linen tablecloth and champagne bubbles popping on her tongue, and the sound of pots and pans clattering in the open kitchen – so she could pull out the scene and re-live it whenever she needed to.

As soon as they'd got home, Emmie had FaceTimed her dad. He'd be just beginning the day she was ending, in California, where he'd moved after her mother died, only months after Emmie left university. *Too many bad memories here*, he'd said. Memories not outweighed, apparently, by the joy of being close to his only daughter. That still stung, even after all this time. Perhaps creating her own family with Toby would finally heal that wound.

Her father's face appeared on the screen: his eyes, the same green as her own, but surrounded by laughter lines, his hair still thick and wavy, but now almost completely grey. He liked to describe himself as a 'silver fox'.

He looked so familiar, and yet the increasing distance between them was apparent in the tan of his skin compared to hers, and the bright morning light of his kitchen contrasting with the artificial glow illuminating her own face.

There was, thank goodness, no sign of Delilah, her dad's 'lodger'. Delilah, who was only a few years older than Emmie, often appeared in the background of their calls carrying a yoga mat or making a smoothie, wearing crop tops and tiny denim shorts displaying long, tanned legs complete with thigh gap, like an advertisement for a healthy Californian lifestyle brand. Even after three years of these regular appearances, they still continued with the pretence that nothing was going on.

Emmie's dad had said all the right things and promised to come over as soon as he could to meet his prospective son-in-law. They were going to love each other, she knew it.

The Universe was still smiling on Emmie the next morning, as when the train pulled in, she could see Iona and Lulu sitting at their usual table opposite a spare seat. Finding a seat near Iona had become increasingly difficult recently, and they often resorted to just smiling and waving at each other from a distance, over the heads of their fellow commuters.

Hopefully Sanjay would join them at New Malden. She couldn't wait to tell her new friends her good news. They were going to be so excited for her! Through Surbiton and Berrylands, Emmie hid her left hand under the table, waiting for Sanjay to complete the audience for her grand reveal. The train pulled to a halt as they arrived at his station, and there he was.

Sanjay managed to push his way through to their table and create enough space to stand next to them. Emmie saw a rather heavy man stand on his foot, making Sanjay wince.

'Sorry,' Sanjay said. He raised his arm to grab hold of a pole to steady himself as the train jerked into motion, and his jumper rose up to expose just a few inches of brown, toned stomach, right at the height of Emmie's nose. Emmie found herself staring. *Stop it, Emmie! Happily engaged women do not look at other men's stomachs. However ripped they might be.*

'Hi, Sanjay!' said Emmie, waving at him, rather showily. The light caught on her diamond and refracted shards of light on to the table in front of them like a miniature glitter ball at a seventies disco. *Look at me*, it shouted. *Aren't I sparkly?* Nobody noticed.

Emmie couldn't concentrate on the conversation, as she was way too preoccupied with waiting for a reaction to her ring. The train stopped at Wimbledon, and disgorged enough people to allow David to get to them.

'Hi, David!' said Emmie. 'Why don't you have my seat? I don't mind standing.' She proffered her left hand, so David could pull her to her feet.

'That's a gorgeous ring, Emmie,' he said, as he took her hand.

'Oh, hallelujah!' said Emmie. 'I was wondering how long it would take someone to notice! I've been waving my left hand around like the bloody Queen on parade since New Malden, and Iona and Sanjay have been totally oblivious, just rabbiting on about who's hooked up with who on *Love Island*!'

'Emmie!' cried Iona. 'You're engaged! When did that happen? How did it happen? When's the wedding? Oh, you must tell us everything! Immediately!'

'That's so exciting!' said Sanjay. 'I'm so happy for you! And for him, obviously!'

All the way through Earlsfield and Clapham Junction, Emmie told them about the proposal. They wanted to know the whole story, which she was more than happy to relay, and were so thrilled for her – especially Sanjay, who was obviously a total romantic. She made a mental note to fix him up with one of her single friends.

'Did you propose, Iona, or did Bea?' asked Emmie, not wanting to move away from the subject, even after they'd exhausted every minute detail of her Friday night.

'Neither of us could for years, sadly,' said Iona. 'Marriage wasn't an option for decades after we got together. We were active campaigners for the legalization of same-sex marriage, and we proposed to each other as soon as the legislation was passed – July 2013. Then we had a wonderful wedding as soon as we could: the thirtieth of March, 2014. We were one of the first legally married gay couples in the country!'

'What about you, David?' said Iona.

'Oh, I'd been carrying the ring around for weeks, waiting for the right moment, and the courage, to pop the question,' he said. 'Then we went to see a play in the West End – *The Importance of Being Earnest*, which had us both in stitches – followed by a wonderful dinner at J. Sheekey. I knew the timing wasn't going to get much better than that. So, when I dropped her home, and she invited me in for a nightcap, I pulled out the ring and the rest, as they say, is history.'

'Oh, that's so lovely!' said Emmie, clapping her hands together, before David ruined the mood by adding, rather morosely, 'Well, it is history now, in any case.'

'I love that play!' said Iona. 'Oscar Wilde. He had a much harder time being queer than we did, poor man. It's the one where a baby is left in a handbag at Victoria station. *A handbag!?*' Iona did remind Emmie a little of Lady Bracknell, actually, but she thought it might not be wise to tell her.

'Are you sure you don't have a baby in yours, Iona?' said Sanjay. 'You have pretty much everything else in there.'

'Insolent child!' said Iona, pretending to clip him around the ear. 'I don't, obviously. But I do have a small pot of nappy rash cream. It works wonders on wrinkles.'

'It's my wedding anniversary in a couple of weeks, actually,' said David. 'Nearly forty years.'

'Why don't you take Olivia back to J. Sheekey?' said Iona. 'I'm pretty sure it's still around. You can remind her of the time she felt the same way about you as Emmie does about Toby.'

'You definitely should, David. After all, it's not over until the fat lady sings. Isn't that right, Iona?' said Sanjay, and Emmie wondered why he looked so sad.

It was fortunate that Emmie didn't have any meetings first thing, because she spent the next two hours filling in all her office friends, who gushed over her ring and seemed almost as excited as she was. Even Joey did a good job of pretending he wasn't secretly dreading the possibility of another director going on maternity leave.

When Emmie finally made it through the throng of well-wishers to her desk, she pulled up her emails. She hadn't noticed the sender of the email with the exuberant title YOUR GOOD NEWS!, so she wasn't at all prepared for the message it contained.

YOU DON'T DESERVE A MAN LIKE THAT.
A FRIEND.

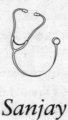

Sanjay

19:00 Waterloo to New Malden

Sanjay wondered whether the vending machine had it in for him, too. It had sucked up the last of his change but was stubbornly refusing to release the Mars bar he'd hoped would fill the hole caused by working through lunch, again.

He balled his hand into a fist and bashed it against the glass. The vending machine laughed at him, as he bruised his knuckles without making the Mars bar so much as quiver, let alone fall into the dispensing tray.

Sanjay's stomach rumbled, churning with a mixture of hunger and frustration, not just at the stupid machine, but at his complete inability to get anything right. No Mars bar, and no Emmie. Stupid, irritating machine. Stupid, irritating Toby with his stupid IT company, stupid beard, stupid skiing holidays and stupid unimaginative engagement ring. Sanjay would have chosen Emmie an emerald, to go with her eyes.

He took a short run up to the gloating hunk of metal and kicked it hard. 'Take that, you arrogant, annoying bastard!' he shouted at it. The machine vibrated slightly, and its internal light dimmed, making it appear surprisingly empathetic, before quickly returning to full power.

Sanjay could sense someone behind him before he saw them. It was an exhausted-looking young mother, holding the hand of Harry, one of his patients from the paediatric oncology ward.

'Are you okay, Sanjay?' asked Harry's mum, who he knew had far more reason not to be okay than Sanjay did. He added abject shame to all his other negative emotions.

'Yes, I'm fine,' he said, bending down so that his head was level with Harry's. 'Sorry about the bad word, Harry,' he said. 'You know how sometimes when life feels really unfair, it helps to let it all out?' Harry nodded. 'But it's still not good to swear, is it?' He stood up and mouthed *sorry* to Harry's mum.

'Don't worry. I've said a lot worse, believe me,' she said.

Sanjay didn't see Harry again until right at the end of his shift, as he was wheeling the blood pressure monitor through Harry's ward. Harry was in bed, his skin as pale as the sheets, and his bald head making him look as vulnerable as a newborn. Actually, given that the chemo had knocked out his immune system, he was probably *more* vulnerable than a newborn.

Harry picked up his pillow, held it in front of him and, with a surprising amount of force, plunged his fist into it several times. 'Take that, you arrogant, annoying bastard,' he said. Thank God his mother had gone home already.

'Did that help, Harry?' asked Sanjay.

'Yup,' said Harry, and it was the first time Sanjay had seen him smile all day.

As Sanjay settled into a seat for his train journey home, his phone pinged with a text alert.

Mum: DAD SAYS YOU LOOKED TIRED WHEN HE FACETIMED YOU. ARE YOU GETTING ENOUGH SLEEP?

Sanjay sighed.

Mum: AND TAKING THOSE MULTIVITAMINS I GAVE YOU?

I'm fine Mum, typed Sanjay. *Just working hard.*

Mum: BY THE WAY, ANITA'S DAUGHTER SAYS IF YOU BOOK AN APPOINTMENT AT HER DEN-TIST SURGERY, SHE'LL GIVE YOU A DISCOUNT ON A SCALE AND POLISH.

Mum, are you meddling again? typed Sanjay. Then he added a smiley face to take the sting out. His mum was more sensitive than she appeared.

Mum: OF COURSE NOT! I'M JUST WORRIED ABOUT YOUR GUMS.

There was a pause before an emoji appeared, which might have been chosen to signify maternal anxiety, or because of the number of teeth it was displaying. Meera had embraced the advent of the emoji wholeheartedly, believing they compensated for the English language's shameful inability to convey the full range and depth of her emotions.

'You look deep in thought,' said Emmie, sitting down in the seat opposite him.

'Oh, hi, Emmie! It's just my mum,' said Sanjay. 'She can't quite come to terms with the fact that I don't need her sorting my life out for me any more. She still messages me every day to check that I'm eating enough fibre and wearing a vest. Honestly, I'm too old to want to discuss my bowel movements with my mother! Is your mum the same?'

He knew immediately from the way Emmie's expression changed that he'd said something terribly wrong.

'I'm sure she would have been,' said Emmie, in the determinedly upbeat tone of someone trying hard not to cry. 'But she died, years ago.'

'I'm so sorry,' said Sanjay, who really, really was. How did he always manage to make such a mess of everything? 'I regularly see mothers dying too early, and it's the most tragic thing. Really unfair.' Sanjay wished he could find some words that didn't sound like empty platitudes. Dealing with death, day in, day out, didn't make the conversation any easier. His mum was right. There were some situations the English language just wasn't up to.

'It must be so rewarding, though, doing what you do,' said Emmie, deftly changing the subject.

'Yes, but it's hard too,' said Sanjay. 'It's physically difficult – hours on your feet, turning patients to relieve pressure sores, dealing with catheters, soiled dressings and bed pans.' Oh God, why had he alerted her to the fact that so much of his job involved other people's bodily fluids? He really should stick only to the photogenic end of his job, like dressing up as one of Santa's elves to deliver gifts to the kids on Harry's ward last Christmas. 'But it's emotionally exhausting, too,' he continued. 'So much sadness.'

'I can see that,' said Emmie, gazing at him as if he were some kind of superhero. 'But at least you're dealing with stuff that *matters*. Life and death. I'm just working on a brief to persuade teenagers to use a new brand of toothpaste.'

'But it must be such fun, doing something so creative,' said Sanjay. 'Anyhow, dental hygiene is important too. That's what my mum's text was about, actually. She wants me to book an appointment with the hygienist.'

Sanjay felt like a fraud. He wanted to tell Emmie about the panic attacks, how sometimes he could only talk himself down by reciting the periodic table in a dark cupboard, but even as he felt the words assembling on his tongue, the train pulled into New Malden.

Sanjay still hadn't eaten, due to the abortive encounter with the vending machine, so he ducked into the coffee shop next to the station. The owner sometimes slipped him a cut-price muffin if there were any left out at the end of the day. He didn't recognize Piers at first, since seeing him here was completely out of context. It was two stops before Surbiton, where Piers lived. He was hunched over a laptop and muttering under his breath.

'Are you avoiding going home, Piers?' Sanjay said. He meant it as a joke, but Piers's reaction made him wonder whether he'd accidentally hit on a truth. Piers looked shifty and slammed down the lid of his laptop, as if he'd been watching hardcore porn. Surely not? There were mothers with kids in here.

'Oh, I just stopped off to answer an urgent client email. You know how it is,' he said.

Sanjay nodded, as if he did know how it was, although he suspected his and Piers's jobs held nothing in common. His day was all swabs, stitches, chemo ports and blood tests. Urgent client emails were not a major feature. Also, Piers's job involved making obscene amounts of money. His, not so much.

Sanjay wondered what it must feel like, never having to worry about your finances. Piers had, no doubt, gone from cashmere babygrows and solid-silver rattles into a job with one of Daddy's friends, by way of the poshest schools. He was quite sure that Piers had never had to nick the individual servings of UHT milk from the staff canteen, because he didn't have enough cash at the end of the month to buy a pint on the way home.

Did he have any idea how lucky he was? Sanjay's entire annual salary after tax wouldn't pay for the ridiculously showy watch on Piers's wrist. Sanjay stopped himself. That sort of thinking could drive you mad with envy.

He wondered what Piers was hiding. Was he having an affair? It would be typical of Piers, who was used to having more than his fair share of everything, to end up with two women when Sanjay couldn't even find his one.

Piers

08:13 Surbiton to Waterloo

Piers was waiting for Martha on their platform at Surbiton station so they could try to find seats near each other for their lesson. Piers had discovered that announcing, 'I'm her maths tutor, would you mind terribly swapping seats?' tended to do the trick, and Martha was learning to deal with the embarrassment. She'd also mostly stopped looking at him as if she didn't entirely trust him. Or like him, even. He was pretty sure that she'd never have agreed to let him help her, were it not for the reassuring presence of hundreds of other commuters, and the recommendation of Iona, obviously.

It was so satisfying, seeing Martha's confidence with numbers grow. She was getting quicker and more accurate with each of their train lessons. Unlike Piers's financial performance, which would definitely be annotated with *must try harder* or *please see me after class* in red pen.

Piers was going into the City later each day so he could match Martha's timetable, and they could miss the most crowded trains, but Candida didn't seem to notice. Nor had she mentioned the fact that he rushed to empty the post box whenever possible, retrieving the envelopes marked URGENT! FINAL REMINDER! which he hid in the back of his sock drawer.

Candida really was extraordinarily unobservant, considering that she could spot the earliest stages of a cobweb the cleaner had missed at twenty paces, or a one percentage point fall in Minty's cognitive ability test scores. He was almost tempted to let a huge ball drop on purpose, just to see if she finally paid some attention to what was going on in his life. But he didn't have the nerve, and he knew that if he dropped one ball, the whole lot would come crashing down.

'How's my best student today?' asked Piers as they waited for the train.

'I'm your only student,' said Martha. 'But good, thanks.'

'Did you manage last night's homework okay?' he said.

'Mostly. I got stuck on the simultaneous equations,' she replied.

'The trick with equations,' said Piers, 'is to stop thinking of them as boring old numbers and see them as patterns. Art, even. They really are quite beautiful. I'll show you.'

They boarded the train and found Iona at her usual table with Lulu holding one free seat. Piers managed to wangle them a second seat by employing a pincer movement of charm and bullying on a middle-aged woman.

As Piers explained the beauty of the simultaneous equation to Martha, he could picture the time he first discovered algebra and started to see the numbers as not just things he could arrange, play with and solve, but as a passport to a whole different life. How ironic that now he was in that life, all he wanted to do was escape.

'So, do you see now?' he asked Martha, who was chewing her bottom lip, as she always did when she was concentrating.

'You know, I actually think I do,' she replied, grinning at him.

'You're not bad at maths at all, Martha,' Piers said. 'You just lack confidence, and I suspect you haven't been taught terribly well. What's your teacher like?'

'I've had loads, actually. They don't have enough proper maths teachers at school, so we keep getting substitutes. My drama teacher even had to stand in for a few lessons. He was almost as useless as me,' said Martha. 'My mum complained, but the head said there's a national shortage of maths specialists.'

'What's your school called again?' said Piers.

'St Barnabus Secondary,' said Martha. 'Why?'

'Just wondering,' said Piers, making a mental note, just in case.

Piers had been ignoring Iona, who he could tell was increasingly frustrated about being left out. She was simmering like a pressure cooker, gathering steam until finally she exploded.

'Look, I know this whole maths thing was my idea – for which I deserve some credit, actually – but could we please give it a break for the rest of the journey, because I need to hear about the auditions for the school play.'

'They're in two weeks,' said Martha, putting her pen

down with rather more alacrity than Piers would have liked. 'They've given us a short section of dialogue to learn and perform. I'll probably end up backstage, doing wardrobe, or lighting, but that's okay. It'll be fun just being involved in some way, and it's already taking my mind off the whole naked pic thing.'

'Backstage, huh? We'll see about that,' said Iona. 'No mentee of Iona's ends up backstage. Have you got the extract there?'

Martha pulled a crumpled piece of paper from her bag, laid it on the table on top of the far more important maths paper, and tried to flatten it with her sleeve. Iona squinted at it, reached into her bag and pulled out some reading glasses.

'I'm doing this for you, dear heart,' she whispered. 'I never usually wear these in public. They make me look old.' Piers was going to quip that it was her age that made her look old, in retaliation for Iona crashing his maths lesson, but decided against it. Prodding Iona was a great sport, but he'd learned that if you did it too hard she'd bite.

'Ooh, look, it's the balcony scene!' said Iona. 'Right, you play Juliet, obviously, and I'll be Romeo. We have three stations to convince Piers and this chap . . .' Iona gestured at the fourth person at their table – an extremely muscular man, wearing only a T-shirt and shorts, despite the cold '. . . that we're falling madly in love with each other. What fun! I'm Iona, and this is Martha,' said Iona to their audience. 'Also known as Romeo and Juliet.'

'Jake,' he replied, holding out his hand. 'Also known as Jake.'

'Oh, yes, it says so on your chest,' said Iona. 'How helpful.' Piers craned his neck to see the words JAKE'S PERSONAL TRAINING printed boldly on Jake's top.

Martha looked utterly terrified, but Piers could see the method in Iona's madness. If she could deal with this humiliation, the audition was going to be a breeze.

Iona

18:17 Waterloo to Hampton Court

What a difference a couple of months make, thought Iona.

It was the end of another rather successful day. She'd spotted Piers and Sanjay on Platform 5 at Waterloo and had managed to corral them into position at her usual table by barging past a young mother with a baby in a pushchair. She'd felt a little guilty about that, until she overhead the woman saying, 'Just ignore the mean old lady, sweetheart,' to her baby.

'There's really no point in her bad-mouthing me to her child,' said Iona to Lulu. 'It's not as if it can understand a word she's saying.'

Ed's executive assistant had put a meeting in her diary, tomorrow at 5 p.m. Until recently this would have sent Iona into a total spin, but now she was quietly confident. Excited, even.

Since she'd started running some of her readers' letters by

Emmie, Sanjay and Martha, and building in the best of their responses, she'd been causing a bit of a stir on 'the socials', her postbag had increased significantly, and her stock in the office appeared to have risen hugely. Then there was the massive coup of landing Fizz, who'd had the whole place in an undignified flutter since she'd joined the team last week.

Yes, this meeting was going to be fun. Perhaps a pay rise was in the offing? She hadn't had one in years, after all. She hadn't dared complain previously, worrying that her relatively modest pay packet was the main reason she still had a job.

Then she had an epiphany. This week was the thirtieth anniversary of her working for *Modern Woman*. Surely this couldn't be a coincidence? Perhaps they'd organized a celebration of some sort? On her tenth anniversary, they'd thrown a surprise party – with champagne and canapés. On her twentieth there had been a cake and some vouchers for Harvey Nichols. What might thirty bring? She must remember to look completely astonished and delighted, or she'd ruin the big reveal.

There were only two things putting a dampener on Iona's mood. The first was the person sitting in the seat behind hers, who was eating an incredibly malodorous hotdog. Did they not know that the Third Rule of Commuting was never to eat hot food on the train? The second was Sanjay, who was looking mournfully into his takeaway coffee, as if it held the secret to his future. The time had come for some tough love.

'Sanjay,' she said. 'I'm afraid it's time to buck up and move on. There are plenty more fish in the sea, and all that.'

'But Iona,' he said, and for the first time since they'd met he seemed to be actually *glaring* at her. 'You said it's not over till the fat lady—'

'She's singing, Sanjay,' interrupted Iona. 'Can't you hear her? She's rehearsing for her gig at the wedding. Sometimes life doesn't work out the way we want it to – I know that better than most, believe me. Anyhow, you shouldn't use the word "fat". It's body-shaming.'

'You used it first, not me,' said Sanjay, glowering at her. 'Look, what if Emmie is *my One*, and she's with someone else?'

'There's no such thing as "the One",' said Iona. 'There are many possible life partners for everyone!'

'Really?' said Sanjay. 'So you could just as easily be with someone other than Bea, could you?'

'Well, not for me, obviously,' said Iona. 'But Toby is clearly the perfect guy for Emmie. She's deliriously happy, and as her friends, it's our job to be pleased for her, however hard that may be.'

'I am happy for her,' said Sanjay. 'I honestly don't care. It was just a stupid crush. I'm over it.'

'We both know that's not true, Sanjay,' said Iona. 'I'm a professional empath, remember. I can *read people*. You're sulking like a petulant toddler and it has to stop.'

Sanjay's phone pinged on the table in front of him.

'I'VE BOOKED YOU AN APPOINTMENT FOR SATURDAY,' read Iona out loud.

'That's my mum,' said Sanjay. 'I think she's trying to fix me up with a dental hygienist, although she denies it.'

'Excellent idea! See, there are plenty more fish in the sea!'

said Iona, picking up his phone and replying with a thumbs-up emoji. Sanjay snatched his phone from her hand.

'Butt out, Iona!' he said, in a voice that sounded much louder than it was, on account of being in an almost silent train carriage. 'I don't need you on my case as well as my mum. My love life is really none of your business. You're just a frustrated old woman with nothing better to do than interfere in other people's lives.'

Iona felt the words like a physical blow. They'd have hurt from anyone, but they were particularly devastating coming from Sanjay, who'd always been so gentle and thoughtful.

Sanjay stared pointedly out of the window, as if he couldn't bear to look at her, let alone speak. Which was rich, given that she was very much the innocent victim here. His accusations were still ringing in her ears: *Frustrated. Old. Interfering.* She wasn't sure which of Sanjay's poison darts stung the most.

Piers was also being uncharacteristically quiet, his head buried in his copy of the *Evening Standard*, like a tortoise retreating into his shell. He certainly wasn't leaping to her defence, making her wonder if she had actually overstepped the mark this time. She remembered all her journeys spent in silence in the past, before the day of the grape. But those were comfortable, relaxing, empty silences, not awkward and loaded like the one loitering malevolently between her, Sanjay and Piers.

When Sanjay got up to leave at New Malden, Piers muttered a cursory *goodbye* from behind his newspaper, but neither Iona nor Sanjay said a word.

Iona just stared out at the evening sky for the next two

stops, watching the colours shifting through the whole palette of reds and oranges as the sun set, and the spectacular and hypnotic morphing choreography of a murmuration of starlings. She'd distracted herself so successfully, by trying to work out how each of the birds knew which way to go and whether they ever bumped into each other, that when they pulled into Surbiton station and a woman's face, which would have been beautiful if it weren't so very *angry*, appeared right at her window, she almost screamed.

'Good God, what's with that lady?' she said, pointing her out to Piers, who was standing up to leave. She was wearing a designer yoga outfit, and had *OM SHANTI* printed across her pert bosom. A phrase which jarred considerably with the vibe she was giving off.

Piers turned in the direction of Iona's outstretched index finger and the colour drained from his cheeks.

'It's Candida,' he said, quietly.

'I think your Jenga tower might have smashed all over the floor,' said Iona.

'I suspect you're right. I'd better go and face the music,' said Piers, then muttered under his breath, 'I suppose it's about time.'

Piers pushed his way towards the doors, then turned around to look at Iona as he got off the train, with an expression much like an errant schoolboy being taken to the headmaster's office, knowing he was about to be expelled.

Iona was left sitting at a table, with just Piers's abandoned *Evening Standard* and a feeling of unease. What on earth could Piers have done to deserve such an irate welcoming committee? It probably involved another woman. These things usually did, she found.

So much for her perfect day. Everything seemed to be going wrong. Suddenly she wasn't quite so confident about her meeting tomorrow with Ed.

Piers

'Candida,' said Piers, deciding to bluff it out. 'How lovely of you to meet me at the station.'

'I found your car in the car park,' she replied, her voice quivering and nostrils flaring. 'So I knew you'd taken the train somewhere. The question is: *where?*'

The people standing around them on the platform had given up all pretence of not watching this drama play out, and their heads were swivelling from one contestant to the next, as if they were watching a particularly aggressive pro tennis tournament.

'What do you mean?' asked Piers, knowing exactly what she meant, but lobbing the ball back to her in any case, playing for time.

'I mean,' she hissed, 'what are you doing getting off this train, all dressed up in your smart business suit, when, according to one of the ladies in my Pilates class, you lost your job *three months ago*?'

Game, set and match to Candida. It looked like he was out of the tournament.

Piers had ten minutes of respite as he and Candida drove back to their house in separate cars. Candida took all the corners dangerously fast in her convertible Mini. It was like following a grenade with the pin pulled out.

As soon as the front door closed behind them, she exploded.

'What were you THINKING, humiliating me like that?' she yelled. 'Do you have ANY IDEA how stupid I looked when Felicia asked how you were coping, and I didn't have A CLUE what she was talking about?' She was so close to him that he could feel a bit of spittle land on his cheek. He left it there, fearing that any sudden movement might trigger an acceleration of her rage.

'I was trying to protect you,' he said, quietly. 'I was made redundant in the last cull, back in January, and I didn't think it was worth both of us worrying to death about it. I thought I'd tell you once I found a new job, but that turned out to be more difficult than I'd expected. Everyone is laying off at the moment, not hiring. And the longer I left it, the harder it became to explain.'

'What are we going to DO?' she said. 'What about the children's school fees? The mortgage? The nanny? How are we going to pay for it all?'

'Don't you see, that's exactly why I didn't want you to know? I was finding it hard enough dealing with the fact that the bank I'd been working for for fifteen years, raking money in hand over fist, giving up my evenings, weekends and cancelling holidays for, had just thrown me on the scrapheap. They gave me a cardboard box and five minutes to clear my desk, watched by two security guards. Then they saw me to the front door and confiscated my pass.'

He felt sick just remembering that day – the humiliation as he was frogmarched across the trading floor like he'd seen happen to so many men, and some women, before him. Some of his colleagues – the ones who thought themselves invulnerable – had chanted *Midas! Midas!* sarcastically as he passed. The more seasoned traders just stared fixedly at their screens, thinking *there but for the grace of God go I*. Few of them, if any, would make it through to a decent retirement age without having to do their own Walk of Shame.

'What did you do with the box?' she asked, with a slight smile, the faintest crack in her armour.

'Chucked it in the nearest skip,' he said.

'Even the photo of me you had on your desk?' she asked.

'I didn't have a photo of you on my desk,' he replied, before he could censor himself. But in the grand scheme of things, this minor infringement was hardly going to matter.

'So where have you been going all this time? What have you been doing?' she asked. And there it was – the inevitable question that would lead to a whole new level of revelations. He took a deep breath, before leaping into the abyss.

'I've been spending the day in various cafés and libraries, applying for jobs,' he said. 'I pulled in a few favours and landed a couple of interviews. But it felt as if they were just going through the motions and didn't lead to anything.'

Then he paused and spun his signet ring around on his little finger, before adding, 'And I've been day trading.'

'Day trading?' she said. 'You mean trading with your own capital?'

He nodded.

'I thought that as I'd spent so many years making money for my clients, why didn't I do the same for myself? For us.'

Her eyes narrowed.

'What capital?'

'My redundancy money,' he said.

'And how's that going?' she asked in a voice that suggested she knew the answer.

'Not brilliantly, at the moment,' he said. 'I've realized it takes a huge mind shift to go from playing with other people's money to risking your own. It takes a while to adjust, that's all.'

'And while you've been *adjusting*,' she said, slowly drawing out each perfectly enunciated syllable, 'how much of your redundancy payment – *our redundancy payment* – have you lost?'

'About two-thirds,' he said, although he knew the precise percentage was seventy-one. Just thinking about it brought back the familiar wave of nausea. 'But don't worry. It's not lost. I'll get it back. I just had a really bad run of luck. That's all changed now, I know it has.'

'You do know you sound exactly like a common-or-garden gambler, don't you?' she said. 'There's no difference between what you've been doing and the man who spends the housekeeping money on the horses or playing the fixed-odds betting terminals at the bookies. It's like the difference between the tramp on the park bench necking methylated spirits, and the "wine connoisseur" who drinks three bottles of Château Lafite over dinner at The Ivy. There is none, apart from the amount of money you spend, and the clothes you wear while doing it. You have to stop.'

'I can't stop now, Candida. Not before I've recouped my losses,' he said.

'And how long have you been telling yourself that, Piers?' she said. He didn't need to answer. She knew. 'It's not worked so far, has it? It's only made things worse.'

'It's too late to turn back now, Candida,' he said.

'It's too late *not* to turn back, Piers,' she replied.

Piers slumped into an armchair and put his head in his hands. He felt the band that was holding him together, and had been winding tighter and tighter for the last few months, snap. For the first time since that ghastly day in January, for the first time since he'd shed his old skin and shrugged on the new, invincible Piers, he cried. And once he started, he couldn't see how it was ever going to stop.

It took a while for Piers to work out where he was. The morning light fell at a different angle than normal, and when he stretched out his arm, the sheets next to him were cold and empty. Then he remembered. He was in the guest bedroom. And the events of the day before came crashing back.

Candida's words seemed to have germinated and taken root as he'd slept, because he could suddenly see his situation with an unwelcome clarity. She was right. He was just another gambler on a bad run, throwing good money after bad and refusing to leave the roulette table until they'd turned off the last of the lights in the casino.

The game, finally, was up.

Piers showered and shaved, mechanically, then walked to his dressing room. His hand hovered over the row of almost identical suits, lovingly fitted by his Jermyn Street tailor, out of habit, before picking out a pair of jeans and a cashmere jumper. There was, of course, no reason for him to wear a suit any more.

But now what?

Piers couldn't bear the idea of the empty day stretching out ahead of him, or of tiptoeing around the house, trying to avoid the wrath of Candida. Or, worse, her disappointment. Even at the points in their marriage when she'd not liked him much, like after the short and ill-advised dalliance with the Dutch au pair, she'd always respected him. She didn't respect him now. Hardly surprising, since he didn't respect himself.

Piers got into the Porsche, inhaling the reassuringly expensive scent of the leather seats, and hearing the throaty roar of the engine. These things usually gave him a little jolt of pleasure, but now he felt nothing. As though all his senses had been cauterized.

He drove, on autopilot, to the station. He parked the car, walked over the footbridge, and found himself standing on his usual platform in his usual place, despite the fact that nothing about him was usual at all. He was a fake. A two-dimensional avatar.

He thought back to the day he'd inhaled that grape, about

two months ago. He remembered how desperately he'd wanted to live, but now he couldn't understand why.

There was no point in him being on this platform. There was no point in him being here at all. There was, in fact, no point in him.

Piers walked to the edge and stared down on to the tracks. A rat scuttled into the shadows. He could hear the slight electric hum of a train, much further down the line, but getting closer with every second. And the louder the hum became, the more the track seemed to call to him. It would be so easy to put just one foot in front of the other and make all of this go away.

The hum became more insistent, more demanding, and he could sense people around him, feel their gazes upon him. Questioning. In a few seconds he'd have missed his opportunity.

The more he looked at the rails, the closer they seemed to be. So, so close. Not a jump, or even a fall. Just a step. The hum increased in volume and turned into a hiss, which sounded very much like *yessssss*.

'No!' said a voice right behind him.

Martha

07:59 Surbiton to Waterloo

Martha found it hard to reconcile the Piers she knew now with the one she'd vomited over just a few weeks ago. She was actually looking forward to seeing him at the station this morning. Partly because she'd managed to finish all her maths homework last night and was secretly hoping for some praise from an interested adult. She didn't include her mother, or her mother's lover, in this description, obviously. And also, because she'd been looking for some distraction.

Today was the day the cast list was going up on the board. She'd allowed herself to feel just a tiny bit hopeful that she might get a part with a few lines. She had, after all, had coaching from Iona, an *actual actress*, most mornings for the past fortnight. Her audition hadn't been perfect – she'd stumbled over one of her early lines before she'd relaxed into it, but it had been okay. Maybe more than okay. She'd felt a tingle of excitement, playing Juliet on a proper stage, and talking to a sixteen-year-old boy, instead of being on a train, flirting with an ancient lesbian.

And Iona had been right. Auditioning for the play had stopped her thinking, for some of the time at least, about *the vagina thing*, and she'd noticed that when she stopped thinking about it, she got fewer barbed remarks or sideways looks. Iona said those thoughts were like catnip to bullies. She hadn't asked what catnip was, but got the general idea. *It's a self-fulfilling prophecy*, Iona had said, *look like a victim, become a target*. Martha tried to imagine Iona ever becoming a target and failed. That woman was bulletproof.

Martha walked down the platform looking for Piers.

She didn't recognize him at first. She'd only ever seen him in a suit. Although Piers in jeans and a jumper looked way smarter than most ordinary people did in their best work clothes. He sort of *oozed* money through his pores. He definitely didn't look like a teacher, that was for sure.

'Piers!' she called, but he didn't react. He was just standing on the edge of the platform, actually over the yellow safety line painted on the tarmac, gazing at the tracks as if he'd just dropped a coin down a wishing well and decided that he wanted it back.

'Piers,' she said again. 'Are you okay?'

It was like he hadn't heard her, although she was right next to him now. He was staring down, hypnotized, and swaying slightly. It seemed to Martha as if her senses had been heightened, because she could hear the people around her – the breathing, shuffling, sniffing – amplified. She could smell the sweat prickling under her armpits. And she could see exactly what was going to happen, the scene playing forward on her retinas in slow motion.

'No!' she shouted, as she grabbed Piers by the arm.

The non-stop fast train to Waterloo charged straight through the station with a speed and power that made Martha feel sick with what might have been. But her relief quickly morphed into embarrassment. Had she overreacted? Was her imagination running away with her? After all, Piers hadn't actually stepped over the edge; he'd just . . . *looked strange*.

The vacuum left by the express train was quickly filled by the stopping train, and the crowd of people around them swarmed towards the opening doors, leaving Martha on the platform, still clutching Piers by his sleeve, feeling even more ill-equipped than usual.

Piers turned to stare at her, his expression blank, as if he had absolutely no idea who she was, or where he was.

'I wasn't going to jump,' he mumbled, as if trying to convince himself more than her.

'Let's go and sit down, shall we?' she said, leading him over to a bench. What would Attenborough say? *The injured lone wolf needs to get back to the safety of his pack.*

'Why don't we call your wife?' she said. He sat, staring straight ahead. He was like an electrical appliance on standby – still plugged in, but not functioning – and she had no idea where to find the remote control.

Martha reached into the pocket of his coat and felt the familiar shape of an iPhone. She took his thumb, wincing slightly as she noticed the skin around it, bitten red and raw, in vivid contrast to his manicured and buffed fingernails, and placed it at the bottom of the screen. Thankfully, it unlocked. She pulled up FAVOURITES in the contact list and found HOME.

It only took Candida fifteen minutes to get to the station. She ran up to them and sat down on the other side of Piers.

'Thank you . . . uh . . .'

'Martha,' said Martha.

'Thank you so much, Martha. I'll take over from here. I don't want to make you late for school. I'm sure he'll be okay. Low blood sugar, probably. He didn't eat breakfast this morning.'

'Sure,' said Martha, who wasn't sure at all.

As she climbed on to the train, feeling sick and shaky, she realized she hadn't asked Candida for Piers's number. How was she going to know if he really was all right? And if adults – proper, educated, married and *rich* adults like Piers – could melt down like that, then what hope did she have? What hope did any of them have?

'Are you okay?' said a voice next to her, as if the tables had been turned, and she was the one staring into the path of an oncoming train. She turned around to see the concerned face of Jake, the personal trainer who'd been her audience a couple of weeks ago.

'I'm not sure, to be honest,' she said. 'Is Iona on the train? I'd love to talk to her.'

'No,' he replied, gesturing over to her usual seat, which someone else was occupying, seemingly with no comprehension of the significance of the seventh aisle seat on the right, facing forwards. 'I've not seen her for a few days, actually. I only found out her name that day I met you, but I'd noticed her for a while, obviously.'

'Obviously,' said Martha, and she could swear she saw a few people around them nodding in silent agreement.

'I used to call her Muhammad Ali,' he said.

'Well, that's a bit unexpected,' said Martha. 'Why? I mean, *you* look a bit like Muhammad Ali, but not Iona.'

'Because she's elegant but fierce. You know, *float like a butterfly, sting like a bee.*'

Martha didn't know, but she nodded anyway since she didn't really want to get into the ancient history of boxers.

'Here, this might help.' Jake passed her an energy drink – the sort of thing her mother would have been horrified by, on account of all the empty calories – but he was right. Just one sip and she could feel her strength returning, her balance evening out.

'I've been wanting to talk to you, actually,' said Jake. 'You see, I couldn't help overhearing your conversation with Iona a while back. About the kids at school. I hope you don't mind.'

'Don't worry,' said Martha. 'It's pretty impossible to ignore Iona's conversations, isn't it?'

'I've been carrying this around for you,' he said, handing her a laminated card. 'It's a VIP pass for my gym. If you can't beat the bullies with this whole *Romeo and Juliet* thing, at least learn how to punch.'

'Thanks, but I can't accept it,' she said, looking at the name of a well-known, hugely trendy, gym on the card, followed by the words ACCESS ALL AREAS. 'It must cost a fortune. Anyhow, Iona says there's a Chinese proverb which goes: *If you stand on the bridge for long enough, the body of your enemy will come floating by.* I think that means they'll get their comeuppance eventually.'

'Mmm.' Jake looked sceptical. 'Look, don't worry about the cost. I own the place. You can pay me back with some good word of mouth.'

'Wow. Well, okay then. That's really kind of you, Jake, thank you,' said Martha, putting the card in her blazer pocket. She wondered who Jake expected her to rave about his gym to. She was hardly an influencer. Quite the opposite, in fact. Her recommendation could be the commercial kiss of death.

'Hey, I'm just building up good karma,' he replied. 'You see, I have a daughter, not much younger than you. And I'd like to think that if she were being treated the way you've been treated, there'd be someone watching who could hold out a hand to her.' Martha smiled, thinking what a gentle, spiritual and generous giant her new friend was.

'Or someone who could track down the fuckers that were bullying her and punch their fucking lights out. You know what I mean?' he continued. 'Sometimes, just hanging around on the bridge isn't enough. Sometimes you need to chuck the body in the river and put your foot on its neck.'

Just a generous giant, then.

'I'll see you at the gym,' he said.

Sanjay

Sanjay wasn't having a good day.

He'd had another restless night, watching the numbers change on his alarm clock. Why was it that time moved so quickly when he was trying to get round all his patients on a shift, yet in the middle of the night any movement was almost imperceptible? He was sucked into a vicious circle – the more he worried about being too tired to cope at work the next day, the more sleep eluded him and the more he worried.

'Sanjay, do you have a minute?' said Julie, and he had to pull himself out of the fog and focus. 'I was really hoping you'd do me a favour. I hate to ask, honestly, but . . .'

'Of course, I will,' Sanjay said, then cursed himself. He really had to stop agreeing to things before finding out the whole story.

'Thanks,' she beamed at him. 'I knew you were the right person to ask. You see, that cold cap hurts like hell, and it's not working. My hair's still falling out in clumps. I keep fishing it out of the shower drain, and when I woke up this morning it looked like I'd left half my head on the pillow. And I can't do it any more, Sanjay. It's like death by a thousand cuts. I want to shave it all off.'

'I get that, Julie,' said Sanjay. 'The cold cap doesn't work for everyone. And we have a great wig guy, you know. Used to work for Vidal Sassoon.'

Julie grimaced. 'I might stick to hats and turbans,' she said. 'But the thing is, I was hoping that you'd do it.'

'Do what?' said Sanjay, finding it difficult to follow the conversation. By the time Julie got to the end of a sentence, he'd lost track of the beginning.

'Shave my head. I know it's way over and above the call of duty, but I can't ask my hairdresser. I suggested she give me a shorter style with more body and, when my hair started coming out as she washed it, she wailed, *Those poor children! They're so young!* As if I were already dead. I left in tears with half my head still covered in shampoo.'

'What about your husband?' said Sanjay.

'I *really* don't want him to do it,' Julie said with a noticeable shudder. 'It's hard enough keeping any romance alive when you have cancer, and this would be the final straw. *Please.*'

Sanjay tried to work out how to say no. That this wasn't part of his job. That he was too busy. That he'd get in trouble – again – for ignoring the necessary boundaries. But he was too tired, and he didn't know how he could turn down Julie, who'd lost so much already.

'I don't know who else to ask, Sanjay. And you're used to

these things, so it won't upset you.' If only she knew. 'I even brought scissors and an electric shaver with me,' she said, sensing him wavering.

'Okay,' he said. 'Let's find an empty cubicle.'

Sanjay stood behind Julie, so she couldn't see his face as he hacked all her hair as close to the scalp as he could, watching the long, chestnut curls fall on to the floor around them. Reminders of a different, happier life, when they'd been teased into up-dos and taken dancing, or had hands run through them while making love. Then he shaved her head, the buzz of the razor masking the trembling of his hand, until it was completely smooth.

Sanjay walked round to face Julie, crouching down and taking her hands in his.

'How does it look?' she said, wiping tears from her face.

'It's fine!' he said. 'Luckily, you have a beautifully shaped head. Some people have really bumpy ones, you know. You don't want one of those on display.'

Julie gave him a half-hearted smile, pulled out her phone and flipped the camera so she could see herself.

'Sanjay, I look like Humpty Dumpty,' she said. She buried her newly bald head in her hands and sobbed. Exposed. Unable to hide behind a comforting curtain of hair. Nothing but naked skin and tears. 'But thank you,' she said through her dripping fingers. 'It's better this way. I'll feel okay about it by tomorrow, I know I will.'

'Is Adam coming to collect you?' said Sanjay.

'I'm meeting him and Sam, my youngest, in the cafeteria,' she said. 'I know they'll look horrified, and I honestly don't think I can bear it.'

'Julie, you wait there,' said Sanjay. 'Put your smiley face on and I'll get them to meet you up here. It's more private.'

Sanjay stared at his watch as he ran down the back stairs to the cafeteria. He was an hour behind schedule already. He was never going to catch up. He spotted Adam and Sam straight away, at a table in the corner, leaning over a colouring book.

'Hi,' he said, crouching down next to Sam. 'Julie asked me to tell you to meet her on the ward. But I wanted to talk to you about something first.'

Sam looked at him, with big brown eyes that were too old and knowing for his face.

'We gave Mummy a new haircut. In fact, we cut all her hair off, like Dwayne "The Rock" Johnson.' You know him?' Sam nodded. 'It's just for a bit. It'll grow back before you know it. The problem is, Mummy's worried that you won't like it. But I know that you'll still think she's beautiful, because she's your mummy, and she's the most beautiful person in the whole world, right?'

Sam nodded.

'So can you try really, really hard not to look sad, and remember to tell her how pretty she is?' Sanjay said, looking up at Adam, who knew this message was as much for him as his son.

'We can do that, can't we, Sam?' said Adam, taking his son's hand in his.

'Great,' said Sanjay. 'I'm sorry, but I have to get on.'

'Thanks, Sanjay,' Adam called after him as he headed out of the canteen.

As Sanjay reached the exit, the man coming in pushed the

swing door so violently that it virtually pinned Sanjay against the wall. 'Sorry,' said Sanjay.

Sanjay paused in the strip-lit, echoing stairwell, clinging to the wall and trying to catch his breath. His heart was thumping, faster and faster, and his palms were prickling with sweat. It was happening again.

He really didn't have time for this. Not now. Not ever.

Sanjay sank to the floor and put his head between his knees, trying to slow his breathing, trying to ignore the truth that had been endlessly nagging at him during those interminable hours of the early morning: he couldn't do this on his own any more.

He was going to have to ask someone for help.

Iona.

Piers

Piers looked at his watch. It was three o'clock in the afternoon, yet he was in bed. The spotless white, pressed and starched bed linen only accentuated how sordid he felt. He was a blemish. An imperfection. He needed to be bleached out of existence.

He was quite sure he'd got up that morning, and he appeared to be wearing clothes. Had he been to work already? He felt the familiar knot form in his stomach. No, he'd not been to work for a while, and now even his facsimile of going to the office wasn't necessary.

He was sure he could remember seeing Martha. Perhaps they'd had a maths lesson?

There was a tentative knock on the door. He was just trying to remind himself how to speak when it opened and Candida came in, carrying a cup of tea. She opened the curtains then sat down next to him, and in a surprisingly sympathetic voice, the sort she only usually used for the children, and even then, only if they'd been hurt or were sick, said, 'Are you okay, Piers?'

Since he didn't know the answer to that question, he said nothing.

'Do you know what year it is? And the name of the Prime Minister?' she said.

'I haven't completely lost touch with reality,' he replied. Then added, 'More's the pity.'

'Don't worry. We'll get through this,' Candida said, stroking his hand.

'I don't see how,' he said, his voice a croak, wondering if she'd offer to kiss it all better, stick a plaster on it and give him some Calpol.

'We'll go through all the finances *together*, work out what we have left, consolidate everything and make a plan,' she said in a firm but calm tone, kicking off her shoes and climbing under the duvet next to him.

How had he managed to underestimate Candida so badly? He'd always thought he was the strong one in the relationship, yet here she was, propping him up. Why hadn't he just told her everything right at the beginning? Was it really possible to salvage something from this terrible mess?

Candida started as something banged against the window, so violently it made the glass reverberate. Piers noticed that all his own reactions seemed delayed. Muffled in cotton wool.

'What the hell?' said Candida, walking over to the window, opening it and looking down at the gravelled drive.

'It was a pigeon,' she said.

'Is it okay?' asked Piers.

'I think it's dead, actually,' said Candida, which seemed unbearably poignant. Piers started to cry again.

'For God's sake, Piers, it's only a pigeon,' said Candida. 'What should I do with it, do you think? Does it go in the regular bin, or in with the food waste? I don't imagine it can be recycled.'

'It's not a pigeon, it's a portent,' said Piers.

'I think you should talk to someone,' Candida said. 'A professional. I don't think you're coping very well.'

She was right. It was only the pretence that had been holding him together. While he was busy playing at being the big swinging dick, he could believe he was still that person. He still felt confident, successful, one of life's winners. He still felt like Piers.

The minute Candida had switched on the house lights, and he was revealed for what he really was, everything fell apart. Stripped of his stage make-up, he was back to being Kevin – the boy he'd been before he'd changed everything about himself, including his name. Kevin with the alcoholic mother, the too-small, second-hand uniform and free school meals. Kevin, whose own father had been useless, jobless and unable to provide for his family. It looked like the apple hadn't fallen far from the tree. His past had been bound to catch up with him eventually. You could only keep running for so long.

'I'll get a recommendation of a psychotherapist from our GP and book an appointment,' said Candida.

'No, don't do that,' said Piers. There was only one person he could imagine talking to about all of this. 'I know someone already. I'll sort it out.'

'Okay, great.' She smiled and patted his shoulder, like he'd just been awarded a merit certificate for 'most improved student'. 'Is he well qualified?'

'She,' said Piers, wondering if being an agony aunt for a women's magazine made you well qualified. 'Yes, she's been in the business for a very long time.' She'd certainly been in *a* business for a very long time, just not the one Candida was expecting. But if Iona couldn't fix him herself, she'd be bound to know someone who could.

Then he turned over and went back to sleep.

Martha

Martha was *in character*. After one of their tutoring sessions, before his meltdown, Piers had suggested she *fake it till you make it*. That philosophy, he'd told her, was the secret to his success. He'd said she should create another persona – one with another name, even – who was everything she wanted to be. So, Martha had. She called her Other Martha.

Other Martha had loads of friends. Not because she was especially pretty, but because she had an innate confidence, a presence, and because she didn't care what anybody thought of her. Not unlike Iona, actually. In fact, Iona and Other Martha were most probably related. Not like a mother and daughter, because those relationships were complicated. More like aunt and niece.

Other Martha was a brilliant actress who'd been talent-spotted while starring in the school play and given a major part in a new Netflix drama. She could come to school wearing a carrier bag as a crop top, and no one would laugh at her. Instead, the next day all the cool crowd would be wearing them.

Other Martha walked down the centre of the school corridor, head held high, unlike regular Martha, who scooted along the edges, looking at her feet. Everyone moved out of the way for Other Martha, the crowds parting like the Red Sea.

Then, she spotted a group of the cool girls, heads together, talking furiously. As she approached, they stopped speaking abruptly and turned to stare at her as one, like a gang of meerkats in the Kalahari. *The meerkat family are always on the lookout – for danger, for food, for a potential mate*, said David Attenborough. No, that image was far too cuddly. They were more like a multi-headed Hydra, which was beyond even Attenborough's narrative capabilities.

Just when she most needed her, Other Martha disappeared in a puff of dry ice, leaving her standing there, exposed. Thanks a bunch. She should have known not to take advice from a man who, it turned out, had more serious issues than even she did.

She fixed her gaze on the stairs ahead of her, and upped her pace, trying to get past her tormentors as quickly as possible.

'Hey, Martha!' said one of them. Could she just pretend she hadn't heard? 'You! Martha! Have you seen the noticeboard?'

She stopped and turned. 'No,' she said. 'Why?'

'Well, you'd better go look, hadn't you?' said another.

Martha considered ignoring them, out of principle, but was too curious, so she turned around and walked back towards the school noticeboard.

'Congratulations!' she heard someone shout. Surely not to her?

As she walked towards the board, people moved away and stared at her. But the good type of stare, not the sort she was used to. The way they might stare at Other Martha.

The cast list was up. Had she been given a part? She held her breath, working her way up through the list of names from the bottom. She wasn't there. She wasn't there. Was this why they were all watching? Because they knew she'd had the audacity to audition and were waiting to enjoy her failure?

Martha reached the last name on the list. Right at the very top.

Juliet – Martha Andrews

The person Martha most wanted to see in the whole world was Iona. Firstly, because she couldn't wait to see her face when she heard that not only had Martha landed herself a part, but she'd landed *the part*. Iona was going to be so thrilled for her. But also, because she had this terrible fear that she'd only got the part *because* of Iona. That all the coaching had been some form of cheating, and as soon as rehearsals started, she was going to be *found out*. And given she'd had two weeks of practice for just one scene, how much was it going to take to learn the whole play?

Perhaps she should just confess right now that she was a fraud, and let someone properly talented take the role?

Iona would know what to do. Iona was the kind of person who never suffered from a lack of self-confidence. Not for a second. She was always sure of the world and her place in it. She was definitely Martha's favourite old person. After David Attenborough. They'd make a great couple, actually, if Iona weren't a lesbian, or married.

Martha knew that Iona took the train from Waterloo at around 6 p.m., so she just had to find a way of killing an hour after school. She put her hand in her blazer pocket and felt the sharp edges of a laminated card against her thumb.

Why not? She'd go and check out Jake's gym. It was exactly the sort of thing that Other Martha would do.

Martha had been standing by the turnstiles which blocked the entrance to Platform 5 for forty-five minutes. Three trains to Hampton Court had been and gone, but there was no sign at all of Iona. Perhaps she'd missed her? No, she couldn't have done. It was impossible to miss Iona.

Martha felt terribly deflated. She kept reminding herself of her fabulous triumph, but without someone to share it with, it felt rather flat. And without anyone to reassure her, it seemed an impossible challenge.

She sighed, put her schoolbag over her shoulder and made her way to the platform to get on the next train home.

Iona

18:40 Waterloo to Hampton Court

Iona ducked into the tourist shop next to the platform entrance, hiding as best she could behind the carousel of postcards. She spun the carousel round slowly, pretending to look at the clichéd shots of Big Ben, double-decker buses and bridges over the Thames. Sometimes all three in one shot. It had been raining outside, so the shop smelled of damp wool, the lingering perspiration of hundreds of tourists and the fake-pine tang of a chemical air freshener.

She caught sight of her own reflection in the shop window. She looked ridiculous. She was wearing what Bea described as her 'Puss in Boots outfit' in anticipation of her thirty-year anniversary party. The party that had turned out to be entirely a figment of her imagination.

Just this morning she'd felt spectacular in her thigh-length boots over tight black trousers, and a double-breasted burgundy velvet jacket, finished off with a black fedora.

Indomitable. She'd twirled around in front of her floor-length mirror like Prince Charming getting ready to bag his Cinderella. Now she felt like a pantomime dame. The Ugly Sister. Mutton dressed as lamb. Foolish, old and a figure of fun. *Oh no, she isn't! Oh yes, she is!* She peered around the entrance, to see Martha finally give up, put her ticket in the barrier, and walk down Platform 5 towards the waiting train.

'Are you going to buy that?' the shopkeeper yelled at Iona. She put down the miniature black taxi she couldn't remember having picked up and walked out of the shop. Then she walked back in, briefly, and stuck her tongue out at him.

Iona watched as Martha's train disappeared down the tracks, then boarded the 18:40 at Carriage 4. A horribly *even* number. A carriage so familiar, and yet totally different. An abandoned, empty crisp packet sat on the table in front of her. No longer needed. Useless. She wondered if she'd ever have the need to catch her usual trains, in her usual carriage, ever again. And that's when she started to cry. Silent tears, pouring down her cheeks, no doubt taking her carefully applied war paint with them. Dripping off the end of her nose and falling on to the Formica tabletop.

The woman sitting at the table opposite Iona's, who was reading a story to her small child, raised her voice a few notches. 'We'll never get to the station in time, Thomas. What are we going to do?' She turned the page and pointed at the picture, trying to draw the child's attention away from the real-life drama on the other side of the aisle, as if Iona's desperation might be harmful to infants.

Iona remembered the column she'd written, back on the day of the grape, about every ending being a beginning in disguise. She'd been wrong. Some endings were just brutally, unjustly final. She cursed her former self with her trite philosophy. No amount of inspirational balderdash was going to make any difference.

People boarded the train at all the usual stops along the line, but for the first time in months, most of the seats around her remained empty. People walked towards her, but quickly diverted on seeing her face, sitting as far away as they could. Standing up, even, rather than face the old woman whose life was falling apart.

And nobody said a word.

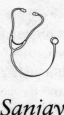

Sanjay

08:19 New Malden to Waterloo

Sanjay had spent some time investigating the possibility of taking a bus to work from New Malden every day, but had reluctantly dropped the idea, on account of it adding around an hour to his journey, depending on traffic conditions. This meant that every morning he was having to avoid both Emmie and Iona. Emmie, because Iona was right. It *was* all over, in fact it had never begun, and seeing her made his heart hurt. And he'd been avoiding Iona because the mere thought of her filled him with guilt.

If his mother had had any idea that he'd spoken to a woman so discourteously, she'd have been furious with him. He knew he had to apologize but hadn't yet worked out what on earth to say.

He thought back, wistfully, to the days when he – like almost every other normal British commuter – knew no one and spoke to nobody on the train. There was a practical reason for this traditional reticence, he'd discovered: trying to evade people on your regular journey added a whole unwanted level of stress to your routine.

He'd seen Emmie several times over the last few days, in the distance. He'd obviously trained himself to pick her out in a crowd, like a hyena homing in on the wounded impala, but with altogether less malevolent intentions, obviously. He hadn't seen Iona at all, however. Which was odd, since she was usually the constant.

For the first time that week, Sanjay made sure he was on Iona's usual morning train and made his way straight to Carriage 3. Today he was determined to find her, to apologize profusely and explain that he hadn't meant any of the cruel things he'd said. He loved the way that Iona cared about him and his life, and she was welcome to interfere any time she liked. In fact, he'd actively encourage her to. He needed her help.

He could tell Iona that he'd not slept properly for months and that the stress and the overwhelming tiredness made him tetchy and irrational, which was why he'd lashed out at her. He could tell her about the panic attacks, and the constant fear of them happening, which was even more debilitating than the attacks themselves.

Perhaps Iona would know what to do. And just talking about it all might help. He didn't want to discuss it with anyone at work, since it demonstrated, surely, that he was completely unable to cope with the fundamental nature of the job. He was a total failure. No wonder Emmie was so far out of his league. Men like Toby never had panic attacks. Quite the reverse. He probably had regular attacks of overwhelming self-importance.

He walked towards Iona's seat. It was empty. In fact, it was the only empty seat in the carriage. He hovered next to it, wondering if it were somehow disrespectful to sit in it.

'She's obviously not coming,' said a familiar voice.

'Oh, hi, Piers,' said Sanjay, as he lowered himself into the seat, feeling like a presumptuous courtier sitting on the empty throne. 'I don't think I've ever seen you in jeans. Has your office gone all casual for the day or something?' There was a long silence, before Piers eventually replied.

'I've been fired. Well, made redundant.'

'Oh my God. I'm so sorry,' said Sanjay, feeling horribly awkward. Despite all his mixed feelings about Piers, he wouldn't wish that on anyone.

'It's okay,' said Piers, looking not very okay at all. 'Actually, it happened a while ago. Back in January. I've not had a job for nearly three months.'

Sanjay was struck completely dumb. The whole time he'd been seeing Piers on the train, flaunting his success and his white privilege, dressed up in his smart suits and status-symbol accessories, Piers had been *fake commuting*. Sanjay wound the tape back in his head, re-examining it from a different angle. Maybe Piers hadn't actually been flaunting anything. Perhaps that was just what he'd wanted to see. Was he just as guilty of stereotyping as everyone else? The thought lodged in his brain like a festering splinter.

'So why have you been taking the train all this time?' he said.

Piers sighed. He seemed to have *shrunk* in the week since Sanjay had last seen him. Collapsed in on himself like an accordion with all the air squeezed out of it. Or perhaps size was also in the eye of the beholder.

'So many reasons,' he said. 'Because I didn't want Candida and my kids to see me as a failure. Because I didn't want to face up myself to *being* a failure. But mainly because I thought I could fix it. Turns out, I can't. I've only made it all worse.'

Sanjay nodded, feeling a bit out of his depth. He'd have felt more comfortable if Piers had revealed he had testicular cancer. That was at least familiar territory, and testicular cancer had an average five-year survival rate of 95 per cent. It was one that rarely gave him sleepless nights. And, although it wasn't ideal, aesthetically speaking, men could operate perfectly well with only one ball. It even had a name: monorchism. Not many people knew that.

'Where are you going now?' asked Sanjay, who was feeling just a little guilty that he liked Piers a lot more now he was so obviously failing and miserable.

'I'm only here because I was hoping to find Iona. I don't have her mobile number, and I really want to talk to her because, well, just because. Actually, I was hoping to employ her on a professional basis,' said Piers. 'You know, as a therapist. You don't have her number, do you?'

'No, I don't. I was looking for her too, in fact. I wonder where she's got to,' said Sanjay.

This couldn't be his fault, could it? Was she the one avoiding him, after he was so rude to her? Surely she had a thicker skin than that?

Emmie

08:08 Thames Ditton to Waterloo

Emmie took the pie out of the oven and placed it on the kitchen table that she'd already laid for two. This recipe always reminded her of her mum. She could feel her standing next to her as she chopped the carrots, onion and celery. *Watch out for your fingers, Emmie. No one wants to find a finger in their shepherd's pie. Unless it belongs to the shepherd. Ha ha.*

Emmie was trying to eat less meat, on account of the planet, but Toby was refusing to give it up entirely. She'd interrogated the local butcher about this lamb, and he'd assured her that it had lived an incredibly happy – if short – life, feeding on lush, organic grass in a Devon field with a view of the ocean. Then he'd smirked, which rather made her wonder if he was taking the mickey.

Emmie usually didn't have the time to cook from scratch during the week, but today she'd been working from home, as she'd started doing increasingly regularly.

Toby was a huge fan of remote working. The commute, he said, was a relic from a pre-internet era. An unnecessary waste of time, energy and money, as well as being a driver of climate change and pollution.

When he and Bill, his business partner, had started their IT consultancy business they'd agreed that an office was an unnecessary expense. They now had twenty or so tech geeks working for them, mainly young guys with bad dress sense and dubious personal hygiene, but everyone worked from home, except when they were on site with clients. Most of their meetings happened by video conference and, when they needed a 'face-to-face', they hired a space in one of the many communal working hubs that had sprung up in the area.

Toby was always ahead of the curve.

'Toby! Supper's ready!' she called.

'This looks amazing!' said Toby, leaning down to kiss her on the back of the neck. 'I love it when I don't have to share you with the office.'

While they ate, Toby told her a story about one of his clients, which involved a mysteriously malfunctioning computer system, an ethernet cable and a cockapoo puppy.

'So, how's your day been?' he said.

'Okay,' she replied. 'Only I'm not really enjoying this toothpaste brief. I really want to pitch for some charity work, something more worthwhile, but I guess I'm just being ridiculously idealistic.'

'Nonsense!' said Toby, taking her hand. 'Your idealism is one of the things I love most about you. I have an idea, actually. It's something I've been meaning to talk to you about for a while.'

Emmie looked at him, simmering with an excitement which should have been contagious, but instead made her feel a little wary. Toby's ideas could range from repainting the downstairs loo, to paragliding in the Alps, with all sorts of craziness in between.

'Go on then,' she said.

'You know how much you like not having to go into the office?' he said. This wasn't entirely true. Toby was more enthusiastic about her working from home than she was, but she didn't want to ruin the mood by correcting him. So she nodded.

'Well, I think you should set up your own business,' he said. 'Quit your job. You're not going anywhere at that company – they obviously don't rate you, and you hate working there. You can set up from home as a consultant. I'll get you started – I've done it all before for my own business – the company registration, tax and legal stuff. Just think! You could be your own boss. You could pick and choose clients who share your philosophy. Like me! I can be your first client! And no more lousy commuting to an antiquated office. Once the money starts coming in, we can build a home office at the end of the garden. Until then, you can share mine.' He leaned back in his chair and beamed at her.

'Oh,' she said, completely taken aback. Toby had obviously thought through every detail of his plan. She really didn't want to rain on his parade, but what he was suggesting was a big change.

'I don't know, Toby. I don't hate my job at all. In fact, I love most of it. It's just some aspects of it make me uncomfortable. I like going into the office. I've got some great friends there, and on the train, even. I think I'd miss it,' she said, trying the words out for size and discovering that she really meant them.

'Oh, Emmie,' said Toby, looking at her as if she'd really let him down. As if she wasn't the woman he thought she was. 'Don't think so *small*. Have some ambition, some guts! Didn't they vote you "Girl Most Likely to Change the World" at your school prom? Well, you're hardly changing the world at that little agency, are you?'

Emmie had been drunk when she'd told him that story. She'd known it was a mistake, but hadn't expected him to use it to goad her like this.

'Do you think Richard Branson ever said, *I can't possibly set up Virgin Records because I'd miss chatting to a bunch of losers by the water cooler?*' Toby continued.

He was probably right, and it was so thoughtful of him to listen to all her whingeing and care so much about her happiness, but Emmie still felt a little hurt at the way he mimicked her, at the sneering tone of his voice, and the casual dismissal of her colleagues. And why did he think she wasn't going anywhere? She'd always seen herself as a success. A high-flyer, even. Had she been deluding herself? Could he see something she didn't?

Emmie lay in bed that night, unable to sleep, turning Toby's proposal over in her head. She ought to feel buoyed by Toby's belief in her; instead, she felt like a loser, who wasn't 'rated' by her employers. The words she'd tucked away into the darkest corner of her memory kept taunting her. *YOU THINK YOU'RE SO CLEVER, BUT WE ALL KNOW YOU'RE A FAKE.* She'd convinced herself that the message had been written by someone who was jealous of her, but perhaps it was just someone being honest, voicing what everyone was thinking.

The idea of setting up her own company and taking a brave leap into the unknown should be really exciting, so why did she feel as if her world kept getting smaller rather than bigger? Why did the thought of not travelling into town any longer, of not seeing her work colleagues or her train gang, fill her with such a sense of loss? A slight prickling of fear, even? Was she a terrible coward?

It was at times like this that Emmie most missed her mum. She loved her father, but even before he'd moved to California, they'd never had the kind of relationship where they'd shared worries and problems. Ever since Mum had died, they'd had an unwritten pact to make every interaction as relentlessly cheerful as possible, as a counterbalance to their individual grief.

Emmie knew exactly who she wanted to talk this over with, who she'd trust to give her the best no-nonsense advice: Iona.

Emmie was sitting at her usual table on the train, but the place opposite her was empty. Was it just a coincidence, or did everyone know it was Iona's seat? And where was she? Come to think of it, Emmie hadn't seen her for a while. Or Sanjay, for that matter.

The train pulled in at Surbiton, and she looked out of the window to see if she could spot Piers on the platform. He wasn't there either, and she couldn't remember the last time he had been. How strange. She felt like she was in a *Sliding Doors*-type movie, where somewhere in a parallel universe the same train was running on the same track with the whole gang aboard, apart from her.

'Emmie?' The voice intruded on her vision. 'It is Emmie, isn't it? Iona's friend? I'm Martha.'

'Oh, hi, Martha. Yes, of course I remember you. *Romeo and Juliet,*' said Emmie.

'Do you think Iona will mind if I take her seat?' said Martha, hopping from foot to foot, as if she were asking for a hall pass from one of her teachers.

'Of course not!' said Emmie. 'She's not here, after all. I haven't seen her for ages, actually.'

'Me neither,' said Martha. 'I've been dying to tell her my news!'

'Can you tell me?' said Emmie.

'Yes! I got a part in the play. Actually, I got *the* part. Juliet,' said Martha with a wide grin that immediately stopped her looking awkward. In fact, for a moment, she looked stunning, like a young Julia Roberts.

'Oh my God, that's amazing! Congratulations! Iona's going to be so proud of you!' said Emmie.

'I know!' said Martha. 'And I really need her help learning the role, you know, her being a professional actress and all.'

'I didn't know that about her,' said Emmie. 'Was she at the Royal Shakespeare Company or something?'

'I guess,' said Martha. 'She's a great coach, anyhow. Much better than our drama teachers.'

'Well, I'm not, I'm afraid,' said Emmie. 'But I can help you with your lines if you like.'

Emmie could see Martha struggling with wanting to learn

her part but being embarrassed about roping in a virtual stranger.

'Is that the script?' she said, gesturing towards the paper Martha was holding. After a beat of hesitation, Martha handed it to her.

'Thanks,' she said, with a shy smile. 'Can you be the nurse? And I'll be Juliet, obviously.'

'Where's this girl? What, Juliet!' said Emmie, which didn't seem to make a great deal of sense, but who was she to argue with Shakespeare?

'How now! Who calls?' replied Martha.

'Your mother,' said Emmie.

She'd miss moments like this if she stopped commuting. All those passing, but heart-warming, interactions with the myriad of people who made up her day. The barista at the station coffee shop, the office doorman, the *Big Issue* seller she chatted to every morning. They all made her feel connected to the world around her, part of something bigger.

Where are you, Iona?

Piers

08:13 Surbiton to Waterloo

Yet again, Piers had had no luck finding Iona. The train pulled into Wimbledon station, and he contemplated getting off and going back home, but since he had nothing else to do with his day, he might as well stay here with Martha, Emmie and Sanjay until the train turned around at Waterloo.

Piers felt more comfortable with the train gang now they all knew the truth about him, and grateful that they didn't seem to judge him too harshly. It made him wonder why he'd let the deceit corrode him for so long.

Piers looked out of the window and spotted David for a second, before he blended back into the crowd. He climbed on at Carriage 3, and walked towards them, finding a seat at the table next door.

'Hey, David, have you seen Iona?' said Emmie, being the first to voice the question they'd all been about to ask.

'Actually, I haven't seen her for more than two weeks,' he replied. 'Is she on holiday?'

'I'm sure she would have told us if she were going away,' Sanjay said. 'She's not exactly one for keeping secrets, is she?'

The faces surrounding Piers all wore various shades of glum. It occurred to him that they were each individual spokes of a wheel, but Iona was the centre, the axis, and without her, the group of them had no purpose at all, and very little in common. If Iona never reappeared, would they eventually stop acknowledging each other altogether? Surely not. At least not straight away.

'Do you think she's sick?' said Martha. 'I mean, you can go downhill quite fast when you're that old. My granny was doing the bingo, Zumba and aqua aerobics every week, then caught pneumonia, and two weeks later she was gone.'

'*That old?!?* Good God, Iona's a decade younger than me, probably. I'm pretty sure she's not even sixty yet, although I've never dared ask, obviously,' said David.

They all looked horrified at the idea of asking Iona her age.

'I'm sorry about your granny, Martha,' said Emmie, 'but Iona's made of pretty stern stuff, I suspect. It'd take *a lot* to keep her off work for two weeks. All the more reason to track her down. But I'm not sure how.'

'When I'm feeling unsure about anything,' said Martha, 'I just ask myself, *what would Iona do?*'

'Me too,' said David. 'Who'd have thought I'd end up basing my life choices on an eccentric lesbian? But it seems to work.'

There was a heavy silence, as Piers imagined they were all asking themselves what Iona would do.

'Martha, you're a genius,' said Sanjay. 'Emmie, Piers, remember the day we first met? Met properly, I mean.' They nodded. 'Well, *that's* what Iona would do.'

Sanjay stood up, looking a little nervous, then took a deep breath, and shouted.

'DOES ANYONE HERE KNOW IONA?' he said. Hundreds of eyes turned towards them.

'She's the one who wears extraordinary clothes. I used to call her Rainbow Lady, before I knew her name,' Sanjay added.

'I called her Crazy Dog Woman,' said Piers. 'On account of her dog, Lulu, and the fact that she's a bit . . . eccentric.'

'Actually, she's the Magic Handbag Lady,' said Martha, 'because more things come out of her bag than is possible in this universe. And she has a daemon.'

'Or Muhammad Ali,' said a man sitting behind them, who Piers recognized as Martha's audience at her first *Romeo and Juliet* rehearsal. Why Muhammad Ali? Piers couldn't understand that one at all, but each to their own.

'If you know who we're talking about, please raise your hand,' said Sanjay.

A forest of hands shot up.

Piers wondered for a moment how they'd describe him. He was pretty sure it wouldn't be flattering. And how many people would care if he were missing? Probably none at all, except possibly Martha. And his kids, obviously.

'Thank you!' said Sanjay. 'Now, if you've seen Iona in the last two weeks, please keep your hand in the air.'

One by one, all the hands were lowered.

'Does anyone have Iona's number?' asked Sanjay. Heads

were shaken and *No, sorry*s mumbled in response. Sanjay sat down, looking dejected. 'That didn't work as well as it did when Iona did it,' he said.

'Did you have a nickname for Iona, David?' asked Martha. 'Before you got to know her.'

'Yes, I did, actually,' he said. They all turned towards him. Until that moment, Piers had forgotten he was there.

'I called her "The Woman On The Train",' he said.

'How . . . inventive,' said Piers.

'I know how we can find her!' said Emmie. 'I can't believe I've been so stupid! Fizz works with her. I'll call Fizz.'

'Not the *actual* Fizz? From TikTok?' said Martha, her eyes like saucers, as if Emmie had said she was going to call Bill Gates or Richard Branson.

'Uh huh,' said Emmie, pulling up a number on her mobile.

'Hi, Fizz! It's Emmie. I'm hoping you can help. I'm worried about Iona. None of us have seen her for weeks. Has she been in the office, do you know?'

They all waited in anticipation, as Emmie uttered words like *No!* and *She didn't? That's awful*, and *You haven't?* Then an explosion of laughter and a *That's so Iona!*

'Fizz?' said David. 'Is that short for Felicity, or Fiona? Surely no self-respecting vicar would allow a child to be christened Fizz?'

Finally, Emmie put the phone down and turned to them.

'Well, that explains it,' she said, drawing out the suspense totally unnecessarily, like the judges did on *Strictly* – which Piers only watched because Candida made him, obviously. And because some of the dancers were seriously hot.

'What?' they chorused.

'She resigned nearly three weeks ago,' said Emmie.

'But she loves that job,' said Piers. 'It doesn't make sense.'

'Fizz said her editor called her in for a meeting. He left the door open deliberately, apparently, so he could humiliate her in public. He told her she was going to have to share her column with some twenty-two-year-old asshole – Fizz's word, not mine – called Dex, so he could *shake it up a bit* and bring her *kicking and screaming into this century*.'

'I can't imagine that went down well,' said Piers.

'It didn't,' said Emmie, 'She called him the c-word, apparently. Then she said something along the lines of, *No, I take that back. I've come across many, many c-words in my day, and all of them have had some level of charm and interest. Some have been quite spectacular, actually. Calling you a c-word would do a grave disservice to c-words. You are a DICK.* And she stormed out. And then Fizz stormed out too, as she was only there because she loves Iona.'

The carriage was usually fairly quiet, with the obvious exception of Iona's table, but right now it was so silent you could hear a pin drop. There was no rustling of newspapers, tinny music emitted from ear-buds or clearing of throats. It seemed everyone was listening to the story of Iona's outburst.

'Blimey,' said Sanjay. 'Does Fizz have her number?'

'Iona had to hand her mobile in, since it was a work phone,' said Emmie. 'Fizz tried to get her home number from HR, but they refused to give it to her, citing data protection.'

'Bloody data protection regulations,' said Piers.

'Actually, they exist for a jolly good reason,' said David.

'So now what do we do?' said Martha.

'I think we should start with what we *do know*,' said David. Everyone turned to look at him in surprise. 'What we do know,' he continued, appearing to expand in stature as his confidence increased, now that he had the floor, 'is that she lives somewhere close to Hampton Court station. So, why don't we all meet there on Saturday, at – say – ten a.m., at the café by the station, and we can track her down. I'll make a list of all the local shops, cafés and restaurants that she might frequent, and we can divvy them all up and see if anyone knows her.'

'That's a great idea, Paul,' said Piers.

'David,' said David. Piers kicked himself. Why did he keep forgetting his name? D.A.V.I.D. It seemed to slide over his memory like oil, never taking hold.

'I can print off a photo of her from the internet – although most of them are very out of date – and we can show it to people, like they do on *Crimewatch*,' said Piers.

'Check the Royal Shakespeare Company website,' said Emmie. 'They might have a headshot from her acting days.'

Piers looked around at all the wheel spokes, now turning efficiently and making progress, and was really happy he was one of them.

Iona

If a tree falls in a forest and no one is around to hear it, does it make a sound? If a person doesn't have a job, and isn't being paid, do they have any value?

Iona certainly felt worthless. Was this it? Was this the end of her productive life? Was she going to spend the next thirty years watching re-runs of *Countdown* in tartan flannel pyjamas, spying on the neighbours and drinking the cooking sherry from a teacup?

There had been a time when she'd have salivated over the idea of three weeks off work. She'd loved the idea of long lie-ins, being able to read novels, travel, indulge herself. But three weeks with no end in sight was an entirely different prospect. It felt flat and featureless. Endless. Pointless.

Iona had been trying to create some form of routine: Breakfast at 8 a.m., dog walk at 8.30 a.m., Jane Fonda at 10 a.m., tea with Bea at 4 p.m. followed by the quiz show with that nice Richard Osman, et cetera, but the repetitive sameness of each day was already dragging her down. How would she feel after three months? Three years? Three decades?

She missed her train friends, who'd become such an important part of her life. She'd even considered taking the train at her usual time, just so she could try to recreate some of that feeling of connectedness. But what kind of weirdo commuted into town every day without a job to go to?

Iona wondered whether she would feel different about being unemployed if she and Bea had had children. Would she be able to shrug off her own ambitions more easily, to put all her passion and energies into helping the next generation to thrive instead? Perhaps she would. But look at David, all lost and bereft in his abandoned nest. Maybe having children just postponed, then accentuated, the sense of emptiness and worthlessness.

Jane Fonda carried on issuing instructions, despite the fact that Iona had stopped listening to her some time ago. *Feel the burn!* shouted Jane at Iona, who couldn't feel anything but numb.

Iona had been this low once before, and the images from back then – October 1991, the ones she'd managed to keep contained for decades – kept intruding. She'd be brushing her teeth when, from nowhere, the memory of a loose molar, rolling around her mouth, and the iron tang of blood would re-emerge. She'd be digging a flowerbed when she'd be floored by a pain in her side – not a new pain, but the memory of broken ribs, kicked in by a steel toecap. The worst time was at night, when the whole scene would replay in her dreams. Iona, lying in the gutter of Old Compton Street, Soho, opening her eyes to see discarded cigarette butts, a

Bounty bar wrapper and the muted rainbow pattern created by the streetlamp shining on a patch of spilled engine oil.

She'd only left the party briefly for a smoke. Not because you couldn't smoke indoors back then, but because she'd promised Bea she'd quit. Even now, she didn't know if they'd been deliberately waiting for her, or if it had been an opportunistic attack – either way, the result was the same.

'Filthy lezzer! Dyke whore!' they'd shouted at her from across the street. She was used to the verbal abuse – the dark underbelly of her increasing fame. She'd turned to face them, cigarette in one hand, and she'd slowly and deliberately raised the middle finger of the other. Petrol poured on flames.

She couldn't remember how she ended up lying in the road, but she could remember the feel of cold, hard tarmac under her cheek, and the kicks that rained down on her back, her jaw, her abdomen. She remembered curling up into a ball, screwing her eyes tight shut, willing it all to end. She remembered hearing flies being unzipped, then the harsh ammonia smell of urine, the sound of it splashing around her accompanied by barks of laughter, and the wet warmth of it seeping into the beautiful silk dress she'd borrowed from Christian Lacroix.

Then, Bea's shouts. How badly she'd wanted to tell her to go back in, to stay safe, but her mouth was full of blood and tooth, and her jaw felt disconnected.

'I've called the police, you bastards!' Bea had yelled. 'Leave her alone!' And they had, but not before calling darling, gorgeous Bea words that even her subconscious couldn't bear to recall.

And Bea had knelt on the road beside her, slipping her hands under Iona's cheek to keep it from the cold, careful not to move her before the ambulance arrived. She'd heard Bea begging passers-by for a coat to stop Iona's violent shivering. She'd felt Bea holding her hand in the ambulance, whispering words of reassurance in her ear, while they injected her with blissful, pain- and reality-removing meds.

'I told you smoking was bad for you, didn't I?' Bea had said, stroking her hair. Iona had tried to laugh before being engulfed by the blissful nothingness.

She'd resigned from the magazine back then too, terrified of going back out so overtly into the world, preferring to stick to the safety of the shadows. But that time they'd been desperate to have her return, had sent flowers every day, cards, and delegations of their most persuasive staff with promises of pay rises and bonuses, and a driver – Darren – to take them to and from events, making sure they were safe in the leather-lined cocoon of his sleek Mercedes-Benz.

It had been Bea who'd got her back on her feet, of course. 'If you give up, they win, darling,' she'd said. 'They *want* us to be small, so we have to stand tall. They want us to be invisible, so we have to be seen. They want us to be quiet, so we have to be heard. They want us to surrender, so we have to fight.'

And fight they did. They'd fought for the equal age of consent, to end the ban on gay people serving in the military and the repeal of Section 28. They'd marched with Gay Pride and campaigned for gay marriage. And she'd won the battle with nicotine, too. She'd never smoked again, mainly as a result of having her jaw wired for several weeks.

But how could she fight now? What enemy was she even fighting? Mother Nature? The march of time itself? Her own, treacherous, deteriorating body?

She couldn't solve this problem by lobbying MPs, marching on parliament, leafleting neighbourhoods or signing petitions. She couldn't solve this problem at all. And neither could her darling, ferocious Bea.

Sanjay

09:10 New Malden to Hampton Court

It felt much like his usual morning, but, at the same time, totally different.

For a start, it was later than usual, and secondly, he was heading south from New Malden, past stations he didn't usually get to see: Berrylands, with a deceptively pretty name, since it seemed to be little more than the sewage plant, and Surbiton. And the people on the train were different. No suits or air of underlying stress, just comfortable clothes, bubbling excitement and lots of noisy kids. Day trippers.

Sanjay had a fear of not being on time. Probably driven by his father, who always decided at the last minute that he'd forgotten something vital, which meant many of Sanjay's childhood memories involved the whole family squashed into a stationary car waiting for him, while his mother checked her watch obsessively, and them all arriving late at the wedding party, football match, or school prize-giving. As a result, he was on a much earlier train than necessary, and hadn't seen any of the rest of the gang.

The train stopped at Thames Ditton. And there she was! Maybe she also built an extra twenty minutes into any journey. Yet another sign that they were meant for each other. They could spend the rest of their lives having someone to chat to whenever they arrived unfashionably early at a party.

'Hi, Sanjay!' she said. She was holding a book, as usual.

'Hi, Emmie! You're early too,' he said. Something about her always made him state the obvious. He nodded at the book. 'What are you reading?'

'*The Girl on the Train*,' said Emmie.

'Ha! That's a coincidence!' said Sanjay.

'Why?' said Emmie.

'Uh, because you're a girl on a train,' he said.

'I guess,' she replied, looking at him as if he were a bit of an idiot, which he clearly was.

'Talking of books, this is just like being in an Agatha Christie novel, isn't it? So exciting!' she said, literally clapping her hands together.

'So long as it doesn't turn into *Murder on the Orient Express*,' said Sanjay.

'Exactly!' said Emmie. 'Actually, I reckon it's the antithesis of the *Orient Express*. I mean, in that story, all the train passengers have a reason to want to kill one of the characters, but in our case, I think we all have our individual reasons for wanting to find her.'

'I do,' he said, before he could censor his words. 'Do you?'

'Yes,' she replied, looking uncharacteristically unsure of

herself. 'I have a big decision to make, and I'd love to talk it through with Iona. What's yours?'

'Uh, I need to apologize to her, actually. I was unforgivably rude to her recently.'

Sanjay couldn't believe he was so stupid. That didn't exactly paint him in the most flattering light, did it? The guy who's mean to old ladies.

'I'm glad I found you again, Sanjay. I've missed you,' said Emmie.

She'd missed him!

'I missed all of you.'

Not so special, then.

'I stopped seeing you on the train for ages. I started thinking you were deliberately avoiding me! Then Iona disappeared too, and Piers, and it felt like I was starring in *And Then There Were None*, as one of the later victims.'

'Oh, I was on nights for a while,' he said, which was the truth, but not, of course, the whole truth. 'And I guess you heard about Piers?' Emmie nodded.

'Just goes to show, you never really know what's going on in other people's heads, do you?' said Emmie.

Sanjay thought it rather fortunate that Emmie couldn't see what was going on in his head, actually. He vowed not to avoid her in the future. It didn't matter if they weren't destined to be together. He could come to terms with that. He'd really love them to be friends. He just had to learn to stop imagining her naked. Argh, he'd just done it again.

'We're here!' said Emmie. The train seemed to exhale as it shuddered to a halt. 'Shall we go and get a coffee while we wait for the others to arrive?'

'Sure,' said Sanjay, sending prayers to the Universe for a signal failure that would prevent any more trains reaching Hampton Court for an hour or two. Why were trains always delayed when you were trying to get somewhere urgently, and never when you were just hoping for a few more minutes of privacy with the girl you secretly loved? He corrected himself quickly: *the girl you wanted to get to know better as a platonic friend.*

'You can fill me in on the wedding preparations,' he said, realizing as the words left his mouth that they were a form of self-harm. He might as well just plunge his own hand into boiling water.

There was a free table on the pavement outside the café, with a clear view of the station exit – the perfect place to wait for the others.

'Emmie, why don't you save the table?' Sanjay said. 'I'll buy you a coffee. What would you like?'

'A cappuccino with soya milk, please,' she said. 'But can you check if the coffee's fair trade? If not, I'll have a green tea.'

And those, it turned out, were the last words he heard from her, as when he came out of the café, carrying two ethical cappuccinos and a slice of banana bread made with fair trade bananas – because who didn't like banana bread? – Emmie was gone.

Piers

09:45 Surbiton to Hampton Court

Piers's life had improved greatly since *the lost morning*, as he liked to think of it, because it made it sound almost romantic, rather than the terrifying reality.

Candida had swept in and assumed control of everything, and he was just going along with the flow and doing what he was told. He had, after all, as she'd pointed out brutally, but in a kindly tone, *made rather a mess of trying to sort it out himself.*

Candida had ring-fenced the remaining redundancy monies and sequestered them away in a low-interest, very safe, savings vehicle. He'd tried to suggest something a little more high-yielding, but she'd just given him one of her looks.

She'd persuaded Minty's school and Theo's nursery, in meetings that she described as *necessary yet humiliating*, to waive the final term's fees of that school year, buying them some breathing space to decide what to do for the future.

The Porsche had gone, obviously, and she'd sold their paddock to the next-door neighbour who'd been coveting it for years. Minty's pony had been rehomed at the local riding school, who were stabling and feeding her for free, on the basis that their pupils could ride her whenever Minty wasn't. The proceeds of the paddock sale had paid off a large chunk of their mortgage. And, finally, Candida had accepted that her boutique was always going to be a cash drain, rather than a resource, and was in the process of selling it to a friend with a husband as wealthy and foolish as Piers had once been.

Candida was settling all the bills Piers had been squirrelling in his sock drawer, paying off the credit card debt where possible, and giving Piers pocket money for expenses. Piers accepted being treated like his wife's third child. He deserved it, after all. He'd lied to her for months and put their whole way of life in jeopardy. And it was strangely relaxing, handing over all semblance of responsibility to someone else, like reverting to a safe, protected childhood he'd never had.

The station platform was much quieter than it was on a weekday, so it was easy for Piers to pick out Martha.

'Martha,' he said. 'I'm really glad I could catch you on your own. I wanted to say thank you, privately. Candida told me what you did that morning. I can't remember much of it myself. It must have been really frightening for you. I'm so sorry. You do know, I would never have . . .' He left the sentence hanging.

'Sure,' said Martha, who didn't look like she believed him at all. 'Honestly, don't mention it. I'm just glad you're okay. You *are* okay, aren't you?'

'Of course!' said Piers, with a great deal more certainty than he felt. 'In fact, I'd love to restart our tutoring sessions if you're game. I need something useful to do with my time!'

Martha grinned and nodded. As the train approached, Piers stood several metres back from the edge of the platform. It drew to a stop, and they could see David through the thick, partially opaque, windows.

Piers knew his name was David, because, determined not to forget it again, he'd written *David* in small letters on the inside of his wrist with a biro, where it was hidden by his cuff.

'Hi, David!' he said, with confidence.

'Piers! Martha!' said David. 'I've saved you seats, and look!' David reached into the backpack on the seat next to him and pulled out a Thermos and some plastic cups. 'I took a tip from you, Martha, and thought to myself, *what would Iona do?* Hence, beverages!' He poured out three steaming cups of hot chocolate, looking as proud as someone presenting their showstopper to the judges on *Bake Off.* 'I hope your mum didn't mind you coming today, Martha?' he said.

'I suspect she was thrilled that she and the boyfriend can walk around the house naked and flirting all morning,' she said. 'I told her I was going to meet some gorgeous but dangerous boys on the Common.'

'Really?' said David, looking a little shocked. 'You didn't tell her you were with us?'

'God, no. She already thinks I'm *not a normal teenager.* If I told her I was spending the day with a bunch of old people tracking down a missing agony aunt, she'd be straight back on the phone to the child psychologist,' said Martha. 'She'd much rather I was smoking weed and having underage sex.'

'She's not an agony aunt, she's a magazine therapist,' said Piers with a wink, 'and steady on with the *old* thing. I'm not even forty, and Sanjay and Emmie are still in their twenties!'

'You might think that's practically embryonic, but from here' – she gestured at herself – 'ancient. Sorry. And you're the kind of person they warn us not to get into a car with, even if offered sweets.'

'Are you sure you wouldn't rather be spending time with gorgeous but dangerous boys on the Common?' said Piers. 'You must think us all rather boring.'

'I prefer spending time with adults, actually,' said Martha. 'Conversation with adults is easy. I know the rules. *Shake hands with a firm, confident grip. Introduce yourself. Maintain eye contact. Avoid controversial topics and don't swear.* Simple. And they tend to really like me. Talking to other teenagers is *way* more complicated. For a start, you can't just go up and talk to anyone. You have to know where they sit in the pecking order compared to you – and I'm almost always near the bottom. Then, even if you *can* speak to them, you have to sort of sidle into a conversation without looking too keen, and you need to know all the right references and language. Which change constantly. It's a minefield.'

'Good grief,' said Piers. Had all those rules existed when he was at school? Perhaps they had, and he'd just instinctively understood them.

They spotted Sanjay as soon as they left the station at

Hampton Court. He was mouthing something to himself, which sounded rather like *aluminium, silicon, phosphorus*, but couldn't be, surely?

'What did you say, Sanjay?' asked Piers.

'Uh, nothing,' said Sanjay.

'Now, we just need Emmie,' Piers said, 'and we've got the whole gang together. We can be the Famous Five. I'll be Julian.'

'No, you're definitely a Dick,' said Martha. Piers was fairly sure she meant it fondly. But not certain.

'Emmie's gone,' said Sanjay, looking forlorn.

'What do you mean, gone?' said David.

'I mean, one minute she was here, sitting at that table over there while I went to get her a coffee. Then, when I came back out, she was gone,' he said.

'Oh dear. We're meant to be finding people today, not losing them. Did you say something to offend her?' asked Piers.

'No, of course I didn't,' shouted Sanjay, looking terribly offended himself.

'I'm sorry,' said Piers. 'It's just that sort of thing used to happen to me all the time when I was your age. Girls were always remembering they had an urgent appointment with a friend in the ladies, or that they had to make a phone call or find another drink.'

Sanjay muttered something else under his breath, which sounded very much like, 'I bet they did.'

'Luckily, there was always another girl around to fill the gap. Ha ha. Usually a better one. Anyhow, don't you have Emmie's number?' asked Piers.

'No, I didn't think I'd need it, did I?' said Sanjay. 'Since she was sitting *right there*.' He gestured at the pavement table next to them.

'Let's not argue, folks, I'm sure she'll turn up,' said David, who was the most unlikely team leader, but – in the absence of Iona – seemed to have assumed the role. 'And, in the meantime, if we're going to succeed, we need to stick together.'

Martha

Martha really hoped they'd find Iona soon, since without her, all the other grown-ups seemed to be squabbling, and going missing. She'd always believed that adults knew all the answers, and that only she was trying to navigate through life without the requisite instruction manual. But it was becoming increasingly obvious that they were often as lost as she was. She wasn't sure if she should find this reassuring or terrifying. Was everyone bluffing?

David was carrying a backpack, which was the sartorial antithesis of Iona's magic handbag and must have once belonged to his daughter, since it had a sticker on it saying 'I Heart The Backstreet Boys' and a picture of some guys looking like One Direction, but with terrible haircuts. He reached into it and pulled out some photocopied sheets of paper.

'Right,' he said. 'I've typed up a list of all the local shops, cafés and restaurants. Each of you has a different section highlighted. Hopefully, we won't need Emmie's list as well, but if we do, and if she's still not shown up, we can split it between us. Piers, do you have the photos?'

David handed round his sheets of paper, each with their names written at the top in block capitals, along with one of Piers's printouts. All he needed to do was to give them all a map, a compass and some waterproof trousers, and it would be just like the orienteering expedition Martha had done on her last school residential trip.

Martha looked at the picture of Iona. She was a fair bit younger, all dressed up for some fancy event, with extravagant false eyelashes resembling over-fed centipedes, and an actual tiara. But it was unmistakably her. Superimposed under Iona's armpit was a picture of a French bulldog, taken from somewhere else on the internet. Piers hadn't got the proportions quite right, and fake Lulu was about the size of a large Labrador.

'Let's do the first one on the list together,' said David. 'That way we can agree the best technique. I'm hoping we'll have her tracked down by mid-afternoon!'

They followed David into the café, and stood awkwardly behind him like unlikely, ill-matched backing singers, as he went up to the counter.

'Excuse me,' he said. The café owner looked a little wary. He most probably thought David was from the food hygiene inspectorate. He certainly had that look about him. 'We're looking for someone and are rather hoping you can help.' David handed over one of the photos.

'Oh, that's Iona!' the owner said. 'Although Lulu looks like she's put on a bit. Not that I can talk.' He patted the ample stomach over which his white apron was straining.

'Gosh, that's jolly good luck. How smashing!' said David, who sometimes sounded like a children's TV presenter from the olden days. 'Do you know where she lives?'

'Somewhere down by the river,' said the manager. 'The newsagent next door delivers her newspapers. He'll know the exact address.' He paused and narrowed his eyes at David. 'You're not a bailiff or anything like that, are you?'

'No, no. We're friends. We're just worried about her,' said David.

'It's not Iona you need to worry about,' said the manager. 'She's indestructible. It's Bea.'

Martha was about to ask why they should be worrying about Bea, but David, displaying a remarkable lack of curiosity, was already making his way to the door. Hercule Poirot, he was not.

David went through the same routine with the newsagent, who pulled out a large ledger and placed it on the counter. He flicked through the alphabet until he reached the page labelled 'I' and ran his finger down the names. His finger stopped towards the bottom of the page, and he peered at them over his reading glasses.

'I do have her address,' he said. They all leaned forwards. 'But I'm afraid I can't give it to you. Data protection, and all that. Sorry.' He paused, his finger still on the page, looked directly at Martha and she was pretty sure he *winked*. He tapped his finger two or three times on the page, then he slammed the book shut and put it back under the counter.

'Damn and double damn,' said David, as they left the shop. Martha could tell it was the closest he ever got to swearing. 'Just as I thought it might be easy.'

'It's Riverview House, Hurst Road,' said Martha. They all stared at her. 'I learned how to read quickly upside down, so I'd know what the child psychologist really thinks of me. It wasn't pretty, to be honest. But knowledge, so they say, is power.'

'Well, I'm not sure it's entirely ethical,' said David, 'but I guess the ends justify the means.'

David plugged the address into his phone, and started doing that thing that old people do with Google Maps, where they turn around and around in circles, staring at the screen of their phone, trying to work out which direction to walk in.

Eventually, he held his phone aloft, and they all followed, like a gaggle of tourists on a sightseeing trip. After ten minutes or so, they were standing at Iona's front door.

It was a traditional, detached house – old and a bit quirky, but in good shape, much like Iona. Through the lead-paned front window, Martha could see a wood-panelled dining room with an open fireplace, an upright piano and a glass chandelier hanging from the ceiling. Martha hadn't thought people did dining rooms any more. They had kitchen islands, breakfast bars and Deliveroo.

David rang the bell, and they could hear Lulu's barking getting louder and louder as she scampered towards them.

Martha wondered if any of the adults were feeling a bit weird about all this. When they'd discovered that no one had seen Iona for weeks, tracking her down seemed the obvious thing to do, but now they were actually *here* it felt a little intrusive and stalker-ish. Maybe she should have found some handsome but dangerous boys to hang out with on the Common after all.

Martha wondered if she was the only one holding her breath as they waited for the door to open. Nothing, just the sound of Lulu yapping at the door. Sanjay bent down, pushed open the brass letterbox and peered through.

'I can't see her, or Bea. But she can't have gone far, because she wouldn't leave Lulu alone for long,' he said.

'You're right. You can't be separated from your daemon,' said Martha.

'I'll see if I can get in round the back,' said Piers. The shock must have shown on Martha's face, because he added, 'I learned to break into houses when I was younger than you. Although I promise I didn't steal anything except for food. Imagine all those people discovering they'd had a burglar, and all he'd done was make himself a peanut butter sandwich!' Good God, Piers was not at all what he'd seemed. Martha erased the picture she'd had of Piers's childhood in a Cotswold stone manor house with an Aga, a larder, a mother who made her own marmalade, and a pair of matching cocker spaniels called something posh people would find funny, like Jeeves and Wooster or Gin and Tonic, and replaced it with . . . what?

'Sanjay, can you give me a leg up?' said Piers. 'I'm not as agile as I was back then.'

Sanjay, rather ineptly, helped Piers over the wooden side gate. David had been rendered speechless by the reckless law breaking. Which was probably just as well.

And again, they waited.

Iona

Iona spotted her train friends standing on her doorstep through the dining room window. She hid behind the curtains, then scuttled into the drawing room at the rear of the house, where she sat on the floor, back against the wall, curled over to make herself as small and invisible as possible, waiting for the doorbell to stop ringing.

Everything had gone silent for a while and even Lulu had stopped barking, so Iona was just beginning to think it might be safe to move, when a face appeared at her French windows. She screamed.

'It's only me, Iona. Piers!' she heard, in the tone of a shout, but with the volume muted by the glass. 'Can you let me in?'

'Go away!' she shouted back.

'Please!' he said plaintively. Then, in a typical male way, and proving the old adage that a leopard never entirely changes its spots, he moved to a more aggressive tack: 'Or I'll have to break the glass.'

Iona sighed and walked over to unlock the windows and let Piers in, cursing him for his arrogant, entitled stubbornness.

'What do you want?' she said.

'We've been worried about you, Iona,' he replied. 'We just wanted to check that you're okay.'

'I'm fine,' she said. 'So you can go now.'

'You're obviously not fine,' said Piers. 'I mean, what are you *wearing*, for a start?' He goggled at her turquoise Lycra catsuit and then pointed at her ankles.

'Legwarmers,' said Iona. 'You know, like The Kids from Fame. *Right here's where you start paying. In sweat!*' she parodied, in a fake American drawl. Piers looked at her as if she'd gone completely mad. Perhaps she had. 'I was doing the Jane Fonda workout. The original, but still the best. See, I'm fine.'

'We heard about your job, Iona. I'm sorry,' said Piers. And with those words, he shattered her pretence and destroyed her bravado. She sank back down to the floor and started to cry. Piers sat down beside her. She really hoped he wasn't going to try to touch her.

He didn't, making her rather wish that he would.

'I know how you feel,' he said. How could he possibly? He was in his *prime*. He had decades to go before he washed up on the same shore as her. He had *no idea*.

'I lost my job three months ago,' he said.

'You're kidding,' said Iona, wiping her nose on the back of her hand. 'But you've been commuting all that time.'

'I was just pretending, because I couldn't face up to the truth. I was too ashamed,' he said. And with those words she felt their disparate worlds connect for a few seconds, and the comforting sensation of being truly seen.

'Piers, you should always remember the First Rule of Commuting,' she said.

'What's that?' he said.

'You need to have a job to go to,' she said, and they smiled at each other.

In the hallway, the doorbell rang again, and Lulu renewed her barking with added vigour.

'Do you think we can let the others in now? They'll have heard you scream. I'm worried they'll call the police,' said Piers.

'Okay. Just give me a minute to wash my face,' said Iona.

By the time Iona re-emerged from the downstairs cloakroom, Piers had opened her front door, and David, Sanjay and Martha had all shuffled into Iona's hallway. They were staring at the wall, which was covered by a massive framed black-and-white photo of a line of life-sized can-can dancers. Their impossibly long legs were thrown up in the air, among a swirl of white, ruffled petticoats. They all wore black opaque tights and identical white frilly knickers.

David was goggling at one of the dancers, right in the middle of the line. His head was at about the level of her breasts, which were spangled with diamanté and shaped into improbable cones.

'Iona,' he said, pointing at the wall. 'Is that you?'

'Oh, well spotted, clever boy,' said Iona, finding that just the presence of her friends had brought back some of her old chutzpah. 'Could you tell by my thighs?'

'No, by your face,' said David, blushing.

'That's a show we did at the Folies Bergère when we were living in Paris,' said Iona.

'That doesn't look like Shakespeare,' said Sanjay.

'No, of course it doesn't,' said Iona. 'Why would it?'

'Emmie told me you were at the Royal Shakespeare Company, before you became a . . . journalist,' said Sanjay.

'Oh, that's my fault,' Martha interjected. 'I told Emmie you were an actress, and she must have just assumed you were at the Royal Shakespeare Company.'

Iona threw her head back and laughed, for the first time since *that day*. The laugh felt like an old, well-missed friend.

'How funny. I told *you* I was *on the stage*, Martha, and you just assumed I was an actress! No, Bea and I were burlesque dancers – it's how we met,' said Iona. 'Look, there's Bea. Bea, short for Beatrice, but also for beautiful.' Iona pointed at the stunning Black dancer she had her arm around in the picture. All the other girls were staring straight at the camera. Iona and Bea were staring at each other. 'Now, you lot. Go and make yourselves at home in there' – she waved towards the drawing room – 'and I'll be right with you.'

As soon as they were out of sight, Iona charged upstairs so fast it made her breathless, and employed her 'emergency five-minute make-up routine'. Then, she found a silver-and-black silk Hermès scarf and concealed her hair in a turban – much easier than trying to deal with it at speed. She tied a wide, silver leather belt around the crimson velvet robe she'd thrown on over her workout gear, removed her legwarmers, and added a pair of high-heeled mules. *Et voilà!*

Iona ran back down to the kitchen and made a pot of Earl Grey tea, which she placed on a tray with five small china cups and some shortbread, and went into the drawing room to entertain her guests. *Brave face on, Iona*, she told herself. Bea always said it was crucial to keep the mood buoyant when you had visitors, even unexpected ones. Presuming you wanted them to come back, which she suspected she might.

Piers, Sanjay, David and Martha were all staring at the wall she called 'The Wall of Fame'. Bea called it, rather rudely, 'Iona's Ego Display'.

There were what looked like hundreds of framed photos of Iona and Bea during the It-Girl years, with all sorts of wonderful people, from Sean Connery to Madonna. There were several gaps, like missing teeth, where she'd removed photos of those celebrities whose pasts had turned out to be not entirely salubrious. They'd been consigned to a dark, locked drawer to have a good hard think about what they'd done. Iona liked to believe that actions had consequences.

Her friends turned towards her.

'We heard what happened at work, Iona,' said Sanjay. 'How are you?'

Iona opened her mouth to tell a lie, and the truth fell out.

'Awful,' she said. 'I mean, I'm *young*. I'm only fifty-seven. I'm in my *prime*. But, it appears I'm redundant – literally. Irrelevant. Surplus to requirements. I don't know what to do with myself, quite honestly.'

'Iona,' said Sanjay. 'You are *not* useless. You are, remember, one of the country's premier magazine therapists. You told me that! And Emmie says your columns are shared all over social media.'

'Thank you, sweet boy,' she said, 'but the thing is, I'm a fake. The only reason I've been causing a stir recently is because I've been stealing all my ideas from you guys. They've replaced me with an amoeba called Dex. No one needs me any more.'

'Iona,' said David, rather sternly, she thought, 'if that were true, we wouldn't be here. *We* need you. We've missed you. Look what an impact you make on everyone! I wish I did. I seem to slide through life without making any impression at all. People often forget having met me, and even if they do remember me, they forget my name.'

There was an awkward pause, as no one knew quite what to say. Luckily, David ploughed on regardless.

'Anyway, how would we sort our lives out without you?' he said.

'Nonsense,' said Iona. 'You don't need me to sort you out. You're just saying that to make me feel better.'

'We do. We're all in a complete mess, of one sort or another,' said Martha. 'Especially the grown-ups.'

Iona was so overcome by this that she sat down on the chaise longue and started crying again. Which was most irritating, because the 'emergency five-minute make-up routine' could not withstand light drizzle, let alone copious tears.

Iona's friends gathered around her, looking awkward.

'Is that you, Iona?' said Martha, in a bid – she suspected – to distract Iona from the uncontrollable weeping thing.

'Yes,' said Iona, turning towards the portrait over the fireplace that Martha was staring at. 'It's a Julian Jessop. He painted me in 1988. I was twenty-six, and he must have been about thirty years older. Bea and I had just come over from Paris and were causing a bit of a stir on the London scene. I sat for him in his wonderful little studio off the Fulham Road, and we sang along to Queen and the Sex Pistols while he painted. He was great fun.'

'I think I saw his obituary recently,' said Piers. 'Wasn't he a notorious lothario?'

'Yes,' said Iona. 'Bea used to make me pack Mace whenever I went for a sitting, just in case. Goodness knows why his wife put up with it all. She loved me, as, being famously lesbian, I wasn't a threat.'

Iona took a handful of tissues from the box on the coffee table and blew her nose.

'Anyhow, enough about me,' she said. 'Tell me, what's been happening with you lot? What's new?'

'Emmie's disappeared,' said Sanjay, with the alacrity of someone who'd been desperate to impart the information at the earliest available opportunity.

'I think that's a bit of an exaggeration, if you don't mind me saying,' said David. 'She was supposed to come with us today, and she met up with Sanjay, but must have changed her mind and gone home.'

'If that's what happened, then why didn't she say goodbye?' said Sanjay, not unreasonably. Emmie had never struck Iona as being bad-mannered. Quite the reverse, actually.

'Sanjay,' she said, in her gentlest voice. 'Did you say something to upset her?'

'Not you too, Iona? No, I said, *Would you like a coffee? Or something like that*,' said Sanjay. 'Then, when I came out of the café with the coffees and some banana bread . . .'

'Oh, I love banana bread,' said Iona, wondering if Sanjay had perhaps brought it with him. Martha gave her a look. 'Sorry, irrelevant,' she said, waving her hand, swatting the words away like a cloud of bothersome flies.

'When I came out of the café, she was gone,' said Sanjay.

'You checked the loo?' she said. He rolled his eyes at her. 'Well, I'm sure she's absolutely fine, but it wouldn't do any harm to call her and make sure.'

'But we don't have her number,' said Sanjay, who was being, Iona thought, a bit wet. No wonder Emmie had buggered off. She was probably worried about drowning.

Piers reached for the teapot to pour himself another cup, and as he did so Iona spotted something on his wrist. A tattoo? 'What does DIVAD mean?' she asked him, before realizing that she was reading it back to front. It said 'David'. How strange.

Piers didn't answer her question; instead, he asked one of his own. One she had absolutely no idea how to begin to answer.

'Where's Bea?'

Sanjay

They all stood and stared at Iona, as the silence grew and grew. Eventually, she sat down and took a deep breath.

'I was wondering when you might ask that,' said Iona, followed by another long pause. 'You see, she's not here. Hasn't been for years, actually.'

She stopped again, and stared at the portrait over the mantelpiece, deliberately ignoring their confused, questioning stares.

'But you said . . .' said Piers, when the silence became unbearable.

'No, Piers, I never said. You just assumed. You have to be careful making assumptions about other people's lives, you know. You should know that better than most, I'd have thought.'

'So where is she?' said Martha.

'Bea was diagnosed with early-onset Alzheimer's, about seven years ago,' said Iona eventually, speaking the words slowly and individually, as if each one were a monumental effort. 'She'd been forgetting things for a while – people's names, then everyday words. I'd find her frozen in front of the washing machine, because she couldn't remember how to turn it on, and she'd ask me the same question several times in one day.

'We thought it was the menopause – you know? No, perhaps you don't. The menopause is to blame for many, many things, but not this, as it turned out. We found ways to compensate: little notes left around the house to remind Bea where to find things, and what she had planned for the day. Then, one evening I had a call from the newsagent by the station. He'd found Bea outside his shop in tears. She couldn't remember how to get home.'

Iona poured herself some more tea with a shaking hand, took a sip and grimaced.

'It's gone cold,' she said. None of them spoke, not wanting to break the spell. Iona paused for a minute or two, before continuing. 'Shortly after that we had an official diagnosis. Initially, I looked after her myself. We stopped going out very much or having visitors. I guess that's when I lost touch with most of my old friends. I found a carer to look after her when I went into the office. It was my job that kept me anchored to the outside world. Other than that, it was just me and Bea, in a little bubble which, despite all my best efforts, she was finding ever more frightening and confusing. Eventually, I just couldn't cope on my own any more. I found her a care home.'

'That must have been really hard, losing your other half like that,' said Sanjay. Iona glared at him. He'd obviously said something very wrong, but he wasn't entirely sure what.

'Bea was not, *is not*, my "other half",' said Iona.

'Er, no. Of course not,' said Sanjay. Wasn't she?

'No woman is anyone's "other half". We are all entire people. Completely whole, and totally unique. But sometimes when you put two very different whole people together, a kind of magic, an alchemy, occurs. Bea said I was like eggs and sugar, and she was flour and butter, and when you mixed us together, we were more than just the combination of our ingredients, we were *a whole damn cake*. And the problem is, when you're used to being a magnificent, mouth-watering cake, it's really, really hard to get used to being just eggs and sugar once more.'

Sanjay wasn't quite sure what to say to that. He decided to skirt around the whole cake analogy and fall back on a more standard response.

'You must miss her terribly,' he said.

'Terribly,' Iona said. 'I feel guilty about it every day. I visit her as much as I can, but she often doesn't know who I am. She feels most comfortable in the past, so we spend a lot of our time there now. Music helps, too. It takes her back. She usually has no idea what day it is, or what she ate for breakfast, but she can remember every lyric of every song released in the 1980s.'

Sanjay had always thought Iona larger than life. Invincible. But right now, she looked shrunken and vulnerable. Eggs and sugar. Broken eggs without their shells. They muttered the tired old platitudes, because what else could they say? *So sorry, how awful for you, poor Bea, nothing you could do*, but the words hung ineffectually in the air.

'That's another reason why my job is so important, you see,' said Iona. 'Almost every penny of my salary goes to pay Bea's care home fees. I'm going to have to move her somewhere cheaper, which I can't bear, as continuity and familiarity are so important to her. Or, I have to sell this house. And this is the only thing I have left of Bea as she used to be.'

'Why didn't you tell us any of this, Iona? How can you make a career out of helping people and not be prepared to ask for help yourself?' asked Sanjay, who was trying to think only of Iona and Bea, honestly, but couldn't help feeling a bit hurt. 'We're your friends, aren't we?'

'Yes, darling, of course you are,' said Iona. 'I just rather liked you thinking me so happy and successful. I let you make all those assumptions. It made me feel like that person again myself, at least for the duration of our little train journeys. And you made me feel connected to the world, you kept me distracted and you helped me hang on to my job for a few extra months. So you did help me, you see, and I'm hugely grateful.'

Iona stood up and walked over to the French windows, skirting around a rather incongruous canary-yellow beanbag. 'Look, why don't I show you around our garden?' she said. 'It's Bea's pride and joy. I'm not half as skilled as she is, so it badly needs a good prune, but it's still spectacular. A bit like me!' She tipped her head back and guffawed, looking exactly like the Iona they knew from the train. The one she so desperately wanted to be.

Sanjay couldn't pay attention to Iona's garden tour, because he was too busy trying to work out how to get her alone so he could apologize privately and salve his prickling conscience. Eventually, he identified his opportunity, and while everyone was gushing over the elegant, and beautifully oriental, koi carp in her fishpond, he pulled her aside.

'Iona, I'm really sorry for being so mean to you the other day. It was completely unforgivable. I honestly thought that was why you'd disappeared,' he said.

'Sanjay, I think we both have to learn that the world doesn't always revolve around us and our problems, don't we?' she said. 'I was, I confess, a little hurt at the time, but it's all forgotten. Really. I suspect you had other things on your mind, didn't you? I was just caught in the crossfire.'

'I did, actually,' he said, looking at the flowerbeds rather than at Iona, lest he lose his nerve. 'And not just the whole Emmie thing. You see, I've been having trouble sleeping. It's my job. It makes me really stressed and anxious, and I can't seem to leave it behind when I go home. It follows me around, even in my dreams.'

'Oh, Sanjay,' said Iona, sounding like she was genuinely concerned about him. 'Your anxiety is the other side of the coin of your empathy. I suspect that's why you're such a good nurse. But there must be a way of finding a healthier balance – to care deeply about your patients while still protecting yourself. Remember the saying *you need to fit your own oxygen mask before you can help anyone else fit theirs?*'

'Well, that's a bit rich, coming from you,' said Sanjay.

'I guess it is, isn't it?' said Iona, with a laugh. 'But what's the point in me asking for help? You can't make me any younger, can you? Nor can you stop the world idolizing youth. And you certainly can't fix darling Bea.'

'So, what should I do?' Sanjay said.

'Surely there's a counsellor or something at the hospital?' said Iona.

'I can't let them know how badly I'm struggling,' said Sanjay, thinking this whole conversation might be a mistake. 'I'll never get a promotion if they know I can't cope. How could they trust me with vulnerable patients if they knew that the smallest thing might trigger a panic attack?'

'Sanjay,' she said, quite sternly. 'I can guarantee that you are not the first medical professional to be having these problems, and you certainly won't be the last. It's a *hospital*, for goodness' sake. If anyone can help you, they can. Look, give it a go. Check the staff noticeboard, for a start. Will you? See if there's a self-help group, maybe? I'm sure it'll be confidential.'

He nodded. 'You know, you should meet my mum,' he said. 'You're quite similar.' As soon as the words left his mouth, he wanted to reel them back in. What was he thinking? Meera and Iona working together, in some kind of maternal pincer formation, would be a total nightmare. He'd have no hope.

'I'd love that,' said Iona. 'Oh, talking of your mum, how was the date with the dental hygienist?'

'I'm not sure you could call it a date,' said Sanjay, cringing at the memory. 'She was wearing a plastic visor and disposable gloves and asking me questions which I couldn't answer because she was in the middle of scraping tartar off the back of my molars with a sharp metal pointy thing.'

'Oh, I can see that wasn't ideal,' said Iona. 'So did you ask her out for a drink or something? Did she seem nice – behind the visor?'

'Yes, but . . .'

'But not like Emmie?' finished Iona. And they both sighed.

'What did I do to make her run off like that?' said Sanjay, desperate for reassurance.

'Oh, I'm sure it wasn't anything to do with you,' said Iona.

He wished he could believe her, but he suspected she didn't even believe that herself.

Piers

Piers was stuck feigning interest in Iona's weird, ugly mutant goldfish, while Sanjay was selfishly hogging all her attention. He was desperate to get Iona on her own somehow. Finally, Iona and Sanjay re-joined them, and they started walking in the direction of a slightly shabby, but still terribly romantic, summer house, almost entirely covered in honeysuckle and jasmine.

Before they got there, Piers seized his opportunity and grabbed Iona by the elbow, pulling her under the pergola.

'Gosh, it's been a few years since anyone's done that,' said Iona, winking at him. 'Are you going to kiss me passionately and ask me to be your girlfriend?' She puckered her lips together, reminding him uncomfortably of a cat's bottom.

'Uh, no, actually,' said Piers, trying not to look as horrified as he felt. 'I was going to ask you to be my therapist.'

'Goodness,' said Iona. 'I suppose that, given our earlier conversation and the whole "fake commuting" thing, it's quite obvious a therapist is required, and I'm flattered that you should think of me, but I don't actually have the requisite formal qualifications. Unless you count being an incurably meddling ex-socialite.'

'I know that, Iona,' he said. 'But I've promised Candida I'd talk to someone, and you're the only person I want to talk to. Why don't we give it a go, and if it's not working for either of us, you can hand me over to a proper professional?'

There was a pause, and he could see Iona considering his proposal.

'Tell you what,' she said, finally. 'Let's ask Lulu what she thinks.' Iona leaned down and picked up the dog, thrusting her face into his. 'Go on, ask her!' she said.

'Uh, Lulu,' said Piers, feeling really, really stupid. 'Do you think Iona should be my therapist?' Lulu said nothing, obviously, but stuck out her tongue and licked his nose, slowly and deliberately. 'Is that a yes or a no, Iona?' he said, wiping the dog saliva off his nose with his Armani sleeve.

'Oh, that's definitely a yes,' said Iona, putting Lulu back on the ground. 'Okay, since Lulu is on board, you can meet me here twice a week. But I can't let you pay me, since I'm only going to talk to you as a friend, not a proper therapist.'

'But you need the money, Iona,' said Piers.

'And so do you, sweetheart,' said Iona. 'Since you're not earning anything either.' She wasn't wrong, actually. Although Iona's potential fees were a small drop in the deep ocean of his monthly outgoings.

'You can bring me a large bunch of fresh flowers whenever you visit. I love having flowers in the hallway.'

'Sure,' said Piers. 'But isn't that a bit like bringing coals to

Newcastle?' He gestured at her flowerbeds, which were a riot of spring blooms.

'Well, yes, but your flowers will be for the benefit of the neighbours. They'll have hours of pleasure gossiping about the handsome young man visiting me several times a week. There's little I like more than being talked about,' said Iona.

'I had gathered that,' said Piers.

'The Major next door will be particularly thrilled,' said Iona. 'He's always described my sexuality as a "lifestyle choice" and "a phase I'm going through". He was the last person who pulled me under this pergola, actually. And he hadn't been looking for a therapist.'

'What happened?' said Piers.

'A neatly but sharply placed knee where the sun don't shine is what happened,' she replied. 'And Bea got her revenge by throwing any snails she found in our flowerbeds over the fence into his garden, until he set up CCTV and caught her at it. Anyhow, he didn't try that again.'

'I bet he didn't,' said Piers, wondering if meeting Iona alone a couple of times a week was a good idea after all. He might not make it out of here alive.

Iona

Iona hummed to herself as she cleansed, toned and moisturized.

Last time she'd looked in her bathroom mirror – just that morning – the reflection that had stared back at her was that of a useless, lonely old woman. The woman looking at her now was very different. She had friends who had missed her, who were so concerned about her that they'd spent their Saturday trying to find her. And she was, it had transpired, needed. Her leather-bound desk diary, which had – apart from her regular teatime visits to Bea – been as featureless and white as the Arctic tundra, now had a whole host of entries, neatly written in turquoise fountain pen.

She had been accosted not only by Sanjay and Piers, but also by little Martha, who'd hung back as everyone was leaving, and told her about the school play. Iona honestly couldn't have been prouder if she'd landed the part herself. And playing a thirteen-year-old virgin would have been a feat at her age, to be honest. Then, Martha had asked Iona if she could come over a couple of times a week after school for help with her lines, since Iona was no longer taking the train. She didn't seem to mind at all that Iona had been a cabaret dancer and not a Shakespearean actress.

She told Martha that she took her role of being *in loco parentis* seriously, so would only agree on the proviso that Martha did all her homework at Iona's dining room table before they started rehearsals. Martha had replied that, as a result of the latest boyfriend, her mother was more *loco* than *parentis*, and she'd be much happier doing her homework with Iona than at home.

Iona climbed into bed, followed by Lulu. Lulu's legs were too short, and her tummy too large, for her to be able to leap on to the bed, so Iona had invested in a bespoke doggy staircase she could use. Bea would have been horrified. Despite being extremely open-minded about most things, she had oddly entrenched, and boringly conservative, views about pets and beds.

Iona picked up her new phone, which she'd bought to replace the one Brenda-from-HR had rudely requisitioned. It was now filled with the contact details of all her train friends, so they could have no excuse for sneaking up on her again before she'd applied her make-up.

She wished she had Emmie's number, so she could find out what had happened to her. What could Sanjay have done to upset her so badly? This had to be some sort of terrible misunderstanding.

Then she had an idea. Emmie was bound to have an Instagram page, wasn't she? Luckily, she was rather an expert on

Instagram. How many fifty-something women could say that, huh?

It didn't take her long to find Emmie's page. She did a quick scroll. Emmie hadn't posted much, just a handful of smug couple pics of her and Toby in impossibly pretty places, eating improbably perfect food and doing a range of activities that showed how energetic, philanthropic and creative they were. Then she spotted a photo that looked awfully familiar. It was her, in her emerald frock coat and Doc Martens, standing by the entrance to the maze. She looked at the caption underneath. *This is who I want to be when I grow up*, it said. She must have taken it when she walked off after that peacock. Iona felt a lump form in the back of her throat and a huge rush of fondness for Emmie. A sort of *motherly* sensation. Or, at least, how she imagined a motherly sensation would feel.

She pressed the button saying 'message' and typed: *Hi Emmie, it's Iona. Just checking that you're okay. If you need me, I'm at Riverview House, Hurst Road, East Molesey. I'm worried.* She added her phone number and some heart emojis, and pressed send. She was probably worrying unnecessarily, but at least now the ball was in Emmie's court.

She turned off her phone and put it in her bedside drawer. She'd written several articles about the deleterious effect of blue light on your circadian rhythms.

Iona and Bea had always loved this magical time, just before sleep. They'd lie there, in the dark, holding hands and touching toes, exchanging snippets of their separate days, using their stories of backstage gossip at the theatre and the latest goings-on at the magazine to knit their worlds closer together. Bea, who was an excellent mimic, could bring the whole of her current cast to life in the quiet of their bedroom, arguing and flirting with each other.

'Night night, Lulu,' she said. She could hear the sound of Lulu licking herself, and tried not to imagine which body part was getting the attention.

As she'd done every night since Bea had gone into the home, Iona pressed play on the old tape deck next to the bed and listened to the soothing tones of the shipping forecast. Far more effective, and less addictive, than a sleeping tablet.

'Mull of Galloway to Mull of Kintyre, including the Firth of Clyde,' said the presenter.

Iona turned towards the side of the bed where Bea had slept for so many years. She'd not washed Bea's pillowcase since she'd left, but however hard she tried she couldn't find a trace of her scent.

'Night night, Bea,' said Iona to the unused pillow. 'I love you.'

'Variable, mainly east and north-east, two to four, showers, good occasionally moderate,' came the reply.

Martha

Martha wasn't really concentrating on assembly that morning. The headmaster had watched one too many TED talks and had taken to delivering overly long inspirational monologues peppered with expressions like *be the best you* and quotes from Brené Brown, Rumi and – because he thought it made him sound contemporary – Taylor Swift. Martha surreptitiously unfolded the papers she had tucked in her blazer pocket, and started reading through act three, scene five, muttering her lines under her breath.

> *Wilt thou be gone? It is not yet near day.*
> *It was the nightingale, and not the lark,*
> *That pierced the fearful hollow of thine ear.*

She'd roughly translated this in the margin as *please don't go yet*. Shakespeare, she'd discovered, never used four words when twenty-six would do. He might be good at the whole play thing, but he'd be useless at writing the emergency evacuation instructions for an airline.

Martha's life had changed immeasurably since she'd first met Sanjay on that train. She still hadn't quite repaired the relationship with her old school friends. Apart from anything else, she found it difficult to trust them, since they'd abandoned her when she'd needed them most. But now, she found herself right in the middle of a new gang: the cast.

These days, when Martha walked into the cafeteria at lunchtime, she didn't have that gnawing fear of having to sit alone or – worse – with the misfits who didn't belong to any of the cliques, and didn't like each other, even. Now, she always found a group from the play, exchanging cast gossip, and testing one another on their lines. It didn't hurt that Romeo was being played by the most seriously gorgeous boy in her year. Well out of her league, obviously, but even being acknowledged by him gave her instant kudos. If the others knew about the vagina pic, and they surely did, they didn't mention it. As far as they were concerned, she was Martha and Juliet: fellow actor and friend.

What's more, Martha's grades had improved along with her social standing. Thanks to Piers, she'd reached the heady heights of the top of the bottom maths set, and her teacher had even dangled the possibility of promotion to the middle set in front of her.

She was doing better in her other subjects too, since she'd started doing much of her homework at Iona's house. Iona wasn't actually any help at all. She said all she could remember from her school days, back in the Dark Ages, was the formation of oxbow lakes, hydrogen burning with a squeaky pop, and her unrequited crush on the netball coach.

However, Iona's enthusiastic ineptitude made Martha realize quite how much she *did* know, which was a great confidence boost. And, as Iona told her constantly, in life confidence was everything. *If you're going to get it wrong, Martha, make sure you get it wrong with PANACHE! Surely they'll give you a mark for style, at least?* Martha had had to explain that that wasn't the way the exam boards worked.

'I'd like to introduce you all to Kevin Sanders,' droned the headmaster. 'Or *Mister Sanders*, as you shall know him.'

'He's quite hot for a teacher,' said a girl sitting behind her.

'Yeah. If you squint, he could nearly be Keanu Reeves,' said her friend.

'You'd have to squint quite a lot,' said the first girl, screwing up her eyes.

Martha looked up and did a double take. It was Piers! Why had the head introduced him as *Kevin*? He so did not look like a Kevin. And he certainly didn't look like Keanu Reeves. She narrowed her eyes. Actually, maybe he did, just a tiny bit. If Keanu ditched his personal trainer and went on a doughnut diet for a few months.

'Mr Sanders is going to be helping in the maths department for the rest of term. He'll be running the maths clinic in the library every lunchtime, for anyone who needs help with their homework or revision. He'll also be holding weekly sessions for those of you who think they might be applying to *Oxbridge*.' The head always said 'Oxbridge' as if it were as thrilling as Hogwarts, which, she supposed, for his generation and profession it was. She doubted they had owls, though. Or talking portraits.

Martha knew where she was going at lunchtime.

Martha watched as Piers patiently explained Pythagoras' theorem to a girl in Year 8.

'Do you see now?' he said.

'Yes!' she replied. 'You make it sound so simple. Thank you.'

Piers seemed genuinely thrilled that he'd been able to help. She wondered how long it would take before he became as jaded and disillusioned as her other teachers. Teaching one-to-one like that was relatively easy. How would he cope if they let him loose on a whole classroom of teenagers? He looked up.

'Martha! I was wondering if I'd be able to find you today! Turns out you've found me,' he said.

'What are you doing here, Piers?' she whispered. 'And why does the head think you're called *Kevin*?'

'Sit!' said Piers, patting the seat next to him. 'It looks like I have a lull between maths patients.' Martha sat, crossed her arms in front of her, and waited for him to explain.

'Well,' he said. 'You told me that your school was short of maths teachers, remember? So I made an appointment with the head, and asked if I could do some work experience.'

Martha kicked herself. She should have remembered that adults often retain information you give them by accident and use it against you, just like Facebook does. And wasn't work experience what Year 11s did? Not old people like Piers. She didn't really mind him turning up at her school;

she was actually quite pleased to see him. She just wished he'd warned her.

'But why do it incognito? Why the Kevin thing? It's not like you're a double agent or anything,' said Martha.

'No, sadly not,' said Piers. 'Kevin is actually my real name. I only changed it by deed poll to Piers when I was eighteen. Remember how I told you to "fake it till you make it"?' Martha nodded, remembering Other Martha. 'Well, Piers was who I wanted to be, my alter ego.'

'So it was Kevin who broke into other people's houses to make himself a peanut butter sandwich?' said Martha, as some of the pieces started falling into place.

'Yes,' said Piers. 'My dad would spend all the housekeeping money at the bookies, and my mum was often too drunk to care, so I was hungry quite a lot of the time. But Iona tells me that it's not exactly healthy to run away from your past, however unpleasant it was. And, to be fair, it could have been much worse. Nobody hit me. Although they often hit each other. So, here I am – Kevin. You can still call me Piers, though, if you prefer.'

Martha wasn't sure that Iona was doing Piers much of a favour, to be honest. All this sharing of feelings and stuff was just weird in an adult, and especially in a teacher. They were supposed to be all buttoned-up and repressed, weren't they? And Piers was a way more interesting name than *Kevin*. Martha had no idea how to respond.

'Cool,' she said.

'Isn't it?' beamed Piers. Kevin. Whatever.

'There is one thing, though,' said Martha.

'What?' said Piers, looking concerned.

'I might need to blank you when I see you on the train, if there's anyone from school there,' said Martha. 'Nothing personal, it's just I'm gradually navigating my way out of Social Siberia, and fraternizing with the staff is not a good look, even if they're a bit like Keanu Reeves. Which you're not, obviously.'

'Sure,' said Piers. 'I'll forgive you.'

He paused for a minute, then added, while pulling in his stomach, 'Keanu Reeves, huh?'

Martha rolled her eyes.

Piers

17:30 Waterloo to Surbiton

Piers was feeling buoyant.

It reminded him, in a way, of his early days on the trading floor – that intense focus required when learning a completely new set of skills, and the huge sense of achievement when you did something right. In this case, however, it wasn't accompanied by the suspicion that he was a pretender, somehow getting away with playing a role that wasn't really his, or the constant gnawing fear of being found out.

In a way, when the bank security men had arrived at his desk with the empty cardboard box, it had been a relief. When the thing you've feared for so long actually happens, you have nothing left to be scared of any more. He'd always known that moment would come; it had just taken fifteen years longer than he'd expected.

This job didn't feel like that at all. He didn't have to

conjure up an alter ego in order to be able to perform. He didn't need the gratifying chants of *Midas! Midas! Midas!*, the Universe-pleasing rituals or the ego-boosting bonuses. It was enough just to be himself, with his love of numbers and genuine desire to do something selfless for a change. He'd submitted his application to join the school's formal teacher-training scheme in September, and hoped that all the unpaid time he was investing would make him a shoo-in.

He was surprised at how much he missed his old train journeys with Iona, which weren't the same without her being a magnet for their little band of misfits. Changing careers was obviously making him sentimental.

Piers looked over at her former table. Emmie was there. He had no idea what to say to her after she'd deserted their expedition with no explanation, so he turned and walked to the other end of the carriage. He didn't want to take the shine off his day with an awkward conversation.

Piers got off at Surbiton and paused at the flower stand outside the station. He picked up an extravagantly showy bunch of white roses, the kind that Candida favoured. The price tag was way out of the league of a teacher's salary, especially one who wasn't getting paid yet, but Candida deserved nothing less. He then stopped at their local deli and chose a home-made boeuf bourguignon and a decent bottle of red, since Candida had sold his fine wine collection.

Piers was ashamed by how badly he'd misjudged Candida. He'd thought their marriage had become a sham, a pretence, an empty shell, like the rest of his life. But it was, he'd discovered, so much more resilient than he'd imagined. As was Candida herself.

Throughout his crisis she had been calm, focused and strong. She'd picked him up and held his hand as he scrambled his way back to sanity, and she'd restructured their finances, so they had a small, but solid, foundation for the future. Tonight, he was going to make sure she realized how grateful he was.

'So,' said Piers, over their candlelit kitchen table, 'I just wanted to say how much I appreciate everything you've done. You're incredible. I honestly don't know how I'd have coped without you.'

'You're welcome,' said Candida. 'I mean, I could hardly leave you on that station platform in a complete mess, could I? You are feeling better now, aren't you? Is the psychotherapist you're seeing helping?'

'Yes. I feel like a totally different person,' said Piers. 'I can't actually believe that was me. And this career change is going to make such a difference to my life. Our lives. I know it'll mean downsizing, fewer holidays, state schools and so on, but I really think that living a simpler, more honest, lifestyle will be good for us all. The kids included. They'll grow up less spoiled and entitled. It'll be a happy medium between your over-privileged childhood and my under-privileged one. A healthy average.'

He smiled at Candida, thinking of their wedding, and how utterly gorgeous she'd looked walking down the aisle towards him. This was just another chapter of their lives. A different one, but better in so many ways. It would bring them closer.

'Piers,' said Candida, her Botoxed forehead forming the

slightest semblance of a frown, 'I'm so sorry if you've mis-understood the situation.'

'What?' he said.

'Look, I'm really pleased things are looking up for you,' Candida said as she placed her knife and fork neatly on her plate next to a solitary abandoned chunk of beef that obviously hadn't met her exacting standards. 'And I wanted to make sure you were back on your feet. You're the father of my children. We're tied together, through them, for the rest of our lives, like it or not. And in some ways, I still love you.' Candida paused.

In some ways?

Piers had the sensation of hurtling towards an immovable object in his old Porsche. He could see what was going to happen, but there was no way he could brake hard enough to prevent it.

'But I thought I'd made it quite clear that that is not the life I want,' Candida continued, as calmly as if she were discussing which Greek island they should holiday on next summer. 'It's certainly not what I bought into. I'm not "Mrs Sanders, the maths teacher's wife". I don't want to live a teacher's small life, on a teacher's small salary,' she said. 'I don't believe that average *is* healthy. When have I ever aspired to be average? I want the kids to have an upbringing that's well *above* average. And, to be frank, I don't want to be married to a *Kevin*. The man I married very wisely chose to leave all that behind him.'

'I know you said that,' said Piers, 'but even if I could find another City job, I wouldn't want it. I honestly think going back to that world would drive me mad.'

'I'm not asking you to, darling,' said Candida. 'I'm just saying, I'm not doing this with you. That's why I've been sorting out all our finances. So we can buy you a flat, some-where near here, and we can co-parent the children. We can be civil and grown-up about all this, can't we? We can con-sciously uncouple, like Gwynnie and Chris Martin. There's no need to waste more of your redundancy payment on expensive lawyers and court battles, using the kids as pawns.'

Piers remembered the dead pigeon. The portent, currently decomposing in their composting bin. He felt as if he'd been flying happily towards his rose-tinted future, without real-izing that there was an impassable sheet of hermetically sealed glass in front of him. He'd flown straight into it and was crashing to earth, stunned and bleeding. How could Candida be so *calm* about all of this? And surely being a single mother with only a modest alimony to live on was not in her life plan either?

A blurred image in his brain gradually came into focus, sharpening and revealing the whole picture.

'You've got the next meal ticket lined up already, haven't you?' he said, feeling intensely weary rather than angry, although he suspected the anger might come later. 'Who is he?'

'No one you know,' said Candida, looking down at her immaculately painted nails. The nails of a rich banker's wife. The nails that were already scratching the back of a replacement rich banker.

'Was he around even before all of this happened? He must have been.'

'Don't be like that, darling,' said Candida. 'A girl always

has to have a Plan B. It was just a silly side-dalliance, and would no doubt have stayed that way if you hadn't blown our lives up so selfishly.'

'You can't do this to me, Candida,' he said. 'What happened to *for better, for worse, for richer, for poorer?*'

'Look, if we're going to argue over occupation of the moral high ground, which would be too unbearably tedious,' said Candida, 'then don't forget you lied to me for *months*, putting your suit on every day and "going into the office". Then you gambled away the children's school fees and, if it weren't for me, we'd have lost everything.'

'But what about the kids?' he said. 'They *need* me. I need them.'

'I know that,' she said. 'But you'll see way more of them than you did when you were working every hour God sends. And think of those long teacher's holidays! Plus, you're welcome to help them with their homework after school as often as you like – you know how much I hate doing that. At least with you being a teacher, we'll never have to worry about hiring tutors. And, if you can get a job in a *proper* school, they might even give you a discount on the fees. There's a silver lining! Look, I'm going to bed. I'll see you in the morning, and we can discuss next steps.'

Candida pushed her chair away from the table, leaving him surrounded by dirty plates and the remnants of a destroyed life. The white roses were still in their cellophane, abandoned in the kitchen sink. She paused at the door, looked over her shoulder, and said, with a tinkling little laugh, 'You know, Daddy always said you were my *starter husband.*'

He couldn't believe how hard his wife was, behind that beautiful face. Peel off the human-like skin and you'd find the Terminator.

Ever since he'd seen her walking down the aisle towards him, on her father's arm, he'd known that he was punching above his weight, that he wasn't anywhere near good enough for her, and he'd always had a niggling fear that one day she'd leave him. Just like the security guards approaching his desk with an empty cardboard box, it had only been a matter of time.

Iona

19:35 Hampton Court to Wimbledon

'Stay still, honey,' said Iona. 'Mummy doesn't want to get soap in your eyes!'

Lulu looked at her through the lavender-scented fug, with an expression that said *I find this all totally humiliating, so please just get on with it.*

Iona lifted her out of the bath, wrapped her in a pale pink fluffy towel, and carried her into the bedroom for the blow-dry.

Considering she was officially unemployed, Iona had been terribly busy.

She'd spent so much time coaching Martha that, should Romeo have a terrible accident on the night, and lose his voice, or a crucial limb, she could easily stand in, although the wardrobe lady might have a challenge on her hands.

Piers had also been dropping in regularly, proffering flowers as instructed. She was slightly concerned that she seemed to spend more time talking to him about herself, instead of him talking to her, which she was pretty sure wasn't the way therapy sessions were supposed to work, so she'd stuck a sign on the wall reading SHUT UP IONA, which was in her eye line, but hidden from Piers's view, and vowed to limit her utterances to words like *How did that make you feel?* and *Tell me about your relationship with your mother.*

It hadn't helped much. She'd never been any good at taking instructions – not even, it appeared, from herself.

She must be doing something right, however, as Piers had more of a spring in his step every time she saw him and was gradually morphing from Eeyore to Tigger. Instead of feeling ashamed of his miserable childhood, and running away from it, she'd taught him to make peace with himself, and to be proud of how far he'd come. *Your past experiences,* she'd explained, *are the foundations on which you build your future. Build them on pride, not shame. Denying your history leaves your house standing on sand, always in danger of collapsing.* She was quite pleased with that analogy. She must use it in her column. Except she didn't have a column any more, did she?

Piers had told her about Candida's declaration last night, along with some story about a pigeon which she'd rather lost track of. But even that didn't seem to have knocked him down too badly. Perhaps it hadn't sunk in yet? He was far more concerned about the kids than his wife, but was quite convinced he'd be even more involved in their lives, not less.

If she were honest with herself, she suspected that Piers's transformation had more to do with his fledgling new career than her 'therapy' sessions. But she could take some credit for the new job too, couldn't she? After all, it was almost entirely her idea.

The problem was, despite every effort to economize – she'd even cancelled her monthly Fortnum & Mason essentials hamper – Iona was burning through her savings. She was going to have to face up to the situation soon and call the estate agent.

She looked around at her home, the foundations on which she and Bea had built their life together, and felt unbearably sad. Lulu, who had been blessed with the gift of telepathy, stared into her eyes, and licked her cheek.

Iona was also worried about Emmie. She hadn't replied to Iona's Instagram message, and no one seemed to have spoken to her since the day she went missing, although they said they'd seen her on the train, so she hadn't been kidnapped or ended up in hospital in a coma. Something was not quite right, she was sure of it. She had a nose for these things.

Iona's phone rang, and for a moment she thought it might be Emmie, conjured up by the power of thought. She snatched it up. DAVID, it said on the screen.

'Hi, David!' she said, squashing her disappointment, and sounding as perky and upbeat as she could muster.

'Iona,' said David. 'What are you doing right now? Could you come over here? To Wimbledon?'

'Darling,' said Iona. 'Is this a booty call? I'm flattered, but you know I'm not that way inclined, don't you?' There was a protracted and awkward silence. Had she embarrassed him, or was he trying to work out what a booty call was?

She must remember that most 'middle-aged' people were not as au fait with modern lingo as she herself was. She decided to put David out of his misery.

'I'm only kidding, dear heart. Yes, I'd love to come and check out *chez David*. Text me the address, and I'll jump on a train pronto.'

Iona could tell it was David's house without even checking the number. All the other properties in the street had been upgraded – they were sporting gleaming glass extensions, fancy electric security gates, and matching pairs of bay trees entwined with tasteful fairy lights on either side of glossy front doors – but this one was stuck in a time warp. Like its owner, it'd not moved on for decades.

'Come in, come in,' said David. 'Are those for me? How lovely, thank you.'

Iona handed him the overly extravagant bunch of white roses that Piers had brought round earlier. Luckily, she'd not had a chance to remove them from their cellophane before David had called. Re-gifting was good for the planet. That would make a good topic for an article. Oh God, she had to stop doing that.

David led her through to a comfortable but fusty living room. Antique rugs were spread across a parquet floor, and dark wood furniture was arranged around the focal point of a large open fireplace. An estate agent would no doubt describe it as *containing numerous original period features and opportunities for modernization*.

David took the flowers through to the kitchen and came back with them in a vase. He was holding a small, white card. 'My darling Candida,' he read. 'Thank you for every-thing. I love you.' It seemed like she wasn't the only one who believed in re-gifting.

'How strange,' she said. Then, unable to keep her curiosity in check any longer, and keen to distract David from Piers's note: 'Do you want me to help you with something?'

'Actually, you've helped me a huge amount already,' said David.

'Really?' said Iona, trying to think what she might have done.

'Yes. You and the others on the train made me realize what a rut I'd got into. So I've been trying to *shake it up a little*. I've signed up for some adult education classes!'

'Great idea,' said Iona. 'What are you learning?'

'I'm doing Russian conversation on Tuesday evenings and learning how to strip down and rebuild a car engine on Thursdays.'

'Excellent,' said Iona. 'You can get a job as a chauffeur for an exiled oligarch.'

David ignored her, which was probably for the best. 'And things are getting better with Olivia, slowly. I'm starting to think that all may not be entirely lost after all.'

'Oh, that *is* good news, David,' she said.

'So I wanted to do something to help you, you see. You know I'm a solicitor?'

Iona hadn't known that, but to admit as much would be to display a remarkable lack of interest in her friend. Had any of them asked him what he did? Her guilt made her nod more enthusiastically than the situation required, while fighting a wave of jealousy. David was at least a decade older than her, and yet it seemed he was still taken seriously in his career. Why was it that men with grey hair and wrinkles achieved *gravitas*, whereas well-preserved women like herself became invisible?

'Well, my speciality is contract and property law,' said David, 'so I'm not much help to you, unless you're thinking of moving house.'

'Sadly, I think that may be the case,' said Iona.

'Perhaps not,' said David, then paused as the doorbell rang. 'Here she is, bang on time as always.'

'David, you're not trying to fix me up, are you?' said Iona to David's retreating back, as he went to open the door.

'Actually, I am,' said David, as he returned with a smart-looking woman in her forties. 'With an employment lawyer. This is Deborah Minks. She works at my firm. I took the liberty of discussing your situation with her. I do hope you don't mind.'

'I guess not,' said Iona, a little warily.

'Can I ask you a few questions, Iona?' said Deborah, who obviously didn't believe in small talk. She guessed one got out of the habit when one charged by the hour. Deborah sat down and took a thin file out of the practical but ugly brief-case which paired nicely with her sensible but dull shoes. Iona nodded.

'I'm right in thinking that you didn't get a pay-off?' she said.

'Yes, because they didn't make me redundant. I resigned. Well, to be accurate, I stormed out, after calling the editor a c—' David held up his hand in an emphatic stop sign.

'Well, our reading of what happened is that this wasn't

actually a resignation, it was *constructive dismissal*. Would you say that the situation was such that you were unable to remain in position?' Deborah peered at her over the top of her glasses. Iona nodded again.

'Could you argue, in fact, that the atmosphere had become completely toxic, and that you felt discriminated against because of your age?' she said.

'Totes,' she replied. The more serious and grown-up Deborah sounded, the more Iona started feeling like a teenager and talking like Martha.

Deborah took a Jaffa Cake from the plate David had placed in front of them, took a neat bite, then put it back down, unfinished. Iona marvelled at the superhuman display of control and restraint. Deborah was definitely the sort of woman you wanted in your corner, despite the shoes.

'Do you feel that, perhaps, you were even manipulated into resigning?' said Deborah.

Iona remembered the way Ed had winked at Brenda-from-HR as Iona threw her lanyard at him, and nodded.

'I don't want to go to court, Deborah,' she said. 'I can't bear the idea of wasting more of my life on that c—' David held his hand up again. He really was a little over-sensitive.

'I don't think it'll come to that, Iona,' Deborah said. 'I suspect they'll be more than happy to settle, and avoid any negative publicity. All we're asking for is that you get paid what you deserve after . . . how long?'

'Thirty years,' said Iona.

'Perfect,' said Deborah, leaning back in her chair and smiling. 'That'll do nicely. Now, you talk, I'll take notes.'

So, she did. She told Deborah about the dinosaur conversation she'd overheard in the toilets, and all the little comments, the *Iona won't understand that*s, the *back in the olden days* jibes, the way they'd exclude her from lunch outings and evening drinks and stop talking when she approached a group standing around the coffee machine. The time when they'd sent out a Christmas card with a picture of everyone from the office on the front, right down to the security guard, and she'd been 'accidentally' missed off.

Iona explained that they'd taken away so many of her responsibilities, one by one, that she spent a large proportion of her day, and her energy, just pretending to be busy and watching the hands of the office clock crawl around their circuit. And then, finally, she replayed the day she was told to check everything she wrote with a boy who peppered every sentence he uttered with things that weren't even words. OMG, IRL, BTW. And, to add insult to injury, when she'd been hired by the magazine in a blaze of glory and gushing PR announcements, he'd not yet been born.

And, as Iona spoke, she felt lighter, as if the weight of years of slights and slurs were being removed from her shoulders. It was, she saw, more subtle and insidious than the bullying Martha had to contend with, but no less damaging.

'Thank you, Deborah, and David,' she said, as she reached the end of her painful and humiliating recollections.

'You're welcome,' Deborah replied, replacing the lid on her pen with a sharp click, as if she were re-holstering a gun. 'Let's go get 'em, shall we?'

Emmie

08:08 Thames Ditton to Waterloo

Emmie thought for a minute that Sanjay was going to come and sit with her, but as soon as she looked up and smiled at him, he turned around and sat elsewhere. Just as he'd done last time. And the time before.

No doubt she deserved the cold-shoulder treatment. She had been terribly rude. But, even so, his behaviour seemed a little over the top. Childish, even. And it stung. Every step he took away from her and every smile he ignored, like a swarm of angry wasps.

Emmie knew she had to apologize to Sanjay, but he wasn't even giving her the chance to do that. Secretly, a part of her was relieved, as she didn't know how to explain what had happened to herself, let alone anyone else. Whenever she replayed the story in her head, it made her look weak, and Toby paranoid and aggressive, neither of which were true, were they?

Had they found Iona? She still longed to talk to her about her fear that her world was shrinking, so that all it contained was her and Toby, in their comfortable, luxurious bubble. Did that matter? Wasn't it enough? Was she just being selfish, expecting more? Iona would have the answers to those questions, she was sure of it.

But almost more than Iona, she found herself missing Sanjay. Over and over again, she pictured him coming out of that café, smiling and carrying her coffee, then discovering that she'd gone. What must he think of her? She'd felt so at ease in his company, so sure that they were going to be friends, and this was how she repaid all his kindness.

Yet again, Emmie thought back to that day, replaying the sequence of events in her mind, trying to work out how the outcome might have been different.

Sanjay had walked into the café, grinning back at her over his shoulder, and she'd sat down at the table outside in the spring sunshine. She'd felt a slight prickling at the back of her neck, the way you do when you sense someone watching you. She'd turned around, and there, parked at the side of the road, on a double yellow line, was a car exactly like Toby's. She'd stared at it, looking for differences – a dent in the wing, maybe, a roof rack, or a *Baby on Board* sticker. Toby, to her knowledge, had never been out to Hampton Court. It couldn't possibly be him.

Even while she was turning that thought around in her head, the window opened and Toby stuck his head out.

'Get in,' he hissed. 'Now.'

Emmie was confused, and concerned. The expression on her fiancé's face was one she'd never seen before. Had something terrible happened? To her dad, maybe? But how did Toby know where to find her? She walked over towards him.

'Toby. Why are you here? What's happened? I don't understand,' she said.

'Emmie, we can't talk properly with you on the pavement, in front of all these people,' he said. 'Why don't you get in the car?'

Emmie walked around to the passenger side, and climbed in. Without saying a word to her, Toby started up the engine.

'Wait! Toby! You can't leave!' Emmie shouted. 'I'm with my friends. We have plans. I have to at least say goodbye, if there's some emergency.'

'*Friends?*' said Toby. 'I only saw one *friend*. I presume that was Sanjay you were looking so *cosy* with.' How was it possible for the word 'cosy' to sound so hostile? 'I saw the way he looked at you, and he is most definitely not just a friend.' Toby slammed the gear stick aggressively into first, as if he were trying to punish his car for something.

'And you lied to me,' he said. 'You told me you were going shopping in the West End.' Toby pulled out into the fast-moving traffic, causing the van behind him to do an emergency brake and blast his horn.

'You'd better put your seatbelt on,' he said.

Emmie felt sick. She had lied, and she knew that lying to the man you loved most in the world, who you trusted enough to spend the rest of your life with, was unforgivable. But Toby, despite never having met them, had an irrational dislike of Sanjay and Iona, of the mere *idea* of them, ever since she'd last been to Hampton Court.

It was just the standard jealousy that went hand-in-hand with intense love. She knew that. Once they'd been married for a few years, he probably wouldn't care less where she went, or with whom, and she'd remember these emotionally charged days fondly. But, in the meantime, it was easier for her, and better for him, if she told a little white lie.

If she were being honest with herself, in some ways she found Toby's jealousy flattering. Reassuring, even. Proof of the depth of his feelings. But she knew it was making her behave in ways she wasn't comfortable with. It had made her deceitful.

'I'm sorry I lied,' she said. 'Truly. But I knew you'd react badly. I don't understand why you have a problem with my train friends, but you obviously do. Anyhow, since we're talking about trust, why have you been following me?'

'I haven't,' he said. 'I just heard on the radio that there was a major problem on the line to Waterloo, so I thought I'd be a hero and give you a lift. I used the Find My iPhone app to check where you were. Imagine my surprise when, instead of you heading north towards London, you were heading south.' He took the corner so fast that she was thrown against the passenger door, the seatbelt digging into her collarbone.

'Toby, please slow down!' said Emmie. She desperately wanted to ask him to take her back, so she could at least say goodbye to Sanjay, but mentioning his name right now would make things one hundred times worse. She wished she'd thought to take his number, but she hadn't expected to need to call him between him going into the café and coming back out again.

'Toby, we agreed to share each other's locations for emergencies, not so we could track each other's movements,' said Emmie. 'I don't think that's right. It's an invasion of privacy. You could have just called me!'

'Emmie, you're the one who lied to me, outright, then went to meet a man in a café behind my back. You're hardly one to lecture me on behaviour and morals. Do you really expect me to believe there's nothing going on? Try to see it from my perspective!' He turned and stared at her.

'For God's sake, watch the road!' she said. 'You'll get us both killed! I can see how it must look, but of course there's nothing going on. I'd never do that to you. He really is just a friend.'

'Well, you're not to see him again,' said Toby, sounding like a petulant child.

'Toby, you can't tell me who to see, and who not to see,' she'd replied, trying to stand her ground, but she was betrayed by a tremble in her voice. 'Anyhow, I can't not see him. We take the same train most days.'

Toby didn't reply, and they drove the rest of the way home in silence. He didn't, in fact, speak to her for the rest of the weekend, and she'd felt unbelievably lonely.

Now, three weeks later, everything was back to normal, and Toby was acting as if nothing had happened. If anything, he was more loving and attentive than ever. But the whole episode bothered Emmie. She could understand why Toby had acted as he had, but since then she'd been on edge. Wary. She knew this was illogical, as Toby worshipped her – he'd never dream of hurting her. If anything, he was too protective.

An uncomfortable question kept going round and round in her head like a moth circling a light bulb, despite being tortured by the heat: *How can you tell the difference between concern and control?*

Emmie had, of course, no intention of avoiding Sanjay because of Toby's jealousy, but it turned out she didn't have much choice, since Sanjay had no intention of talking to her. Whenever she'd spotted him in the distance, he'd been walking in the opposite direction. Deliberately.

Emmie was determined to make things right between them. She picked up her handbag and walked down the aisle towards him.

'Hi, Sanjay,' she said. 'Do you mind if I sit here?'

Sanjay

08:19 New Malden to Waterloo

'Thanks,' said Emmie, as though he'd invited her to join him, which he hadn't. She sat down on the seat opposite him, nonetheless. 'I've been desperate to find out if you tracked down Iona. Is she okay?'

'Yes,' said Sanjay.

'Yes, you found her, or yes, she's okay?' said Emmie.

'Both,' said Sanjay. He knew she wanted more information, but he didn't think she deserved it. She'd made it quite clear that she didn't want to spend any time with him. He'd seen her in the distance a few times over the past weeks. So, she'd obviously not been abducted by aliens or a religious cult, nor was she suffering from amnesia after a terrible head injury. She was just rude, and not the girl he'd thought she was. He'd made the classic mistake of judging a book by its cover.

'Look,' said Emmie. 'I know you're angry with me, and I don't blame you. It was horribly bad-mannered of me to disappear without an explanation, and I'm really, really sorry.'

Sanjay didn't say anything. He was damned if he was going to make this easy for her. He looked out of the window, as the relatively lush, open landscape of the suburbs was replaced by the densely packed brick, concrete and plate glass of central London.

'My fiancé showed up. There was a bit of an emergency. It was a really difficult day,' she said.

'That doesn't explain why you didn't even say goodbye,' said Sanjay. 'I bought you coffee. And banana bread. Made with fair trade bananas.' He cursed himself. That was hardly the point.

'Well, he was a bit cross. I wasn't where I said I'd be, and he gets a little jealous sometimes. I guess it's flattering, really,' said Emmie. She smiled at him nervously, and he wasn't sure who she was trying to convince: him, or herself.

Sanjay felt his emotions shift from anger, through confusion, before settling on concern.

'Emmie, was he *following you*?' he said.

'Not exactly, no,' she replied. He waited for her to elaborate. 'We share locations on Find My iPhone. You know, for emergencies. He heard about a huge problem on the train line and just checked where I was, to see if he could help me. Which was super thoughtful.'

Sanjay didn't trust himself to say anything. It was entirely possible – probable, even – that his unease had nothing to do with Toby, it was just desperation in disguise. The need to find some reason to dislike Emmie's fiancé, some chink in his 'Mr Totally Perfect' persona.

'Toby's always wanted to look after me, protect me,' she said. 'Right from the beginning. It's how we met, you know. I'd had my wallet stolen on the Underground. He found me at the turnstile with no ticket and no money, and he rescued me.'

Bloody Toby. The man was a walking cliché, with his whole knight-in-shining-armour act.

'Wow. How romantic,' he said. Did that sound sarcastic? He did hope not. 'Emmie, I don't want to interfere or anything, and I know it's none of my business, but just be a bit wary of the whole jealousy thing.' He could see Emmie trying to interrupt him, but he ploughed on regardless, not stopping to question what he was about to say, lest he lose his nerve. 'You know I used to work in Accident and Emergency? Well, I saw many women whose partners "got a bit jealous". They'd tell me that in the beginning it was all wildly, obsessively passionate, but then he'd start dictating where they could and couldn't go, who they could and couldn't see, what they could and couldn't wear and how they spent their money, if they were allowed any. And, after a while, they'd find that when they stepped out of line they'd end up "falling down the stairs" or "walking into a cupboard". Then, finally, they'd find themselves sobbing on my shoulder in the family room, telling me that they knew they had to leave, but couldn't see how. I don't want that for you.'

Sanjay paused, and looked nervously at Emmie. She'd gone very quiet and very still, looking down at her fingers as she clenched and unclenched her fists. He'd gone too far. He wished he could grab those words with both hands and swallow them back in, but he knew that even if he could, they'd make him choke.

'Sanjay,' she said, almost in a whisper. 'I know you mean well, but you honestly don't know what you're talking about. You don't know me, and you certainly don't know Toby. He loves me, and I love him. So, please, just go back to your patients, who do need your help, and leave us alone.'

'Okay, Emmie,' he said. 'I know I don't know Toby, but I'm not the one planning to marry him. You are, so please just make sure that you really, really do know him. You're always so keen to ensure that everyone is treated ethically and fairly; just make sure that you are, too.'

'I'm not *planning* to marry Toby, Sanjay. I *am* marrying him,' said Emmie, glaring at him. And with terrible timing, the train shuddered to a full stop at Waterloo station. Before Sanjay had even stood up, Emmie was out of the doors and on to the platform, weaving her way through the crowds and away from him.

All day, Sanjay replayed the conversation, questioning his motivations, re-looking at Toby's actions from every viewpoint. Sometimes a seemingly obvious set of symptoms could add up to a whole different diagnosis. A suspected malignancy could often be completely benign. He knew that.

Maybe Toby was just Mr Perfect. Desperate to look after his beloved fiancée and to make sure that she was safe and happy. And he could hardly blame Toby for being a little jealous, could he? After all, Sanjay had spent weeks simmering with jealousy, and that didn't make him an abuser.

Perhaps he'd just jeopardized any possibility of a friendship with Emmie over nothing. If he'd kept his stupid mouth shut, then he could be there for her as a support if things did go badly.

In a rare quiet moment, Sanjay dashed to the canteen, bought himself a cup of tea and a KitKat, and sat down at a table. He pulled up the app he used to check his train line on his phone and typed in *train delays Hampton Court Waterloo* and the date of their trip to find Iona. He searched and searched, but there was nothing. No delays, no problems, in either direction. Not until the early evening when there was a broken-down train outside Vauxhall.

Either Emmie was lying to him, or Toby was lying to her.

Emmie

All day at work, Emmie had taken out the phrases Sanjay had uttered and re-examined them in her head. *He'd start dictating where they could and couldn't go, who they could and couldn't see, what they could and couldn't wear and how they spent their money.* And she'd picture Toby, telling her she couldn't see Sanjay any more. Then she'd remember the suit he'd bought her as a surprise present just last week, the one that was beautifully well cut and horribly expensive, but made her look like a demure version of a middle-aged British Airways air hostess. *Now you're going to be a company owner, you need to look the part*, he'd said, beaming at her. *That means no more miniskirts or low necklines . . .* He seemed to have ignored the fact that she'd not yet decided to quit her job. As far as he was concerned, it was a done deal.

Emmie remembered Toby's insistence that their salaries were paid into a joint account, how he'd go through their statements with a highlighter pen and how, increasingly, he questioned her purchases. *We're saving for our wedding, Emmie. You can't keep spending money on frivolities like make-up.* Then, as always, salving the burn with words of love: *Anyhow, I think you're beautiful just the way you are.*

Then a thought more devastating than all the others. The words that Emmie hadn't discussed with anyone, because they made her feel ashamed and afraid: *THAT PINK SKIRT MAKES YOU LOOK LIKE A TART. WE ALL KNOW YOU'RE A FAKE. YOU DON'T DESERVE A MAN LIKE THAT.* She batted the words away, hard. Toby adored her. He'd never deliberately undermine her confidence that way.

Surely it was Sanjay being over-protective, not Toby. He was making her paranoid, inadvertently driving a wedge through the middle of her perfect relationship. She felt as if she were staring at that dress that broke the internet a few years back. What do you see? Is it really black and blue, or white and gold? It can't possibly be both.

Emmie stood on her doorstep, trying to calm her breathing. Toby was taking clients out for dinner this evening, so she'd have some time to herself to think.

'Hi, Toby!' she said in her normal voice, taking off her shoes and her coat, placing them in their authorized areas, in her normal way.

Toby came out into the hall. 'Hey, Emmie! What's the matter? Are you okay?' he said. Not so normal, then.

'Just tired,' she replied. 'Hard day.'

'Poor baby,' said Toby. 'The sooner you quit that job, the better. Why don't you have a hot bath and an early night? You haven't forgotten I'm out this evening, have you?'

'No,' she said. 'Probably just as well. I wouldn't be good company right now.' Sometimes the easiest lie is the truth.

Emmie went through all the usual motions on autopilot. She felt as if she were re-running an old movie of herself, shot in very different times. The image looked like her, but it was two-dimensional and flimsy.

To distract herself, Emmie pulled up her Instagram feed. She rarely looked at her personal Instagram. When you spend so many of your working hours dealing with social media, doing it at home loses its appeal. She opened her messages. One stood out, from an account she didn't follow: @ionabeaandlulu. She clicked on it. *Emmie, if you need me, I'm at Riverview House, Hurst Road, East Molesey.* Then a mobile number, and the words: *I'm worried. Iona.* It had been left weeks ago. On the day they'd gone to find her. The day the cracks had started to appear in her perfect world. The cracks that seemed to be widening into chasms.

Emmie's finger hovered over the screen, but she had no idea how to reply. Where did she even begin? She'd leave it till later. But she hugged Iona's concern to her like a lucky talisman.

Finally, the front door closed behind her fiancé, and the corset crushing her ribcage loosened a little.

How well do you really know him, Emmie? said the voice in her head, paraphrasing Sanjay's words from that morning. She *did* know him, surely she did? They'd been together for two years, living together for months. And there were advantages to Toby's obsession with decluttering, and his philosophy of *a place for everything, and everything in its place.* She knew what every drawer and cupboard in their house held, and – being a new build – there were no loose floorboards or hidey-holes concealed inside ancient chimney breasts. Nowhere he could hide secrets from her.

There was only one place that had always remained an enigma. Toby's study, which he often referred to, with a laugh, as his *man cave*. Emmie only ever went in when he was there and, even then, only after knocking.

Emmie opened the door to the study. The scent of Toby still hung in the air. Her heart was pounding in her chest, and all her senses were tuned to fight or flight, as if his hand might come down on her shoulder at any minute.

The room was as pristine as the rest of the house. On his desk, just a blotter, a fountain pen, a letter rack and an antique silver letter opener, all arranged in perfect straight lines, at right angles to each other. In the silence, the gentle tick-tock of an antique carriage clock on the bookcase sounded as loud and sinister as the countdown mechanism of a primed bomb.

Emmie sat in Toby's desk chair, feeling a sigh as the padded leather seat gave slightly beneath her, adjusting to an unfamiliar weight and shape. She ran her hands over the polished desktop. Fake Edwardian, fake mahogany. Was Toby fake, too?

She placed her fingers cautiously on Toby's keyboard. She'd used his computer once or twice, when her laptop had been playing up. She'd remembered laughing as he'd told her the password. Emmie20111990. Her birthday. He'd not have given her the password so freely if he had anything to hide, would he?

She typed it in, and the screen sprang into life.

Emmie scanned through his emails and his files. Toby's hard drive was as neat and organized as everything else in his life. She couldn't see anything untoward. What was she doing, invading his privacy for no reason? Committing exactly the crime she'd accused him of so recently.

She pushed her chair away from the desk and pulled out the desk drawers one by one, revealing neatly stacked passports, papers, photographs – nothing unexpected, nothing out of place. She should stop this now. She had no valid reason for behaving like this, other than an unsettling conversation on her commute. What was she even looking for?

Then, she reached for the bottom drawer, and it wouldn't open. Emmie pulled again on the shiny brass handle, but it was locked. There was no sign of a key anywhere. She groaned out loud in frustration.

Think, Emmie. Think. Why would Toby keep a drawer locked? Maybe just to keep the contents safe from burglars, or perhaps to keep them away from her. *How well do you really, really know him, Emmie?*

She picked up the letter opener – shaped like a miniature dagger – and shoved the tip into the small keyhole. She wriggled it up and down while simultaneously pulling and pushing on the drawer handle.

Eventually, more through a combination of luck and force than skill, and with a small splintering sound, the drawer opened. It would be immediately obvious to Toby what she'd done, she realized, fear stabbing her between the ribs. How was she going to explain that to him?

Emmie peered into the drawer. She couldn't immediately see anything in it at all.

Trying to stay calm, she reached back into its depths, and felt the slim, neat shape of an iPhone. Toby's old phone. The one she'd assumed he'd had recycled when he upgraded last Christmas. She pressed the button on the side, expecting the battery to be dead, but it lit up almost immediately. It needed a four-digit pin. She tried his birth year. Then her own. Then 2017, the year they'd met. And she was in. All his passcodes were about her, but now, instead of that making her smile, it made her shiver.

The phone must have been restored to factory settings, because there were none of Toby's favourite apps. Nothing apart from the basic features. She held her breath as she tapped on the message icon. Only one message, and she knew every word of it as if it were branded into her soul. *YOU THINK YOU'RE SO CLEVER, BUT WE ALL KNOW YOU'RE A FAKE.*

The walls closed in around Emmie, suffocating her. She placed a trembling finger on the mail icon, knowing already what she'd find. Two emails, both sent to her. From a.friend@gmail.com. The phone burned in her hand and she dropped it on the desk, then reached into the back of the drawer again.

Her fingers closed around something so familiar that her prints were moulded into the battered leather. Emmie forced herself to keep breathing, trying to strangle the snakes writhing in her stomach. It was her old wallet. The wallet that had been stolen out of her bag on the Tube, the day she'd met Toby. Toby, who'd found her, helpless, on the wrong side of the ticket barrier, without a ticket. Toby, who'd scooped her up and rescued her. Her knight in soft cashmere.

She opened it up and there it was – the photo she'd thought she'd never see again, of her and her mother. All the bank and credit cards she'd had to cancel, but no cash. Had he bailed her out by loaning her her own money?

And why keep the wallet? Because he was intending to confess, and return it some day? Or was it some kind of trophy? His equivalent of the stuffed head of a lion mounted on the wall of a country house, or a butterfly pinned in a glass display case.

Suddenly everything was clear. Toby was not her rescuer, he was her captor. He always had been. He'd created a gilded cage for her, and she'd just walked into it – gratefully and lovingly, smiling and wearing a diamond solitaire ring. He'd been undermining her confidence, making her doubt herself with his anonymous messages, then started cutting off all her escape routes, alienating her from any potential saviours, her train friends and her work colleagues. *You love working from home, Emmie.*

How could she have been so blind? Was she so desperate to believe in the happy-ever-after that she couldn't see what was staring her in the face?

She pulled the ring off her finger and placed it in the middle of the desk. Then she moved it, three inches to the left. Toby hated anything being off-centre.

Picking up her wallet, she ran up the stairs to their bedroom, pulled a suitcase down from one of the top cupboards, and started throwing her clothes into it. As she did so, she played back the Instagram message from earlier in her head: *If you need me, I'm at Riverview House, Hurst Road, East Molesey.*

Emmie paused in the hall and walked over to the serried ranks of Toby's shoes, neatly paired and facing forward, like soldiers on parade. With shaking hands, she picked up one of each pair, and, as she walked down the road towards the station, tossed them in a neighbour's skip. Then, she threw up in the gutter.

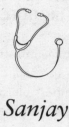

Sanjay

19:15 New Malden to Hampton Court

On his way out of the hospital, Sanjay stopped at the main staff noticeboard. He scanned the collage of job opportunities, of things lost and found, flats for rent and bicycles for sale, until there, right in the bottom corner, he found it. A small, unadorned notice saying CLINICIANS SUPPORT GROUP MEETING, EVERY MONDAY AT 1PM. ALL WELCOME, followed by the name and number of the organizer. He pulled out his phone and took a photo of the notice. It wouldn't hurt to go along once, just to check it out, would it?

Sanjay climbed the final flight of stairs up to his apartment and rounded the corner. He'd thought he might be imagining the faint smell of biryani, but no. There, sitting on his doorstep, was a bulging carrier bag with a folded piece of A4 paper on top, his name written on the front in bold capitals.

Sanjay unfolded the note: FOR YOU TO SHARE WITH A FRIEND, it said, in handwriting almost as familiar as his own: his mother's. At the bottom, she'd added, as always: P.S. HEAT THROUGH SLOWLY. DO NOT MICROWAVE.

Sanjay's mum, Meera, demonstrated her love through food, but found catering for two, now that he and his siblings had all left home, impossible. She cooked in huge vats, served with giant ladles, and just couldn't do small portions. So, whenever his dad's firm had a taxi fare out in the direction of New Malden, she would load up the driver with leftovers for her son.

Meera had a key, too. She'd insisted on it, for emergencies. In the early days of Sanjay living with his workmates, she'd turn up unannounced from time to time, and springclean their apartment. After a couple of rather embarrassing incidents, involving a used condom, and Ethan's secret porn stash, they'd all agreed that she was no longer allowed inside without warning, unless one of them was on the brink of death. And even then, she had to be accompanied by a member of the emergency services and wasn't allowed to touch anything.

Sanjay's flatmates loved his mother's cooking almost as much as he did, and it was a great excuse to get some beers in and eat proper Indian food while watching a movie together. But, looking at the note, Sanjay realized he had another friend he wanted to share tonight's dinner with. Very much so.

He pulled out his phone.

*

'Come in, Sanjay!' beamed Iona. 'There's only one thing better than a handsome young man turning up on one's doorstep, and that's a handsome young man bearing dinner.' He handed her the carrier bag.

'This is so exciting!' said Iona. 'Is it difficult to prepare? I'm a dreadful cook. Bea used to say that whenever she wanted to lose some weight, she'd just ask me to take charge of the kitchen for a month.'

'Not difficult at all,' said Sanjay. 'You just bung it in the microwave. Oh, but don't forget to tip it out of the foil containers first, otherwise the microwave will explode. Ethan did that once. It took ages to scrub the turmeric off the ceiling. Anyhow, what have you been doing, Iona? You look a bit . . . hot,' said Sanjay.

'How kind of you to say so, darling. No one's called me "hot" for some time,' Iona replied, with a lewd wink. He wasn't sure whether she'd deliberately misunderstood him, or not. 'Lovely Martha is still here. I've been teaching her the can-can. Come and join us – we can work up a good appetite before heating up the food. You'll need a skirt.'

With some trepidation, Sanjay followed Iona into the dining room. The table and chairs had been pushed to one side, and the rug rolled back, revealing a polished parquet floor.

'Hi, Sanjay!' said Martha, who was looking even hotter than Iona. She was still wearing her school uniform, but over the top of her regulation navy skirt was a voluminous one, in a multitude of colours and ruffled layers.

'Here you go!' said Iona, passing him a similar garment, with an elasticated waist.

It was quite clear to Sanjay that dissent was not an option. He pulled the skirt on over his trousers.

Iona walked over to an old-fashioned record player. 'We've been using the classic can-can by Offenbach, *Orpheus in the Underworld*,' said Iona. 'A bit cheesy, but great fun.'

And within a few minutes, Sanjay was twirling his skirts and kicking his legs like a professional. He remembered bumping into his flatmates on the way to the station, and their teasing when they'd discovered he was taking food round to a 'girl'. *Ooh, Sanjay's got a date. About bloody time.* If they could see him now. He'd never live it down.

Martha stared at him and started laughing. More than the situation warranted, in his opinion. She was laughing so hard that he was worried she wouldn't be able to breathe properly. She collapsed on the floor, then lay on her back, staring at the ceiling through dilated pupils.

'Argh, the room is spinning,' she said.

'Martha,' said Iona, looking rather concerned. 'When you went into my kitchen to get a glass of water, you didn't eat one of my cookies, did you?'

'Yes, I did, actually,' said Martha. 'I was starving. I didn't think you'd mind. They're very moreish. The weird thing is it seems to have just made me *more* hungry.'

'Oh, bugger,' said Iona. 'Those are my special cookies. I take them for my arthritis.'

Sanjay looked at Iona, and he looked at Martha, and suddenly it all made sense.

'Iona, have you given Martha a cannabis cookie?' he said.

'I didn't *give* it to her, sweetheart. She took it. Don't worry, it'll wear off soon. She'll be fine. And she won't be getting any pain in her joints for a while.'

'I'm fine now, actually! More than fine,' said Martha. 'Just don't tell my mum.'

The combination of music and Martha's laughing was so loud that the doorbell must have been ringing for some time before they heard it.

'Iona! What's that ringing noise? Is it in my head?' yelled Martha, above the noise.

Iona lifted the stylus off the vinyl.

'It's my doorbell. Gosh, I've not had this many surprise guests since Bea put the chip pan on the hob before wandering off for a bath and forgetting about it. We had the whole Kingston Fire Service round for supper. It was every heterosexual woman's fantasy. Quite wasted on us. Wait there, I'll go see who it is,' said Iona.

Sanjay checked his phone. There was a text from his mum:

Mum: DID YOU FIND A FRIEND TO SHARE DINNER WITH?

He was about to reply when Iona came back into the room.

'Look who's coming to stay for a while,' she said. Walking behind her was Emmie. And a suitcase.

Yes, typed Sanjay.

His mum sent a smiley-face emoji, a party popper and a heart in reply.

Meera often used emojis inappropriately. She'd got into

all sorts of trouble with the misuse of the aubergine. But in this instance, she'd managed to describe exactly how Sanjay was feeling.

But Sanjay's elation swiftly morphed to concern, as Emmie just crumpled into a little heap on the dining room floor and sobbed.

Piers

08:13 Surbiton to Waterloo

While Martha worked on the equations Piers had set her, he scrolled through the latest local properties on Rightmove. They'd had an offer on the house already, so they were looking for a more modest place for Candida and the children, and a nearby apartment for him. The problem was, modest wasn't a descriptor Candida was well acquainted with, so it was taking a while.

Piers was amazed at how little he minded selling their home. It had been chosen by Candida, furnished by an interior designer, and maintained by a whole host of workmen. He'd paid for it all, but it'd never really felt like his. It struck him as deeply ironic that he'd bought this obscenely massive house, and yet he spent all his time gravitating to its smallest, cosiest corners. He was secretly looking forward to creating his own home, somewhere unpretentious, relaxed and comfortable. Somewhere Minty and Theo would love coming to after school and at weekends.

Martha handed him her paper, confidently.

'You're not going to need me for very much longer, Martha,' said Piers, scanning down all the correct answers and meticulous workings-out.

'I am getting better, aren't I?' she said. 'Hey, did you take your old suits to that charity for the long-term unemployed I suggested?'

'Yes. They virtually ripped them out of my hands. They said they'd be perfect for their clients' job interviews. I kept one, for old times' sake. Martha, can I ask your advice about something?'

'Me?' said Martha, looking stunned at the role reversal.

'Yes, you. You see, the headmaster called me in last week. He said he's really pleased with the job I've been doing, and he offered to let me teach an actual class,' said Piers.

'Oh, wow! That's brilliant!' said Martha.

'Well, it's not, actually. It was a total disaster, in fact,' said Piers, cringing at the memory which had been replaying over and over in his head on a mortifying loop. 'They didn't pay me the blindest bit of attention. They just kept talking to each other, chucking balls of paper around and scrolling on their mobile phones, which I didn't have the courage to confiscate. There were a handful of kids in the front seats who were valiantly trying to follow the lesson, but it was impossible with all the racket. I'm a total flop, Martha.'

It struck Piers that just a few months ago, he'd never have dreamed of having a conversation like this, one that exposed his failure, weakness and lack of confidence. Certainly not with a teenager, definitely not on public transport. But his own journey to the edge of the abyss, and his subsequent 'therapy' sessions with Iona, seemed to have given him this need to *share*. He hoped that was a good thing, because he didn't know how to reseal the lid on Pandora's box.

'Oh, don't worry,' said Martha. 'That's just par for the course. We do that with all the substitute teachers. It's like an initiation test. Although most of them don't come back again.'

'But I've got another lesson today,' said Piers, feeling sick at the thought. 'And what happens if the head drops by and sees the utter carnage in my classroom? I can say goodbye to my place on the teacher training course.'

'Have you ever watched a David Attenborough documentary?' said Martha, in what seemed a complete non sequitur.

'Yes, of course I have,' he replied.

'Well, what you have to realize is that teenagers are like wildlife in the Masai Mara. You need to understand their psychology. Believe me, I've spent years studying this stuff,' said Martha. 'It's the only way I've survived this long.'

'Okay, tell me more,' said Piers, trying not to sound sceptical.

'When you go into a classroom – the watering hole, if you like – you have to be the alpha male. You know, like the big gorilla,' said Martha. 'Do they have gorillas in the Mara? I'm not sure they do. Let's say we're in Rwanda. Anyhow, you need to *show no fear* and, crucially, you must *not* try too hard. If you try too hard or seem to care in any way what they think of you, you give them the power. The alpha doesn't have to try, he just is. You see?'

'Yes, I think I do,' said Piers, thinking back to his days on the trading floor, which was a veritable jungle of monkeys, man-eating lions and venomous snakes.

'And you need to work out who the wannabe alpha is,' Martha continued. 'There'll be one kid who everyone looks up to, who'll compete with you for dominance. You need to isolate him or her, and *take them down*. Right at the beginning. Then the troop – that's the collective noun for gorillas, by the way – will look to you for leadership.'

'How do I "take him down"?' asked Piers.

'Or her, or them,' added Martha, sternly.

'Or her, or them,' said Piers, resisting the urge to roll his eyes. 'You're not expecting me to bare my teeth and beat my chest, are you?'

'No, obviously not,' she said in an exasperated tone. 'You mustn't take these analogies too seriously. Do it like the stand-up comedians do with hecklers. Not mean or aggressive, but clever and witty. And firm. You can do that, I know you can.' Piers felt ridiculously chuffed with her faith in him. 'So, when you go into that classroom, remember Attenborough. Think *look at all those silly chimpanzees. I am the big gorilla*. Honestly, I take Attenborough with me everywhere,' said Martha. 'He's the best.'

The train pulled into Vauxhall station, and Martha scanned the crowd on the platform, as she did at every stop. But now she did it with anticipation, not fear. Piers could see a group of boys in the school uniform which matched hers.

'Sorry, Piers. I've got to go,' said Martha. 'I'm going to sit with Romeo, from the play.'

He saw Romeo wave over at Martha. Piers knew his real name was Aaden. He was one of the boys who'd turned up to Piers's Oxbridge entrance talk, a Somali asylum seeker who, apparently, couldn't speak a word of English just two years ago. Now Piers was giving him private advanced maths coaching and was determined to help him apply for a Stormzy Scholarship to Cambridge.

'Is there something going on between you two?' said Piers.

'Hey, Mr Sanders. Boundaries, remember. Teachers can't ask questions like that. It's creepy,' said Martha. 'Good luck with the class!'

She walked over to Aaden, who put his arm around her shoulders. It looked like he was right. He resisted the urge to punch the air in celebration.

Emmie

08:05 Hampton Court to Waterloo

Emmie missed Toby. Not the real Toby, obviously, but the man she'd thought he was, and the future she'd thought they had together. Rationally, she knew she should hate him, but a piece of her heart, buried deep within her chest, had yet to catch up. It was still in love with the man who'd adored and protected her. The one who'd never existed. She was left with such a confusing mix of emotions: a deep grief, but accompanied by guilt for feeling that grief, all overlaid with anger and what felt like a frisson of fear.

Emmie's left hand felt empty without the ring on it. She'd mentioned this to Iona, who'd said, *It's not empty, dear heart, it's LIGHT. That ring was weighing you down! It wasn't a declaration of love, it was a symbol of OWNERSHIP.*

Iona was doing her very best to keep Emmie cheerful and occupied. The minute she spotted her moping, she'd suggest a Jane Fonda workout, a bread-making session, or a 'spot of gardening'. It was exhausting, frankly. Her stomach muscles were killing her, the bread always came out like bricks, and she still couldn't tell the difference between the weeds and the flowers. Iona was thirty years older than Emmie yet seemed to have twice the energy.

The train pulled in at New Malden. She smiled as she saw Sanjay standing on the platform, waving at her. Something about him always made her smile.

'Hi, Emmie! How's it going?' he said, as he reached her table. He looked at her searchingly, as though he wanted the genuine answer, so she decided not just to give him the usual platitudes.

'I'm much better, thanks, Sanjay,' she said. 'But it's still so hard.' Words that didn't even begin to describe the complexity of her feelings but were, at least, true.

'I'm sure it is,' said Sanjay. 'It's bound to take time to get over something like that. Does work help take your mind off things?'

'Definitely,' said Emmie. 'Although in a way it's made my job feel even more pointless and frivolous.'

'You should listen to my mum,' said Sanjay. 'She says the best way to heal is to give back, to focus on someone other than yourself. Perhaps you should have a think about how you can use your marketing skills to do something really good. You know, as a side hustle.'

Sanjay's phone pinged on the table.

'She's a very wise lady, your mum,' said Emmie. 'That's exactly what I've been wanting to do.'

'She is, but I wish she'd stop texting me all the time. She does love to interfere. In capital letters,' said Sanjay, putting his phone in his pocket, but not before Emmie read the words DID YOUR FRIEND ENJOY THE BIRYANI? She wondered who Sanjay's 'friend' was, and felt a tiny pang of jealousy. She slapped it down like an irritating fly.

Of course someone as lovely and gorgeous as Sanjay would have a girlfriend. She was sure it wouldn't stop him spending time with her. She was *delighted* for him, obviously.

'Your mum's probably just a bit bored and lonely now you've left home,' said Emmie.

'Hardly!' said Sanjay. 'She's a human rights lawyer, doing mainly pro-bono work. I honestly have no idea where she finds the time to meddle!'

'Wow. That's seriously impressive,' said Emmie, feeling herself blush. What sort of terrible feminist was she, assuming that Sanjay's mum was a housewife just because she liked to cook and was interested in her son's life?

'Sure,' said Sanjay. 'But what about my Human Right to a little privacy?'

'Talking of meddling women,' said Emmie. 'I've been wanting to talk to you about Iona. She's really missing these train journeys and having a routine. And she badly needs a job, not just for the money, for the self-esteem.'

And as she said those words, two seemingly unrelated thoughts collided, creating a shower of sparks. *Use your marketing skills to do something really good* and *Iona really needs a job.*

'Sanjay,' she said, hoping that voicing her fledgling plan wouldn't jinx it. 'I think I may have an idea.'

'Hi, Sanjay, Emmie,' said David, who'd joined the train at Wimbledon. He sat down at a recently vacated seat at their table. Emmie was about to say hello when a Facebook notification appeared on her phone, making her head swim and her vision blur. She placed her phone face-down on the table and buried her head in her hands, as if not seeing the message could make it disappear.

'Emmie, what's the matter?' said Sanjay.

'It's Toby,' she said, through her fingers. 'He won't stop messaging me. I've blocked his number, but he keeps finding different ways to get to me. It's starting to scare me, actually.'

'Emmie, what happened with your young man? It all seemed so perfect!' said David, with the sort of fatherly concern in his voice that she'd missed from her actual father.

'I've left him, David. I realized I'd mistaken control for love. Don't worry, I'm sure he'll give up hounding me eventually,' she said, hoping he'd believe the words more than she did.

The silence between the three of them was shattered by Emmie's phone ringing. Unknown number.

'That'll be him,' Emmie said, feeling sick. Toby must have bought a vast number of SIM cards to get around her block. She tried to inhale, but her breath stuck in her throat, as if Toby were right behind her, strangling her.

'I . . . can't . . . breathe . . . Sanjay,' she said, her words escaping between shallow gasps. She grabbed his arm, trying to steady herself and stop the world spinning around her.

'It's okay. You're just having a panic attack,' said Sanjay. 'It's the fight-or-flight response. It's nature's way of keeping you safe. You know what I do when I feel like that? I inhale really deeply, and I repeat the periodic table in my head in order of atomic number. *Hydrogen, helium, lithium.* I know it sounds stupid, but I find it really helps.'

'*Beryllium, boron, carbon, nitrogen,*' whispered Emmie, opening her eyes and concentrating on Sanjay's face.

'OMG. I've never met anyone else who can do that, apart from other nerdy medics,' said Sanjay, looking at her as if she'd just split the atom.

'I was a geek at school, too,' said Emmie, releasing the words between the breaths that had slowed a little. She unpeeled her fingers from Sanjay's wrist. She'd been clutching it so hard she'd left indentations. 'I'm so sorry. I feel like such a fool.'

She'd forgotten about the phone on the table in front of her, until it started ringing again. Before she could pick it up to switch it off, David answered it.

'Who is this?' he said. Then paused, before saying in a tone Emmie had never heard him use before, 'I'm Emmie's lawyer, and if you come anywhere near her again, I'll slap a restraining order on you faster than you can say stalking, harassment, ruined reputation or custodial sentence.'

David placed the phone back on the table.

'A little unethical, as it's not my area of law at all, in fact, and I didn't have permission to act on Emmie's behalf, but it seems to have done the trick,' he said.

'Wow, David. You've really changed,' said Sanjay.

David beamed at them. 'My wife says the same, actually.'

Iona

12:05 Hampton Court to Waterloo and return

Since it was a Saturday, Iona was treating herself to a lie-in. She was trying to sink back into a half-finished dream that involved herself, Bea and all the Spice Girls except Posh Spice, who she'd never liked on account of the whole refusing-to-smile thing, when there was a knock on her bedroom door.

'Enter!' she said.

Iona opened her eyes and, for a moment, thought she'd gone blind, before realizing that she was still wearing the self-heating aromatherapy eye-mask she'd put on when she'd gone to bed.

She lifted up the mask, to see a large bunch of multi-coloured helium balloons moving along the foot of her bed. Was she still dreaming? And, if so, where had the Spice Girls buggered off to? They'd been having such fun.

'Happy Birthday, Iona!' said Emmie.

'Good God, so it is!' said Iona. 'How on earth did you know?'

'It was on one of the invitations on the wall of your downstairs loo,' said Emmie. '*COME CELEBRATE IONA'S 29TH BIRTHDAY, THURSDAY, JUNE 19TH, WITH A NIGHT OF DEBAUCHERY AT MADAME JOJO'S.*'

'Oh, yes. That party was a hoot. Feathers, sequins and drag queens all over the place.'

The helium balloons made their way up the doggy staircase on to Iona's bed, tied – she now saw – around Lulu's ample belly.

'I've made you breakfast,' said Emmie, passing Iona a tray laden with fresh pastries, fruit salad, orange juice and a cafetière of fresh coffee. 'And this is for you.' She handed Iona an envelope.

'Darling, you are too, too kind. Isn't she, Lulu? Thank you. I'm feeling quite overcome,' said Iona, sniffing theatrically. Lulu must have felt the same, because she emitted a delicate, but surprisingly deadly, fart, then used the ensuing fracas as a cover while she stole a croissant from the tray.

Iona opened the envelope to find a birthday card, signed by Emmie and all of the train gang, and two tickets. One outward, from Hampton Court to Waterloo, and one return.

'Gosh. Train tickets. How sweet of you,' said Iona, doing her best to sound thrilled. It was, so they said, the thought that counted.

'Actually, the tickets aren't the present. The present is what's on the train,' said Emmie. 'The 12:05, to be precise, so you'd better get moving.'

*

'Bye, Bea!' said Emmie, as they left the house.

Iona had hoped that having a house guest for a while would stop her talking to her absent wife, but instead Emmie had started doing it too. Now they both looked unhinged.

Iona spent the ten minutes it took to walk to the station trying to find out what her birthday present was.

'Darling, you know how much I hate surprises!' she said. 'I do like to be able to plan my reactions. Nothing worse than being caught on the hop, especially in public.' But Emmie refused to budge.

'You know, Bea threw me a surprise party once. I ended up walking into a crowded room in my undies,' said Iona. Emmie entirely missed her cue. She was supposed to ask Iona to elaborate on one of her favourite anecdotes.

'Quick, Iona,' she said, instead. 'We can't miss the 12:05!'

'Lulu can't walk any faster, she has short legs,' said Iona. 'And I think the balloons are causing additional friction.'

Emmie picked up Lulu and the balloons with one arm – the girl was surprisingly strong for one so slight. That was no doubt due to the magic of Jane Fonda. She tucked the other arm into Iona's, pulling her towards the platform, where the train was waiting to depart.

They jumped on at the first available door, just as the guard blew his whistle, and started walking through the train towards their normal carriage.

As Iona reached the final door to Carriage 3, she noticed that it seemed busy, despite the rest of the train being virtually empty. She opened the door and was met by a cacophony of noise.

'HAPPY BIRTHDAY!' they all said in unison. All the train gang – Piers, Martha, David and Sanjay. Even Jake, Martha's gym friend, and Deborah, the scarily efficient employment lawyer with a mundane taste in accessories.

'Emmie! What's everyone doing on the train on a Saturday?' she said.

'Well, since it's your birthday today, and we've all missed you on the commute, we thought we'd throw a train party. We have drinks, balloons and music, and everyone brought a plate of canapés.'

'I think I ought to sit down,' said Iona. 'I'm feeling a little overwhelmed.'

Iona progressed down the aisle towards her table, feeling like one of the brides at a wedding. By the time she reached her seat, she'd ruined all her eye make-up. Luckily, she had supplies in her handbag.

The table in front of Iona was covered with mismatched plates of food – ranging from the humble snack to elaborate canapés. She picked up a Cheesy Wotsit in one hand, and a smoked salmon blini in the other. She tried to match the plates in front of her with each of her friends, which was more difficult that she'd imagined. Take Piers, for example. A few months ago she'd have definitely said sushi, but now she wondered whether he weren't more of a Twiglet kind of guy.

'This really is the best birthday present ever,' she said.

'Actually, we haven't got to the present yet,' said Emmie. 'Deborah and David, why don't you start?'

'Excellent,' said David, placing a large brown envelope on the table in front of them. 'Well, the first part of your present is in here. It's actually from Ed Lancaster – your old editor – following a couple of meetings with my good friend Deborah.' Lulu growled, menacingly.

'Sorry, David,' said Iona. 'Lulu growls whenever she hears *that name*.'

'Deborah?' said David, looking confused.

'No, silly. Ed Lancaster,' said Iona. Lulu growled again. 'She's not forgiven him yet, as you can see.'

'Well, this was extracted from *that person*, I must confess, under some duress,' said Deborah, giving Lulu a side-eye, which silenced her immediately. Lulu always knew who not to mess with. 'He must have missed the memo about the joy being in the giving.'

Iona ran her manicured fingernail under the sealed edge of the envelope. 'It's the initial out-of-court settlement offer from *Modern Woman*,' Deborah continued. 'We think we can push it up a little, but it's in the right ballpark. Take a look.'

Without even taking the paper completely out, Iona peered at the contents of the envelope, her eye running down the neat type until she reached a number comprising several zeros. She gasped.

'Oh, my goodness, that's way better than I'd dared hope for. Thank you so much, both of you,' said Iona, pushing the paper back in quickly, in case exposure to the light would make the numbers on it disappear.

'I have something too, Iona,' said Piers, handing over a similar brown envelope. 'It's a tax-efficient investment vehicle for your pay-off. It should give you a steady monthly return to cover most of Bea's care home fees.' Iona's face must have betrayed her, because he added, 'Don't worry. I'm extremely good at investing other people's money, just not my own. I'll take you through it in detail another time,' Piers said. This was a relief, as Iona's head was swimming too much to be able to feign financial acumen.

'We wanted to help you sort out Bea's situation,' said Emmie, 'but you also need a career. So, I've revitalized *Ask Iona*.'

'Oh, darling, that's a kind thought, but *He Who Shall Not Be Named* was right about one thing. *Ask Iona* was a little bit out of date. It wasn't getting half the mail it used to. He just put it out of its misery before it died a long, painful and humiliating death,' said Iona, who'd thought much longer on this topic than Emmie had. 'It was probably the humane thing to do.'

'That's not true,' said Emmie. 'You saw what happened when they shared some of your content on social media. It's not *Ask Iona* that's outdated. People will always need help with their problems – just look at all of us!' Emmie gestured at the group around them, who all nodded on cue. 'It's *Modern Woman* that's out of date. Ironically.

'We're going to take *Ask Iona* on to YouTube. We'll shoot footage of you addressing a problem. Either with someone in person if they're brave enough, or – if they'd prefer to stay anonymous – reading them out from your mailbox. Then we'll post it on your channel and share it all over the socials. Over time, as your subscriber base builds up, you'll get a really decent income in ad revenue and sponsorship. Joey, my boss, has said you can use our studios whenever there's one free, in exchange for an agency credit on your videos, and potential sponsorship opportunities for our clients. He says you'd bring in a hard-to-reach demographic. He even said it was exactly the sort of innovative creative vehicle the agency is famous for. He's probably boasting about it to our biggest brands right now.' Emmie looked at her nervously, waiting for her reaction.

Iona didn't know what to say. She was grateful that her friends had such faith in her, but it was too late. She was too old. Past it. She'd been pretending for years, and she was tired of it. Her fingers ached from clinging on to the cliff edge so hard. All of her ached.

'Emmie, darling,' she said, groping for a good reason to turn her down politely. 'No one's going to want to watch these videos. They won't waste their time staring at saggy old, baggy old me,' said Iona.

'Well, if there's one thing all this proves,' said Emmie, gesturing at the party around them, 'it's that everywhere you go, you find an audience. Plus, we have a secret weapon: Fizz. She's already agreed to plug *Ask Iona* from all her channels. She even said she'll come on as a guest, with a problem for you to solve. So, what do you think?'

'I think you're a genius, obviously,' said Iona. 'But I can't possibly let you spend so much of your time trying to make me feel relevant. It's not fair on you. You have your whole life to lead. Your own career to concentrate on.'

'But Iona,' said Emmie, 'I *want* to do it. It would mean I can use all my skills doing something that will actually help people and do some good. Change lives, even. It would make me feel better about myself, honestly it would. You'd be doing *me* a favour, to tell the truth.'

Iona paused, and looked at her friends, all watching her eagerly. She took a deep breath, trying to steady her voice, before replying.

'Thank you. I'm terribly grateful, truly I am. But no. I'm not doing it. It's too late for me and, to be honest, I'm at peace with that now. Let's just enjoy the party, shall we?' Iona poured herself another drink, concentrating on the glass and the bottle so as not to see the disappointment on Emmie's face.

'Just think about it, will you, Iona?' said Emmie. All the energy and joy had leached from her voice, which Iona knew was entirely her fault.

'Sure,' she said, still not meeting Emmie's eye.

The train pulled in at Platform 5 at Waterloo, but none of Iona's friends got off. It seemed they were all intent on staying for the return journey. Even the train guard had stopped trying to check tickets, and was joining in.

'Iona,' said a voice to her left. It was Martha. 'I have something for you, too.'

She handed Iona a small envelope. It was obviously a mystery envelope kind of a day. Iona opened it, and discovered, for the second time in a matter of hours, two tickets.

'They're for the opening night of my play, next week,' said Martha. 'It would mean so much to me if you'd come. Will you?'

'Darling, I wouldn't miss it for the world!' said Iona. 'But what about your mum and dad? I can't take their tickets. They do want to come and see your performance, don't they?'

'Don't worry,' said Martha. 'They're not totally useless

parents, just a bit preoccupied. They're coming together, in fact, on the last night. Hopefully they'll make it to the end of the performance without yelling at each other like the Montagues and Capulets.'

'Well, in that case, I shall be there with bells on!' said Iona. Then, seeing Martha's face, added, 'Not literally, dear heart. It's just an expression.'

Iona spotted Piers further down the carriage and made her way up to him. She checked she was out of Martha's earshot.

'Piers,' she said. 'You have an "in" at Martha's school, don't you?' Piers nodded.

'I guess you could say that,' he said. 'If you mean "in" as in "unpaid intern".'

'Do you think you could acquire some extra tickets for the opening night of the school play?' she asked him.

One thing Iona had learned from her years in and around show business was that it was impossible to have too big, or too enthusiastic, an audience.

Martha

The school hall was totally transformed, yet it still felt familiar, much like the time when Martha had gone to see Santa at her primary school Christmas fair, and had realized that the man under all the lavish robes and the extravagantly flowing beard was actually her best friend's dad.

The audience were sitting on proper chairs, wearing their evening finery, and the hall was dimly lit and humming in anticipation, but beneath it all was the faint echo of the school assembly. A melange of parental perfumes and aftershaves overlaid the usual scent of disinfectant, teenaged sweat and hormones, and Martha knew from experience that if you ran your hands under any of the chairs, you'd find dried-up balls of chewing gum.

Martha remembered a word she'd had to look up, from the first paragraph of *The Handmaid's Tale*, which Iona had insisted she read. *Palimpsest*. Something revised or altered but still bearing visible traces of its earlier form.

Tybalt peered out from behind the curtain.

'There are so many of them!' he said. 'And there's the most extraordinary woman, right in the middle, holding a dog dressed in an Elizabethan ruff like a mini, furry Elizabeth I. It's hilarious!'

'Surely dogs aren't allowed in the building?' said Benvolio. 'Unless it's a guide dog. Is she blind?'

'Well, that would explain the outfit,' said Tybalt.

There was only one person they could be describing. Martha peered out beside them and, sure enough, there was Iona. She was taller than most people already, but when you added the extra three inches her elaborate Elizabethan-inspired hairdo provided, she became a definite restricted-view hazard. Martha could see the people behind her whispering and shuffling their chairs, trying to see around her. Martha smiled. She'd expected nothing less.

What Martha hadn't expected, though, is that her personal fan club would take up a whole row of seats. There was Piers, obviously, since he was a teacher of sorts, but also Emmie, Sanjay, David and even Jake, her friend from the gym.

While Martha was thrilled to see them all, it just made her even more nervous. When she was being humiliated and bullied at school, she'd always had her train gang to fall back on. Her little oasis on rails. Her safe space. She couldn't bear the idea of terminally embarrassing herself in front of them, too. Where would she be able to escape to then?

Martha rubbed her eyes. She thought for a minute her fear had made her hallucinate. There, making her way along the row towards the empty seat between Iona and Emmie, was Fizz from TikTok. She was sure of it. No one else could carry off that crazy dip-dyed hair look, as if someone had immersed one side of her head in a pot of pink paint, then stuck her fingers in an electrical socket. The rows of seats were so close together that everyone had to stand to let Fizz through, like a Mexican wave, announcing her presence.

A buzz of chatter began backstage, quickly growing in volume and intensity. She obviously wasn't the only one to have spotted the arrival of their celebrity guest.

OMG! Fizz has come to see OUR PLAY. How come? Do you think she'll post us on her channel? I'm super nervous now. How many followers does she have? Yes, I'm sure. Yes, the actual Fizz. Look! Over there.

Martha walked away from the stage, into a dark corner piled high with props, trying to calm her breathing, and her thoughts. She couldn't shake the memory of the dream she'd had every night that week. Over and over again she'd walked on to the stage, blinded by the lights, and delivered her first line, only to be met with howls of derision. She'd looked down to discover that she was totally naked. Behind her, beamed up on a huge screen, was *that picture*, and the headmaster was standing at a lectern, pointing at her notable features with his laser pen.

Martha felt like she was going to vomit. She pulled out her phone and called Iona, hoping she'd ignored the instruction to the audience to turn off their mobiles. Sure enough, Iona, always the rebel, picked up.

'Iona,' she whispered. 'I can't do this. I'm going to be sick. I can't remember any of my lines. I'm never going to live it down.'

'Martha,' whispered Iona back. 'Every great actor feels

exactly as you do now before going on stage. I had to cajole Bea out of the toilet before every opening night, you know. Even after decades in the business. The directors always had my number on speed dial. It's the adrenaline that's making your heart pump and your palms sweat. But adrenaline is your friend. It'll carry you through the performance. Triumphantly! As soon as you've got going, it will all come back to you. Just focus on the first line, then let go. Now breathe. Long, deep breaths. We're with you.'

Everything went quiet, and Martha heard the confident, booming voice of George in Year 9.

> *Two households, both alike in dignity,*
> *In fair Verona, where we lay our scene,*
> *From ancient grudge break to new mutiny,*
> *Where civil blood makes civil hands unclean.*

Martha breathed in and out, letting the poetry of the familiar words wash over her, watching as Tybalt, Benvolio and Romeo took their places on the stage. Moving out of the way while the backstage crew, dressed in head-to-toe black like theatre ninjas, executed seamless scene changes. Waiting until she heard the nurse call, just as Emmie had on the train, all those weeks ago:

'Where's this girl? What, Juliet!'

The walk to the centre of the stage felt endless, the spotlight that followed her progress was dazzling, the anticipation of the audience palpable.

Long, deep breaths. We're with you.

'How now! Who calls?' she replied in a voice that sounded

as if it were coming from elsewhere. Then, just as Iona had promised, the audience fell away, and all the words, all the movements came back to her, like muscle memory buried deep in her subconscious.

She wasn't scared, lonely Martha any more, or even bold, popular Other Martha. She was Juliet, a thirteen-year-old girl, caught up in a family drama not of her making, promised to one boy, while falling in love with the one she could never have.

Sanjay

They all rose to their feet, and the hall echoed with the reverberations of clapped hands, stamped feet and assorted whoops and cheers, ranging from the reedy sopranos of the Year 7 girls to the deep bass of some of the fathers. Even Lulu got over-excited and emitted a volley of high-pitched barks.

Martha had been a triumph. Within minutes, Sanjay had forgotten that he knew her, that she was anyone other than thirteen-year-old Juliet Capulet. She had that indefinable, mesmeric quality that drew your eye to each of her quiet, understated movements.

He watched her, beaming at the audience, transformed from the terrified and awkward schoolgirl he'd met, somewhere between New Malden and Waterloo, just a few months ago.

Romeo leaned down and kissed her. Either he was a much better actor than even that performance indicated, or it was more than just a staged kiss.

Iona reached into her bag and pulled out a single red rose. She threw it towards the stage. It lighted, trembling, on the shoulder of an obese, balding father, who retrieved it and tossed it forward, to land at Martha's feet. Romeo picked it up and passed it to her, one hand pressed against his heart, causing an increase in the intensity of the cheers and whistles, along with the inevitable shout of *Get a room!*

'Wasn't she amazing?' said Jake, whose wildly enthusiastic claps made Sanjay's look like the fragile fluttering of butterfly wings.

'I'm so proud,' said Iona. 'I'm her mentor, you see. I taught her everything she knows.'

Next to Sanjay, Emmie sniggered at Iona's inability to totally relinquish the limelight. She was still wiping her eyes, having sobbed through the funeral scene.

Fizz was holding her phone aloft, pointing it at the stage, while the cast took endless curtain calls from an audience who didn't want to let them go.

All this heightened emotion, all this positive energy, all this talk of passionate love – surely this was Sanjay's moment? What better time could there be?

He reached over, clasped Emmie's hand, closed his eyes, summoned all his bravado, and, feeling like Tom Daley, poised at the end of an Olympic diving board, stark naked apart from his tiny Union Jack trunks, took the plunge.

'Emmie,' he said, whispering into her ear. 'I've been meaning to tell you how much I like you.'

Emmie turned towards him, and smiled her warm, natural smile. The smile he'd been in love with ever since he'd first spotted her on his train, more than a year ago.

'Oh, I really like you too, Sanjay,' she said, making his heart leap with hope. 'I can't tell you how lovely it is to have a male friend who isn't just trying to get me into bed. I've never had a brother, but I imagine this is just what it's like, without all the sibling rivalry, obviously.'

Sanjay had studied enough anatomy to know that a heart doesn't actually break. But if it was just an expression, then why did it hurt so much? He stared at the words written on the front of the programme in his hands: *For never was a story of more woe than this of Juliet and her Romeo.*

The audience were crammed into the dining hall, where there was a choice of warm white wine for the adults, and sticky fruit punch for the children. Sanjay was holding one of each, trying to work out which had the least offensive aftertaste. The jostling of the crowd led to inevitable spillages, and the floor under his feet was tacky, and slightly crunchy due to an earlier accident involving a bowl of crisps.

Sanjay was eavesdropping on the buzz around him, trying to forget his abortive, humiliating attempt to seduce his own Juliet.

Have you seen? Fizz has already posted a video of the curtain calls on her channel. It says, 'What a Juliet! My friend Martha was AWESOME!'

How does Martha know Fizz? Do you think she'll introduce us?

I'm definitely inviting her to my party. D'you think she'll bring Fizz?

Look. Martha's holding hands with Aaden. Seems like Romeo and Juliet are an actual thing.

No mention of *that photo*, as Martha called it. Iona had been right; she'd obliterated all that malicious gossip with something far more interesting.

Martha and Aaden were surrounded by a group of well-wishers. Two little magnets on a plate of iron filings. They made the whole 'boy gets together with girl' thing look so effortless. How did they do that? And why couldn't he?

Sanjay watched as a tall girl with an expression that looked like she'd just bitten into an apple and found half a maggot pushed her way through the crowd. He recognized her, he realized. She was one of the gang who'd been on the train, the day he and Martha had met.

'Hey, Juliet!' she said, loudly enough to cut through the hubbub. 'Have you shown Romeo that picture of your vagina yet?'

The noise level dropped, as an anticipatory silence rippled around Martha. Everyone waited to see what she'd say. But she didn't say anything. Instead, she pulled back her right elbow, at shoulder height, and punched the bigger girl right in the face.

There were gasps, and a few stifled cheers, as the girl staggered back, her hand pressed against her nose.

Piers was pushing his way through the crowd towards Martha.

'You'd better come with me, young lady,' he said, in an utterly deadpan teacher voice, his face tight with controlled anger.

The crowd parted to let them through. Piers was holding Martha by the offending arm, steering her towards the exit.

As they passed Sanjay, Iona and Jake, he heard Piers whisper, 'Nice one, Martha. Let's get you out of here while things calm down a little.'

'I'm so proud,' said Jake to Iona. 'I'm her mentor, you see. I taught her everything she knows.'

'Is there a doctor in here?' called another teacher, who was holding a tissue up to the girl's bleeding nose.

'Ooh, Sanjay! This is déjà vu all over again!' said Iona.

Sanjay sighed, then called out, 'I'm a nurse!'

They walked back to the station together, through the bustling, lamplit streets of Westminster, high on Martha's success.

'Were you terrified, before you came on stage?' asked Sanjay, still sporting a smattering of blood from the smashed nose.

'Totally!' said Martha. 'I'd expected there to be way less people, to be honest.'

'Way fewer,' said Iona. 'Fewer, not less. Sorry, sorry, it's just after decades of working with words I have a bit of an obsession with grammar.'

'I couldn't care fewer about grammar,' said Martha.

'Nobody does any more. I should try to let it go, since I'm no longer a writer,' said Iona, looking bereft.

'Iona,' said Emmie. 'I can't believe you're going to let those assholes at that magazine define you. You mustn't let Ed Lancaster win.' Lulu snarled at her, but she ploughed on, regardless. 'You need to show them what you can do! You are not past it. You're still a writer, and a therapist – it's in your bones. If anyone is the real deal, it's you.'

'Emmie, darling,' said Iona. 'You're very kind, and I know what you're trying to do. I know you want me to agree to your YouTube thingy, and I admire your tenacity, but the answer, I'm afraid, is still no.'

Iona

Iona and Bea sat in the large bay window of the nursing home, looking out over the ancient parkland. Iona could picture the ghosts of shooting parties from a bygone era, returning from a day hunting deer, retiring to this same drawing room to drink tea and boast of their exploits, their proximity to death just making them feel more alive.

Today was neither the best day, nor the worst. Bea hadn't recognized her but had – at least – known her to be a friend, and not someone to be scared of. On her best days, like the day Iona had brought the Dictator along with her, Bea knew exactly who she was and where she was, and it felt much like old times. The days when Bea looked at her with confusion, or even fear, flickering in her eyes, then flinched from her outstretched hand, were the ones she really couldn't bear.

Iona reached into her bag and brought out the old leather photograph album. She loved being able to touch these photos, rather than having them floating around in the Cloud, mingling with millions of other memories exiled by thousands of strangers. All those holidays, weddings and birthday parties jumbled up together in the ether, just waiting to be called down for their moment in the sun, or thrown up as a random Facebook memory.

The album fell open at a page titled '1 December 1992 – WORLD AIDS DAY'.

'Do you remember this, Bea?' said Iona, pushing the album in front of her. 'We joined the march on Downing Street, and you were arrested for hitting a policeman over the head with our placard.'

Bea ran an index finger over the photographs.

'It was such a fuss over nothing. The policeman was wearing a helmet, and the placard was made of cardboard and soggy from the rain, for goodness' sake. You'd have done less damage trying to attack a hammer with a jelly. They were just racist homophobes looking for an excuse,' said Iona, transported back to that time. She could still feel her fear as she tried to push her way through the police barricade to reach Bea, her anger and impotence as she watched her being handcuffed and bundled into the back of a police van.

And here she was, still desperately trying to reach the woman she loved, but the distance between them now was so much greater and harder to navigate than a police cordon. It shifted over time, dark and changing shape, filled with obstacles that she couldn't see, just had to grope for and feel her way around.

Bea mumbled something under her breath.

'What's that, my darling?' said Iona.

'If you give up, they win,' she said.

'That's right, Bea,' said Iona, clasping her hand. 'Remember, that's what you said to me when I quit my job after coming out of hospital. And we said the same every time we marched, petitioned and lobbied. *They want us to be small, so we have to stand tall.'*

'They want us to be invisible, so we have to be seen,' said Bea.

'They want us to be silent, so we have to be heard,' said Iona.

'They want us to surrender, so we have to fight,' they both said together as Bea leaned in towards Iona and rested her head on her shoulder.

A question lodged itself in Iona's head, and grew and grew, pushing everything else aside, until she could think of nothing else.

When had she stopped fighting?

She knew the answer. When she'd finally had to accept that she couldn't make Bea better, that no amount of fighting was going to fix her, she'd stopped fighting for herself, too. She'd waved the white flag, laid down her arms and surrendered.

Something Bea would never, ever have done.

Iona folded herself into her ancient blancmange-pink Fiat 500 and slammed it into first. The Fiat's engine protested, unsure why its driver had become so aggressive. As she drove home on autopilot, crashing through the gears, the words she'd spoken with Bea reverberated around her head, jumbled together with the ones Emmie had said to her last night.

We have to be seen. We have to be heard. You need to

show them what you can do. You are not past it. They want us to be small. You have to stand tall. You are not insignificant. You have to fight.

Iona could feel a building tingle of excitement, a sense of purpose, mixed with a shot of adrenaline, almost as if she were standing in the wings back in the old days, about to go on stage and listening to the murmuring of a full house. That knowledge that something magical was about to happen.

She unlocked the front door and swung it open so violently that the doorknob hit the hallway wall, enlarging the existing dent and sending a small shower of fine plaster on to the tiled floor. She put her bag down and picked up a folded umbrella from the coat stand.

'EMMIE!' she shouted. 'EMMIE, WHERE ARE YOU?'

Emmie appeared at the top of the stairs looking alarmed.

'EMMIE!' repeated Iona, brandishing the umbrella like a sword. 'WHAT ARE YOU WAITING FOR, WOMAN? LET'S DO THIS THING!'

Piers

Piers couldn't quite believe that he was sitting in a sound-proofed recording studio in a hyper-trendy digital agency in Soho. It was about as far removed from his old trading floor as you could get.

He'd been invited by Emmie and Iona to watch the inaugural recording of *Ask Iona*. Actually, that wasn't quite true. He'd had a morning with no lessons and had begged them to be allowed to come until they'd eventually capitulated.

According to all the usual key indicators, Piers's life had deteriorated significantly. Yet he was happier than he'd ever been. He found himself identifying silver linings and counting blessings like a modern-day Pollyanna.

Six months ago, he'd lived with his beautiful wife and two children in a house that the *Daily Mail* would call 'a mansion', but Candida described as 'adequate', set in acres of grounds. Now, he lived on his own in an ordinary two-bed flat near the station, overlooking a supermarket car park.

The carpet was bald in patches, the curtains didn't meet in the middle, and there was a damp patch the shape of Africa in the corner of his bedroom ceiling. But whenever Piers added a new cushion, a set of plates or a candlestick, he felt a sense of achievement. Of progress.

He'd taken Theo and Minty to IKEA. They'd had such an adventure, following the floor arrows around the vast store, choosing furniture for their bedroom and not caring if anything matched or was in fashion. In fact, they'd declared, the less fashionable the better. Then they'd celebrated their successful bounty hunting in the canteen, a bonded trio of retail musketeers, feasting on Swedish meatballs and Daim bars.

He missed Candida much less than he'd imagined he would. He realized that their relationship had been held together by little more than joint obligations, timetables and shared tasks for years. Ironically, the time they'd felt closest was the period when she'd been secretly executing her exit strategy.

Things with Candida now were as amicable as could be expected when one partner had been secretly screwing their rich neighbour, while the other had been secretly screwing their finances. He was guilty, admittedly, of loading up the kids with sugar and artificial preservatives before sending them back, bouncing off the walls, to their mother, whenever he knew she had a date lined up. But he'd never claimed to be a saint.

Piers had been accepted on to the teacher training scheme, starting next term, and, in the meantime, was trusted to cover lessons for absent teachers. He knew that much of his job would involve admin, handing out detentions and trying to make the basic principles of mathematics stick in the heads of pupils who dreamed of being reality TV stars, or celebrity gamers, and didn't see the point of algebra. But already, just once in a while, he had the sense that something he'd said or done had made an impact. That perhaps, in a small way, he would be able to change somebody's future, rather than just move numbers from one place to another in order to make rich people richer while giving himself a stomach ulcer.

Piers had been placed in a dark corner, at the back of the tiny, airless recording room, and instructed not to interfere. At the front, lit by spotlights and hovered over by a large microphone on a long pole, were two small armchairs, one of which was occupied by a slight, grey-haired lady called Louisa who ran the agency catering company and was only here because Emmie had bribed her to take part.

'Bea says one should never trust a skinny caterer,' Iona whispered to him. 'It's like having an obese personal trainer or finding out your relationship counsellor had a messy divorce. She says anyone who can spend their whole day preparing food and not eat too much can't really love what they're making.'

'Or they have a cocaine habit,' said Piers.

'Gosh, do you think so?' said Iona, eyeing Louisa suspiciously.

'No, Iona, I don't,' said Piers.

Emmie was standing behind a state-of-the-art camera on a tripod, wearing large headphones and looking terribly professional. Piers recognized her hot-pink pencil skirt as the one she'd worn on the day they met. If you could describe a near-death experience as a 'meeting'.

'Okay, let's go, Iona,' she said.

Iona introduced herself to Louisa and sat in the vacant armchair. She turned towards the camera, and Emmie said, 'Action!' just like they did in the movies.

'Good morning, everyone!' said Iona, with a broad smile circled in bright red lipstick. 'And welcome to the first ever episode of *Ask Iona*! I'm Iona Iverson, and today I'm joined by the lovely Louisa. Welcome to the show, Louisa!'

Louisa's face was frozen in a rictus grin.

'Thank you, Iona,' Louisa said, in a thin, high-pitched voice. 'Hello, everyone!' She gave a nervous wave to the camera.

'So, tell us why you're here today, Louisa,' said Iona.

'Um . . . I wanted . . . I wanted to ask you . . . about . . .' Piers held his breath, wondering whether the first ever guest was ever going to be able to get to the end of her sentence.

'. . . the change,' she said, the final two words tumbling over themselves.

'Oh, yes. *The change*,' said Iona. 'Isn't it funny how we call it that? As if we get to a certain age and turn into a werewolf, or the Incredible Hulk!'

'Well, it does feel like that sometimes,' said Louisa. 'You know, the weird temperature fluctuations without warning, the lack of sleep, the irrational anger, constantly walking into a room then forgetting why you're there, and finding your lost car keys in the fridge.' Piers wondered if it was actually safe to put this woman in charge of the lunchtime sandwiches. 'You get that feeling that you're no longer any use to anyone. You become invisible.'

Louisa was definitely warming up. Disturbingly so. Was it really a good idea to discuss such personal matters so publicly? Wasn't it important to retain some level of mystique? In eight years of marriage, for example, he and Candida had never left the bathroom door open while they were on the toilet. That sort of thing was the death of romance. Although, to be fair, all the romance in their marriage had died long ago and been replaced by lists of instructions and passive-aggressive digs, despite the lack of communal ablutions. Did Candida and her new man pee in front of each other with abandon? Perhaps they did.

'Darling, you are not alone!' said Iona. 'I've been there! And, as someone who's out the other side, I have to tell you that there are huge *benefits* to the menopause!'

Louisa looked more than a little sceptical. As well she might.

'We women spend the majority of our lives as slaves to our pesky hormones. We have to deal with messy, painful, expensive periods!' Piers felt a little queasy. She could at least use a handy euphemism, like *getting the painters in*, or *meeting Aunt Flo*. 'Not to mention PMT! And all that oestrogen makes us desperate to nurture everyone except for ourselves. Men don't have to put up with any of this nonsense. They just motor on, regardless, revelling in the gender pay gap. But what they don't realize is that post-menopause is *payback time*. We get to be selfish for once. We find a whole new lease of life and, often, a triumphant second act!'

'I'd never thought about it like that,' said Louisa. 'That makes me feel a whole lot better about it, actually.'

'Do you remember Tina Turner's *Private Dancer* album?'

said Iona. Louisa nodded. 'It was her most successful ever. Her comeback after years of commercial purgatory. You know how old she was when she released it? *Forty-five!* And she was only getting started. She did her last world tour aged seventy.'

'Okay, but what about the hot flushes?' said Louisa, who was obviously a realist and, let's face it, no Tina Turner.

'Sure. You need to find a way to ease the transition,' said Iona, coming back down to earth. 'If you talk to your GP, they'll check your personal risk profile and take you through the options, like Hormone Replacement Therapy or acupuncture.'

After some more discussion about hair thinning and memory fog, Emmie made a 'wrap it up' motion with her hands.

'Thank you so much, Louisa, for joining me on *Ask Iona* – also known as Iona's post-menopausal second act – and thank you, everyone, for watching.'

'Go to officecateringsolutions.com for all your office catering needs! Never beaten on price or quality!' said Louisa, in a rush.

'You can send your problems to me by email at Iona@askiona.com,' interrupted Iona. 'If you're a little shy, you can send them anonymously, or you can be like Louisa, and join us live in the studio or by video link.'

'Well done, Louisa and Iona!' said Emmie. 'You were amazing!'

Piers gave a round of applause from his little corner, and everyone jumped as if they'd forgotten he was there.

'Next time, we'll hopefully have some remote guests,

too,' said Emmie. 'We've been using this new technology called Zoom which allows you to record a video conversation from two different locations via a web link. It's the way of the future, apparently.'

Piers snorted. He'd been asked to invest in that little company, but had turned them down. Nothing could properly replace a face-to-face meeting. It was never going to catch on. He had an instinct for these things.

Sanjay

Sanjay had been to three sessions of the Clinicians Support Group. He couldn't believe he'd not discovered them before. It hadn't stopped the panic attacks altogether, but they were definitely less frequent. Staring his anxiety in the face seemed to have stripped away some of its power.

The biggest change, however, was that he no longer felt so alone or ashamed. Hearing other people, from top consultants to junior nurses, describe the same insecurities that hounded him and the fear that followed him was extraordinarily cathartic and reassuring.

Just last week a senior heart surgeon, the sort that's always followed down the hospital corridors by a gaggle of acolytes, had confessed that he still threw up before every single major operation. He said he'd accepted his anxiety now, as he saw it as a sign he still cared, and he didn't ever want to stop caring when someone lay unconscious on his operating table.

He watched as Julie walked up to the large brass bell, hanging from a pillar right in the middle of the chemotherapy waiting room. It was a tradition in this ward that whenever a patient finished their final session, they got to ring the bell. In a room where the air was usually thick with a palpable sense of disease and distress, the bell always provided a momentary but welcome interlude of joy and hope.

Julie grabbed the cord hanging from the bell with both hands and pulled it three times, causing the bell to swing from side to side. The chimes reverberated around the room, along with applause and cheers from the waiting patients. She walked up to Sanjay and threw her arms around him. She was much smaller than she'd been a few months back, the chemo having peeled away all her curves, but her hug was fierce, nonetheless.

'Ever since I first heard that bell ring, I've been waiting to do that,' she said. 'I can't believe it's finally my turn.'

'Well, much as I've loved getting to know you, I don't want to see you back here in a hurry, okay, Julie?' said Sanjay.

'I'll do my best to stay away,' she said.

'Is Adam taking you home?' said Sanjay.

'Yes, but he's got to pick the kids up from school first, so he'll be another half-hour at least,' she said.

'Well, I have my break now. I usually work through it, but I've been told I have to stop doing that, so you'd be doing me a favour if you had a farewell cup of tea with me in the canteen,' said Sanjay.

'It's a date,' Julie replied.

'You're looking great, Julie,' said Sanjay, as he put the plastic tray laden with tea and cakes on the table in front of her. She raised her rather inexpertly drawn-on eyebrows at him.

'You're a real charmer,' she replied, 'but I know I look terrible.' She pulled off her multi-coloured beanie and rubbed her shiny bald head with the heel of her hand.

'I'm not talking about the hair,' said Sanjay, 'I'm talking about the fact that you seem so much happier. Just a month ago you told me you didn't see the point in getting out of bed any more.'

'I know,' said Julie. 'But I had a revelation. I realized I'd been spending all my time worrying about my future, or lack of it. I was living with this constant, gnawing fear, like rats chewing on my innards.'

'Eew,' said Sanjay.

'I know,' said Julie. 'Sorry, that image came from a rather nasty torture scene in *Game of Thrones*, which I've been watching when I was too sick to get off the sofa. Anyhow, the point is I know that this cancer could come back and bite my ass at any time, but I'm not going to think about it. Life is short, mine possibly shorter than most, and I refuse to waste a single day more stressing about something I can't control.'

'I worry too much, too, you know,' said Sanjay. 'I always imagine the worst-case scenarios in any situation. But you're right. Life is too short to live in fear.'

And right then it hit him. He knew what he was going to do. What he had to do.

'You know what? I'm going to go for it,' he said, before he could censor himself.

'Go for what?' Julie said. 'A promotion? Ooh, is it a girl? Please say it is!'

Sanjay nodded, staring into his tea.

'Well, ask yourself this. It's easy to love someone when they're all young, radiant and filled with the joy of life, but take a long hard look at me. Would you still love this girl of yours if she had no hair, eyebrows or eyelashes? Would you massage her back while she vomited through the night, and drive for hours at three a.m. to find mint-flavoured ice cream because it's the only thing she can bear to eat?' she said, staring at him earnestly.

'You know, I really would,' said Sanjay. 'I mean, she's got great hair and eyelashes, but they're like *way* down the list of all the things I like about her.'

Julie was about to say something, but stopped, looked over his shoulder and beamed.

'Julie!' shouted Adam. 'You're done! I'm so proud of you, baby.' And Adam picked her up and crushed her to him, kissing the top of her bald head over and over again before covering it tenderly with her beanie.

As they walked towards the doors, Julie looked back at him.

'That's what you want, Sanjay,' she said. 'Make sure you get that.'

Sanjay put the empty cups and plates on to a tray and carried them over to the counter. A couple of student nurses, laughing so hard at a shared joke that they weren't watching where they were going, knocked into him, causing everything on his tray to slide precariously to one side.

Sanjay felt the apology hovering on his lips, but bit it back and just stared at the two students. Waiting.

'Oh. I'm so sorry,' said one.

'Yes. Sorry,' said the other.

'No harm done,' said Sanjay with a smile.

Martha

08:13 Surbiton to Waterloo

As the train pulled into Surbiton station, Martha saw Iona sitting with Sanjay. Iona waved, pointing at Martha, then at Lulu sitting next to her. This was her code for *Lulu's saved you a seat*. Martha felt like one of the chosen ones.

'Hi, Iona! Hi, Sanjay,' she said as she reached their table. 'No Emmie today?'

'No,' said Iona. 'She had a breakfast meeting with the toothpaste people. I'm joining her at the agency, for our next recording session. Sanjay very kindly met me at Hampton Court so he could help me sort through the *Ask Iona* emails. You can join in, if you like? We have some from students worrying about their exam results. You might be able to give me some insight . . .'

'Sure,' said Martha. 'I'm totally convinced I've screwed up mine. Except for maths, perhaps.'

'Okay, I'm sure you haven't, but we'll come back to that,' said Iona. 'What have you got next, Sanjay?'

Sanjay shuffled through a pile of email printouts, all marked up with highlighter pens and Post-it notes. He passed one over to Iona, who whipped her reading glasses out of her bag and peered at it.

'Oh, this *is* an interesting one. It's from another Anonymous,' she said, scanning down the page. 'He tells me that he's been secretly in love with a girl for ages. They see each other almost every day and have become great friends. But she recently came out of a disastrous relationship and thinks of him like a brother. He wants to be so much more than that. Is it hopeless? How can he get her to see him differently?'

Iona placed the paper back on the table in front of her.

'So, how are you going to answer that one?' asked Sanjay, looking at Iona intently.

'Well, my darling,' she said. 'I'll tell him that the line between best platonic friends and lovers is wafer-thin. Have you watched *When Harry Met Sally*?' Sanjay shook his head. 'Well, you must. You see, having wild, passionate sex with someone is the easy bit. Forming a great friendship, like Harry and Sally's, based on kindness, mutual respect, similar values and a shared sense of humour – which something tells me is exactly what he has – *that* is really hard. It takes time and effort on both sides. But when you combine that with sexual attraction, that's when you become *the whole damn cake*. You see?' Sanjay nodded.

'Anyhow,' Iona continued. 'When the shit hits the fan, as it does in any relationship at some point, it's the friendship that gets you through, not the sex. You know that, Sanjay. You work on a cancer ward, so you must see relationships being tested all the time.'

'So do Harry and Sally get together, then? In the movie?' he said.

'Yes! Although it takes them twelve years and three months,' said Iona.

'That's not exactly reassuring,' said Sanjay. 'For Anonymous.'

'Well, I'm sure it won't take him anything like as long,' said Iona. 'Because he has me to help.'

'So, how does he go from being her friend to being more than that?' Sanjay asked, as if it mattered just as much to him as it did to Anonymous. Sanjay, Martha decided, was one of the most empathetic adults she'd ever met.

'Well, that's where you – he – needs a *grand gesture*. Something to make her sit up and pay attention, to question her previous assumptions, see him in a different light,' said Iona.

'Like what?' asked Sanjay.

'Well, think of the Hollywood movies again. Richard Gere standing in the limousine clutching a bunch of flowers and declaring his love to Julia Roberts? Hugh Grant and Andie MacDowell kissing, not noticing the rain? But he can't just steal one of those, it should be something that's very personal to her, to them,' said Iona. 'For example, my wife and I met on the stage. That was our shared passion. So, when I wanted to let her know how I felt about her, I told her I'd left something behind at the theatre one evening. We went back there, and it was all dark and empty.

Then a live band started playing, and a spotlight came on. Picture it, my darlings!'

Iona flung out her arm, gesturing at an imaginary stage, and stared into the middle distance.

'I walked up to the microphone and started singing Cole Porter's "Let's Do It". And that was the beginning of a life-long romance. Luckily, she wasn't put off by the fact that singing is not one of my many talents. So, I'll suggest Anonymous thinks about how they met, about what's unique to their relationship, and works from there.'

'So, if they met on a train, for example . . .' said Sanjay.

'Well, then he could think of a grand gesture that involves a train journey,' said Iona, beaming. 'Why not? And what does he have to lose?'

'But what if that doesn't work?' said Sanjay.

'The only way to be guaranteed of failure, dear boy, is not to try,' said Iona. 'Love is the greatest risk of all, but a life without it is meaningless.'

'That's really poetic, Iona,' said Martha. 'Who said that?'

'I did, dear girl,' replied Iona. 'Just now.'

They moved on to a quick discussion about the emails asking for help with exam stress, then, as the train pulled into Waterloo, Sanjay dashed off to make his shift, leaving Iona and Martha collecting all the papers together.

'Iona,' said Martha. 'I didn't want to butt in or anything, and you're the expert, obviously. But are you really sure it's a good idea to suggest someone makes a grand romantic gesture *on a train*? I can't think of anything more embarrassing.'

'Oh gosh, you may be right, dear child,' said Iona. 'The

problem is, I'm just so desperate to watch. Having been so intimately involved since the beginning, I couldn't possibly miss the denouement.'

Martha had no idea what Iona was talking about. The email had been anonymous, so how on earth was Iona expecting to get a ringside seat?

Emmie

08:05 Hampton Court to Waterloo

Emmie was finally getting back to her normal self, which was strange, since she hadn't realized she *wasn't* her normal self when she was with Toby. He'd chipped away at her so slowly, so insidiously, that the changes hadn't been at all apparent. She'd felt protected, when she was being smothered. She'd felt adored, while she was being isolated. She'd felt supported, while he was destroying her self-confidence. How could she have been so blind?

She'd made herself a hard and fast rule: No More Men. At least not for the foreseeable future. Not until she'd repaired all that damage and could trust her own judgement again.

Emmie was sitting with Iona, who was travelling into town to meet with yet another journalist. *Why is it that they find 'woman gets new career in her late fifties, and can use social media' so extraordinary?* Iona had asked, not unreasonably. *Now, learning Pitman's shorthand and operating a Telex machine, or a telephone switchboard – that was hard!*

Emmie suspected that much of the media interest was, actually, down to Iona herself, who had a habit of adding a layer of 'extraordinariness' to anything she touched. Still, it was a great bonus. All the free PR had driven Iona's metrics through the roof.

Iona, who was scrolling through her emails, snorted so loudly that Emmie looked up in alarm.

'Oh, look!' said Iona. 'There goes the body of my enemy! You remember my favourite Chinese proverb?'

'If you stand on the bridge for long enough, the body of your enemy will come floating by?' replied Emmie, who'd been waiting for some time to spot Toby in the river. 'Whose body is it?'

'He Who Shall Not Be Named,' said Iona, gesturing at Lulu. 'My old editor. Listen to this.' Iona peered at her iPad screen, where she'd enlarged the type, so as to avoid being spotted in her reading glasses.

'*Dear Iona,*' she read, mimicking Ed's pomposity. '*I've been so thrilled to see all your great success.* I bet you have, you slippery little sucker. *I am glad that we managed to come to such a generous arrangement and parted as good friends, because I'm hoping that you and your little YouTube channel* . . . LITTLE channel? My subscriber base is double yours, asshole . . . *will consider a paid partnership. I'm sure the relationship would be hugely beneficial to us both. Will you join me for lunch at the Savoy Grill to discuss? You can bring your lovely dog. Yours,* et cetera et cetera.'

'Blimey,' said Emmie. 'How are you going to reply?'

'How about: *Dear Ed, fuck off*?' said Iona. Lulu growled.

'A bit blunt, maybe?' said Emmie.

'You're right, as always, sweet pea,' said Iona. 'No need to sink to his level. Remember what dear Michelle Obama says: *When they go low, we go high!* I'll soften it a little.' She paused and typed away with two index fingers, slightly hampered by her long, scarlet-painted nails. 'Here you go. Better?'

Iona passed the iPad to Emmie, who read the response Iona had already sent.

> *Dear Ed,*
> *Fuck off.*
> *Best wishes,*
> *Iona x*

The train pulled into New Malden. Emmie looked out for Sanjay, but couldn't see him. She felt a lurch of disappointment, which was silly. There was no rule that they had to travel on the same train, after all. Then she saw two faces that looked a little familiar.

'Iona,' she said. 'Remember when we met Sanjay's flatmates on the train the other day?' Iona looked up and nodded. 'Well, isn't that them?'

They both peered out of the window at the two young men standing on the platform. Everyone else was rushing to pile on to the train, but they just stood alongside the carriage, waving at Emmie and Iona. Then, they bent down simultaneously, and stood up again, holding up a large piece of card between them.

Written in bold, black capitals was one word: EMMIE.

Emmie frowned, and stood up to leave the train to find out what was happening, but as she did so, the train lurched forward, and the two faces on the platform slid to her left, and out of view.

'What's going on, Iona?' she said, as she sat down again.

'Search me, cupcake,' said Iona, examining her nails.

Emmie frowned. One thing she'd learned about Iona was that the more innocent she looked, the guiltier she was.

It only takes three minutes for the train to travel from New Malden to Raynes Park, so before Emmie had had a chance to solve the puzzle, they were slowing down at the next platform.

There, standing as still as a bollard in a road of moving traffic, was Jake. As the train stopped, he waved at them. He reached down and picked up a piece of card, just like the one at New Malden, only this one read WILL YOU.

The three minutes from Raynes Park to Wimbledon felt like forever. This time, she wasn't surprised to see David, and a woman she presumed was his wife, Olivia, standing on the platform. They smiled and held up two pieces of card. One read GO and the other read ON.

'Emmie. Will you go on . . .' muttered Emmie. 'Iona, it's a message for me.'

'Gosh, do you think so?' said Iona, trying and failing to look surprised. Emmie had no idea how she could have imagined her a Shakespearean actress.

It took four minutes before the next platform, Earlsfield, came into view, along with Martha and her boyfriend, Aaden. Their cards read A and DATE.

The distance between Earlsfield and Clapham Junction was the longest yet. A full six minutes. Emmie sat on the edge of her seat, her nose almost touching the window. She spotted him from some distance. Her friend. Sanjay. He was holding up a piece of card reading WITH ME?

Iona was scrabbling around in her giant handbag. She pulled out two pieces of card, and pushed them over the table towards Emmie. One read YES and one read NO.

'Sorry,' said Iona. 'There's no *I'm not sure, can I think about it for a bit* card. You'll just have to go with your gut instinct. But quickly. Before the train starts moving again. Chop chop!'

Emmie thought about how happy and comfortable she felt whenever she was with Sanjay. Could that be the starting point for something else? She remembered her disappointment just now, when Sanjay wasn't at New Malden, and how he was the person she most wanted to spend time with. She thought about how utterly gorgeous he was, how the sight of his toned stomach all those weeks ago had made her breath catch in the back of her throat, and about her irrational stab of jealousy when she'd thought he was dating someone else. She remembered Sanjay talking her down through her panic when Toby kept calling her. The only other person she knew who'd memorized the entire periodic table in order and loved Daphne du Maurier.

Perhaps it was already something more, and she'd just not noticed. She'd been so busy looking over her shoulder at her lost life that she'd not seen what was right in front of her. Kind, lovely, utterly gorgeous Sanjay.

But, having thrown herself so willingly into a relationship

that had nearly destroyed her, how could Emmie trust herself again? She couldn't. But she could trust Iona. Iona, whose index finger was edging one of the cards in her direction, silently urging her to choose it.

Emmie almost reached for it, before remembering her new hard-and-fast rule: No More Men.

Still, one thing Iona had taught her was that rules were there to be broken. Spectacularly, and with panache.

Emmie leaned forward and picked up the card saying YES.

Martha

Sometimes, Martha found it hard to remember that Mr Sanders was actually Piers. He looked so at home, sitting among the other staff on the stage in the school hall, in his regulation teacher corduroy trousers and burgundy lambs-wool jumper from Marks & Spencer, that it was impossible to reconcile that image with the brash, arrogant, designer-clad man she'd vomited on months ago. The man who used to talk too loudly on his mobile and who occupied far more room and sucked up way more oxygen than his fair share. Now, he was on his way to joining the small group of teach-ers who managed to navigate the tightrope between cool-and-relaxed and unable-to-maintain-discipline.

There was a rumour flying around that Mr Sanders and Miss Copeland – the art teacher – were *an item*, on account of them being seen leaving the art supplies cupboard together, but Martha wasn't trading in the gossip. She'd spent too long at the wrong end of the gossip chain to believe everything she heard. Perhaps Piers had been in dire need of some modelling clay. Or some sticky-backed plastic.

As Martha was filing out of the hall, Mr Braden – her drama teacher – pulled her aside.

'Martha,' he said, with an expression so inscrutable that it was impossible to know if she was in trouble or not. She guessed years of drama school gave you ultimate control over your own facial features. It was probably a compulsory module. 'I have a letter for you and your parents. Once you've had a chance to discuss it, let me know what you decide.' He handed her a slim envelope, and disappeared back into the crowd before she could ask for any more detail.

Martha didn't open the letter until lunchtime, despite it burning a hole in her schoolbag like a radioactive isotope. She'd carried it around all morning, waiting until she could meet up with Aaden. For some reason, she felt this wasn't an envelope she should open alone.

The lunch room was already crowded when she got there. She scooted around the outlying tables of loners and misfits, with whom she still felt an affinity, and headed towards Aaden's table, right in the centre.

She would never have dared to sit here a few months back. It would have broken every unwritten code of cliques and pecking orders. She was still the same person. Still gangly and gawky, still unable to grasp the latest language, wear the correct accessories, or idolize the right celebrities, but through some incredible alchemy, what had been seen as *weird* had now become *individual*.

'Hey, Martha!' said Aaden, shuffling along the bench to make room for her. 'I've missed you!'

'It's only been two hours, dickhead,' said Martha. 'Look, Mr Braden gave me this. I haven't dared open it yet. It's probably something really boring, but . . .'

'Do you want me to read it for you?' said Aaden.

'No. Thanks, but I'll do it. I just wanted you to be here,' replied Martha. 'For moral support.'

Martha opened the envelope and pulled out a folded sheet of notepaper. She scanned the words, reading them several times in her head, trying and failing to make them take hold, before handing the page wordlessly to Aaden, who read the letter out loud.

Dear Martha,

Nick Braden, your drama teacher, very kindly sent me some footage of your recent production of Romeo and Juliet. *I have to say, I was most impressed by your performance.*

I'm currently casting for a play at the Young Vic Theatre. There's a small, but significant, part I'd love you to audition for.

If you're interested, perhaps you could ask one of your parents to call me to discuss details, dates, etc.?

I hope to have the pleasure of meeting you soon.
Yours,
Peter Dunkley
Theatre Director

'Martha, this is epic,' said Aaden, looking at her as if she'd just levitated several metres above her chair. Which, to be fair, would be no more surprising than what had actually happened.

Martha couldn't speak. She just sat, staring at the paper in her hand.

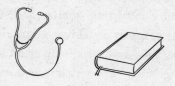

Sanjay and Emmie

'Where does this go, Emmie?' asked Sanjay, holding up a china teapot.

'Wherever you like!' said Emmie. 'This flat is going to be filled with a jumble of things that are neither useful nor "spark joy", all in random places. I've had it with Marie Kondō.'

A reasonably priced flat had become available in the neighbourhood Sanjay, James and Ethan lived in, and Emmie had jumped at it. It was the perfect solution: three stops closer to Waterloo, and near enough for easy sleepovers, while still allowing Emmie as much space as she wanted. Sanjay was very much hoping that one day, in the not-too-distant future, she'd ask him to move in, but he wasn't going to push her. The last thing Emmie needed was someone else trying to control her. And besides, they had all the time in the world.

Jake had offered to supervise the extrication of Emmie's belongings from Toby's house and, as a result of him standing by the front door like a presidential security detail, it had all gone relatively smoothly.

'Emmie,' Sanjay said, as he opened the next box with a Stanley knife. The comforting smell of well-thumbed books mingled with the scent of the flowers Sanjay had bought as a house-warming gift, and the spring clean they'd given the flat that morning. 'Can I ask you a question?'

'Sure,' she replied.

'Would you like to meet my family? I thought we could go for lunch on Sunday,' he said.

'I'd love that, Sanjay!' she said. 'I've been dying to meet Meera. I know I'm going to love her.'

'Not as much as she's going to love you,' said Sanjay. 'You have been warned.'

He pulled out his phone and started to type.

Mum, can I bring my girlfriend home for lunch on Sunday? There was a momentary pause before the screen filled with the word GIRLFRIEND?!?, followed by a flurry of emojis, seemingly chosen at random. He took that as a yes.

Sanjay carried an armful of the novels over to the bookcase and started stacking them on the shelves. One stopped him in his tracks, transporting him back months in time. *Rebecca* by Daphne du Maurier.

'What are you looking at?' asked Emmie, sitting down next to him.

'*Rebecca*,' said Sanjay. 'I loved that book.'

'Me too,' said Emmie.

'What did you think of Mrs Danvers?' asked Sanjay but, just like the last time he'd asked her that question, she didn't answer him. Instead, she just leaned over and kissed him, so hard that it made his head swim.

The room, with its half-emptied boxes and piles of Emmie's belongings, fell away. All his senses were focused entirely on the two of them – the touch of her fingers on his skin, her breath on his neck, his lips on hers.

Sanjay knew now that he hadn't loved Emmie when he'd first seen her on his train, all those months ago. He'd loved the idea of her. The fantasy he'd created around all her perceived perfections. But now he loved the *actual* her, with all her quirks and imperfections. All the things that made her uniquely Emmie.

Sanjay wasn't thinking about what might go wrong, or what the future held. After all those hours listening to the Headspace app, trying to master mindfulness, he'd finally achieved it. There was no moment except this perfect one, right here and right now.

He ran his hand through her hair, twining it around his fingers, breathing in the scent of her, and knew he'd never want to be anywhere else.

Iona

'Hello, beautiful Bea,' said Iona.

Bea was sitting in her armchair, looking out of the window at the setting sun. She turned to face Iona and smiled. Iona felt herself relax. It was obviously a good day today.

'It's you again,' Bea said. 'I know you, don't I?'

'Yes, darling, it's me. Iona,' said Iona.

'Iona. That's the name of my love. She's in Paris, you know. Look. She's gorgeous, isn't she?' said Bea, pointing to a frame on the mantelpiece, which held a smaller version of the can-can picture from Iona's hallway.

'You're gorgeous too, my dearest,' said Iona, following Bea's lead. Trying to correct her just made her more confused and upset.

There were, Iona had learned, some problems that you really couldn't solve. You just had to find a way to live with them. And if Bea could no longer join her in Iona's world, then she would join Bea in hers.

'Shall we take a trip to Paris?' Iona said, walking over to the old-fashioned record player on the sideboard. The Cole Porter album she wanted was already on the turntable, so she just lowered the stylus on to the right track: Ella Fitzgerald singing 'Let's Do It'.

'Oh, this is our song!' said Bea, clapping her hands together.

'Might I have the pleasure of this dance?' said Iona.

She held her hand out to Bea, who stood up, placing one hand on the small of Iona's back, and taking her hand in the other.

Iona sang the lyrics of the song softly, as her cheek rested against Bea's. She closed her eyes, and they were back on the stage at La Gaîté, while the band played from the orchestra pit at their feet, and they took their first steps on a journey that would last a lifetime.

They whirled around the polished floor, in a dance that encircled all the ones that had come before: spinning like tops, arms outstretched and heads tipped back, in the rain on a lamplit Champs-Élysées. Laughing out loud as they twirled each other round the dance floors at all those launches and awards ceremonies, lit by the flashbulbs of the paparazzi. The beautifully choreographed first dance at their wedding, dressed in matching silver tuxedos sprinkled with rose-petal confetti.

'I love you, Iona,' said Bea.

Iona wasn't sure if Bea was talking to her, or to the memory of her, but right now it didn't really matter. Either way, those words belonged to her, just as they'd always done, just as they always would.

'Not as much as I love you, darling Bea,' she replied.

'We're the whole damn cake,' said Bea.

'The whole damn cake,' echoed Iona.

AUTHOR'S NOTE

I have spent a significant proportion of my life on buses, trains and the London Underground. I often saw the same faces and, like Iona, I would make up nicknames for my fellow commuters, and imagine what their lives away from our shared journey must be like. That was how my passion for storytelling began.

I never spoke to any of these people. Nor did anyone speak to me. That would have been *weird*. I once saw the face of a very smartly dressed man on the Underground begin to turn green. We all looked at him askance, until eventually he put his expensive leather briefcase on his knee, opened it up and vomited into it. He then closed it again and got off at the next stop. Nobody said a word. That's what it's like to be a Londoner.

Every so often I would read stories in the *Evening Standard* about men who would commute in a suit to central London for months after losing their jobs, because they were too ashamed to tell anyone, even themselves, the truth.

I was fascinated by these stories, and wondered what would make someone behave like that. That question lodged in my subconscious and eventually became Piers.

I grew up in a house by the River Thames in East Molesey. The house, in fact, that Iona lives in. I described that house from my memories of the 1980s, so I apologize to the current owners who have, no doubt, extended and modernized it. Every day my dad took the train to work from Hampton Court to Waterloo and, when I was a teenager, I took the same line to school in Wimbledon. I remember a particularly nasty gang of girls from a rival school who would ridicule me for always having my head in a book. That memory, along with my adolescent crush on David Attenborough, inspired Martha.

I also need to beg forgiveness from anyone who currently commutes on the Hampton Court to Waterloo line. You'll have noticed that I took some liberties with, as Iona would say, *the actualité*. The train usually leaves from Platform 3 at Waterloo, but Platform 5 just rolled off the tongue a little more neatly. Also, at some point over the last decade, the layout of the trains was reworked to remove all the tables. Iona would have been horrified! Where would she put her cup of tea and her papers? Luckily, the joy of fiction is that it's enabled me to correct this egregious error of South Western Railway.

Now I work from home and in libraries and cafés, and I never expected to miss those days of crowding into dirty, smelly railway carriages. But then, the pandemic hit, and I found myself looking back on those times with an incredible sense of nostalgia. I also started to wonder what would have happened if I'd ignored the unwritten rule of commuting and had been brave enough to talk to my fellow passengers. What adventures might those conversations have taken me on?

And that thought became this book.

A note about names. I've learned that names have power. Nominative determinism is real. As a new character starts to form in my head, the correct name slowly appears beside them. Then, once that name is attached to them, it begins to inform their behaviour. This is most true of Hazard in my debut novel, *The Authenticity Project*.

Iona's name has a particular resonance. I used to have a wonderful friend named Iver (due to his Nordic heritage). Iver was a farmer and a builder – as strong as an ox. A few years ago, he decided to go to Tanzania for a couple of months to use his skills helping a charity build affordable housing for people in need. While he was there, he had a massive heart attack and died. Iver's daughter, Iona, is my goddaughter, and his widow, Wendy, is one of my closest friends. So, Iona was named after both Iona and Iver, and once I'd given her that name it started to mould her. Iona developed Iver's eccentricities, his *joie de vivre* and his dress sense, along with my goddaughter Iona's bravery, intelligence and immense kindness. I still miss Iver every day, and hope that, somehow, he knows about his namesake and loves her as much as I do.

I have always used writing as therapy. As a way of making sense of the world and exploring things that bother me. This is what I did with the wonderful Iona. You see, I spent nearly two decades in the heady world of advertising. I loved it in the early days. It was buzzy, creative and more than slightly wild. When I was just thirty years old, I was promoted to the board of J. Walter Thompson. I was the youngest board director, and one of the only women. Less than a decade later, I looked around and realized that, at thirty-nine, I'd become one of the oldest people in the office. I was also treated differently. I was at the height of my powers, and yet I was viewed as a dinosaur. Out of date and irrelevant.

It makes me furious that, as men age, they gain *gravitas*. They become *silver foxes*. Women, however, become invisible. We cannot allow this to happen, my friends. We must all *be more Iona*. We all deserve, like Iona, to have a Triumphant Second Act. Writing is mine. I had my first novel published at the age of fifty, and I am grateful every day to all the readers all over the world who've bought and recommended my books. You have, quite literally, made my dreams come true. Thank you.

ACKNOWLEDGEMENTS

This story would never have been told were it not for three incredible non-fictional women.

The first is my agent: Hayley Steed. The title 'agent' comes nowhere near to describing the role Hayley plays in my life. She is my mentor, my sounding board, my psycho-therapist, my business manager, my cheerleader and my friend. She's also supported by an amazing powerhouse of a team at the Madeleine Milburn Literary Agency, including the phenomenal Madeleine herself, Giles Milburn and Elinor Davies, the foreign rights team – Liane-Louise Smith, Georgia Simmonds and Valentina Paulmichl – and the film/TV agent Hannah Ladds.

The other two extraordinarily talented women I need to thank are my editors: Sally Williamson at Transworld in the UK, and Pamela Dorman at Pamela Dorman Books in the USA. Working with Sally and Pam, and their assistants, Lara Stevenson and Marie Michels, is such a privilege. As an author, it's often difficult to see the wood for the trees.

You know that something isn't quite right, but you're too close to the words to know what. My incredible editors always have the courage and sensitivity to tell me when something isn't working, the creativity and vision to see how the story can be improved, and the enthusiasm to keep me going.

Being a storyteller is the best job in the world, but it can be hard and very lonely. Like many authors (especially women!), I suffer from terrible imposter syndrome, and often doubt my own talent. This is where friendships with other writers are so important. I'd like to thank Write Club – a fabulous writing group formed when we all did the CBC novel-writing course back in 2018. Thank you for all your support, wisdom and humour, Natasha Hastings, Zoe Miller, Max Dunne, Geoffrey Charin, Maggie Sandilands, Richard Gough, Jenny Parks, Jenni Hagan, Clive Collins and Emily Ballantyne. Huge thanks also to the D20 Facebook group – a group of fellow debut authors who share the dubious honour of having their first novels published in the middle of a global pandemic. Somehow, we got each other through.

Thank you also to my wonderful author buddy, Annabel Abbs, and my trusted first readers – Caroline Skinner, Caroline Firth and Johnny Firth.

Which brings me to my husband, John. We've been together for more than two decades, and while his inability to load a dishwasher still infuriates me, marrying him remains the best decision I ever made. None of my books would exist without his support and belief in me.

Huge thanks, as always, to my mum and dad for their

tireless cheerleading, and to my amazing three children. This book is dedicated to my eldest, Eliza, but please understand that this does not mean that she is my favourite child. I, of course, love them all passionately and entirely equally. I would, however, like Charlie to note that he will never get a book dedicated to him until he makes an effort to read at least one of them!

It takes a huge team of incredibly talented and dedicated people to put this book in your hands, and I am grateful to them all. Here they are:

Editorial
Sally Williamson
Katrina Whone
Viv Thompson
Josh Benn
Judith Welsh
Lara Stevenson

Copy editor
Eleanor Updegraff

Proofreaders
Jessica Read
Barbara Thompson

Marketing
Vicky Palmer
Lilly Cox
Aoifé McColgan

Sales
Tom Chicken
Laura Garrod
Emily Harvey
Gary Harley
Louise Blakemore
Chris Wyatt
Natasha Photiou
Laura Ricchetti

Publicity
Becky Short
Alison Barrow

Production
Cat Hillerton
Phil Evans

Audio
Alice Twomey
Oli Grant
Nile Faure-Bryan

Design
Irene Martinez

Operations
Alexandra Cutts

Finance
Derek Bracken
Anshu Kochar

Contracts
Rebecca Smith

Reception
Jean Kriek

ABOUT THE AUTHOR

Clare Pooley graduated from Newnham College, Cambridge, and spent twenty years in the heady world of advertising before becoming a full-time writer.

Clare's first novel – *The Authenticity Project* – was a BBC Radio 2 Book Club pick, a *New York Times* bestseller and the winner of the RNA debut novel award. It has been translated into twenty-nine languages. *The People on Platform 5* is her second novel.

Her funny and brilliantly blunt memoir – *The Sober Diaries* – has helped thousands of people worldwide to quit drinking.

Clare lives in Fulham, London, with her long-suffering husband, three children and two border terriers.

You can find out more at www.clarepooley.com or on Twitter @cpooleywriter and Instagram @clare_pooley

If you enjoyed *The People on Platform 5*, you'll love Clare Pooley's feel-good debut novel about the power of honesty and the kindness of strangers

Read on to discover the heart-warming, poignant and uplifting story . . .

Monica

She had tried to return the book. As soon as she realized it had been left behind, she'd picked it up and rushed after its extraordinary owner. But he'd gone. He moved surprisingly swiftly for someone so old. Maybe he really didn't want to be found.

It was a plain, pale-green exercise book, like the one Monica had carried around with her at school, filled with details of homework assignments. Her friends had covered their books with graffiti of hearts, flowers and the names of their latest crushes, but Monica was not a doodler. She had too much respect for good stationery.

On the front cover were three words, beautifully etched in copperplate script:

The Authenticity Project

In smaller writing, in the bottom corner, was the date: *October 2018*. Perhaps, thought Monica, there would be an address, or at least a name, on the inside so she could return it. Although it was physically unassuming, it had an air of significance about it.

She turned over the front cover. There were only a few paragraphs on the first page.

> *How well do you know the people who live near you? How well do they know you? Do you even know the names of your neighbours? Would you realize if they were in trouble, or hadn't left their house for days?*
>
> *Everyone lies about their lives. What would happen if you shared the truth instead? The one thing that defines you, that makes everything else about you fall into place? Not on the internet, but with those real people around you?*
>
> *Perhaps nothing. Or maybe telling that story would change your life, or the life of someone you've not yet met.*
>
> *That's what I want to find out.*

There was more on the next page, and Monica was dying to read on, but it was one of the busiest times of the day in the café, and she knew it was crucial not to fall behind schedule. That way madness lay. She tucked the book into the space alongside the till with the spare menus and flyers from various suppliers. She'd read it later, when she could concentrate properly.

Monica stretched out on the sofa in her flat above the café, a large glass of Sauvignon Blanc in one hand and the abandoned exercise book in the other. The questions she'd read that morning had been niggling away at her, demanding answers. She'd spent all day talking to people, serving them coffees and cakes, chatting about the weather and the latest celebrity gossip. But when had she last told anyone anything about herself that *really mattered*? And what did she actually know about them, with the exception of whether they liked milk in their coffee, or sugar with their tea? She opened the book to the second page.

My name is Julian Jessop. I am seventy-nine years old, and I am an artist. For the past fifty-seven years I've lived in Chelsea Studios, on the Fulham Road.

Those are the basic facts, but here is the truth: I AM LONELY.

I often go for days without talking to anyone. Sometimes, when I do have to speak (because someone's called me up about payment protection insurance, for example), I find that my voice comes out in a croak because it's curled up and died in my throat from neglect.

Age has made me invisible. I find this especially hard, because I was always looked at. Everyone knew who I was. I didn't have to introduce myself, I would just stand in a doorway while my name worked its way around the room in a chain of whispers, pursued by a number of surreptitious glances.

I used to love lingering at mirrors, and would walk slowly past shop windows, checking the cut of my jacket or the wave in my hair. Now, if my reflection sneaks up on me, I barely recognize myself. It's ironic that Mary, who would have happily accepted the inevitability of ageing, died at the relatively young age of sixty, and yet I'm still here, forced to watch myself gradually crumble away.

As an artist, I watched people. I analysed their relationships, and I noticed there is always a balance of power. One partner is more loved, and the other more loving. I had to be the most loved. I realize now that I took Mary for granted, with her ordinary, wholesome, pink-cheeked prettiness and her constant thoughtfulness and dependability. I only learned to appreciate her after she was gone.

Monica paused to turn the page and take a mouthful of wine. She wasn't sure that she liked Julian very much, although she felt rather sorry for him. She suspected he'd choose dislike over pity. She read on.

When Mary lived here, our little cottage was always filled with people. The local children ran in and out, as Mary plied them with stories, advice, fizzy pop and Monster Munch. My less successful artist friends constantly turned up unannounced for dinner, along with the latest of my artist's models. Mary put on a good show of welcoming the other women, so perhaps only I noticed they were never offered chocolates with their coffee.

We were always busy. Our social life revolved around the Chelsea Arts Club, and the bistros and boutiques of the King's Road and Sloane Square. Mary worked long hours as a midwife, and I crossed the country, painting the portraits of people who thought themselves worth recording for posterity.

Every Friday evening since the late sixties, at 5 p.m. we'd walk into the nearby Brompton Cemetery which, since its four corners connected Fulham, Chelsea, South Kensington and Earl's Court, was a convenient meeting point for all our friends. We'd plan our weekend on the grave of Admiral Angus Whitewater. We didn't know the Admiral, he just happened to have an impressive horizontal slab of black marble over his last resting place which made a great table for drinks.

In many ways, I died alongside Mary. I ignored all the telephone calls and the letters. I let the paint dry solid on the palette and, one unbearably long night, destroyed all my unfinished canvases; ripped them into multi-coloured streamers, then diced them into confetti with Mary's dressmaking scissors. When I did finally emerge from my cocoon, about five years later, neighbours had moved, friends had given up, my agent had written me off, and that's when I realized I had become unnoticeable. I had reverse metamorphosed from a butterfly into a caterpillar.

I still raise a glass of Mary's favourite Baileys Irish Cream at the Admiral's grave every Friday evening, but now it's just me and the ghosts of times past.

That's my story. Please feel free to chuck it in the recycling. Or you might decide to tell your own truth in these pages, and pass my little book on. Maybe you'll find it cathartic, as I did.

What happens next is up to you.

Monica

She Googled him, obviously. Julian Jessop was described by Wikipedia as a portrait painter who had enjoyed a flurry of notoriety in the sixties and seventies. He'd been a student of Lucian Freud at the Slade. The two of them had, so the rumours went, traded insults (and, the implication was, women) over the years. Lucian had the advantage of much greater fame, but Julian was younger by seventeen years. Monica thought of Mary, exhausted after a long shift delivering other women's babies, wondering where her husband had gone. She sounded like a bit of a doormat, to be honest. Why hadn't she just left him? There were, she reminded herself, as she tried to do often, worse things than being single.

One of Julian's self-portraits had hung for a brief period in the National Portrait Gallery, in an exhibition titled *The London School of Lucian Freud*. Monica clicked on the image to enlarge it, and there he was, the man she'd seen in her café yesterday morning, but all smoothed out, like a raisin turned back into a grape. Julian Jessop, about thirty years old, slicked-back blond hair, razor-sharp cheekbones, slightly sneering mouth and those penetrating blue eyes. When he'd looked at her yesterday it had felt like he was rummaging around in her soul. A little disconcerting when you're trying to discuss the various merits of a blueberry muffin versus millionaire's shortbread.

Monica checked her watch. 4.50 p.m.

'Benji, can you hold the shop for half an hour or so?' she asked her barista. Barely pausing to wait for his nod in response, she pulled on her coat. Monica scanned the tables as she walked through the café, pausing to pick up a large crumb of red velvet cake from table twelve. How had that been overlooked? As she walked out on to the Fulham Road, she flicked it towards a pigeon.

Monica rarely sat on the top deck of the bus. She prided herself on her adherence to health and safety regulations, and climbing the stairs of a moving vehicle seemed an unnecessary risk to take. But in this instance, she needed the vantage point.

Monica watched the blue dot on Google Maps move slowly along the Fulham Road towards Chelsea Studios. The bus stopped at Fulham Broadway, then carried on towards Stamford Bridge. The huge, modern mecca of the Chelsea Football Club loomed ahead and there, in its shadow and sandwiched improbably between the two separate entrances for the home and away fans, was a tiny, perfectly formed village of studio houses and cottages, behind an innocuous wall that Monica must have walked past hundreds of times.

Grateful for once for the slow-moving traffic, Monica

tried to work out which of the houses was Julian's. One stood slightly alone and looked a little worse for wear, rather like Julian himself. She'd bet the day's takings, not something to do lightly given her economic circumstances, on that being the one.

Monica jumped off at the next stop and turned almost immediately left, into Brompton Cemetery. The light was low, casting long shadows, and there was an autumnal chill to the air. The cemetery was one of Monica's favourite places – a timeless oasis of calm in the city. She loved the ornate gravestones – a last show of one-upmanship. *I'll see your marble slab with its fancy biblical quotation and raise you a life-sized Jesus on the cross.* She loved the stone angels, many now missing vital body parts, and the old-fashioned names on the Victorian gravestones – Ethel, Mildred, Alan. When did people stop being called Alan? Come to think of it, did anyone call their baby Monica any more? Even back in 1981 her parents had been outliers in eschewing names like Emily, Sophie and Olivia. Monica: a dying moniker. She could picture the credits on the cinema screen: *The Last of the Monicas.*

As she walked briskly past the graves of the fallen soldiers and the White Russian émigrés, she could sense the sheltering wildlife – the grey squirrels, urban foxes and the jet-black ravens – guarding the graves like the souls of the dead.

Where was the Admiral? Monica headed towards the left, looking out for an old man clutching a bottle of Baileys Irish Cream. She wasn't, she realized, sure why. She didn't want to speak to Julian, at least not yet. She suspected that approaching him directly would run the risk of embarrassing him. She didn't want to start off on the wrong foot.

Monica headed towards the north end of the cemetery, pausing only briefly, as she always did, at the grave of Emmeline Pankhurst, to give a silent nod of thanks. She looped round at the top and was halfway back down the other side, walking along a less-used path, when she noticed a movement to her right. There, sitting (somewhat sacrilegiously) on an engraved marble tombstone, was Julian, glass in hand.

Monica walked on past, keeping her head down so as not to catch his eye. Then, as soon as he was gone, about ten minutes later, she doubled back so that she could read the words on the gravestone.

ADMIRAL ANGUS WHITEWATER
OF PONT STREET
DIED 5 JUNE 1963, AGED 74
RESPECTED LEADER, BELOVED HUSBAND
AND FATHER, AND LOYAL FRIEND

ALSO, BEATRICE WHITEWATER
DIED 7 AUGUST 1964, AGED 69

She bristled at the fact that the Admiral got several glowing adjectives after his name, whereas his wife just got a date and a space for eternity under her husband's tombstone.

Monica stood for a while, enveloped in the silence of the cemetery, imagining a group of beautiful young people, with Beatles haircuts, mini-skirts and bell-bottom trousers, arguing and joking with each other, and suddenly felt rather alone.

Julian

Julian wore his solitude and loneliness like old, ill-fitting shoes. He was used to them, in many ways they had grown comfortable, but over time they were bending him out of shape, causing calluses and bunions that would never go away.

It was 10 a.m., so Julian was walking down the Fulham Road. For five years or so after Mary, he often didn't get out of bed and day morphed seamlessly into night, the weeks losing their pattern. Then he'd discovered that routines were crucial. They created buoys he could cling to to keep himself afloat. At the same time every morning, he went out and walked the local streets for an hour, picking up any supplies he needed on the way. His list today read:

Eggs
Milk (1 pint)
Butterscotch-flavoured Angel Delight, if poss

(he was finding Angel Delight more and more difficult to track down)

And since today was a Saturday, he would buy a fashion magazine. This week was *Vogue*'s turn. His favourite.

Sometimes, if the newsagent wasn't too busy, they would discuss the latest headlines, or the weather. On those days, Julian felt almost like a fully functioning member of society, one with acquaintances who knew his name, and opinions that mattered. Once, he'd even booked an appointment at the dentist, just so he could pass the time of day with someone. After spending the whole appointment with his mouth open, unable to speak as Mr Patel was doing goodness knows what with a selection of metal instruments and a tube that made a ghastly sucking noise, he realized this was not a clever tactic. He'd left with a lecture on gum hygiene ringing in his ears, and the resolution not to return for as long as possible. If he lost his teeth, so be it. He'd lost everything else.

Julian paused to look in through the window of Monica's Café, which was already filled with customers. He'd walked this road for so many years that in his mind, he could picture the various reincarnations of this particular shop, like peeling back layers of old wallpaper when you're redecorating a room. Back in the sixties it was the Eel and Pie Shop until eel fell out of favour and it became a record shop. In the eighties it was a video rental store and then, until a few years ago, a sweet shop. Eels, vinyl records and VHS tapes – all consigned to the dustbin of history. Even sweets were now being demonized, blamed for the fact that children were getting larger and larger. Surely it wasn't the fault of the sweets? It was the children to blame, or their mothers.

He'd definitely chosen the right place to leave The

Authenticity Project. He liked the fact that he'd ordered tea with milk and not been asked all sorts of complicated questions about what specific type of leaf he wanted and what sort of milk. It came in a proper china cup, and no one demanded to know his name. Julian's name was accustomed to being signed at the bottom of canvases. It did not sit comfortably scrawled on a takeaway cup, like they'd done in Starbucks. He shuddered at the memory.

He'd sat in a soft, scarred leather armchair in the far corner of Monica's, in an area lined with bookshelves that he'd heard her call The Library. In a world where everything seemed to be electronic and paper was a rapidly disappearing medium, Julian had found The Library, where the smell of old books mingled with the aroma of freshly ground coffee, wonderfully nostalgic.

Julian wondered what had happened to the little notebook he'd left there. He often felt like he was slowly disappearing without trace. One day, in the not too distant future, his head would finally slip under the water and he'd leave barely a ripple behind. Through that book, at least one person would see him – properly. And writing it had been a comfort, like loosening the laces on those uncomfortable shoes, letting his feet breathe a bit more easily.

He walked on.

Hazard

It was a Monday evening, and getting late, but Timothy Hazard Ford, known to everyone as Hazard, was avoiding going home. He knew from experience that the only way to escape the comedown after a weekend was to just keep on going. He'd begun pushing the start of the week further and further back, and bringing the weekend further forward until they almost met in the middle. There was a brief interlude of horror at around Wednesday, and then he was off again.

Hazard had been unable to persuade any of his work colleagues to hit the City bars that evening, so instead he'd headed back to Fulham, and stopped off in his local wine bar. He scanned the sparse crowd for anyone he knew. He spotted a reed-thin blonde, her legs entwined round a high stool and her torso leaning over the bar, looking like a glamorous bendy straw. He was pretty sure that she was the gym buddy of a girl his mate Jake used to go out with. He had no idea what her name was, but she was the only person available to have a drink with, and that made her, at this moment, his very best friend.

Hazard walked over, wearing the smile he reserved for exactly this sort of occasion. Some sixth sense caused her to turn towards him and she grinned and waved. Bingo. It worked every time.

Her name, it turned out, was Blanche. Stupid name, thought Hazard, and he should know. He poured himself lazily on to the stool next to hers and grinned and nodded as she introduced him to her group of friends whose names floated into the air around him like bubbles, then popped, leaving no impression at all. Hazard was not interested in what they called themselves, only their staying power and, possibly, their morals. The fewer the better.

Hazard slipped easily into his usual routine. He took a roll of banknotes out of his pocket and bought a showy round, upgrading requests of glasses to bottles, and wine to champagne. He reeled out a few of his well-tested anecdotes. He plundered the long list of his acquaintances for mutual ones, and then spread, possibly even invented, a flurry of salacious gossip.

The group coalesced around Hazard in the way it always did, but gradually, as the large station clock on the wall behind the bar ticked past the hour, the crowd thinned out. *Gotta go, it's only Monday*, they said, or *Big day tomorrow*, or *Need to recover from the weekend, you know how it is*. Eventually, only Hazard and Blanche were left and it was just 9 p.m. Hazard could sense Blanche getting ready to leave and felt a rising sense of panic.

'Hey, Blanche, it's still early. Why don't you come back to

mine?' he said, resting his hand on her forearm in a way that suggested everything yet, crucially, promised nothing.

'Sure. Why not?' she replied, as he knew she would.

The revolving door of the bar spat them out on to the street. Hazard put his arm around Blanche, crossed the road and strode down the pavement, not noticing or caring that they were occupying its whole width.

He didn't see the small brunette standing in front of him like a traffic obstruction until it was too late. He barrelled into her, then realized that she'd been holding a glass of red wine which was now dripping rather comically off her face and, more importantly, was spreading like a knife wound over his Savile Row shirt.

'Oh, for fuck's sake,' he said, glaring at the culprit.

'Hey, you walked into me!' she replied in a voice cracking with indignation. A drop of wine trembled at the end of her nose like a reluctant skydiver, then fell.

'Well, what on earth do you think you were doing just standing in the middle of a pavement with a glass of wine?' he yelled back at her. 'Can't you drink in a bar like a normal person?'

'Come on, leave it, let's go,' said Blanche, giggling in a way that made his nerve ends jangle.

'Stupid bitch,' said Hazard to Blanche, keeping his voice low so the stupid bitch in question wouldn't hear. Blanche giggled again.

Several thoughts collided when Hazard was woken by his strident alarm. One: *I can't have had more than three hours' sleep.* Two: *I feel even worse today than I did yesterday, what on earth was I thinking?* And three: *there's a blonde in my bed who I do not want to deal with and whose name I can't remember.*

Luckily, Hazard had been in this position before. He slammed off the alarm while the girl was still asleep, mouth open like a Japanese sex doll, and carefully picked up her arm by the wrist, removing it from his chest. Her hand dangled down like a dead fish. He placed it carefully on the rumpled, sweaty sheets. She appeared to have left so much of her face on his pillow – the red of her lips, black of her eyes and ivory of her skin – that he was surprised she had any left. He eased himself out of bed, wincing as his brain clattered against his skull like a ball in a game of bagatelle. He walked over to the chest of drawers in the corner of the room and there, just as he'd hoped, was a scrap of paper with a message scribbled on it: HER NAME IS BLANCHE. God, he was good at this.

Hazard showered and dressed as quickly and as quietly as he could, found a clean piece of paper and wrote a note:

Dear Blanche, you looked too peaceful and beautiful to wake. Thanks for last night. You were awesome. Make sure you close the front door properly when you leave. Call me.

Had she been awesome? Since he had virtually no memory of events after around 10 p.m. when his dealer had shown up (even quicker than usual on account of it being a Monday), it hardly mattered. He wrote his mobile number at the bottom, carefully transposing two of the digits, in order to avoid it being at all useful, and left the note on the pillow next to his unwelcome guest. He hoped there'd be no trace of her when he returned.

He walked to the tube station on autopilot. He was, despite the fact that it was October, wearing sunglasses to protect his eyes from the weak glare of the new day. He paused as he reached the spot of his collision last night. He was pretty sure he could see a few splatters of blood-red wine still on the pavement, like the remnants of a mugging. An unwelcome vision floored him: a feisty, pretty brunette, glaring at him as if she really, really hated him. Women never looked at him like that. Hazard didn't like being hated.

Then a thought struck him with the vicious sideswipe of an inconvenient truth: *he hated himself too. Right down to the smallest molecule, the tiniest atom, the most microscopic subatomic particle.*

Something had to change. Actually, *everything* had to change.

Monica

Monica had always loved numbers. She loved their logic, their predictability. She found making one side of an equation balance with the other immensely satisfying, solving x and proving y. But the numbers on the paper in front of her now would not behave. No matter how many times she added up the figures in the left-hand column (income), they wouldn't stretch to cover the total in the right (outgoings).

Monica thought back to her days as a corporate lawyer, when adding up the numbers was a chore, but never something to keep her awake at night. Every hour she spent poring over the small print on some contract, or leafing through endless statutes, she'd bill the client two hundred and fifty pounds. She'd have to sell *one hundred* medium-sized cappuccinos to make the same.

Why had she allowed herself to make such a monumental life change with such alacrity, and for such emotional reasons? She who found it difficult to choose a sandwich filling without running through a mental list of pros and cons, comparing price, nutritional values and calorie counts.

Monica had tried every café on the commute between her flat and her office. There were the soulless ones, the tired and grubby ones and the identikit, mass-produced chain ones. Every time she handed over money for an overpriced, mediocre takeaway coffee she'd picture her ideal café. There would be no brushed concrete, moulded plastic, exposed pipework or industrial-style lamps and tables; rather it would feel like being invited into someone's home. There would be comfy, mismatched armchairs, eclectic art on the walls, newspapers and books. Books everywhere, not just for show, but ones you could pick up, read and take home with you, so long as you left another one in its place. The barista wouldn't ask your name in order to misspell it on your cup, he (or she, Monica added quickly) would know it already. They'd ask after your kids and remember the name of your cat.

Then, she'd been walking down the Fulham Road and noticed that the dusty old sweet shop, which had been there for ever, had finally closed. A large board on its front announced TO LET. Some local wag had painted a large I in between the letters O and L.

Every time Monica walked past the vacant shop she could hear her mother's voice. In those last few weeks, the ones that smelled of disease and decay and were punctuated by the constant electronic beeps of medical machinery, she'd urgently tried to impart decades' worth of wisdom to her daughter, before it was too late. *Listen to me, Monica. Write it down, Monica. Don't forget, Monica. Emmeline*

Pankhurst didn't chain herself to those railings so we could spend our lives as a tiny cog in someone else's wheel. Be your own boss. Create something. Employ people. Be fearless. Do something you really love. Make it all worthwhile.
So, she had done it.

Monica wished she'd been able to name the café after her mother, but she was called Charity, and it seemed like a really bad business decision to give a café a name that implied no need to pay. Things, as it turned out, were hard enough.

Just because this café was her dream didn't mean anyone else would necessarily share it. Or, at least, not enough of them to cover her costs, and she couldn't keep making up the shortfall for ever; the bank wouldn't let her. Her head was throbbing. She walked over to the bar and poured the remainder of a bottle of red wine into a large glass.

Being the boss was all very well, she told her mother, inside her head, and she loved her café, the essence of which had seeped into her bones, but it was lonely. She missed the office gossip around the water cooler, she missed the camaraderie forged over pizza during late-night working sessions, she even found herself remembering fondly those ridiculous team bonding days, the office jargon and impenetrable three-letter acronyms. She loved her team at the café, but there was always a slight distance between them, because she was responsible for their livelihoods, and right now she couldn't even manage her own.

She was reminded of the questions that man – Julian – had asked in the notebook he'd left on this very table. She'd approved of his choice. Monica couldn't help herself judging people by where in her café they decided to sit. *How well do you know the people who live near you? How well do they know you?*

She thought of all the people who'd come in and out today, the bell ringing jauntily with each arrival and departure. They were all connected, more than ever before, to thousands of people, friends on social media, friends of friends. Yet did they, like her, feel like they had no one they could actually talk to? Not about the latest celebrity eviction from some house, or island, or jungle, but about the important things – the things that keep you awake at night. Like numbers that wouldn't obey your command.

Monica shuffled her papers back into their file and pulled out her phone, loading up Facebook and scrolling through. There was still no sign of Duncan, the man she'd been dating until a few weeks ago, on her social media. She'd been ghosted. Duncan, the vegan who'd refused to eat *avocados* because the farmers exploited bees in their pollination, but who thought it perfectly acceptable to have sex with her and then just *disappear*. He cared more about the sensitivities of a *bee* than he did her.

She kept scrolling, despite knowing this would not be a comfort, more a form of mild self-harm. Hayley had changed her relationship status to 'engaged'. Whoop whoop. Pam had posted a status about her life with three kids, a boast thinly and inexpertly disguised as self-deprecation, and Sally had shared her baby scan picture – twelve weeks.

Baby scans. What was the point in sharing those? They all looked the same, and none of them resembled an actual child, more like a weather map predicting an area of high pressure over northern Spain. And yet, every time Monica saw a new one it stopped her breath and floored her with a wave of yearning and a humiliating stab of envy. She felt, sometimes, like an old Ford Fiesta, broken down on the hard shoulder, while everyone sailed past her in the fast lane.

Someone had left a copy of *HELLO!* on a table today; it screamed a headline about a Hollywood actress's 'baby joy' at forty-three. Monica had scanned the pages during her coffee break, looking for clues as to how she'd done it. IVF? Egg donation? Had she frozen her eggs years ago? Or had it happened easily? How much time did her ovaries have left? Were they already packing their suitcases for a relaxing retirement on the Costa Brava?

Monica picked up her glass of wine and walked around the café turning off all the lights and straightening any errant chairs or tables. She went out on to the street – keys in one hand, glass in the other, locked the café door and turned to unlock the door to her flat above.

Then, out of nowhere, a large bloke, towing a blonde like a motorbike's sidecar, careered into her so hard that she was momentarily winded, and the glass of wine she was holding erupted, all over her face and his shirt. She could feel rivulets of Rioja coursing down her nose and dripping off her chin. She waited for his abject apology.

'Oh, for fuck's sake,' he said. Monica felt a heat rising from her chest, making her face flush and her jaw clench.

'Hey, you walked into me!' she protested.

'Well, what on earth do you think you were doing just standing in the middle of a pavement with a glass of wine?' he said. 'Can't you drink in a bar like a normal person?' His face, with its perfectly symmetrical planes, would have been classically handsome, but it was split by the ugly gash of a sneer. The blonde pulled him away, giggling inanely.

'Stupid bitch,' she heard him say, deliberately pitching his voice just loud enough for her to hear.

Monica let herself into her flat. *Honey, I'm home*, she said, as she always did, silently and to no one, and thought for a minute she was going to cry. She put the empty glass down on the draining board of her kitchenette, and wiped the wine off her face with a tea towel. She was desperate to speak to someone, but she couldn't think who to call. Her friends were all caught up in their own busy lives, and wouldn't want her inflicting her misery on their evenings. There was no point calling her dad, since Bernadette, her stepmother, who saw her as an inconvenient backstory to her new husband's life, acted as gatekeeper, and would no doubt announce that her father was busy writing and couldn't be disturbed.

Then Monica saw, sitting on the coffee table where she'd left it a few days ago, the pale-green notebook labelled *The Authenticity Project*. She picked it up and turned again to the first page. *Everyone lies about their lives. What would happen if you shared the truth instead? The one thing that defines you, that makes everything else about you fall into place?*

Why not? she thought, feeling the thrill of being uncharacteristically reckless. It took her a while to find a decent pen. It seemed a bit disrespectful to follow Julian's careful calligraphy with a scrawl in manky old biro. She turned to the next clean page, and began to write.

Look out for Clare's new funny and heart-warming novel

HOW TO AGE

Disgracefully

When age makes you invisible, secrets are easier to hide

Coming 2024
Available to pre-order now